PRAISE FOR KENNE

FICTION

"Johnson successfully draws the reader into the emotional turmoil that his characters experience. Indeed, one of the strengths of Johnson's writing is how much we come to care for the characters and their journeys . . . He is above all else a visually-oriented writer, and is intent on creating memorable visuals."

—BookPleasures.com

"Johnson is especially effective . . . at introducing disparate, unrelated stories and slowly having them collide with one another throughout the course of the story."

—*Pittsburgh Post-Gazette*

"Without question Kenneth Johnson is the closest our generation will come to the great Rod Serling. His understanding of the human mind has created some of the most developed and understood characters ever. When Kenneth Johnson puts something out, it is always quality."

—ScaredStiffReviews.com

FILM

"The cerebral Kenneth Johnson, who created the [*Incredible Hulk*] series . . . went to great lengths to dramatize a cursed life—the kind chronicled in the novels of Victor Hugo, Robert Louis Stevenson and Mary Shelley."

—*The New York Times*

THE
MAN
OF
LEGENDS

THE
MAN
OF
LEGENDS

KENNETH JOHNSON

47N◉RTH

Text copyright © 2017 by Kenneth Johnson
All rights reserved.

Published by 47North, Seattle

www.apub.com

Amazon, the Amazon logo, and 47North are trademarks of Amazon.com, Inc., or its affiliates.

ISBN-13: 9781477819685
ISBN-10: 1477819681

Cover design by Rex Bonomelli

Printed in the United States of America

For Bill and Stella Pence,
who have been guiding lights

A VERY IMPORTANT NOTE

To each of the people who allowed me to record their eyewitness accounts of the mysterious and frightening supernatural adventure we all shared, I must again express my indebtedness. Their ages at the time are listed, and I endeavored to transcribe their voices and speech patterns exactly as I heard them.

Their experiences were interwoven with my own account of the astonishing and dangerous events to which I was both a witness and a participant. Together with mine, they formed an oral documentation that became the original *New York Times* edition of this book, published sixteen years ago.

I was, and remain, humbled by the lovely reception which that publication received from both the public and my peers.

But I was always frustrated that a vital element of this history was missing: it had been impossible at the time to get a first-person narrative from the remarkable man who was the principal player in all that occurred, a man who, on a great number of occasions, had altered the course of human history.

Then, only a few months ago, I was amazed when he reappeared in my life. And I was blessed to receive from him a copy of his own perspective of those incredible days.

His generosity allowed me to entirely reedit and greatly expand my earlier publication. His invaluable material has been blended into all I'd previously gathered to create this comprehensive and definitive new edition.

The words that begin on the next page, and are interspersed on so many new pages herein, are those of the subject himself and have been faithfully rendered. For sharing his side of one of the most unique stories the world has ever known, I am grateful to him, and I will be, eternally.

Jillian Guthrie
New York City, 2017

ONE

Will, age 33...

The images were so vivid, so tangible, so minutely detailed, that all of my senses confirmed I was in the midst of total reality. It never occurred to me I was dreaming.

The overlapping sequences varied wildly in time and place, but they were laced to one another by a strong common thread, by the recurrent theme of my nightmares: once again I was fleeing to avoid capture.

Lightning flashed outside the massive stained-glass rose window portraying Saint John's vision of the Apocalypse. I heard the voices of the two priests pursuing me. The younger cried out in French, "Stop him!" The older shouted hoarsely in Latin, "He has opened the sacred reliquary! Touched the treasure! He must not escape!" But I was determined to do so, yet again.

I lifted the hem of my coarse black monk's robe so it would not catch in my sandals as I rushed desperately up the marble steps from the dank crypt below. Reaching the top of the staircase, gasping for breath, I ran out from beneath the rough-hewn wooden scaffolding designed to support artisans during their construction labors. It was tied together with thick ropes and lined the walls of the dark, deserted Gothic cathedral.

More flashes of lightning from outside blasted into the lofty church's spectacular interior with momentarily blinding illumination. Rain gusted down through the stone tracery of the fifteen magnificent but unfinished windows that surrounded me, towering fifty feet overhead. I remember thinking that in another year or so, perhaps by AD 1248, their openings would be filled with stunning stained glass, and the interior of Sainte-Chapelle de Paris would remain dry during a storm. But on this night the cathedral was still open to the elements, wet and miserable, chilling me to the bone. The rainfall had extinguished most of the torches, creating a smoky haze. My thick wool robe was heavy with the rain and smelled like a wet sheep.

I blinked from the drops of rain spattering my face as I strained to run through the vast, vaulted sanctuary. Some dark, invisible force made me feel as though I were trying to run underwater. Struggling past the central altar, I heard discordant shouts from other angry voices and the running footfalls of King Louis's royal guards approaching from the palace cloister to the north. The guards had been roused by the cries of the two priests pursuing me. The younger one reached the top of the marble steps behind me, shouting angrily as he ran, "I command you to stop!"

But I did not. I reached the lofty cathedral's main entrance, the Portal of the Last Judgment. As I lifted the massive iron locking bar, I glanced up at the statue of lithe Saint Etienne, shadowy within his niche above. Graceful Etienne gazed down upon me, then, during a flash of lightning, I saw his pale marble face come alive with a nightmarish, eerie smile that raised the hair on the back of my neck. His shining eyes followed me as I pulled open the ornately carved portal door beneath him and rushed through it into . . .

The Red Garter Saloon. The 1859-era barroom was packed with boisterous prospectors plus the requisite con men, gamblers, and whores hoping to relieve the miners of their hard-earned silver or gold dust.

The surreal transition didn't seem unnatural as I looked around, panting from exertion. Brightly lighted by candelabras and kerosene lamps, the Red Garter was typical of many saloons in Nevada's burgeoning boomtowns, but the amazing Comstock Lode had made Virginia City a beguiling destination.

I hurried away from the back door, pushing through the scruffy prospectors of mixed ethnicity and age. Unshaved, in serviceable clothes and muddy boots, most wore sidearms. Still breathing heavily, I caught a glimpse of myself in the gilded mirror behind the bar and saw I fit right in: my clothes were like theirs; a four-day beard stubbled my face; from under my sweat-stained cowboy hat light-brown hair hung shoulder length and itched because I needed delousing; a long-barreled Colt Navy revolver was holstered on my hip. I was Caucasian, stood five foot ten, looking as though I'd weathered some thirty-three rough years.

The people and images swirled weirdly around me. I hurried past a piano player in a dented bowler with a cigar clenched in his wickedly smiling, stained teeth while he pounded out "Camptown Races" on a tinny piano. Boozy clientele hung about his battered upright, adding their inebriated voices; several spat with uneven accuracy at one of the many spittoons on the pitted wooden floor. I squinted from the thick tobacco smoke, the breath of cheap alcohol, and the sweet or very sour smells of wildly divergent hygiene.

"Hey! W.J.!" I saw the smiling, bushy-haired reporter, Sam, shouting to me from across the room, waving me over. But I kept moving. Casting a furtive glance back over my shoulder to see if my pursuers had yet followed me into the saloon, I bumped into a full-bodied, redheaded prostitute with a beauty mark on her chin. I inhaled the fragrance of her rose water and saw the flesh of her bosom blossoming upward from her flouncy scarlet bodice. She had a good deal of eye shadow, rouge, and mileage.

Her fine white teeth gleamed as she grinned at me with come-hither, wanton eyes and murmured in a deep, near-masculine voice, "How about a return match, Will?"

I waved her off. "Sorry, Rebecca." I elbowed on through the jostling mob toward the saloon's entrance, but sensing something, I glanced sideways through the cheery men and painted women. I saw that sitting at a rustic gaming table was a fastidious gambler wearing a black suit and ruffled white shirt with a black silk string tie.

With a swoosh, everyone else suddenly grew hazy. Their voices melded and echoed as from a great distance, and the room darkened. The gambler and I were suddenly the only two clearly visible in a cloudy limbo. He expertly shuffled cards with elegantly manicured fingers. The gambler was a sleek young man in his midtwenties, clean shaven with neatly trimmed dark hair and brows. His faintly smiling eyes were riveted upon mine in greeting. We knew each other, sharing a history that was long and most certainly out of the ordinary. The gambler nodded toward an empty chair at his gaming table, inviting me to sit. His intense gaze gave me a chill yet was also very seductive. Then I heard a shout from the back door behind me.

"There he is, Sheriff! That's the man!"

The boisterous saloon burst fully alive again around me. Turning quickly, I saw a Catholic priest pointing at me across the jovial crowd. The sheriff and his deputy drew their revolvers, pushed past the priest, and began battering their way through the tangled mob toward me.

I shot a last glance in the direction of the smiling gambler, but he had disappeared. I turned and ran toward the saloon's front entrance as the sheriff fired his pistol upward, shouting, "Don't let that man escape! There's a big reward!" Suddenly I felt a dozen hands grasping at me, but I ducked, spun, and twisted with surprising agility, shouldering my way through the swinging doors . . .

As I bolted outside, my head was spinning. Fighting dizziness, I registered that I was wearing a three-piece 1930s business suit and a white Panama hat, and carrying an old leather briefcase. Then I saw the big black Packard, gleaming under the streetlamps, speeding up Chicago's rain-slicked 18th Street right toward me. One of the Boss's fedora-wearing enforcers leaned out the front passenger window, another out the back window, both aiming tommy guns that began blazing at me. I opened my mouth and screamed, but no sound emerged.

I tried to dive for cover behind an iron mailbox, but my move was too late. The Thompson submachine gun had originally been named the Annihilator. And for good reason, I realized, as a half dozen .45-caliber ACP bullets blew through the briefcase I was clutching and continued through my worsted suit and deep into my body. The impact of the hot lead blew me backward as it cut down across me in a diagonal line starting at my left collarbone. Though the bullets came nearly instantaneously, I felt the first slug shatter my clavicle and the second go cleanly through my left lung, ricocheting off the brick building behind me. The third shot splintered my sternum and must have also grazed my aorta, because I saw my blood immediately fountain out. The next slug entered at my navel and slammed into my spinal column, paralyzing me from the waist down. The fifth and sixth ripped through the soft tissues of my spleen and liver. The pain was overwhelming. The world around me became even more illusory.

Blood poured from my wounds as I fell into the filthy water streaming along the gutter. Barely conscious, my cheek against the gritty pavement, the image of the wet Chicago street swimming in my head, I caught a quick glimpse of someone watching sadly from the shadows of an alley. It seemed to be the same dark-haired, sleek young man from the saloon, but now in a smartly tailored 1930s suit with spats. His eyes were on mine as he shook his head at my plight.

I heard the big Packard's tires screeching in protest. From my sideways perspective on the pavement, I saw the driver swerve through a 180-degree turn in the next intersection at State Street. I was vaguely aware of echoing screams from pedestrians as they leapt out of the car's path. The gangsters were coming back to finish me.

Struggling against the agony of mortal wounds, my flowing blood mixing with the gutter's polluted stream, I clawed at the rough macadam, pulling my battered body toward a steaming manhole that was partially open. I heard the Packard's throaty engine accelerating toward me from a block away.

I pushed at the manhole cover, which seemed impossibly heavy, but I knew I had to keep the bullet-ridden briefcase out of their hands. I got the weighty manhole cover slightly more open and shoved the briefcase in ahead of myself just as the machine guns started snapping like a string of firecrackers. The bullets ricocheted off the pavement, blowing chips of concrete off the curb. Though my legs were numb, I felt the punctuating pressures as several slugs struck and cracked the bones inside them. My mouth was filling with blood, choking me, as I grasped the edge of the open manhole and made one final agonizing exertion to pull myself headfirst into it. I fell downward into the darkness . . .

And landed atop the corpses of four ragged men, two women, and three children that were strewn haphazardly in the medieval wooden cart. I saw that their eyes were rolled back sightlessly, their skin was mottled with black pustules and running sores, and their gaping mouths showed blackened tongues, marking them as the latest victims of the plague. I hazily remembered that the pustules had been developing in my own groin and armpits. The pain was intense, consuming.

Lying helplessly in the wagon, clad in a tattered brown monk's robe, I heard the heavy clip-clop of a horse's hooves on cobblestone. Turning my head, I saw that the old wooden cart was being slowly pulled by a decrepit mare along a dark, bleak eastern European street. Acrid smoke was drifting. I hazily glimpsed ragged people with torches setting fire to the shacks that served as peasant dwellings in about AD 850.

I tried to drag my agonizing body to the edge of the cart, but another dead body landed atop me, heaved onto the cart by two burly men with rags tied around their faces. I fought the dizzying waves of pain, darkness, and nausea that coursed through me.

Then I sensed gravity changing. Instead of pulling from beneath me, gravity was suddenly over my head. My disordered mind indistinctly realized that the cart was being tipped, and I was sliding headfirst off of it, along with the corpses. I landed atop still more jumbled dead bodies at such an angle that I felt my neck crack. Almost immediately, another consignment of the limp, ragged deceased was unloaded into the crude pit, landing atop me. I was tightly pinioned. The weight on me was such that I could hardly draw a breath.

As I gasped, my nostrils caught the unmistakable scent of oil. Through one jaundiced eye, I saw by the flickering, nightmarish torchlight the villagers on the lip of the pit with their faces and hands swathed.

Suddenly I heard urgent shouts in Hungarian. "No! Wait!" From my half-inverted angle I caught sight of several Benedictine friars rushing onto the macabre scene. "If he is among them we must have him!"

"Too late," the nearest villager yelled back as he and others sloshed oil from rustic wooden buckets onto all the diseased bodies, of which I was the only living part.

The priests protested, shouting that they spoke with the full authority of Rome. Several of the locals grabbed and restrained them. One infuriated Benedictine bellowed, "I tell you we must have the bastard! His Holiness the Pope commands it!"

I saw a blurred shimmer of torches appear closer by as the villager responded curtly, "Tell His Holiness you were too late."

I tried to cry out, but my hoarse voice was too feeble to be heard. A torch landed upon the corpses near me. The oil ignited with a whoosh, and I was engulfed in searing flames.

A squealing, tortuous screech snapped my eyes open.

I blinked, thoroughly disoriented for a moment. I realized I had been dreaming and was wary that I still might be.

Then I glanced around, realizing I had dozed off while seated in the rapidly moving New York subway car on the number-nine train of the Broadway Line. It lurched sharply again, causing another screech of heavy metal wheels stressing against unyielding steel rails.

I drew a slow, grateful breath, relieved to be free from the grasp of my painful, recurrent, all-too-vivid dreams.

Lights flashed by in the dark tunnel outside. The surface of the window beside me was deeply etched with late twentieth-century graffiti. I looked at my reflection in the distressed glass. In two ways it was quite different from my image in the Red Garter's mirror: I was clean shaven, and my brown hair was clean and much shorter, if still a bit scruffy and needing a little trim. But otherwise the face looking back at me was the same: that of an everyday man in his thirties, with features that I supposed some might compare to an old Roman statue. My nose was definitely of that variety, my forehead and cheekbones broad and more or less sturdy. My face had a healthy color with smile lines around the eyes. I actually had been smiling a good deal in recent days, days which—dark dreams aside—I felt held much positive promise.

My eyes were light brown, and I had often been told that there was something out of the ordinary about them—something indiscernible that occasionally people had characterized as either oddly arresting or somewhat unsettling.

I gazed into them myself for a moment longer, as though sharing with a close friend my optimism about the days immediately ahead. Then I looked around the jostling, half-full subway car at my fellow passengers, wondering how the events of the next few days might affect each of them. At least seven distinct variations of multiethnicity were represented, including an East Indian boy who was about six and spoke to his mother in a dialect I recognized as Gujarati. When his large and innocent brown eyes met mine, I winked at him and said hello in his native language. He shyly returned my smile.

Like the others around us, he was dressed as I was: for midwinter in New York. I wore faded jeans, a white wool turtleneck, sneakers that were comfortable for walking, and a warm navy-blue peacoat I had long since broken in.

I stretched a cramp out of my right leg, and my gaze fell upon the small brass rivet securing the pocket seam on my well-worn Levi's. A faint smile crept across my face as I recalled the first time I ever saw such a rivet on denim.

The subway loudspeaker interrupted my recollection, announcing the 116th Street station. The train decelerated to a squealing stop. The doors rattled and hissed open, and I stepped out onto the old tiled platform, very much enjoying the unique buzz of contemporary New York around me. I walked toward the exit stairs at the end. A beggar sat on the floor with his back to the wall, his tousled gray head slumped forward. I dropped some coins into the man's cup and continued down the platform.

A clean-cut young black preacher wearing an inexpensive but cared-for suit handed out pamphlets nearby. He spoke cheerfully to passersby, saying, "You have only two days to get right with God, brothers and sisters! Two days until January first, when His Glory will finally be revisited upon us!" He reached out a pamphlet to me. "Here, brother, God bless you."

I received it with a polite smile and moved toward the exit. The spring in my step reflected the positive spirits that were coursing happily inside me. But as I approached the exit stairs, I glanced down the dark subway tunnel and slowed my pace. I sensed that something lurked deep within the tunnel's obscurity—something disquieting.

Was that a slender shadow I glimpsed moving past a distant yellow warning light in the dark tunnel? Did I really hear a faint whisper from a familiar voice saying something like, "Isn't it about time we talked?"

I paused, narrowing my eyes, but still unable to penetrate the darkness, to divine the presence I sensed down the tunnel.

All the while the young minister behind me continued passing out his pamphlets, saying, "Two days until the Son of God returns to judge the quick and the dead. Forty-eight hours until you will face blessed Redemption or eternal Damnation. Do not tarry, friends. He is coming."

His words distracted me from the tunnel's ominous darkness and brought some comfort. With a grateful heart I glanced back at the reverent minister, inhaled, and climbed the exit stairs toward the bright December sunlight.

TWO

Jillian Guthrie, age 27, journalist...

I was really pissed at my editor. About the only thing George hadn't messed with was my byline, which the typesetter at least managed to spell correctly this time: Jillian with a *J*, not a *G*.

Not that George's changes were all bad. Some of them, I grudgingly saw, actually improved the flow of the read. But I was still angry because he'd made other changes just for the sake of making changes. Justifying his damn job. I hated that shit. Different, but no better. I would have argued against them but hadn't had a chance to see them until the tabloid hit the streets that morning. I had just snagged a copy of the latest edition before heading up to 116th Street in the taxi.

It was the week after Christmas, 2000, so the seasonal decorations were still everywhere along Amsterdam Avenue.

I bailed out of the cab at 116th, stepping over the grungy remnants of gutter snow, and blinked when I saw my exact double staring back at me. Actually it was me, mirrored in a liquor store window, complete with grumbly face: shortish at five three; hair cropped in a wash-and-go do; figure kept trim by activity, nerves, and excessive caffeine; simple eyeglasses in thin wire frames, no contacts, my eyes were too dry. Normally I wore pants, but that day I was wearing a soft, loose skirt under my car coat to appear more feminine and accessible to the people I was en route to seduce.

I walked west along 116th at the brisk pace that was my norm. You snooze, you lose, in a New York minute. Clichéd, yes, but accurate. I tucked the tabloid under my arm while fumbling to pull out the address I had scribbled on the back of a Ray's Famous Pizza receipt. Then I ran headlong into someone.

He was a fortyish Latino with a round face and a drooping mustache; he gestured an apology and kept going. But I froze, snagged by the sharp memory of my childhood sidewalk in our low-rent area of Brooklyn.

I was five, zipping along on my trike in the spring sunshine when I collided with Mr. Ramirez. He was a fortyish Mexican, with a round, cherubic face and a drooping mustache. He wore a neatly pressed and starched white shirt. He always did, every time I saw him afterward. But that was the first time. He smiled kindly and helped me up, speaking in Spanish-accented English: "Sorry, *chiquita*. Are you alright?" Behind him, I saw a moving van unloading his belongings into a small house. My ever-friendly, petite Romanian mother smiled, extended her slender hand, and welcomed him to our neighborhood. I also vividly remembered Mr. Ramirez pressing her hand and whispering something confidentially into my mom's pretty ear. From her reaction, I knew it was a flattery.

Standing there at 116th and Broadway on December 30, 2000, I felt the memory tighten my face, which made me grit my teeth. But the light changed, so I sucked it up and headed on to my appointment, walking west across Broadway, frowning.

Will...

I was cheerfully walking east across the Broadway intersection along with two dozen other pedestrians. I dodged between the numerous people walking in opposition. I noted that some were frowning or merely preoccupied with their various concerns, but others were like me: simply enjoying the ambience of the Upper West Side. Cloaked with

Christmas decorations that sparkled in the clear December morning, the avenue was buzzing with the unique energy of quintessential New York: striving traffic moving in a herd, innumerable people heading in all directions, wafting scents of cinnamon and charred chestnuts, echoing music from various radios, all part of the ambience of the great city.

I inhaled deeply, enjoying the bracing, chilly air, blue sky, and bright sunlight on the many still-white patches of snow as I crossed onto the Columbia University campus. I felt an effervescent enthusiasm within my chest.

As I looked ahead, the particular configuration of the university buildings, the snow still blanketing much of the broad campus lawn, and a custodian pulling a trash cart toward me caused me to slow with déjà vu.

The campus momentarily became a snowy countryside in Germany; the custodian was a medieval peasant pulling a small hay cart toward me, smiling a friendly greeting. In the distance, I could see Altenburg Castle. Its tall central tower commanded a view across the snow-covered meadows where I stood and on to the distant bishopric at Bamberg.

As I came back into the moment, standing there at Columbia, I noted that an NYPD officer, rocking on his feet to keep the blood flowing, was taking my measure. Always wishing to avoid any questioning, I discretely continued across the campus, giving the appearance of someone who belonged there and was going about my business the same as the other people. The people who were normal. Unlike myself.

I saw an urbane young mother of East African descent talking on her cell phone, her breath making puffs in the cold air above the colorful scarf wrapped around her throat. Her two-year-old daughter sat patiently in a stroller, bundled against the winter weather, playing with a string of brightly colored wooden beads in her mittened hands. The child's large brown eyes locked onto me and followed me strangely. Then she spoke quietly to me with a dark voice that sounded oddly like an adult male. "You oughta just give it the hell up, man."

I blinked and stared at the toddler. She had looked away and was cheerfully occupied with her string of beads, completely unaware of my existence. But the child's mother gave me a sharp glance that clearly said, *Stop looking so intently at my child, creepy stranger.* She wheeled the stroller away.

I watched them go, feeling the same disturbance in my gut as when I tried to see into the darkness of the subway tunnel. Then I drew a breath and continued walking eastward. As I passed a newsstand, a grisly cover of *National Geographic* arrested my eye. It showed a face, recognizable as having been human, but now resembling a shrunken head. The entire visage was brownish black. The eyes were squinted tightly closed; the mouth with its broken teeth was open grotesquely as though crying out in pain; the stringy hair extended down beneath a bristling rope that was wrapped tightly around the shriveled neck. The headline proclaimed, "Bog People: Sacrifice Victims Preserved in Danish Marshes." The image churned up a queasy memory within me, which I suppressed as I continued on.

Eleanor Edgerton, age 61, vagrant...

It was too damn cold that morning to have your ass right on the freezin' concrete bench, so I was snuggin' my blue blanket up under me when I seen ol' Roland comin'.

Blind as a goddamn bat, ol' Roland is. I seen him lots, waddlin' along beside Lucie, his guide dog. Black lab, sweet pooch. One time Roland ast if he could "take a look at my face." With his fingertips, y'know? They was soft, like a woman's. I told him my face was gonna feel like a map crisscrossed with a lot of rutted roads. Too much sun, too many ciggies. But he was sweet, said I felt pretty to him.

Ro ain't never passed me without him droppin' somethin' into my cup. Did that day, too. "There's a fiver, Ellie," he says, and I thanked him kindly.

So I set there beside my shoppin' cart startin' to juggle my three beanbags and watchin' him walk away when I seen that thirty-sompin' guy comin' toward him. Sorta sandy-brown hair, wearin' one o'them navy peacoats, walkin' in my direction. Ain't never seen him before, but ain't never gonna forget that first time, 'cause it was the damndest thing: Ol' Roland come to a dead stop like he had *caught sight* of the guy comin'! Then Ro's head turned real slow, like Ro was watchin' the guy pass. *Watchin' him*, you understand? But Roland's been flat-out blind for seventy-odd years. I ast him 'bout it later and he said he couldn't make head nor tail of it neither. But said he sure as shit knew that somebody—or some *thing*—unusual was goin' by.

But that ain't the damndest thing. Nuh-unh. You ain't heard the god-damndest thing yet. What happened next made me drop my beanbags.

The peacoat guy walks on past Ro, and he passes a statue at the corner of the park near to where I was squattin'. Now lemme tell ya, I seen that ol' statue rain and shine, summer and winter for years. I know it good. But when this guy walked past it—the head o'that goddamn statue turned to watch him go by!

Yeah, I know, I know, I seen weird shit before. But only when I been seriously boozin'. Hey, if I was someplace I couldn't get liquor, I'd buy me some vanilla extract and slug that down. Mostly alcohol, y'know. I'd get drunk as a skunk, but smell like a cupcake. And I'd end up behind some stinkin' dumpster seein' them black and yellow snakes wriggling around my feet. But I'd seen 'em or such like 'em before. Plenty. I knowed it was 'cause of all the hooch.

But this statue thing was different. I was stone-cold sober, and I ain't never seen something I knowed was real steel or bronze or some shit come to life and turn its goddamn head to watch a guy!

I seen the guy slow down a mite, like he sensed somethin' bizarro behind him. But he didn't look back at it, no ma'am. Then he seen me starin' at him, and I got all airy in my chest. Scared, y'know? But when he smiled it was just an ordinary, friendly smile. So I swallows hard and just holds out my hand like usual. "Got some spare change, boyo?"

"Sure," he says, fishin' out a coupla twenties! Whoa, jackpot! But before I could thank him, he says, "If you'll take a little walk with me."

"Hey," I snapped back at him right smart, statue come to life or not. I pushed back his damn money and pulled down my old knit cap, the one with the beer tabs sewed on it. "Hey," I snaps at him, "I ain't no goddamn whore."

And he grinned at me, sorta chucklin'-like, and says, "Ah, just my luck. But walk a little up the way with me." He reached down easy, but I clutched myself tight. He talked real calm, sayin', "It's okay, I used to be with the Show."

That stopped me cold. He knew the Code: *I'm with the Show* was how you'd let someone know you worked with the carnival. Then he says, "I'm a free-a-zend."

Okay. Now he had me. That was secret carny lingo we all used when we didn't want a mark to know what we was sayin' to another carny. Like instead of saying "Piece of shit," a carny'd say, "Pia-zeese of she-a-zit." So "free-a-zend" was "friend."

But I was still eyein' him close. "How'd you know I was with the Show?"

He eased them twenties into my hand and picked up my three grungy beanbags; juggled 'em hisself like a pro. He'd seen me doing it. Jugglin' was what we mostly did when we were just killin' time on the midway waiting for a mark.

Twenty-three years I spent travelin' with the cheap shows all over hell till me knees give out. So I know people, huh? And marks. And cons. Ain't nobody gonna play the outside on me. Ain't nobody gonna bullshit this ol' bullshitter.

But this guy.

This guy.

There was somethin' . . . I can't . . . Shit, I still don't know what the hell it was. But he made me feel, I dunno. Safe. Kinda comfortable-like. And it wasn't just 'cause of him being a carny. It was somethin' else, too.

So I let him help lift up my old creakin' bag of bones. And we wheeled my cart up the street, walkin' slow. He ast my name, and I just told him Eleanor 'cause he seemed okay, but you never know, so I kept my eye on him, wary-like.

We walked along Amsterdam, and then I seen where we was headin': that big-ass Cathedral of Saint John the Somethin' or Other. I pulled up short. "Naw, naw," I says to him, figurin' now that he's one of them evangelicals or some shit, "I ain't no goddamn churchy type neither."

"I understand," he says real calm and logical with a friendly glimmer in his eye, "but maybe a warm-food-and-dry-place type? They're not pushy in there, believe me."

I stared right into them light-brown eyes o'his. Crotchety as I felt, there was somethin' about this guy. He had this calm but juicy sorta nature that perked you up. He didn't press, but he sounded so damned encouragin', and like I'd be doing him a favor. "Nothin' to lose, huh?" He nudged me, real gentle. So after a minute I gave in and let him help me across the street.

I was inside that big church once a long time ago. But I didn't remember it being so goddamn humungous. He took me up to this Chinaman who had a name tag that looked pretty official and ast him to look after me. Then he says, "Have a doctor examine her, too. She's diabetic."

I 'bout dropped what teeth I had left. Musta sounded pretty goddamned stupefied when I ast him, "How the hell'd you know that?"

The guy just smiled at me and gave my arm a friendly sorta squeeze as the Chinaman started to ease me away, but I hooked the guy's sleeve and zeroed in sharp on him. "Why'd that statue turn its head to look at you?"

Will...

That caught me off guard, and I saw the kindly Korean frown at me questioningly. So I just said matter-of-factly, "I have absolutely no idea, Eleanor. But you take care now." I patted her hand and gave a subtle look to the Korean to silently transmit, *The old dear must be fantasizing about something.* The Korean indicated understanding and gently led her away through the apse of the great cathedral. I was pleased to have made her a bit more comfortable, even though I thought that in a few days she might be looked after far more grandly.

But I was troubled hearing that Eleanor had seen the statue's movement. It was disturbing to know that someone other than myself had witnessed such an unreal occurrence. That indicated a new escalation, a new and more aggressive offensive by the dark and potent forces that I knew were at work.

I stood alone in the apse for a moment, trying to let the peaceful ambience of the massive House of Saint John the Divine, and also John's predictions, outweigh the underlying tension I'd been trying to ignore.

As I emerged, frowning, from the cathedral and turned north on Amsterdam, I sensed that behind me, high up on the ornate balustrade, one of the stone gargoyles was slowly turning its ugly, demonic head to watch me.

Rather than giving it the pleasure of seeing me look back, I casually raised my fist over my head in its direction, then stuck up my middle finger.

It amused me momentarily, until I turned west on 120th Street and felt the sudden pain stabbing my brain like a nail being driven into my skull. It staggered me, as it always did. I heard myself mutter, "Ahk. Wrong way, dummy," as I leaned with both hands on a battered wire-mesh trash can and tried not to vomit.

I turned and stumbled back the way I had come, and when I regained Amsterdam, the pain abruptly stopped, as I knew it would. As always, it stirred up uneasy thoughts that I didn't wish to contemplate. So I didn't. I drew a fresh breath of the chilly December air and walked eastward.

THREE

Chuck Weston, age 52, singer-songwriter...

The double malt tasted good that cold morning. Janie'd been needling me about it. Saying it seemed to her it'd been tasting a little *too*
good to me in the last few months. And how she didn't enjoy facing up
to a mike with me and getting a lungful of whiskey fumes. Hard to get
through a song, she said, much less a whole set. I knew she was right,
but I can be kinda dogged sometimes. Outright pissy, truth be told. So
I was relieved when she and our two tweener girls headed off to our
place in Tahoe the day after Christmas.

I took me another swig. Mmm, that Scotch was smooth stuff,
lemme tell ya. I had the bottle in a brown paper bag, and I was sittin'
there just like some vagrant might've. 'Cept I was sittin' there waiting
for my limo on the stoop of the classic brownstone facing Morningside
Park we'd lassoed for five point six. I was wearin' my usual Stetson;
my boots that Nudie made and monogrammed for around two grand;
my long, slick leather duster from Neiman's—also known as Needless
Markup. And I guess the Louis Vuitton grip that matched my guitar
case was sort of a tip-off that I wasn't exactly destitute.

But I sure as hell felt like it. And the double malt tasted good. I was
lifting the brown bag to take me another slug when I noticed this guy

walk past me, then pause and look back curious-like, sayin', "Excuse me . . . Chuck Weston?"

I glanced at him and grumbled, "Used to be." Then I looked at him again, closer. Friendly-faced guy with light-brown hair, tad shy of six feet, midthirties, wearing a peacoat.

But there was somethin' else. Somethin' about his eyes and the way he was lookin' at me. Studyin' me, like. I studied him right back for a few shakes, then finally squinted and said, "Do I know you, pardner?"

"Just a fan," he said, smilin'. "I saw you play in Tokyo."

That brought back a memory sweeter than the double malt. The Japanese had treated me like royalty. I nodded to the guy. "That was a good one, alright."

"Considerably better than good, Mr. Weston," he said, like it was the understatement of the year. "I was also privileged to see you in Nashville, with your wife. Truly extraordinary."

I snorted. "Oughta tell my damn record company." I took another disgruntled swig and saw that he was eyeing the guitar case.

"Is ol' Betsy in there?" he asked, and I nodded. He stood there on the sidewalk starin' at the case for a very long moment. Finally he said, "Would you mind if—" He stopped short, seemed right shy about it. "Would it be possible for me to just take a quick look?"

"At this point you can have the bitch." I waved my hand dismissively, giving him permission to take a gander. He was a bit startled. I guess I did come off kinda cavalier about it, so I reined in a mite and said, "Go on, son, s'okay."

I can read people pretty well. Spend a buncha years workin' your way up through lots of grubby backwater Texas clubs, you kinda get a sixth sense about folks. Doin' a little time in the Big House don't hurt, neither. This guy was a genuinely nice feller, and the way he unsnapped the case super-carefully made me feel I could trust him. "What's y'name?"

"Will," he said as he sat down on the step beside me and opened the case real slow. Then he just stared at Betsy nestled there in her sheep-skin-lined case. A curious sorta smile workin' on his face. "That's her alright," he whispered soft and low, downright reverent-like. "Nineteen sixty-four Gibson Epiphone FT 98 Troubadour."

"Only a couple hundred ever made," I said. In spite of feelin' grumpy, I was still proud of her.

"Two hundred and ten." He nodded as he studied her while I sussed him out. I was about to ask who he was when he went on. "But Betsy is the only one I've ever seen with a single black pickguard."

"Yeah," I said, surprised. "Most of 'em have two—"

"White ones. Yeah. I love the way they worked the spruce and the maple." He touched it very lightly, like it was a baby bird. "I think this is the best flattop Gibson ever made."

"Gotta agree with you on that one. You play, huh?"

He shrugged kinda shy-like. "A little."

I reached my gnarled hand in and lifted her out by the neck. "Take her for a ride, Will." He seemed downright stunned when I held her out to him. He shook his head no. It made me smile. "Go on ahead."

He took and held her like a newborn baby, resting her on his knee. Then he thrummed the strings lightly. She was just slightly off, and damned if he didn't hear it. He glanced at me. I nodded for him to tune her up.

He looked up at her slim neck. "Are these gold tuners?"

"The originals, yep."

As he tuned her gently, he said kinda offhand, "I haven't heard you much lately."

"You ain't alone," I sniffed. "Stuff ain't sellin' worth shit."

"Sorry to hear that," he said as he finished tunin' her. He just sat there and felt her in his hands a moment. Then he said, "I love that lick you do in 'Glory.'"

I was lifting my brown bag for another sip, but froze halfway up 'cause of what he did next: he launched into one of the most incredibly intricate blues riffs I ever played. Took me a month to get that sucker down, and even then I still messed it up regularly. But this son of a gun didn't miss a note. And I mean to tell ya his fingers were flyin'!

But that wasn't all: after he zipped through it once, he started improvisin' off of my lick and doin' shit that woulda made Jackson Browne's or Keith Richards's jaws drop. Mine sure as hell did. He whipped it up into this final machine-gun frenzy of notes that ended on such a sustained high, I had absolutely stopped breathin'.

When he finished, he just smiled at me like it was the most natural thing in life. And I just sat there starin' like a teenage boy seein' real titties for the first time.

Finally I managed to laugh and say, "Well shit, boy, you done practiced a mite."

He grinned and said, "I've practiced a *lot*." He punched that word like it meant way more'n I could imagine. "And whatever you practice is what you get better at." Seemed like he glanced down kinda pointedly at my brown bag o'whiskey. Then he looked me straight in the eye and said, "But I don't have the gift for poetry you've got."

I blew out a puff that hung a second in the cold air. "Yeah. I'm so goddamn gifted I ain't written a hit for six years."

He shrugged. "That's because what you've been writing is pure crap."

It was like a splash of ice water in my face. I blinked.

He played another nifty riff while he said, "You've succumbed to the populist trap, Mr. Weston: writing what you think the fickle public wants to hear or what the suits in big corporate record companies think they can market easiest, instead of doing what you used to." He drew a big breath. "Woody Guthrie always said you've got to plumb the depths of your own soul's unique experience." I saw his eyes go sorta distant as he went on like he was remembering: "Riding on top of that boxcar with the starry night sky spread overhead and the dawn barely starting to creep up on the horizon, Woody would just soak it all in, filter it through the people he'd met and had an empathetic connection to, and then he'd turn it into art. He wrote like you used to—right from your heart." This guy made me feel like he'd been sittin' there right beside ol' Woody. Then he turned to look at me, real keen eyed. I felt like he was drawing a bead on me down the barrel of a Winchester. "You need to get back to that, Chuck. Back to your roots. Back to Austin."

He held Betsy out to me with a tight, sorta challengin' grin. "There's a lot to sing about." Then this strange kinda twinkle came into his eyes, and he said, "If we're lucky, there'll probably be even more to sing about in a couple of days. But either way, you should quit crying in your double malt and get your shit together, Chuck. Be better for all of us." He placed Betsy lightly into my hands. "Yourself included."

He kept gazin' steady at me a second, then grinned one last time, nodded, and walked on down the sidewalk, leaving me starin' after him.

I didn't see him again until the horror that happened in that old warehouse.

FOUR

Will...

Having his Betsy in my hands and actually playing her had been a rare and extraordinary treat. I'd played a lot of guitars over the years, but never a finer one. And the fact that it belonged to an artist I much admired made it all the more pleasurable. The experience put a spring in my step and helped disperse some of the uneasiness I had been feeling. I was further cheered as I crossed Morningside Park when I saw a stocky, bearded Caucasian man speaking energetically through a megaphone to passersby.

"And the Glory is near at hand, my friends," he said with a confident smile. "'They shall hunger no more, neither thirst anymore.'"

I automatically finished the quote. "'For the Lamb shall return to be their shepherd.'"

The sidewalk minister glanced at me with surprise and an appreciative smile, saying, "Amen, my brother."

Nicole Jackson, age 23, student, part-time bartender...

It'd been a rough morning. I'd had another dream about Casey. He was running ahead of me, and I couldn't catch up. It was like the air was real thick and I was running in slow motion. No matter how hard I tried, I couldn't run fast enough. I knew he was in danger, and I called out to him, but he just kept going, getting farther and farther away. I was crying very hard as I ran. Sobbing. When I woke up, the sleeve of my cotton nightshirt was soaked with tears.

I dragged myself out of bed feeling like a bag of wet sand, shuffled to the bathroom, and pulled my hair back. I hate my hair. Every black woman I know says the same thing. I tied it into a ponytail to start my routine. But when I saw how puffy my eyes were I didn't bother with any makeup. I held an ice cube against them before I left for work. On the subway from Queens I just felt dead.

I usually only worked weekends, but a couple of people were gone for Christmas and since CCNY was closed for the break, I covered. When I got to the bar up in Harlem, I dug another piece of ice out of the bin for my eyes. It was still early afternoon, so there weren't many customers yet, and that was fine by me. I didn't feel like talking or getting hit on.

It wasn't really a bad place, though: an old vintage hangout across from the Apollo that'd been there on 125th just east of Frederick Douglass since the '20s—all wooden on the inside and homey. The place had seen Harlem go from chichi to crummy and now back to trendy again. My dad had seen it all. He grew up just a few blocks north on 131st, still knew everybody in the neighborhood, like the old woman who owned the bar. That's how I got the job.

There were only two men sitting at the bar drinking beer. One was a buff black teamster guy I'd seen a few times. The other was a newcomer, a white guy in a peacoat with light-brown hair, sipping a Corona. I saw their eyes lock onto this curvaceous cocoa-skinned chick in a lavender-blue fuzzy Angora sweater, who came swishing in. She passed close by. I could smell her powder. The teamster eyed her like I'd eye a piece of double–Dutch chocolate cake.

He nudged the Corona guy and I heard him mutter, "Be nice to *feel* warm and fuzzy, huh?" I shook my head sourly and turned to check the stock. Men. Are they predictable, or what?

But in the mirror I saw that Corona had looked away from the girl, not rising to the bait. The teamster was leaning out to check her booty, but the guy in the peacoat was just looking kind of wistful, like maybe remembering an old love.

The teamster blew out a final appreciative puff, tossed down the rest of his Bud, nodded good-bye to Corona, and waved to me with a "See ya', Nicole," as he left.

I picked up his glass and wiped off the bar. Corona must've noticed that my eyes were still puffy, because he asked, "Job, illness, or boyfriend?"

I was in no mood for him and glanced up, intending to give him a glare that would slam on his brakes. But when I saw his eyes, I paused.

There was something about them. About his gaze. It was, I don't know, *open* you might say. He wasn't on the make. He was genuinely sympathetic. My own eyes suddenly filled up with tears. "Wow," I said, wiping them with a dry corner of the bar rag. "Sorry." My voice was so shaky. I was like totally startled. I couldn't believe how just looking at him had made me come all unglued.

"No, no," he said right away, holding up a hand, palm toward me, "I'm the one who should apologize." He turned a little bit away, like to give me some privacy. He seemed kind.

I pushed the water button on the soda hose to pour some for myself and sort of distract me. Even then it took me a minute to find my voice. When I finally managed it, all I could get out was a whisper. "Dog." He looked back at me. I swallowed, barely holding on to my voice. "It was my dog."

He looked at me for a long moment. A whole bunch of thoughts or emotional stuff seemed to be going on inside him. Then he just said, "Oh." But he said it in a soft kind of way that made me think he knew exactly what I was feeling. Maybe more than anyone ever had. "That can be even worse," he went on. "I'm truly sorry. What kind was it? How old?"

"A golden. Thirteen."

"That's a rough one. Sorry."

"Yeah." I was determined not to cry. "Had him since we were both pups." He sipped his Corona and didn't say anything at all. But the expression on his face kind of invited me to keep talking. It was strange. I was the one always listening to customers unloading. This guy turned the tables. But once I started, it was actually really comforting.

"It's just so weird," I said, pondering. "I mean, I really loved my grandmother Gertie, too. She was this funny, cantankerous, wonderful old dame. She died a couple months ago, and of course I cried. But"—I was embarrassed to admit—"when Casey died last week it was . . . I dunno, it was so different. I really came apart. Sobbing and . . ." A tear was tracing down my cheek again. I wiped it off. "I mean, just look at me."

A sad smile crossed his face. "It's because you didn't know your grandmother when she was a pup."

I looked at him curiously. "But she told me a lot of great stories about when she was young here in Harlem. Showed me scads of photos of her back then."

He leaned his arm on the bar, glanced at my name tag, and explained patiently. "But it's not the same, Nicole. With Casey you actually saw his *whole life cycle*. While he lived it. Beginning to end."

My eyes drifted away as I recalled. "Yeah. I remember sitting on the floor on my ninth birthday. We'd moved from Harlem out to Queens. An actual house. A real backyard. Then Daddy brought home the best present I ever got. That happy little bundle of golden fur, y'know? With those needle-sharp puppy teeth—"

"And that wonderful puppy breath?"

"Yes!" I laughed. I loved this guy. He really understood. "He whined in his crate beside my bed every night for the first two weeks."

He smiled. It was clear that he was happy to listen.

"I've got so many memories of Casey all jumbled together: the puppy peeing on my rug, then learning to sit."

"And in about a year he got sorta gangly, like a teenager?"

"Yeah, and without me really noticing, day by day he grew up into this big, handsome adult who used to jog alongside me under the Whitestone Bridge. When we'd stop to catch our breath, he'd always come lick my cheek or hand. Momma used to say, 'That dog just can't control his licker.'"

"Then he started getting gray around the muzzle," Corona said, knowingly. "Became a sugar face."

I sighed. "Yeah, he was really a gray old gentleman by the time I started City College. We didn't play as much, but that seemed okay with him. Then he started having trouble getting up. And last week . . ." The sadness was welling in me again; my throat was tightening. "Last Tuesday morning he couldn't get up at all. I lay down beside him, put my face on the floor right by his while I just stroked his cheek over and over. Then after a while I realized he was gone."

He sat there without speaking while I leaned on the bar, just thinking about it all for several quiet minutes.

Finally I said, "I guess you're right. When you see the whole thing like that, the whole life of someone you love from beginning to end. That's what makes it hurt so much."

He was silent. I looked over at him and saw that his eyes were downward, but not focused, like he was somewhere else, thinking about losses of his own. "Yes," he finally said, "that's what does it."

I took a big breath and blew it out as I stood up straight. "I'd never do it again, I tell you. It's not worth the pain."

"Well, you may feel a lot less pain by next week." He looked up, smiling kinda oddly.

I was going to ask what he meant, but right then a Harlem prince and princess breezed in like they were walking onto a yacht, y'know? Martin and Lateesha. Their parents were flush cotillion types, and they were grad students at some Ivy League college. They leaned on the bar right in front of me and Corona as Martin said, "Couple microbrews." I opened the cooler to get them while Martin turned to Lateesha, saying, "Look, there's no denying Pascal was one of the great minds of the seventeenth century, but he was definitely more a scientific philosopher than a theologian."

Actually I knew Pascal was both, and Martin sounded so pompous I wanted to hit him with a pie. Lateesha was also cynical. "Oh yeah, Martin? So that's why he said, 'Man was ultimately nothing'?"

"No no," Martin corrected her smugly, "Pascal said, 'Man was the ultimate measure of everything.'"

Lateesha shook her neatly cornrowed head. "Wrong. I am telling you what he said was—"

Will...

"'Qu'est-ce que l'homme dans la nature? Un néant à l'égard de l'infini, un tout à l'égard du néant.'" I hadn't meant to say it in French, but it automatically came out the exact way I'd first heard it. Nicole and the other two looked rather startled. So I translated quietly, "'What is man in nature: Nothing in regard to everything and everything in regard to nothing.' A middle between everything and nothing. That's what Pascal said. But I wish he hadn't said it with such bad garlic breath."

They stared at me. I glanced away, realizing I was unintentionally showing off. But occasionally it just comes out, particularly when I'm confronted by such a pretentious pair. I'm only human. More or less.

I also found my eyes drawn to the curvaceous young woman in the inviting Angora sweater. The teamster had been right; she was extraordinarily attractive. I felt a feral sexual warmth within me, and instantly I heard a familiar voice speaking in an ancient tongue: "She would be just the beginning."

I glanced behind the bar, but instead of Nicole standing there I saw the darkly handsome, sleek young man. He was dressed in an expensive black suede Windbreaker over a camel cashmere turtleneck. His eyes were as friendly and dangerous as ever. His attitude was charming and casual when he spoke again in the ancient language: "How about it?"

I stared at him a moment, then I responded in the same long-dead language, "How about you pound sand up your ass?"

Nicole...

"What!?" I said, startled. I was standing there holding the two cold microbrews in my hand. Corona blinked as though he had been looking at someone else and was surprised to see me—even though I hadn't moved more than a foot.

"Oh. Nothing," he said, shaking his head peculiarly.

Martin and Lateesha were also staring at him as I handed them the beers. Lateesha asked him, "What language was that?"

"Aramaic," Corona replied. "Dead language." Then he went on in a sorta singsongy voice, "'As dead as it can be. It killed the ancient Hebrews. And now it's killing me.'"

The two grad students decided he was a weirdo and sidled away. Corona seemed to enjoy their slight discomfort—and he saw that I did, too. He winked at me as he took out a twenty and pushed it across the bar toward me. He tossed back the last of his beer and stood up to go, but seemed to have a last-minute thought. "Hey Nicole, you know the pound over on Powell?"

I remember scrunching my face a little, curiously. "Yeah?"

"I think they've got some pups they're going to put down tomorrow."

Then he finger waved a friendly little good-bye to me and walked out.

I didn't see him again until five days later—when we were trapped together inside that warehouse. That unbelievable nightmare. Not everyone got out alive.

FIVE

Jillian...

As I rode the A train down from Harlem, I was looking through my article again, still peeved at George for the stupid changes he'd made. I was determined to make sure he didn't mess with the new story that I'd just locked up the exclusive rights to.

I got off at 42nd Street and came up inside the Port Authority Bus Terminal. One of my least favorite places in Manhattan. Huge, lofty, always smelling of disinfectant and the bustling people headed in all directions at once. Sixty-seven million people came through there every year, and I swear to God I thought fifty-six million of them were illegal Hispanics. With annoyance I pushed my way through the latest bunch who had just jumped the fence.

(It's embarrassing and extremely painful for me to write those last two sentences—and many that are upcoming. Only with great difficulty can I admit how I harbored such unbridled intolerance. But that's who I was at the time, for what I thought were very substantial reasons. In documenting this story, I realized it was vitally important for me to be completely truthful and brutally honest about who I was—about what had been my mindset for years, and why. Only by presenting myself as I was then, warts and all, can I expect anyone to truly appreciate the magnitude of the startling transformation I underwent over the next few mind-bending days—as a direct result of the unique man I was destined to encounter.)

I came out on Eighth and briskly walked the long block to Ninth, squinting into the cold wind from the Hudson that was whipping my face and under my glasses. As I approached the newsstand near the corner, I slowed down. My eyes, as usual, went right to the front page of the *New York Times*. I'd always loved the classic font that the paper's name was set in. That typeface was regal and in itself lent a weight and seriousness of purpose to what had become "America's newspaper of record." I had known everything about the *Times* even before I got to NYU: how it was called "the Gray Lady" because of its formal style and somewhat staid appearance; the ninety-five Pulitzers from covering the World Wars in 1918 and the 1940s, through the Pentagon Papers and Vietnam revelations, up to reporting on the latest Taliban travesties. I knew it was, bottom line, the most prestigious paper that every journalist would kill to work for. Certainly there were other excellent papers like the *Washington Post*, the *Los Angeles Times*, or the *Boston Globe* in which a reporter would be proud to have her byline, but the Gray Lady was absolutely the crown jewel.

There were still a few copies of the *Times* left, waiting to be bought by thoughtful, intelligent New Yorkers, those who were anxious to read "All the News That's Fit to Print."

Nearby were stacks of tabloids, including the *National Register*. It always made me smirk and think, *All the News That's Print to Fit.*

I heaved a frustrated sigh and headed toward the old office building nearby where I unfortunately worked. The big modern metal sign over the main entrance announced "The National Register—America's Favorite Paper!"

I shook my head every time I passed under it, because I knew that from a mass-circulation standpoint, the statement was true. And, therefore, I knew that America was in deep trouble.

I generally referred to it as the *National Regurgitator*. It depressed the hell out of me to be working there, but jobs in print journalism for a recent grad student, particularly in New York, were incredibly hard if not outright impossible to come by. The quickly evolving Internet was looming like a very dark cloud. After months of pounding the pavement, my choices finally came down to waiting tables or at least getting my foot in the door—even if it was the door to an outhouse. I was, however, determined to bloom where I was planted, to play the *Register*'s tawdry game to the hilt, all the while praying that instead of having it make me a journalistic anathema, I might somehow parlay it into snagging a position at a serious paper.

As I walked into our bull pen area on the eleventh floor, I saw George standing at the layout board, considering a pasteup of a front page. There was a big blank space waiting to be filled by some bizarre photo, and next to it, in fifty-point type, the headline screamed, "Elvis Found Alive—as a Woman!"

George Purvis stood frowning over it with his tie loosed and his Target dress shirt pouchy as always. He was in his characteristic thinking pose: head tilted forward, chin in (which made him look as though he had no chin at all), his right forefinger pressed flat against his lips in the manner that suggested he was shushing someone. He was a balding, graying, bookish man in his upper fifties, who looked more like a small-town banker than the editor of "America's Favorite Newspaper." He was nodding thoughtfully to Steve Snyder, a sweet younger reporter with unruly hair, who was very nearly as thin as the pencil in his lanky hand. I'm sure I'm not the only one to have Disney's version of Ichabod Crane pop into my head when looking at Steve.

George nodded to Steve as they scrutinized the front-page mockup. "That's pretty damn good, pal."

"Okay, George," I said saucily as I passed by, "I got 'em."

But George was focused on Steve. "So now go find a female Elvis impersonator—"

"Who'll say she had a sex change, right, chief," Steve said, completing the thought. Then his face lit up. "Ooo ooo, subhead: 'The King Becomes a Queen!'"

George's gray eyebrows arched up, always a sign of approval. "That's good, too, buddy boy." Then without looking at me he added, "Got who, Jilly?"

"Those black Siamese twins," I said as I shirked off my coat. "Exclusive."

He was still contemplating the Elvis headline as he asked offhand-edly, "How much?"

"Just eighty-five hundred," I said as a throwaway, hoping the "just" would make it sound like a bargain. But nope: George's attention swung fully onto me.

"Eighty-five?"

"That's max." I cut him off, waving my hand, then digging into my carry bag for the folder. "It'll only be four grand if they don't survive the separation—and the doctor says it's eighty-twenty against."

He was shaking his head. "That's still a pretty big pile of dough. I told you not to go over four—"

"Look at these photos." I plopped them down on the desk beside him, and his eyes widened immediately. I prodded him optimistically, saying, "Huh? . . . Huh?" as though I had just placed the Holy Grail before him.

He shuffled slowly through the truly grotesque photos of the con-joined eight-month-olds one at a time, his face twisting into a grimace as he turned one sideways, then upside down and back, trying to under-stand what he was looking at. Finally, he muttered the words I longed to hear. "Holy shit . . ."

"Exactly what your readers'll say," I agreed, scooping up the stack of pictures. "At two bucks a copy."

"I dunno," he said tentatively. "I mean, if it bleeds it leads, and gross always sells, but those are really . . ."

"Extreme." I nodded proudly. "Yeah."

Steve had stepped closer and was looking at the photos in my hand as I straightened them up. His eyes went wide, too, as he offered another welcome and equally literate review. "Yow!"

"Right. And 'Yow' is exactly what our beloved publisher wants. You know that, George." I quoted her mantra, "'The public is jaded. We've got to keep pushing the envelope.'" I turned away, muttering to myself, "At least for this paper. Inquiring minds want to know . . . God help us."

I weaved my way through the maze of desks and other reporters and copyeditors toward my own. In addition to being a newspaper office with the appropriate phones, computers, printers, TVs, Post-it notes, coffee setup, scattered files, and papers, the place was also a serious rival of Ripley's Believe It or Not Museum. There were old *Register* front pages, with photos of eerie people, framed on various walls to inspire us. Others trumpeted past landmark headlines like "Live Baby Found in Watermelon." In addition to them, various physical artifacts from the paper's probing journalistic investigations crowded shelves and cluttered the tops of file cabinets. A stuffed two-headed wombat, for example, shared space with a dried brown mummy's hand and a rusty telescopic rifle sight allegedly excavated near the infamous grassy knoll. The office was a treasure trove for those who delighted in the macabre. It was the Smithsonian of the Lowest Common Denominator.

My fellow Registerians were an equally eclectic lot: men and women of varying ages. Many, like myself, doubtlessly viewed their employment here as a stepping stone to more substantive newspapers. A few had indeed managed to move on out and up successfully. But many others had settled in and found a permanent home. And why not? Their pay was often twice what they could've gotten at a more prestigious paper or mag, many of which were actually downsizing because of Internet pressure. Geraldine Hecht, the publisher of the *Register*, was very shrewd in that regard. She knew that to attract reporters who could even spell their names, she had to offer them something other than possible Pulitzers. And money worked. What a surprise.

As I walked through the busy office, Kiko intercepted me. She was a pert Asian girl, from Laos or someplace, who had gone goth with wild spiky black hair and an eyebrow piercing. As she handed me some phone messages, she said, "Hey. That really nice guy, Doug? From down in accounting? He came by looking for you again. You could definitely get a commitment there, girl."

"If I wanted it," I bantered offhandedly as I slowed down to flip through the notes.

"Why wouldn't you? Doug's smart, sorta cute in a nerdy way, and—"

I interrupted her when I reached my desk and saw that it was extremely neat. That really annoyed me. I called off to the Mexican custodian who was putzing around with a trash can a few desks away. "Conchita?"

The stocky woman looked up at me with a winning smile. "*Sí?* Yes, Miss Jilly?"

I indicated with both hands. "My desk?"

"*Sí, sí,*" she said in her heavy accent with enthusiastic pride, "I clean up for you."

"No, Conchita," I sighed, fighting my homicidal urge, "I said please *don't* touch it."

She smiled more broadly, moving away happily and convinced that she had pleased me. "*Sí, sí, de nada*, Miss Jilly."

As I stared daggers at her, I flashed back to standing in our tiny Brooklyn kitchen when I was five. My ever-patient mother correcting me in her heavy accent whenever I used a word in her native Romanian: "English, Jilly. We speak English. I came here so you can be American girl."

Standing in the tabloid office, I grumbled to Steve, "Wouldn't they expect me to learn Spanish in Mexico?"

Steve had ambled over to me on his long, thin legs. "Perhaps. But for the record, she's from Costa Rica." I shrugged dismissively. "And check the census: this almost *is* their country." Then he looked again through the photos I had shown to George, and grimaced. "God, I never saw real Siamese twins. Or I guess the PC is 'conjoined,' huh?"

"Yeah. That's the PC, but people get 'Siamese' better. Sells more papers." I was disarranging my desk back to the way I liked it. Steve kept staring at different photos.

"God. Can you imagine being their parents? Or them?"

"You getting soft, Steve? Where's your journalistic detachment?"

"Is that what it's called?" His tone made me glance up. I caught him scrutinizing me like an anthropologist might have. "This place is getting to you, Jilly."

I exhaled a little puff of disregard. He sat on the edge of my desk. "I mean, I know they pay us pretty well, but you oughta be doing Woodward-Bernstein stuff at the *Times*, not Siamese—"

"I know, I know." I held up my hands defensively. It wasn't the first time he'd broached the subject. "I do know, Steve. I've been looking."

"For a better gig? Or at least something to get their attention? Like the cool investigative work you did when we were at NYU?"

"Yeah, I am." I was proud of the serious work I had done for the *Washington Square News*, particularly a strong piece about AIDS in the Bowery. And I did know that chasing Siamese twins was decidedly not the same.

"Good," Steve said, nodding emphatically. "I'm really glad to hear it, girl. I need a friend at a hot paper who can help me get a job there, too." Then he stood up. "But meantime, I need a good Elvis pic from your Millennium stash."

"You got it," I said, pulling open the file cabinet beside my desk. "You want young and sexy? Or I've got a great old sweaty sperm whale." I lifted out the thick folder of pictures I'd been gathering for our paper's upcoming special photo edition.

Shortly after I joined the paper the previous year, 1999, I'd put together an end-of-the-Millennium photomontage, "Faces of the Last Thousand Years!" The public had eaten it up. It played right into all the press hype, hoopla, and outright nonsense that went on during the transition to the year 2000. And it sold a gigantic amount of extra papers, more than the *Register* ever had previously.

George and publisher Geraldine Hecht naturally wanted a repeat performance, but didn't want to wait another thousand years. I gave them an excuse: pointing out that the *true* end of the Millennium would actually arrive at midnight on the upcoming New Year's Eve, when 2000 gave way to 2001. George thought it could be not just a photo section, but an entire special edition of the paper featuring "More Faces of the Last Thousand Years!" I was a bit surprised by their enthusiasm. I knew that no one but the most ardent religious zealots or calendar nerds were paying any attention to the upcoming milestone.

"And this time put in more elephant men, dwarfs, and grotesqueries," the ever-elegant Mrs. Hecht had personally directed.

I had outwardly professed my eagerness to oblige while inwardly I sighed and vowed that 2001 would also be my year to escape her tabloid cesspool.

As I opened the overstuffed folder, a few of the pictures spilled out onto my desktop, and one threatened to fall off so I grabbed it. "Or how 'bout this one, a great Gandhi?"

Steve waved it off with a chuckle. "Doesn't sell like Elvis."

"No shit, Sherlock. That's the tabloid spirit." I looked at the photo of Gandhi. I knew it was from 1948. It showed him dressed as always in one of his signature white Indian dhotis and laughing with someone. I knew it had been taken at his home at Birla Bhavan in New Delhi only a day before he was killed by an assassin.

My eyes were momentarily drawn to a man who was standing just behind Gandhi and watching him with a smile. Though the picture was black and white, had I taken the time to study it carefully, I would have guessed that the man's hair was a medium brown; his eyes seemed about the same shade. I would have said that he was in his early thirties.

But at that particular moment I barely noticed him.

SIX

Tito Brown, age 17, a mixed-race tagger...

I been out cruisin' the night before. Freezin' my motherfuckin' ass off. But it'uz worth it when I spotted the target. Up on West 112th. Near where they been knocking down them old buildings. It'uz one o'them old trailer things you drive yourself. What they called? Yeah, yeah, motor homes, thas what I'm talkin' about. And lemme tell ya, this one was butt ugly. Sorta the color of puke. But a virgin target, know what I'm sayin'? Big wide flat sides with lotsa space under the window. And it ain't never been tagged.

So next day I drift by it a couple times, y'know, kinda casual-like. Don't look like nobody's at home. So I move in closer, all the time watching for cops, but it's like the week after Christmas and they ain't much shit goin' down. I got right up to the window and can't see nobody inside, so I set down my bag and get goin'.

First I pulled out a Krylon 2206. It's one o'them cool-ass ad-o-nized colors. Looks like metal; 2206 is Dark Bronze they call it. I been usin' that one a lot lately. I shook the can till I could hear them balls inside clickin' good. Then I smacked the lid on the sharp edge o'the curb to pop it off and pulled off the spray cap. Them caps they come with ain't worth shit. My cousin Ray taught me that. "Gotta work up your own caps, Tito, from other kinds of cans: wide tips from carpet cleaners all the way down to real narrow suckers for doin' thin-line work, know what I'm sayin'?" Ray had it down, man. Ray was somethin'.

Ray was.

I snapped on a medium cap and started right in layin' out my name reeeeal big: *TITO*! Sure as shit ain't nobody gonna miss it as big as I done it: from the top o'the window all the way down the side to the bottom. I'uz smilin', too, 'cause I knew somebody'uz gonna be drivin' this rig all over so lotsa people'd see it. Like the subways used to, before the suckers figured out how to make them cars with some sorta no-stick surface they could wash down. That was the shit. No more sneakin' into the layup yards in the Bronx with Ray where we could paint them trains all night.

After I done my name, I decided to rough in a sorta skyline behind it, like my name was painted gigantic 'cross the whole fuckin' city. I used a 3542 Castle Rock for that. Castle Rock, man? Some of them names they come up with kill me: Fresh Salmon, Grape Frost, Tidepool, Woven Tapestry. Shit, I don't even know what the hell them last two's s'posed to be. Anyways, after I roughed the skyline I used a 3545 Stonewashed Denim and outlined me a pair o'eyes at the back end of the bus like they'uz lookin' at my name and all. I'uz concentratin' real hard on doin' the long eyelashes, so I didn't notice the guy till he said, "You got some skills."

Yo! Scared the piss outta me! I whipped around ready to take off if he's a cop. But he was just this ordinary white dude in one o'them peacoats like my cousin come home from the navy wearin'. Light-brown hair and eyes, 'bout like Krylon 2504. Little taller than me and wearin' that coat, I couldn't tell if I could take him or not. Least not without my shiv, which, like a fool, I left in my ditty bag. So I started edgin' toward the bag while I says, "Oh yeah? You think so, huh?"

"Yeah, I do," he says, all the time looking at my tag real careful-like. "But you're lazy."

"What the hell you talkin' about?" I was almost to my bag as he started movin' closer. But not like he was comin' to get in my face. He was really just lookin' at my tag.

"You've got an excellent eye for color, Tito. It is Tito, right?"

"Could be, yeah."

"Hey. I'm Will," the guy said, all the time eyeing my tag. I'uz still tryin' to figure his game.

"The hues and tones and blending are all good, but there's an inconsistency of style."

"Say what?"

He pointed at the big pair o'eyes I done at the back. "This design here and those there"—he meant the skyline and my name—"they don't share any artistic unity." I just stared at him. Tryin' to get my head around what he was sayin'. "Can I see your preliminary sketch?"

"Don't do no sketch shit."

"Just what moves you in the moment, huh?"

"Thas it, yeah. I just jump in," I said, proud-like.

"Which is exactly the way to work."

Yo. Now that made me feel better. But then he kept goin' with a big *if*.

"*If* you're an Impressionist trying to capture a fleeting moment in the changing quality of light. But your work is clearly in a bolder, more populist graphic style, which would benefit from a bit more thought regarding design and intent."

"Well." I shrugged like it don't matter none. "I know some taggers do that sketch shit, but it's too much work."

"Too bad you feel that way," he says. "What you've done here," he says, "and there . . ." He pointed at the eyes and then the rest again. "It's well conceived."

"Yeah, so?"

"But they lack the power they could have, Tito, if they were more cohesive. There's also no subtlety."

"Hey asshole." I'uz getting' pissed. "Hell-lo? I'm using fuckin' *spray cans!*"

"Right," he says, starin' hard at me with this tight little grin. "Why exactly is that?"

I couldn't tell if it'uz one o'them shit-eatin' grins like guys give ya when they're bustin' your balls, or somethin' else. I blinked and stared back at him, trying to figure out what this dude was all about. And where he was goin' with this shit.

"Well," I said. For some reason I was feelin' kinda shifty, back-pedalin'-like. "'Cause . . . like, that's what all the brothers and sisters use, man."

"Ah." He looked at me sorta sideways, then said, "I pegged you for being a bit more independent."

He kept on starin' at me. Felt like a dare. Then his cell phone rang.

Will...

I kept my eyes level on Tito, trying to judge if he was getting my point. When the phone rang for the third time, I answered it without looking away from the boy. "Hello?"

"Mr. Bloom . . . ? W.J. Bloom?" I thought I recognized the voice, but the signal was a bit thin.

"Yes, that's right. Mr. Smith, is it?"

"Yes, sir, Walter Smith down at the Rainbow."

The image of his SoHo art gallery came immediately to mind, though I hadn't been there in quite a while. I envisioned the proprietor, Walter Smith, likely wearing a tailored tweed blazer and slacks, his bald head shiny even under the gallery's discreet lighting. As Smith spoke I imagined him looking across his polished oak counter at a wall hung with several paintings done in a strong, evocative style, somewhat like Manet. At the same time, I noticed that Tito was looking off at his graffiti on my rig with slightly different eyes than before.

44

Smith was saying, "We sold your study of the street vendor and the pauper."

"I'm happy to hear that."

"I knew you would be. And we managed to get you the full price," he said, obviously to underscore his astute agenting on my behalf. His subtle self-aggrandizement made me smile and didn't trouble me at all. I needed someone to handle such details, and Walter had been quite effective and efficient over the years. "Seven thousand, minus our commission," he went on. "I should transfer it to your Chase account?"

"As usual, yes. Thank you."

"Uh, Mr. Bloom," he said in a manner that made it clear there was something additional, but which he was somewhat hesitant to approach. "The woman who bought it was most anxious to meet you."

"Well, Walter," I said patiently, having been through this numerous times in the past, "you know I avoid that, so—"

"Yes, yes, of course I do know. But this lady is quite elderly and said it was very urgent. She also gave me the distinct impression she had met you before. Do you know a Hanna Claire?"

I drew a breath. Even Tito, preoccupied as he was with reconsidering his graffiti, glanced over at me when he sensed the change in my demeanor; he recognized that something had just had a strong personal impact on me. Hearing that name unexpectedly after so many years stirred profoundly deep, fond, yet extremely mixed, emotions. I stood silently for a long moment, peering into the past: toward the River Seine flowing beneath Pont Saint-Louis at night.

Finally I heard Smith's voice inquire, "Mr. Bloom?"

"Yes," I said, bringing myself back into the moment even as my mind weighed and considered the possibilities. "Yes, I'm here." I paused. "Please tell her . . ." I struggled to determine the best and most suitable reaction. The yearnings that had welled up in me upon hearing her name were surprising and intense. Yet I knew that first and foremost, I had to consider her feelings. I certainly understood why she would want

45

to see me again, and I her. But I knew from past experience that whatever joy she might gain would ultimately be far outweighed by grief.

With a heavy heart, I concluded that the best approach was the gentlest. I quietly said, "Please tell her that you haven't been able to reach me."

"You're certain, Mr. Bloom? I know she'll be very disappointed that—"

"I'm sorry, Mr. Smith . . . I have to go now." I flipped the phone closed and stood looking vaguely at it. I finally realized that Tito was gazing at me.

I managed a faint smile and said, "You should check out the Met's stuff."

He shook his closely cropped multiethnic head. "Naw, man. I'm Yankees."

"Not those Mets." I chuckled as I took out my keys. "The Metropolitan Museum of Art."

"Get the fuck out, man." His face wrinkled as though he'd just tasted a bitter root. "I don't do museum shit."

"It's on Fifth at Eighty-Second. Go into the Romantic rooms." I moved past him toward the motor home. "Examine the chiaroscuro."

"Who's he?"

"Look it up." As I unlocked the door I was amused to see his face go completely slack.

"Yo, hang on, hang on." He was totally confused. "This here's *your* wheels?"

I smiled at him as I stepped up into the doorway. "What was your first clue?"

His dark-brown eyes stared at me. "And you ain't pissed that I . . . that I . . . tagged your . . ." He was waving his hand toward his artwork.

I shook my head. "I'm just disappointed that you didn't do a better job." Then I had an additional thought and said, "Tell you what: meet me day after tomorrow on East One Twenty-Sixth by the river." I nodded toward his large artwork now adorning the side of my rig. "You shouldn't have any trouble finding it, huh?"

"Naw," he half laughed. "I mean, yeah. I can find it. But why?"

I shrugged, smiling. "Why not?"

He studied my face for a moment, then finally nodded slowly. I nodded back and watched him collect his paints and bag, and then shuffle off along 112th, a wiry teenager in his incredibly baggy, clown-sized jeans.

Tito...

So I'm walkin' away thinkin', *What the hell was that all about?!* When I got to the corner, I snuck a look back. He was just standin' there in the door o'his van, watchin' me. I already thought he was the strangest fuckin' dude I ever met. But I didn't have no idea just how strange. Shit man muthafucker, no, not yet I didn't. Not by a long shot.

Will...

Tito looked back at me curiously once from the corner, then disappeared out of sight.

Once he was gone, my gaze gradually drifted beyond into what has been called a thousand-yard stare. Into the distance. Into the past. As I turned her dear name over in my mind . . .

Hanna.

SEVEN

Hanna Claire, age 85, former United Nations envoy...

I simply don't get being eighty-five.

I heard Dorothy Parker on the radio back during the war say, "You're only as old as you feel."

Then in 1948 I became a big fan of Satchel Paige. Brilliant pitcher hired for Cleveland from the Negro Leagues. At forty-two, Satchel was the oldest rookie in Major League history. Or was he forty-three? Or forty-four? Nobody ever quite knew for sure. We weren't really sure he knew it himself. He had a couple of wonderful quotes on the subject: "Age is a question of mind over matter. If you don't mind, it don't matter."

But my very favorite of his has to be "How old would you be if you didn't know how old you was?"

In my case, about twenty-eight. Certainly not eighty-five.

And certainly not looking anything like the wrinkly-faced old biddy with the snow-white hair that I see staring back at me in the gilded mirror I bought in Canterbury in the '60s. I've just never understood aging. I feel as rambunctious as ever, like a spring chicken trapped in this ridiculous octogenarian shell. I don't get why I can't just throw on my scruffies and take my horse jumping or sail solo across Long Island

Sound or jog down to the Battery like always. I still do throw on my scruffies every day, but now I have to pay more attention to how I move just because of a stupid tumble six years ago. It made me mad when the doctors chastised me, saying that a seventy-nine-year-old shouldn't have been out rock climbing.

I liked to think that my eyes were just as blue as they ever were, though. Crystal blue, Will called them. Crystal blue. It still gave me a sweet lightness in my chest when I thought of him. He was one of a kind, Will was. And that was certainly something of an understatement.

Anyway, the doorman rang and told me who was downstairs asking to see me. I hesitated. Even though the person below might be my only hope; even though Walter Smith had just phoned from the gallery to say he couldn't contact the artist and doubted if he'd ever be able to, in spite of my offer to pay twice the price for the painting. Still, regarding the man waiting in my lobby, I had serious second thoughts.

But I realized I had no other choice. I told the doorman to send him on up. I was hoping he might provide a lead for me, a way to contact Will. But I also knew I was swimming in dangerous waters and had to be extremely careful about how I approached the man who was on his way to meet me.

When my doorbell rang, Methuselah looked up sleepily and yawned. He's my very opinionated and, being male, very rare calico. He was nestled in his favorite spot: the northeast-corner window of my town house on 84th at East End.

I opened my front door and greeted the man in the hall. He was slightly taller than my five feet ten and had an imposing persona. He wore a trench coat buttoned to the top. His hair had perhaps been dark brown, but was now salt and pepper. I guessed his age to be somewhere in the late forties. He had a full, roundish face and on that day had dark circles under his eyes as though he hadn't slept much or well.

His eyes themselves gave me a chill. They were very pale, almost ghostly. They made me feel disquieted, even a little fearful, but I didn't let it show. Having worked for decades in various services for the UN, I had become a master of astute diplomacy. His voice was heavily accented with French as he said, "Miss Claire?"

"Yes. Please come in. May I take your coat?"

He bowed slightly, with continental courtesy. *"Merci."*

"De rien," I responded automatically, and his gauzy eyes glanced at me, pleased.

"Ah, vous parlez français?"

I smiled, reverting to my native Bostonian English, which has often caused some to flatteringly compare me to Katharine Hepburn. Don't I wish. "I once spoke French quite well, but I've gotten a bit rusty, I'm afraid."

"No matter." He shrugged, adding with barely disguised disapproval, *"L'anglais* is the language of the world nowadays."

He entered as he unbuttoned the gray coat, revealing his clerical collar beneath. "St. Jacques would seem a good name for a priest," I said, smiling. "And your given name is . . . ?"

"Paul."

"Ah. Also appropriate. Hang your coat just there if you would, Father Paul." I indicated the mirrored walnut coatrack I'd rescued from an antique shop in Edinburgh. It felt right at home among the other late-Victorian pieces in my eclectic old town house. "I've just made some tea. Would you like some?"

"Certainement, merci, just black," he said as his pale eyes locked onto the painting above my mantle and then darted around the rest of the room. I saw him quickly scan the dozens of framed photos sprinkled across my baby grand and other shelves and tables. I knew precisely what he was searching for: the special photos I had carefully hidden away when he had first telephoned several days earlier. I was anxious to draw him out, though, in hopes of getting more information from him than he'd get from me.

He walked closer to the fireplace, making a show of warming his hands near the flames, but I knew darn well he was studying the painting over my carved mahogany mantle.

"You have a beautiful home," he said cordially. "For how long have you lived here?"

"Over forty years."

He looked out the window over Methuselah's wary head. The calico's piercing eyes were sizing him up as carefully as I was. He seemed somewhat uneasy because of Methuselah's presence as he said, "The view is wonderful."

I stepped closer, handing him the thin china teacup and saucer. "That window was the reason I bought the place back in the fifties. That's Carl Schurz Park out there."

"Ah." He nodded, sipping the hot Irish Breakfast tea. "Where the mayor has his Gracie Mansion, is it not?"

"It is, indeed. And the bridge beyond is the Triborough."

"Over the East River, yes," he said, looking out at the imposing suspension bridge.

"Actually it's the original 'bridge over troubled water,'" I said. "It spans the confluence, where the Harlem River, there on the left, meets the East River flowing in from Long Island Sound. They're in constant conflict with each other and the tide. It's very rough."

"And dangerous, I would imagine."

"Yes. That particular spot is called Hell Gate." As he gazed at it I remember thinking, *An appropriate name, under the current circumstances.* "But I know you didn't come to look out my window." I gestured toward the fireplace. "Is that the painting you phoned me about?"

He turned to look at the framed Impressionist oil painting above my mantle. "Yes. Yes, it certainly seems to be. And very nice, although I must confess I know very little about paintings. A businessman friend in Rome asked me to inquire about it while I was here. He's quite a collector of such work." For a professed novice Father Paul certainly seemed to study it carefully, with the seasoned eye of a connoisseur. I noted a subtle, peculiar smile working on his face.

I baited him. "It might easily be mistaken for a work by Manet, don't you think?"

"Alas, Miss Claire," he begged off, "I am not schooled enough to offer an opinion."

Was he trying to pull the wool over this old dame's eyes? "Well," I said, "others have felt that. But, as you can see, it is signed by a different artist." Indeed, he was already carefully investigating the lower right-hand corner, where appeared the letters *W.J.*

Then he turned his attention to the painting's brushstrokes, which, while small and precise, were also bold and evocative. The color palette suggested a late afternoon. A Parisian street vendor was at his crepe stand just outside the Louvre.

"This was obviously sometime before the glass pyramid was erected in the courtyard," Father St. Jacques noted.

"Considerably before, yes." I smiled, adding, "I'm afraid that is not my favorite architectural addition."

"I hate that ridiculous thing," he said as he gave me a warm, comradely smile. He was a shrewd man, encouraging my confidence. He looked back at the painting. The vendor was smiling and leaning down toward a disheveled, barefoot street urchin. The vendor's left hand was touching the child's right shoulder, as though to get her attention. In his right hand was a fresh crepe he was offering to her. The girl had just turned to glance at the vendor. The look of surprise on the urchin's face at the unexpected benevolence was what elevated the picture from a mere glimpse of Parisian street life to the level of poetry. There was a faint glow of amazement to the girl's face, and when combined with the simple tenderness in the expression of the vendor, the painting shone with a truly humanistic magic.

I watched him carefully as I asked, "Your businessman friend saw it in that magazine photo of me?"

"*Oui.* Yes." He turned his attention fully onto me, along with his charm. "It was quite a lovely article that *Vanity Fair* did about the UN High Commissioner for Refugees. I was most impressed to learn of all your work with them."

I nodded a polite thanks, but said, "Well, I think they talked a bit too much about me and not enough about the others."

"Were you at the headquarters in Geneva?"

"Often, yes. But also wherever the work took me. And what of you, Father Paul?" I was eager to probe his real reason for being here. "I take it that travel is also part of your job description?" I sensed his antennae react to my specific inquisitiveness.

"Yes, of late," he responded.

"When you phoned initially you were calling from Rome, weren't you?"

"Yes." He nodded pleasantly, sipping his tea again, but he clearly wanted to change the subject. Not so fast, buddy boy.

"You came all this way just to have a closer look at this painting?"

"No, no," he said, just a little too quickly.

Father Paul St. Jacques, age 48, Catholic priest, translated from the original French entries in his personal journal...

I felt as though I had spoken just a bit too quickly, so I tried to smooth it over. "No, I am here on other business, Miss Claire. When my friend heard I was coming, he asked if I would call upon you."

"What sort of business do you do for the church?" she asked. I had already been uncertain whether she was merely curious or much more shrewd than her soft, elderly appearance suggested. She possessed an airy, youthful attitude, and she did not smell like an old woman. There was a citric fragrance of the fresh outdoors about her. Nor did she dress her age. Rather than a dress or skirt, she wore casual but stylish slacks. I increasingly sensed that within her lurked a brisk, sharply spirited, no-nonsense New Englander, who might be trying to discern my true mission on your behalf, My Father.

So I presented my standard answer, sounding very professional indeed. "My work is primarily clerical research. I'm afraid you'd find it very boring indeed. Even I often do." I looked again at the painting, desirous of steering back onto the correct heading. "May I ask how you acquired it?"

"It was a gift from the artist."

She knew him!? My heart skipped a beat. I fought my intense desire to look at her, to study her expression. I feared, though, that my eyes would betray too much. I sought strength from My Father's Almighty Grace as I endeavored mightily to keep my breathing at a level pace and my tone casually conversational. "Really? How did you come to make his acquaintance?"

"He saved my life," she said with a smile. "Quite literally. Rescued me from the Seine one night."

Now it felt appropriate to glance at her curiously. "You had fallen in?"

"No," she chuckled. "I had jumped."

"What? On purpose!?" I said with genuine surprise. Her smile grew bemused.

"Yes, I'm afraid your church would not have been pleased with me."

"Mon dieu." I automatically made the sign of the cross upon myself. "You intended to drown yourself?"

"Mmm." She nodded, and her smile took on a mild irony. "Things, how shall I put it? Hadn't been going well. I was young, romantic . . ." Her voice trailed off as she looked deeply at the painting, or more accurately, looked into it. Then she put considerable feeling into her next word: "Passionate . . . and very near drowning, when suddenly there was someone splashing beside me in danger of drowning himself."

I inclined my head, encouraging her to continue.

"I was confused and quite annoyed I had been interrupted," she went on, "but found myself swimming to his aid. He fought me at first, but as I grew angrier and shouted at him, he finally relented and let me help him to the side. We dragged ourselves out and sat there on the stone river wall beside Pont Saint-Louis under the streetlights of Paris."

Her eyes had grown distant. "I can still see the back of Notre Dame lighted against the darkness behind him. We were soaked and shivering as we sat sharing our troubles. I told him about the gorgeous Parisian graduate student I had stupidly followed from Oxford, with whom I thought I was oh so madly in love and who professed to return my devotions. Until that very night, when I had found him in flagrante with a sixteen-year-old gamine. Sitting there by the river, I was about ready to throw myself in again and finish the job, when he shook some water from his still-dripping hair and said to me, 'Well, you know those Frenchmen. Always anxious to share their big baguettes.'"

I smiled at the humorous remark.

She nodded, saying, "Yes, he made me laugh, too. He completely defused my depression."

I tried to sound just ordinarily curious. "And why had he sought to drown himself?"

There was a twinkle in her eye as she recalled, "I realized rather quickly that he'd only pretended to be in peril to rally me."

"Really?" I raised an eyebrow. "Seems an unusual choice."

"But a wise one, Father Paul. He knew that if he had just tried to rescue me, I would have fought him. But by presenting himself as he did, well . . ." She gestured as if to say, *Here I am.*

"I'm very glad that he was successful." I continued to maintain a purely conversational tone as I probed. "He was French, I take it?"

"No. Though he spoke it like a native."

"Where was he from?"

"Actually, I was never completely certain."

Was she getting wary? I had to be more obtuse. "Ah." I smiled. "A common subterfuge. Very likely he was married. He was older than you?"

Hanna...

Boy, he is really pressing, I thought. I wondered how much I should tell him. I felt he already sensed I was being cautious. But what the heck. I figured the more I volunteered, albeit carefully, the more I was likely to get out of him. I tried to toss it off casually: "Oh, I would say early thirties. He was not gorgeous like my Parisian had been, but handsome."

"And nothing hinted at his nationality?" He tried to sound like he was surmising it, but I knew he was digging.

"Not really," I said. "A bit shy of six feet. Sandy-brown hair and light brown eyes that were, how shall I say, arresting?"

"Hmmph. Fascinating. And when did all this happen?"

"In April," I told him, as I looked back at the painting. "Of 1937."

I heard Father Paul draw a slight breath.

But I barely noticed. I had been caught up again by the magic of the painting. It was a common, mesmerizing occurrence for me: remembering when he first put it into my hands.

For a sweet moment I was alone with the painting and my memories. My crinkly, aging fingers lightly touched the precious antique strand of petite pearls that always encircled my neck, and I remembered it all.

My hair, long and honey colored then, was still damp from the Seine. I was wrapped in a sheet that was warm from our wonderful, intuitive lovemaking. It had happened spontaneously and had not at all been like a first time. Rather, it was as though we were old, dear friends and long-since lovers. The soft amber light in the small room enhanced the nature of his painting, which was leaning against a wall.

Everything around us enhanced the warmth and romance of that evening. Glenn Miller's "Moonlight Serenade" was playing from someone's radio in a nearby flat. The nighttime sounds and springtime fragrances of the City of Light drifted in through the garret window, which looked out over the rooftops of Paris. Like the other rooms I came to share with him, it was rented for only a day or two. Or three. Never more than three.

The voice of Father St. Jacques intruded upon my reverie, sounding as if it came from another dimension. "How long did you know him?"

I slowly came back into the moment with what I imagine was a wistful smile. ". . . Not long enough." My unintended intonation very likely suggested our intimate connection.

The priest did his best to sound casual as he asked, "What was his name?"

Should I tell him? And if so, which name? I had pondered the dilemma ever since he had first telephoned, and I still had not arrived at a satisfactory decision. But the moment he asked, the name was on my lips: "Willem James Logan."

I noted a faint glimmer immediately appear in the priest's ghostly eyes. He asked, "Have you seen him recently?"

I endeavored to keep my voice level. "Not since before the war."

"World War Two?"

"Yes."

"Is he still living?"

"I presume so; I've not heard otherwise." Then it was my turn to have a go: "And why are you trying to find him, Father Paul?"

"My friend wishes to offer him a commission for a painting" was his ready answer, though I knew better.

"Really?" I said with an innocent smile.

"Yes. My friend considers him quite extraordinary."

"Well," I said lightly, "he certainly is that."

"Have you had any recent contact with him, Miss Claire?"

"No. But I'd very much like to." I paused to review the bidding: it didn't appear I was going to get anywhere with him unless I was slightly more straightforward. "In all honesty, Father Paul, that's why I encouraged your visit. When I heard of your interest in his painting, I became hopeful that you might have some information for me regarding the artist's whereabouts. I'm obviously not getting any younger. One foot in the grave and the other on a bar of soap, as my grandmother used to say. I should very much like to see him again before I shuffle off to Buffalo and beyond."

He made a noncommittal gesture with his hand. "Alas, Miss Claire, I fear that I am not in possession of any specific information that would be of help to you."

"So you have no idea where he is, Father?"

"No." The priest shook his head negatively. "Indeed, I was hoping that you might."

I breathed a sigh as I turned away for a moment. I gazed out the corner window toward Hell Gate. The tide was coming in. It was the time of greatest turbulence.

Only a month earlier my kindly young doctor, Sandra Mader, had taken over the practice of her father, Herbert. He had been my physician and friend for forty years. I had watched Sandy grow from infant to quiet child to scholarly teenager to medical student. Now she was my doctor. And she had told me she feared I was exhibiting some early but telltale signs of Alzheimer's.

Though I'd had vague suspicions myself, it was a stunning blow to hear it put so clinically. Particularly since, in most all other respects, I was still pretty healthy and vigorous for an old dame. No one wants to lose their memory, of course. But the thought of losing my memories of Will, without ever seeing him again when there might be even the slimmest possibility, was unbearable.

I knew I must tread very carefully, however. I knew I was playing a very dangerous game: trying to use Will's arch nemesis to help me locate him for myself. I recognized the serious jeopardy I might unintentionally bring down upon him. I truly didn't want to do that. But I'm embarrassed to admit that my own selfish desires to find him, to see him, to hold him again, were just too compelling. My time was running out. My hourglass was draining. The grains of sand now had a finite number. Let me tell you, my dear, an old woman's heart can be a very determined force.

I looked down at Methuselah lying on the sill. His eyes were fixed upon me with a depth of intelligence that positively seemed to understand everything I felt. And to encourage me.

"Father Paul," I began, as I slowly turned back to face the priest. "Do you have a Bible with you?"

He looked slightly nonplussed. "Uh . . . not at this moment, I'm afraid."

I moved to the large bookcase that was built in along one entire wall. "Not a problem," I said, withdrawing a volume. "I do." Then I walked to where he was still standing on my navy-and-scarlet Persian rug before the fireplace and the painting. "There may possibly be some additional information I can give you, Father Paul, but first I need you to swear something to me."

"Of course, madam," he said with a furrowed brow designed to connote utmost sincerity.

Father St. Jacques...

I knew it. The devious crone had been toying with me. I would of course agree to whatever oath she asked in order to accomplish my mission in the service of Mother Church. I could cite numerous historical precedents in which soldiers of the Cross such as myself, pursuing the greater interests of the Holy See, had been required to bear false witness in order to achieve their important goals. It was meet and proper that they do so, that your will, My Father, might be fulfilled.

And certainly there was no goal in the history of the Roman Catholic Church that was more vital nor more imperative to achieve than that upon which I, and others like me, had been dispatched. It was a mission to which I had earnestly devoted the last twenty-three years of my life. And to which I was committed to devoting all my energies until I breathed my last breath and rose to join thee in thy glory, O My Father.

She held out her Bible to me. I placed my right hand firmly upon it. She looked me in the eye and spoke in a more formal manner befitting a solemn oath. "If you should chance to discover his whereabouts, you will notify me immediately. You further give me your personal promise, and also your pledge as a representative of your church, that no harm shall come to him . . ."

Yes, yes, I thought. *Get on with it, old woman.* I felt nervous indigestion beginning to burn in my stomach.

". . . Nor any restraint of any kind placed upon him."

"Restraint, madam?" I asked, feigning puzzlement. "Why should that even be a—"

"Nor shall any restraint of any kind be placed upon him," she repeated emphatically, adding, "by you or the church." Her eyes were fixated upon me. "This you swear before God."

I drew a resolute breath. "I do so solemnly swear, madam. The sin upon my immortal soul." Then I impulsively took the Bible from her hand and kissed the book to seal the contract, at least in her eyes.

She stared at me in silence for fully fifteen seconds, as if still weighing her choice. Finally she walked to a rolltop desk that was inset into her bookcase wall. From a narrow slot beside it, she withdrew a thin wrapped package that was slightly over a square meter in height and width. I spotted a small, colorful label on the back denoting that it had come from an establishment called the Rainbow Gallery.

She rested the object upon the desktop and looked at me again with her eyes slightly narrowed, as though she were trying to peer into my soul, to assure herself of my pledge. I held up the Bible that was still in my hand and cocked my head toward her for emphasis and assurance.

She then turned her attention to the package and carefully unwrapped the paper and the protective plastic bubble material around it.

"A gallery in SoHo saw the same article about me and my work at the UN that you saw," she explained. "They also noticed the painting behind me in the photograph and called to see if I'd be interested in something they had."

My pulse rate quickened, but I kept my voice calm and professional. "Really? Would you consider it to be a companion piece?"

"It's very possible. Judge for yourself." She removed the last of the wrapping and turned the painting to face me.

O My Father, who knoweth all the secrets of my heart and my deep yearnings to fully serve thee, you knew as well as I the feelings stirred within me when I looked upon that new painting.

It was in the identical, if slightly matured, style as the painting over her mantle. It also depicted a street vendor offering food. But instead of presenting a crepe to a Parisian urchin, the kindly vendor was extending a small skewer of meat and vegetables to a shabby, destitute woman. The framing was a mirror image of the Parisian scene, but the gentle body language of the vendor, his hand touching the vagrant's shoulder and the surprise on her face, imbued this new work with exactly the same poetic quality as the one painted in France in 1937.

Rather than the setting being outside the Louvre, however, in the background of this new work was the Museum of Modern Art. In present-day New York. Yet it bore the identical signature: *W.J.*

I glanced at Hanna Claire, who was watching me very closely. She obviously saw that I discerned the two paintings appeared to have been crafted by the same hand. She seemed to be considering whether to tell me something else. I prompted her, inquisitively, "Yes, Miss Claire?"

She finally said, "There's another very similar one in the Met. Dated 1883."

"But not signed the same," I said innocently.

"Actually, it is." Her eyes held my own. "Imagine that."

I shrugged at the only possible conclusion. "But surely a different artist."

She spoke with a lack of expression that I believe is referred to in English as *deadpan*. "Surely."

I looked at the new painting again. "Can't the gallery put you in touch with the artist who painted this one?"

"Not so far. I even tried to bribe them. But perhaps I just don't have enough weight." She looked at me pointedly. "Or enough resources."

I nodded affirmation. "If I am able to locate him, you shall be notified immediately."

"As you have sworn."

Her gaze remained fastened upon my own as we each tried to divine the other's secrets.

I nodded again, most solemnly. "As I have sworn."

EIGHT

Minos Volonikis, 24, graduate student...

I was born and grew up on the Greek island of Mykonos, so New York in time of winter was very hard on me. I missed my village, Plakias, where the houses all look like big white sugar cubes. I missed the most my warm turquoise Aegean. Particularly on that freezing cold day.

I had arrived in New York only one week before to prepare for studying mathematics in the next semester at Columbia University. Olympic Air was still trying to find my lost suitcase. They thought possibly it had gone to Prague. Very bad news. In that suitcase was the heavy coat I bought in Athens, so I was not dressed well for the cold. Also the office for student loans was closed for Christmas holidays. So I had not much money, only for the room I rented. I was hungry and my spirits were low.

With my head down in the icy wind from the Hudson River, I was walking across Riverside Park and saw a man standing near a park bench. On a tripod he had a Canon SLR like one I have, taking photos of the George Washington Bridge. As I walked past, he said to me in Greek, "Turkey on wheat, lettuce, tomato, mustard, mayonnaise."

I was surprised. I stopped to look at him, and he pointed to a white paper bag that was on the snowy bench. "Go ahead. Take it," he said in Greek. His accent was very good. Like a Peloponnese. But I'd heard stories about New York and crazy people. My uncle in Athens had told me, *Watch out.* But this man was busy with taking a photo and seemed friendly. I looked at the white bag. Then I remembered about maybe anthrax or something.

He looked at me and smiled, talking more in Greek: "It's fresh. I'm just not hungry."

"How did you know I was?" I asked to him.

His face showed wisdom. "I've been there."

"And Greek?" I was very curious.

He laughed a small bit. "I've been there, too. And that little Greek cross around your neck. But you're not Peloponnese; you sound more like the Cyclades. Andros maybe, or Naxos?"

"Mykonos," I said, smiling a little then.

"Lovely. Beaches with sand like talcum powder."

That really made me smile. "Yes, exactly!"

Then he picked up the sandwich bag and put it into my hand. "Please. It's good food. It's safe. It will go to waste if you don't take it."

"But I can't pay you," I told him. "My student loan is lost in the mail, so I really—"

"Have a cash-flow problem," he said to me, with a nod to his head. Then he took out two American twenty-dollar bills. Uh-oh. I thought about what my uncle told me. *They all want something,* he said. Watch out. I backed up. Waved to him: no thanks.

"Come on, I need the write-off." He saw me not understand and explained, "It means that I benefit as much as you do."

Will...

I eased the money into the young man's pocket and said in Greek, "Welcome to New York." I enjoyed the amazed expression on his face as I answered my cell phone. "Yes?"

A woman's perky voice responded, "Mr. Marshall? J.W.? It's Laura at Gotham. Have you got a sec?"

I envisioned cheerful thirtysomething Laura Rakowitz, with her oversize glasses and curly hair swirled up into a clip, sitting amid books and proof pages in her cluttered office at my publisher's mid-Manhattan building. The office was small, but Laura had a nice view of other skyscrapers. She was an excellent young editor out of Yale with a bright future.

"Laura, I've got all the time in the world," I said as I waved a goodbye to the still-befuddled Greek student. "At least till January first."

"Well, I just e-mailed you the final cover art, and we're about to go to press with your latest volume. But our researcher said he still can't find any other historical sources from the 1100s that mention a beauty mark on Eleanor of Aquitaine's derriere."

I laughed. "I'm afraid you'll have to trust me on that one, Laura."

"Hey, the way your history books sell, I certainly will, J.W., and I've gotta tell you, this one's the best yet." I could hear her fanning through the proof pages of my new volume. "Just like always, this one reads like you'd actually *been in the room*. This time with ol' King Henry, Eleanor, and their dysfunctional brood."

I enjoyed a private smile. "Good, Laura. That's exactly the eyewitness quality I strive for."

"Well, you succeeded once again. And I love how you weave in your philosophy, about the most ideal results coming when people treat others ethically, with respect."

"Not exactly a complicated concept, huh? Wish more people would get on board."

"Let me tell you, J.W., your examples really inspire 'em to. Oh, oh and . . . Sorry, I know I'm gushing, but those brilliantly smooth little asides needling organized religion are always such eye-openers. Big breaths of fresh air. There. I'm done."

I laughed. "Best review I could hope for. Thanks, Laura. But tell me how your own book is coming."

Laura Rakowitz, age 31, junior editor, Gotham Sons Publishing...

I heaved a long, pleased sigh. That's why I always loved speaking to him. With so many big authors it's all about them, you know? But not him. He was always seriously interested, even in a fledgling like me. "That's so nice of you to ask, J.W. And after all the phone calls we've had, it was wonderful to finally meet you face-to-face last week." On that day of his visit he told me he hadn't been in New York for a very long time and wanted to take advantage of the opportunity to meet me personally. I felt honored.

I held the phone closer, glancing out my office door to be certain no one else was hearing, and said to him, sort of *entre nous*, "And let me tell you: out of all the authors I deal with, you're the only one who ever asked if maybe I was a writer, too."

"I apologize on their behalf."

"Oh, you more than make up for it, believe me, J.W.," I said expansively. "And I actually have made a little headway, thanks. The notes you gave me on those pages I sent you were like, like . . . wow!" I suddenly felt like an idiot. "Boy, that sounds really literate and articulate, huh?" I heard him chuckle as I searched for the right words, feeling a bubble of enthusiasm. "But they really did trigger a lightbulb moment: you focused me on evaluating all the different options to make each sentence be the absolute best it could be."

"Well, nobody's ever completely successful, me especially, but—"

"Are you kidding?!" I burst out laughing at his understatement. "We've got preorders up the ying-yang for your latest. Not just from libraries, colleges, and the usual suspects, but more and more from the public, too. Can't we pul-eeze get you to make some PAs this time? Maybe do a lecture or two? A dozen universities have asked for a personal appearance." I shuffled through my papers, trying to find the list. "I even got a call from one of Oprah's producers."

"No, no," he said, and I could hear the modest smile behind it. "I'm really not very good at that sort of thing, Laura. Prefer staying under the radar."

I found one special Post-it note I definitely wanted to ask him about. "Well, how about this one at least: I got a personal visit from a very nice French priest who said he was a big fan."

There was an unexpected silence. What I'd said seemed to give him pause for some reason. But he maintained a neutral voice. "Really? When was that, Laura?"

"Just this morning. He wanted to know all about you." Anticipating his response, I continued quickly, making it clear that I'd kept all the details of his relationship with us completely confidential like he'd always asked us to. "The priest did say he'd love for you to attend a history conference in Rome. Said the Vatican would love for you to make an appearance there."

"Mmm, I'll bet they would," he said dryly. It seemed like more to himself than to me, but I took it as encouragement.

"Well, he left his contact info if you ever change your mind, said they'd pay all expenses. Mine, too, if I could talk you into it and wanted to come along."

"Well." I heard him chuckle again, but with a slightly sardonic quality this time. "They certainly can afford all that, huh? But no, Laura. Let's maintain our party line: no public appearances."

"Okay," I sighed, "you're the boss, J.W. Just keep these manuscripts coming in. To be perfectly honest, the first time they assigned me one of your books, I sorta groaned. I was never a big fan of history, but you make it so vibrant, so completely alive."

"Well, I'm delighted that I've sparked—"

Will...

A growling voice nearby interrupted me. "What are you waiting for?"

I looked around and saw a passing woman's sleek young Doberman straining at its leash toward me. Its breath was hot in the frigid air. It was staring strangely at me. I heard my own voice trailing to finish my sentence to Laura: ". . . sparked your . . . imagination . . ."

The Doberman's lips curled into what almost looked like a human smirk, then it turned and trotted haughtily away with its mistress as I watched it go.

NINE

Father St. Jacques...

Energized by my meeting with the Claire woman, I hurried north across Carl Schurz Park. The winding pathways along the East River were lined with barren winter trees and concrete sandboxes dusted with snow. Passing through Germantown, I bought a chicken sandwich and ate it as I walked. It combined with my enthusiasm to trigger my usual heartburn. At the 86th Street Lexington Avenue subway I took the express train south. As the lights and local stations flashed past, I was focused on my exciting task at hand but also felt the deep, visceral hum of the powerful electric motors that drove the subway train. Their vibration within me echoed my own personal drive.

I smiled, recalling my lackluster brother seminarians who'd always postulated what drove me so determinedly. Little did they understand as they jested and mocked me, Heavenly Father, my consuming desire to achieve at least some modest personal success that I might better serve thee. Always in service to the greater glory of thee, O My Lord, Most High. Amen.

I greatly enjoy writing in this journal. I am thankful that my study of Saint Augustine's *Confessions* years ago inspired me to record my own musings, though I have not the most humble hopes that mine might ever see publication.

I credit thee for delivering all the goodness and opportunities that ever came my way. And when adversities occurred, I have looked upon them as challenges set before me by thy same Divine Hand.

As the subway train lurched and sped southward past 77th Street, I closed my eyes and again dutifully recited my daily catechism of thankfulness to thee.

I praised thee again for delivering me from the clutches of my savagely dysfunctional family and bringing into my life the Most Reverend Francois Beauvais, Archbishop of Paris. Had not his path been guided to cross mine during His Excellency's visit to Chartres, this young seminarian should never have had the grand opportunity of coming under Beauvais's gaze, of being found pleasing to his eye and helpful to his needs. Both professional and personal.

I again gave thanks for being invited to join Archbishop Beauvais's retinue. To accompany him to Paris at so young an age was honor enough, but to have become the archbishop's true and closest intimate opened up entirely new worlds and pleasures for me. On so very many levels.

I gave thanks for the early years under the guidance of the archbishop's gentle hand in Paris, years which were filled with study and wonder. I relished those days and nights: my healthy adolescent body maturing along with the inquisitiveness of my mind under the wise and worldly tutelage of Beauvais. And also the development of my soul, which belongs only to thee, My Father.

I was grateful to become secretary to Archbishop Beauvais for seven years, to serve the church by conscientiously serving him. Thou knowest I have often confessed the sin of pride when he complimented me on the thoroughness with which I always labored. But such attention to detail and tireless efforts were merely my nature.

I shall always give thanks for soon becoming Archbishop Beauvais's primary aide-de-camp in all matters both public and most private, so that I was the first to learn of the personal trial that had been set upon the archbishop: his testicular cancer with its dire prognosis.

Riding on the subway I again confessed how that knowledge had weighed heavily upon me thrice over: that I would lose my loving mentor was naturally my greatest sadness. But with the loss of Archbishop Beauvais would go the position, albeit modest, to which I had risen. And any further ascension in the hierarchy of my beloved church, so that I might better serve thee, seemed impossible.

As the archbishop's sundown was approaching, there was much to put in order, and I set about it in my usual industrious manner, to be found worthy in thy Divine Eye.

The most important matter was the visit from His Holiness, Pope Paul VI. I felt an ethereal thrill on that remarkable day in May of 1977 when the famous, prestigious, Most Holy Father was conducted into the archbishop's bedchamber, where I sat dutifully at His Excellency's bedside. There came with Pope Paul's person such a presence, a weight of office, a corporeal sense of power that swelled the room and swept over those in attendance like an ocean wave. I thanked thee again most heartily for that experience.

The pontiff's face at eighty years was leaner than I had expected; his thinning hair was as white as his skullcap, but his gait was strong as he swept into the room. His luxurious creamy-white papal robes lightly brushed the floor around his polished red Prada shoes (red, I knew, for the blood of Our Lord Jesus). He gestured casually for his entourage to remain behind outside. They responded instantly to his minute signal and gracefully bowed out. I later reflected upon how it must feel to have such a position as the pope; to be a man, yet much more than a man; to have such dominance over a vast, international multitude; to be the possessor of such quiet, unquestioned power. How must that feel?

I had come to my feet instantly. "Your Holiness," I said nervously, in Latin, bowing low. My heart fluttered. I was actually in a room, *in camera*, with the pontiff. The sovereign of the Vatican city-state.

"Ah," Pope Paul said, extending his ring, to which I pressed my young lips as His Holiness continued in perfect French, "the bright and talented Father Paul of whom I have heard. God's blessings upon you, my son."

"And upon you, Your Holiness," I replied in French. Glancing up at him, I noted a somewhat cagey, mischievous twinkle in his eyes as he assessed this young priest. As though he knew secrets about me.

"Your master has frequently mentioned your name to me," he continued. "With considerable praise."

I bowed again, saying, "I humbly pray that I may prove myself worthy in all respects, Most Holy Father."

The pope studied me a moment longer, then stepped closer to the heavily carved mahogany bed upon which Archbishop Beauvais lay propped up. The archbishop tried not to show his considerable pain despite the strong medications. As Archbishop Beauvais kissed the pontiff's proffered ring, Pope Paul saw how pale he appeared.

"Francois, what am I to do with you." The Holy Father shook his head as he looked down at Beauvais teasingly, like one might have regarded an errant child. "You have upset my plans. At the next consistory I had intended to fit you with a red hat. Now I'll have to go with *Ratzinger*."

The archbishop groaned disparagingly, but I was distracted by my own internal reaction. I confess that I felt grave disappointment hearing I had just lost the opportunity to serve a cardinal and thus the chance to advance myself in some meager way, so that I might better serve God, of course. I listened only halfheartedly as Archbishop Beauvais and the pontiff reminisced as old friends do. Then I was startled to hear the archbishop say, "You have received my assessment of Father St. Jacques? And my recommendation?"

The pope nodded. "I have, Francois. The tribunal is vetting him as we speak." The archbishop frowned with concern, but the pontiff gestured lightly with his forefinger, saying, "It is a mere formality, I assure you. It shall be as you wish."

The archbishop's frail hand sought the pontiff's and squeezed it. He whispered, "I am counting on you, Giovanni."

I blinked. It was unprecedented to hear the archbishop address the Most Holy Father by his given name.

"You may rest peacefully, my brother," Pope Paul said as he leaned down and kissed the archbishop's fevered forehead. "Your worthy young friend shall enjoy complete access to our presence. And our resources."

My heart fluttered as it had when His Holiness entered. My head was buzzing with confusion and possibilities as the pontiff made the sign of the cross over Archbishop Beauvais and delivered his Latin blessing upon him. The pope held Beauvais's gaze for what each of them knew would be the last time until they would meet again in God's heavenly presence.

Then as the pope stood to leave, his eyes met mine and he said, "Two Pauls are better than one, wouldn't you say, Father?"

My bewilderment continued. "Your Holiness?"

"We shall make an excellent team, Father Paul." He extended his ring for me to kiss. After I had done so, the pontiff nodded a final goodbye, smiling with portent as he said, "Until Rome, then." He turned and swept out through the tall doorway to lead his waiting, attentive retinue.

I stared after him, entirely uncertain of what I had heard and what had just transpired. I looked back at the archbishop, who seemed amused by my consternation. Beauvais gestured weakly toward the departed pontiff. "At my insistence Giovanni is arranging—" He flinched faintly as a wave of pain arced through him. "Arranging a very important position for you within the cardinalate. Once you have settled my affairs you will go to Rome, to Cardinal Boleslaw Filipiak."

I knew the name. He was a Pole and the well-respected dean of the Sacred Tribunal. The archbishop said weakly, "Sit closer, Paul, it's getting difficult to speak." I did. "You know something of my early life in the church. My many travels."

"As a missionary, yes, Excellency," I said. The archbishop's expression became a secretive smile.

"On a mission, Paul, yes. But not as a missionary." His eyes grew distant. "And I almost achieved my goal once, in Buenos Aires. We nearly trapped the bastard."

I frowned with curiosity. "Trapped whom, Excellency?"

Beauvais turned to me. His smile had undergone a strange transformation. There was a frightening look in his eyes that bespoke such unconscionable evil that it erected the hairs on the back of my neck. "I will give you the combination to my personal safe, Paul. In it you will find the journal I kept in those days. There is only one other copy, kept at the Vatican under highest security deep within the crypt beneath Saint Peter's Basilica. Only the tribunal and the pope, and soon you, have access to that vault and knowledge of its other contents. You will work in conjunction with them."

It was thus that I learned to my amazement that I had lost the opportunity to serve an archbishop and a cardinal only to find myself suddenly in the direct service of the Most Holy Father! My spirit soared as I contemplated the new possibilities that my diligent efforts, and thy will, of course, had opened before me, Heavenly Father.

I laughed inwardly in that moment, and often since, as I imagined the expressions that would have appeared on the faces of my niggardly father and the woman he referred to as my whore of a mother had they heard of the heights to which their unwanted, misbegotten son had ascended. Thus far.

As I rode on the subway through the underground darkness, I thanked God that now, after twenty-three years on the trail, I could afford to smile. I felt closer than ever to achieving the success that had eluded Archbishop Beauvais and so many others before him who had been charged with this incredibly important mission.

I knew the successful completion of my mission, the capture and containment of my quarry, would drastically alter the future of our Mother Church and indeed stir the entire world.

I smiled as I contemplated what my place might be in that new world. And, of course, I gave thanks to God for allowing me the opportunity to rise to such an extraordinary height.

I stepped off the subway at Prince Street and climbed up the urine-smelling stairway to the fresh air in the area of Lower Manhattan known as SoHo. I knew it was so called because of its location south of Houston Street. Near the corner of Prince and Mercer Streets, I saw the small but elegant Rainbow Gallery. It occupied the bottom floor of one of the old large-windowed buildings that had originally been a workhouse in this garment district.

Upon entering, my eyes were immediately drawn to two other paintings clearly fashioned by the same hand as those in Hanna Claire's possession. The artistic style was identical, and the subject matter also bore a connection. Both paintings were decidedly humanistic, though bordering, I sniffed, upon the overtly sentimental.

I introduced myself to the dapper gallery owner, Walter Smith, whom I immediately surmised was a homosexual, and proceeded to inquire about the artist.

"He's very eccentric," the fastidious Smith said, smiling with his plucked eyebrows raised and a slight inclination of his shiny bald head to imply that he was understating the matter. "Enigmatic. But he has a great sense of humor."

"And physically?" I asked.

Smith drew a breath and stroked the goatee of his neatly trimmed gray Van Dyke. "Well, I only met him face-to-face once actually. In the Hamptons, years ago. Light-brown hair and eyes, as I recall. Average height. In his thirties, back then."

"And you're obviously still in communication with him."

"Oh, indeed yes, he sends two or three new works every year. As you can see." He gestured toward the nearby paintings.

"Where is his studio located?"

"I really don't believe he has a permanent location," Smith said. "The paintings have come in from all over the country and the world."

"But surely there are return addresses?"

Smith shook his carefully groomed head. "Only that of the FedEx or DHL office he sent it from. He apparently travels constantly."

I couldn't withhold a knowing smile. "So it would seem." I turned to carefully scrutinize the paintings, knowing I had to bait the hook subtly. "The work is quite lovely. I find it very moving."

"Are you a collector, Father St. Jacques?"

"Yes." I replied casually, as though it were obvious. "Are these two spoken for?"

"Not at this moment," Mr. Smith said. "But I do have considerable interest in each of them from three, no four, separate parties."

Don't overplay your own hook baiting, you little queen, I thought. "And your asking price?"

"Only six thousand for each," Smith said with a plaintive little sigh. "I've told him I could sell them for much more, but he prefers that I not."

"How unusual. But if you never see him, how does he receive payment?"

"I'm afraid that's confidential, Father."

"Of course, of course." I pretended to study the paintings even more carefully. "Seems an exceedingly reasonable price." Then I pretended that an amusing thought had just occurred to me. "Does he by any chance send letters accompanying them?"

"Occasionally, yes, but again, with no return address."

"And I wouldn't presume upon his privacy. But I am curious about his handwriting."

"I beg your pardon?"

I shrugged innocently, trying to sound a bit embarrassed. "Oh, I'm something of an amateur student of handwriting and what it suggests about a person. It would be interesting to get a sense of that in conjunction with owning these two pieces of his. And perhaps commissioning another." I saw that Smith was near the snare. "You do take American Express, I assume?"

The art dealer couldn't hide the flicker of conquest in his eyes. "Whatever is your pleasure, Father St. Jacques." He spoke it with a slight twinkle of sexual double entendre.

"Do you think I might have a peek at one of his letters?"

Smith paused only a split second, then crinkled his nose cutely and whispered *entre nous*, "Well, I don't think there's any harm in that." As he turned toward his tidy desk I made certain the front of my raincoat was slightly open. I watched Smith extract and examine a letter for any information he might not wish to share, then it apparently passed his censorship, because he handed it to me, saying, "This came with the very paintings you're interested in, Father St. Jacques. As you can see, it's merely a description of them."

The letter was handwritten in the script I knew so well. I held the letter out slightly, as though to accommodate my eyesight. My other hand surreptitiously triggered the equally small camera in the buttonhole of my jacket. I snapped several frames to be certain of obtaining a clear digital photograph. "Very interesting."

"What can you tell?" Smith was genuinely curious, sidling closer to glance at the letter. I could smell his Zizanie aftershave and wanted to make him feel like an intimate confidant.

"Well," I said, pretending to study the familiar penmanship, "he seems to be a man of extremely strong opinions; see how his strokes are forward leaning?"

"Mmm, yes," Smith intoned. "The strokes."

"Yet he is buffered by softer, humanistic, almost feminine tendencies. See the smooth gentleness of the curving characters?"

"Fascinating." Smith's blue eyes flashed up at me, his voice so delicate that he might have been asking for a tryst. "You are obviously a person of many talents, Father Paul."

You have no idea, little man, I thought, but said, "Modest, indeed, Mr. Smith. And solely by the Grace of God." I returned the letter, asking, "Could you try calling him for me? I'd very much like to discuss a commission."

"I'm happy to try, but I'm afraid it's a waste of time."

Smith inserted the letter back into a folder and poked at the phone on his desk. I edged closer, watching carefully, memorizing the number. I noted that it was an area code for Philadelphia, the city to which I had most recently tracked my elusive quarry. I felt a slight excitement rising. I knew I was getting closer than I had been in years.

TEN

Renji, age 43, a Rastafarian busker...

"No, no, mon," I said to da old black dude, name of Zack, sitting beside me on da bench dere on Amsterdam. He seemed to be having him trouble understanding my calypso dialect. So I spoke to him more sloooowly. "What I be tellin' to you is dot you and me, we both be descended from da lost tribe of Israel. Even though you be from Alabama and I be from Jamaica. Even though you not a Rasta like me, we both be black, you see?"

I was taking a break from playin' my steel drum. Da buskin' was go slow dot day. I figured the people musta spent all dere spare change on Christmas. But I was talking energetic-like, trying again to make da old dude understand us Rastas, but also to keep my mind offa da cold. It was getting to me, too. Mon, I longed for my old commune outside Kingston near Catherine's Peak. "Winter dere was warm, like blessed Africa," I often said to da old man, "not freeze-your-balls-off cold like sittin' on dis bench on Amsterdam Avenue."

Da ganja helped me a little. I was holdin' it with da tips of my thumb and finger. To make it easy I'd cut off da fingertips of dees old wool gloves I found. I took anudder hit and held out da joint to da old black dude, but he shakin' his head.

"I don't do drugs, son." Zack was pokin' through his shopping cart heaped with da castaway goods dot was all his belongings.

I smiled my pearly whites, explaining, "No, mon, to us Rastas da ganja is spiritual." Then I went on, explaining, "So listen, Alabama or Jamaica don't matter: our ancestors both been stole by dem slavers, you dig? But we both still subjects of Jah."

Old Zack pulled his raggedy coat tighter and scrunched his face real sour-like. "Who de hell is Jah?"

"He da Emperor, mon! Da great ol' Haile Selassie. Become emperor of Ethiopia in 1930."

"So how come you think we his subjects?" He pulled his knit cap lower over his hairy ears. "Slave stealing happened way long before 1930, son."

"Ah, but dots what the faith be about, my brotha. Because Jah be da first black man dot all da world recognize as an emperor. He have da Great Dignity, see? Dot's why dey call him da Lion of Judah. Like Brother John told in Revelation 5:5: 'And one of da elders saith unto me, Weep not: behold da Lion of da tribe of Judah, da root of David, hath prevailed to open da book and to loose da Seven Seals.' Ol' Haile, he be da Lion of Judah, mon! And when da Glory Time comes, dot great ol' King of Kings himself goin' to come down from da heavens—"

"Now just hang on, Renji boy." Da old man was wavin' his arthritic hand and shaking a finger in my face. "It's Jesus who's going to come down at the 'Pocalypse."

"Yeah, yeah." I'm noddin' hard with my dreadlocks bouncin' and wavin'. "He gonna come, too. But Jah comin' special to gather in his lost *black* sheep, mon. You and me, bro. And all da brothas and sistahs."

Da old man stared at me, thinkin' it over in his old gray head. Dot's when I saw da man in da peacoat walkin' down Amsterdam toward me and old Zack. I saw him glance toward us and heard him say into his cell phone something like, "Sorry, Walter, but tell da gentleman I can't take on no commissions."

Will...

I had paused near the Rastafarian and the old man, digging into my pocket. Turning the phone away from my mouth, I leaned down toward the Rasta and pressed some money into his hand. "Hey, brother, go buy some iron tablets, okay? Your red-blood-cell count is down." I saw his confused expression and pointed down to his fingertips, which were peeking out of his wool gloves. "See how white your nails are?"

I saw the Rasta realize I might be right and also realize that the bill I put into his hand was a fifty. The old black man also spotted it with widening eyes, but I had to refocus on my phone conversation, saying, "No, Walter, it's not a matter of money, you know that."

Then I heard something from Walter that brought me to a stop and darkened my mood. "Wait. He's a priest?" Hearing Smith's confirmation, I paused to weigh the best approach, then said, "Sorry, but no, Walter. And please tell the good father as little as possible about me."

I flipped the phone closed, clicking my teeth together slightly as I often did when thinking something through. At the same time I was peeling off another fifty for the old black vagrant, saying, "Happy Christmas, pal."

But when I turned to hand it to the vagrant, I was startled to see instead the sleek young man sitting on the bench in his black suede Windbreaker and cashmere turtleneck. His dark eyes looked knowingly into mine, and his voice was patient and friendly as he said in Latin, "You'll never buy your way out. Pal."

I drew a breath to respond, but in an eye blink he was replaced by the old vagrant, who received the fifty with great appreciation. The old fellow stood up shakily, nodding thanks with his gray head. "God bless you, sir." Then he turned and hobbled away from me, pushing his overloaded shopping cart.

I watched him a moment, then called after him cheerily and in Latin, "You're getting nervous, huh? Only one day to go?"

But the old black man didn't look back nor did the sleek young man reappear. I stood there, trying to stay expectant and positive. But I was feeling increasingly nervous myself, knowing that the critical moment of truth was rapidly approaching. It was barely over twenty-four hours away.

Father St. Jacques...

The round-faced East Indian doorman nodded a friendly greeting, saying, "Welcome back, Father St. Jacques."

"Thank you, Satyajit," I responded, shaking the Indian's hand. Then I entered through the lovely wood-framed door being held graciously open for me. The doorman was one of the aspects I particularly liked about the old Wyndham Hotel. Unlike the gargantuan Plaza directly north across 58th Street, the Wyndham was small, but exceedingly comfortable and homey. Indeed, many people, particularly theater people, did make their home there.

I had once seen Gerard Depardieu speaking in easy camaraderie with Meryl Streep in the understated elegance of the polished-paneled Wyndham lobby. Being a fellow Frenchman, I might have approached Depardieu had he been alone. Instead, I had lingered for an extended time in a corner, ostensibly checking an airline schedule, that I might better observe the pair of film stars.

In confession I have often admitted having a fascination with theater people, those who strut and fret their hour upon the stage for the benefit of an adoring public. I thought how wonderful to them must be the sound of applause for their work, how delightful to be lauded and sought after. Not only theater people, I supposed, but all manner of persons who achieve a celebrity level, bringing instant facial recognition by their peers and the public.

Entering the Wyndham one afternoon during my last visit, I brushed past Liza Minnelli as she was leaving. On a whim I had turned and followed her. She walked west to Seventh Avenue and then turned south along the wide sidewalk. I was amused and quite amazed to see how very many heads did turn to note the passing star, to take a closer look at a true celebrity. I had watched her pause when one person asked her for an autograph, and how genially she obliged.

Always affecting the modesty appropriate to my station, I was pleased that none of those people looked twice at the lowly priest who was walking somewhat behind her. That was as it should be. I contend that such is the appropriate life for a servant of the Heavenly Father. In my prayerful contemplation I frequently say, "If wider recognition ever comes to me for my dedicated service in thy Holy Name, My Father, it is not because I desire or strive for it, but solely because it is in thy gift, part of thy divine will, O Lord of all."

When I saw Miss Minnelli finally disappear into a building, I came to a stop looking southward into Times Square. There, above the heads of the teeming ordinary people, were enormous advertisement billboards, many bearing the faces of the famous. One of them was of Liza Minnelli herself.

I wondered how it feels to people such as them, to have heads turn in their direction each time they passed by or entered a room. Did they ever grow so accustomed to it that it escaped their notice? Or did they continually exult in it? I truly wondered.

My small suite at the Wyndham was nicely appointed as always, with floral patterns and comfortable furniture that gave me the feeling of being in the preferred guest room of a fine private estate rather than at a hotel. I always requested an inner room, thus avoiding the clanging and clattering of the garbage trucks that collected the Plaza's refuse across 58th Street at three in the morning.

Of course I would have been quite content in a more modest hotel, but the tribunal was flexible. They appreciated the sacrifices I had made on behalf of Mother Church over the last two decades and were understanding that I should betake myself of certain creature comforts when those comforts were available. The cardinals knew from my many detailed reports that as a consequence of my mission, I often had to sleep in unclean or unsavory surroundings, sometimes in a parked car or even open country. Thus, when I suggested that I might be allowed an occasional nice room in a pleasant hotel, it was considered by them to be not unreasonable, and they agreed that the Vatican treasury could certainly afford the relatively small cost.

It was early evening in Manhattan and thus about one in the morning in Rome. I was sure that when my call awakened Father Benedicto, the young priest had not been happy. But over the years as one of my key assistants in the Vatican, Benedicto had grown accustomed to the time differences that frequently required such interruptions to his sleep when he was the one on call. He was a very dedicated and smart young man who had survived my stringent requirements for extreme efficiency, clearheadedness, and personal hygiene. He was also handsomely athletic, and I was pleased to have him representing my office and my tastes.

"You should have just received my e-mail," I said to him in Italian. My facility with Benedicto's native language was superior to Benedicto's with French, so I often condescended. "Do you see it?"

"Just a moment, Father Paul," he responded. I heard Benedicto yawn and imagined him squinting and shaking the sleep from his eyes as I had so often seen him do. I also heard the clicks of Benedicto's computer keyboard. "I'm looking for it." He then mumbled some profanity about his glasses while I sat in the Wyndham suite drumming my fingers impatiently on my laptop.

I finally prodded, "Well?"

"Yes. It's decrypting now, sir. A jpeg file? Looks like a letter?"

"Correct."

"A new handwriting sample?" His sleepy voice had suddenly gained clarity and focus. He understood that I was on the scent, and he was immediately an attentive Watson to my Sherlock Holmes.

It made me smile, somewhat slyly, as I confirmed, "Correct again, Benedicto. And very recent."

"Excellent, sir."

"Yes, it is." I felt a bit smug and made a note to confess that later.

"I'll begin an analysis and comparison immediately."

"Call me as soon as you have a result."

"Of course, sir. Have you met with the New York archdiocese?"

"I placed an urgent call to Archbishop Malloy's office. He's out of town until midday tomorrow but is seeing me immediately upon his return."

"Good luck with him, Father."

"Thank you, Benedicto, but I'm sure I shan't need it. By tomorrow I'll have the full weight of the archdiocese behind me. Ciao." Ending the call, I went down my mental checklist to see if there was anything I had forgotten. There was not.

I did my ablutions and then my beloved evening devotions to thee, My Lord of Hosts. But afterward I found that I was too invigorated to think of sleep, and my stomach was troubled with anticipation. I elected to take a short walk.

Stepping out onto the sidewalk of 58th Street, I felt that a chill wind had begun to blow.

I wondered if my quarry was also feeling it at that moment.

ELEVEN

Tito...

The guy shoutin' popped my eyes wide open out of a dead sleep: "Last day for our gigantic end-of-the-year sale!"

Man, I hate them too-loud-and-cheery radio dicks. He went on yellin': "Today, December thirty-first only! Half price on everything at Dress for Less celebrating the end of 2000!"

I wanted to bust a cap in that punk's ass next door. Dumb shit knew the crap walls in the projects is paper thin. His screamin' radio in the next apartment waked me up, and the sun wudn't even come up. I glanced over at my twin cousins Chico and Juan, but they'uz still totally snoozin'. Them six-year-olds could sleep through fuckin' World War Three, and sometimes they even slept through the gunfire in this hood.

I rolled up the lumpy old futon I slept on every night and stuffed it in a corner of the room my aunt let me hang in. Up in the South Bronx at 161st Street at Walton. One of them old red brick project buildings built in the '50s. She had three rooms up on fourteen looking east over ratty Kilmer Park. I looked out the window at the trees down there, all scarred up with no leaves causa it being winter. The grass was scruffed down to bare patches. What'uz left of the snow was grungy that mornin', December 31. It'uz still dark.

The sky was flat black, but out at the horizon it'uz deep red. Like Krylon Cherry Red 2101, but darker even, like the blood on the wall down on the first floor. Where the Knights did Ray.

Ray'd been the twins' brother. Two years older than me. I'uz twelve when Ray got clipped by a fuckin' hailstorm of bullets. When Ray went down I felt like they'd killed me, too. It'uz fuckin' devastatin'. Ray'd been like my only real family.

Ray's momma's my aunt. She took me in when my momma died, but was never happy 'bout it. I'uz only seven then, but I learned quick to stay the fuck outta her way when she came in glary eyed, sayin' how there was *one too many* livin' in her place. But Ray was always cool. Tellin' her to chill and always treatin' me like we'uz equal. Like bros.

I like idolized Ray, man. He taught me how to boost cans of Krylon, how to use them different nozzles when we was taggin'. Ray always had a rag tied over his nose when he was paintin' to lessen the fumes. Ray had asthma.

But then the Knights cured him. Permanently. "With a fuckin' Uzi," I told the cops. "No good reason, neither," I tol' 'em, tryin' not to cry so much. "Ray weren't no banger, no hopper, neither. Maybe he'd seen them Knights smoke somebody or somethin'." But the cops never found out why the gang had done him.

I watched the building's super try to clean the walls and even white-wash 'em. But Ray's blood had soaked in. It'uz still down inside there. Finally the super spread on some real thick paint. You can't really see Ray's blood no more, but I sure as shit can still see it, know what I'm sayin'?

Okay, so that New Year's Eve mornin' I'uz curious about the Will guy, so I caught a train down to 125th and walked east toward the river. I pulled my cap around frontways so it'd block the cold wind cuttin' at my eyes. It also kep' my face part hidden, because a lone half-Spic who ain't a homeboy cruisin' through East Harlem ain't always the swiftest move to be makin'.

Finally I seen his rig with my big tag on it over near First Avenue. It'uz parked under the overhead ramp that runs out onto the Triborough.

When I got closer I heard a fiddle playin' some kinda symphony shit. Sounded like a zillion notes sprayin' up and down really fast. But just before I got to the door, the music turned into that knee-slapping hillbilly stuff played on a country fiddle. I ain't down with that country shit neither, but I sure knew that whoever was playing had him some serious skills; that fiddler's fingers was flyin'.

When I knocked on the door the music stopped. Will opened it, holdin' the fiddle. He was wearin' old Levi's and a pink shirt about like Krylon 3534, called Ballet Slipper. He had a couple of shirt buttons undone showin' some skin and chest hairs, and right then I thought, *Uh-oh, I bet he's a fag.*

"Hey, Tito," he says t'me, smiling.

But I'm like wary now. I just says, "Yo."

He waved his fiddle for me to come in, sayin', "Mi casa es tu casa."

Okay, now I'uz sure he's a fag. So when I stepped up and in, I'uz edgy and made sure I had me a clear shot to get out the door, case he starts comin' on. Didn't want nobody tryin' to pack my fudge. But I'uz stayin' cool, tryin' t'seem casual-like, and said, "Fiddle sound pretty good."

Will shrugged, modest-like. "Thanks, when they're made as well as this one is, anybody can sound good. Take a look."

He handed me the fiddle. I'uz careful. I mean I ain't never held no fiddle before, but even so, I could scope that this one'uz prime. The wood was real fine grain; it'uz polished deep. "This here's an oldie, huh?"

"From 1709," Will said. He had stepped over into the tiny kitchen. "Want some coffee? Hot chocolate?"

"Naw, thas awright." But really I'uz still cold from walkin', so I says, "Hey, yeah. Some chocolate, maybe." While he fixed it, I'uz peekin' through one of them *S* cutouts on top of the fiddle. I could jus' barely make out some kind of name writ down inside, Strad something. "Seventeen oh nine, huh? Didn't know they made stuff like this way back then."

"They made 'em long before that, Tito," he told me while whippin' up some kind of special chocolate stuff. "But not as well as that one: spruce on the top. Best for the harmonic board. Then willow on the inside and maple for the back and neck. The man who made that one treated his with special minerals like borax and potassium silicate, then finished them off with a varnish made from Arabic gum, honey, and egg white."

I'uz surprised. "Honey and egg white? No shit?"

"No, he didn't use any shit," Will said straight-faced. Then he grinned 'cause he seen me smirk when I got the joke. "But it was quite a laborious process."

He went on talkin' about it while I scoped out his place. Looked like he lived in it a long time. Everything'uz clean and neat, but there'uz lotsa weird stuff: strange lookin' little gadgets and old thingies, teeny statues made outta wood or stone. Some looked like they's African, others like I seen in pitchers my momma showed me from her home down in the Yucatan.

There'uz old, antiquey-like toys, too, and what looked like small, weird science-kinda tools inside glass cabinets.

Under my feet'uz one o'them Aladdin rugs with lots of swirly patterns in it. Dark colors mostly, deep reds and greens and blues. Hangin' in front of a window there'uz a couple stained-glass pitchers done in soft pastels. I looked close and seen a girl's name: *Tiffany*. I guessed she's the one what did 'em.

There'uz a pricy-assed sound system and a cabinet with a shitload of books, some lookin' really old. I seen writers' names like J.W. Marshall, W.J. Sloan. There'uz also a newer set of books 'bout history that had them J.W. initials, too.

Hangin' on the cabinet was an eight-inch hoop with a spiderweb of string in it. Beads and feathers wuz attached.

"It's a dream catcher," Will 'splained. "The Navajo hang them where their loved ones sleep. To catch bad dreams. Then the first rays of morning sun cleanse them away. Pretty sweet, huh?"

"Yo. Could use me one of them sometimes."

"Well, at least for the rest of today," Will said with a smile that made me think he knew some kinda special secret.

"Just today? Somethin' gonna be different tomorrow?"

He leaned against the kitchen counter and breathed out this long sigh. "Well, you never can be sure, Tito. But yeah, maybe everything'll be different tomorrow." He said it in a strange kinda tone. Then he shrugged. "Or maybe nothing will be. Here you go."

I took the steaming cup and sat on a chair by the foldout table. Then I sipped the chocolate, which surprised the shit outta me. "Whoa!"

"Whoa good or whoa bad?"

"Way good. Like melted Hershey bars or somethin'."

"Very old recipe." Will sipped his own. "One thing I never get tired of, one of the few things." He said that with kind of a sigh, too.

There'uz somethin' for sure strange about Will. I looked at him over my cup. "So how come you moved clear over here 'cross town?"

"I'm a mobile kind of guy." Clearly he didn't want to gimme the straight shit. Then he reached for a tote bag and laid it on the table 'tween us.

"Whas that?"

"It's for you, Tito."

Will...

Seeing the boy's expression register utter confusion, I wondered how long it had been since anyone had given Tito a gift of any kind. "Go ahead, take a look."

He pulled out the sketch pad and the nice set of acrylic paints. He still seemed puzzled so I said, "More subtle than spray cans, huh? Thought you might like to try 'em out." He still looked pretty dumbfounded, particularly when he realized there was something else inside the bag. He carefully took it out.

"What up? A camera?"

"Yep." It was the new digital Canon I had tested out the previous day. "To photograph the graffiti you've done on walls or," I needled him lightly, "on the sides of motor homes."

Tito looked at all the items. "So, like, what'chu mean? You loanin' me this?"

"No, I'm giving it to you."

The youth stared at me in disbelief. "Say what?" I nodded confirmation and Tito asked warily, "How come?"

"Because you need to work up a portfolio." I saw Tito's blank expression. "A portfolio is a collection of your sketches and paintings."

"What I need that for?"

"To get into art school."

He burst out laughing. "What're you, trippin', man?"

"You want to be an artist, don't you?"

Instead of answering the question he got gruff. "I can't afford no fuckin' art school."

I plunked down a thick brown envelope in front of the boy. "Scholarship applications. You're minority, which is good. But asshole is bad. You'll have to work on that."

Tito stared at me. I could see that his mind was whirling, and I liked that. He finally said, "C'mon, man, I ain't even finished high school."

"You still go?" Tito looked away from me, guiltily. "Well, that's your call, kiddo. Even a GED helps. But a couple of these places might take you anyway. They're more interested in your artistic potential than your grades. Would your parents get behind it?"

"Can't get behind nothin'. My momma's dead."

I took a breath and spoke more softly: "I'm sorry. What happened?"

"She had that breast cancer shit. I was seven."

Tito...

That memory's like an ice pick stab into my brain. And bitter, know what I'm sayin'? Always gonna be, I guess. I just sat there, quiet.

Will'uz quiet, too. Then he said, "Must have been very hard on you."

You ain't got no fuckin' idea, man, I'uz thinkin'. But I sucked it up, put on my best unruffled 'tude and shrugged. "Naw, I'm cool."

"Your father?"

"He ain't no good. To hisself or me neither. Still got eight or nine years to go up at Fishkill."

"Do you live with family? A guardian?"

"My momma's sister, yeah. My *aunt*." I tried to say it so's he'd get a feelin' 'bout what a double-barreled bitch she was. Meantime I kept staring at the camera and the paints and shit. Finally I just come at him head-on. "Okay, so what's the dealio? Why the fuck you doin' this, man?"

"Because you're such a fuckin' charmer." He said it with a little smile and poured us more chocolate.

I squinted at him real sharp; I knowed this sucker was up to some kinda shit. "And what the hell you want from me?"

He nodded at the stuff. "I want you to take advantage of it."

I stared at him, tryin' to figure it out, but feelin' dumb as a box of rocks. Before I could talk he axed, "You get to the Met?"

"Naw, I ain't yet."

"Well, when you do go, spend the day." He folded out a map of that museum place. "I know you'll be more interested in the modern and contemporary works, but first hit the European collection. Take a look at how different artists handled light and design. Check the chiaroscuro. Did you look that up yet?"

"Ain't like my aunt got a 'cyclopedia."

"Well, ask 'em when you get over there." Then he circled some parts on the map. "Look at the differences between Vermeer and the

Impressionists. Might give you some ideas." I seen him remember somethin' and smile. "Oh, and while you're there go into the Sackler Wing and check out the Temple of Dendur."

"Like in *Star Wars*?"

"No, that was *Endor*," Will chuckled. "Dendur, like in Egypt. Like in 15 BC, two thousand years ago. I want you to see the graffiti on it, from Napoleon's army in 1799."

I'uz amazed. "You shittin' me! Guys was taggin' stuff way back then!?"

"Oh yeah. And without using spray cans. People have always been tagging things, Tito."

I'uz still tryin' to figure out what the hell'uz up with him. Then, 'cause his shirt'uz open some, I seen he had a thin leather string round his neck with a tiny, old, hand-carved wooden cross hangin' on it next to a small antiquey locket. "Okay," I said, nodding, thinkin' I figured it out. "So what: you not just some kinda good fairy goes around handin' out shit to people, right? You some religious guy tryin' to born me again, huh?"

"No way," Will laughed. "Let's just say I like to invest in possibilities, which you have definitely got . . . And also I'm eternally hopeful."

And right that second we heard this loud squawk from outside. We both looked through the frosty side window and seen this huge muthafuckin' raven sitting on a skeleton branch of a tree out there. Swear t'God that big, sleek black sucker was starin' in, starin' *right directly at Will*, with big, dangerous red eyes.

It squawked again, but even creepier: sound like a mockin', sarcastic kinda laugh. Like how my aunt'd curl her lips up into that deadly smile and shoot me an ugly, hateful laugh that was really a buzz saw.

Lemme tell ya', that huge raven with them fiery eyes like to scare the livin' shit outta me.

But it wudn't nothin', *not nothin'*, compared to the scares I'uz gonna get with this guy.

TWELVE

Jillian...

I knew I was right up against the deadline for the special photo spread and that at any moment George was going to come lean over my shoulder. I had the candidates laid out all over the big conference table in the *Register* office when I heard his voice.

"'More Faces of the Last Thousand Years!'" George said casually as he meandered into the room. "Gonna be great, Jilly." I knew he was trying to give the impression that he wasn't concerned about the impending deadline. But I also knew the sword of Damocles and Geraldine Hecht was hovering over my head. And George's.

I pushed up my glasses for a second to rub my eyes as I spoke around the pencil I had clenched in my teeth. "And I know it has to go to press very soon, George. Just making the final pick."

"Thought this might help." He handed me a mug of coffee. I thanked him as I poured it into a Styrofoam cup and set the mug aside. He looked at me curiously for a beat while I juxtaposed three photos into a different sequence. "Why do you do that?"

"Because they look better that way."

"Not the photos; I mean why do you always switch the coffee into a cup like that?"

I was preoccupied, busy perusing the photos. "Mugs get broken. I don't like things that can break."

"Because . . . ?"

"I don't like the responsibility," I said as I swapped out a Grover Cleveland for a Teddy Roosevelt.

"Ooookay," George said, widening his eyes. "Strange answer but better than none." He watched me work for a moment. "That why you've ducked my offer to take over the photo division?"

I shrugged, dodging the question again. Besides, something in the Roosevelt picture had caused a frown to catch in my brow. I squinted through my glasses at the shot of Teddy barnstorming for the Bull Moose Party from the back of a train.

"You coming to the New Year's Eve party tonight?" George inquired. "Couple people asked me about you. That Douglas guy from accounting, particularly."

I was busy shuffling among the strewn photos to find my magnifier. "George. This guy look familiar?"

"Teddy Roosevelt. You didn't answer about the party."

"Not Teddy, this guy." I pointed to a man who was standing beside the back of the train near Roosevelt.

George looked closer at the man I indicated. In the black-and-white photo, his hair and eyes looked to be a medium shade, probably light brown. He appeared to be in his midthirties. George scrunched his eyes, adjusting the magnifier for the maximum effectiveness. He studied the man and shook his head. "Nope. Should I know him?"

"Coulda sworn I've seen him somewhere else." And something about that fact was disturbing me, though I couldn't put my finger on exactly why. I started searching through other photos as George gave up on getting an answer to his question.

"Well, that New Millennium of yours officially begins in about twelve hours," he said. "But your deadline hits in three."

"And thirteen minutes," I muttered distractedly. As George hung in the doorway for a moment, I could feel that he was looking in at me with a touch of fatherly sadness, and then he left.

But I was gazing hard again at the Roosevelt photo and at the man in it who affected me so curiously.

Tito...

After I come off the subway at 86th I walked west, then turned south down Fifth Avenue. Yo. Sure as shit not *my* hood, man. I'uz real uptight bein' so far outta my zone. All them fancy buildings 'cross from Central Park with them uniformed door guys. Shit, them places got some serious money workin'.

Then I come to a dead stop 'cause I caught sight of it. Whoa! It'uz glowin' in the sun up aheada me. The fuckin' Metropolitan Museum. I'uz amazed. It'uz so huge-assed I could see it from blocks away. Ain't nothin' like it in the Bronx. Look like it come right out of some movie like *Gladiator*. Made me nervous, swallowin' uncomfortable, y'know? I knowed that place definitely couldn't be my kickin' spot.

I'm thinkin' Will's crazy. They ain't gonna let some sorry ass like me go in there. When I got up right 'cross the street I seen they was about a hundred steps climbin' up to the entrance from a big ol' wide sidewalk along Fifth. Even though it'uz freezin', lotta people'uz sittin' on the steps, having hot dogs and coffee and shit. I'uz surprised how most of 'em'uz just regular people, not dressed snooty or nothin'. I seen blacks and Latins and Asians all different ages and all mixed in. I even saw a couple of street punks who looked just like me. I felt they'uz scopin' me out, threatenin'-like, but then a couple just popped their heads, acknowledgin' me. I nod back subtle, tryin' to give off like I comed here all the time. Then I climbed up them steps 'tween the people and went through these huge-ass iron doors.

When I stepped inside, my guts jumped. It'uz like *in-tense*! My eyes went wide as a big momma's ass, and I whispered right out loud, "Whoa, muthafucka!"

If I thought these digs'uz big on the outside, on the inside it seemed even more gi-normous. I felt fuckin' microscopic standing on this wide stone floor there in what'uz the biggest room I ever seen in my life. All made of this gray-whitish stone. All round me was these columns goin' up fifty feet to a balcony with a stone fence round it. I seen lotsa people walkin' up there. Lookin' even higher up I seen skylights with the noonday sunshine streamin' down in. Made me feel like I'uz on the terrace of some kinda outdoor garden, specially 'cause they'uz potted plants and flowers all round. There'uz a buncha flowers big enough for somebody to hide in sittin' on toppa this circle counter in the center.

I ain't never even imagined a buildin' like that place. I heard some touristy guy nearby to me sayin', "Magnificent." I heard that word before somewheres but never had somethin' to 'ply it to till just that minute. It'uz weird: so big it made me feel puny-like.

But jus' the same it'uz so, I dunno, *grand*, it like lifted my spirits up. Know what I'm sayin'? Gave me this surprisin', it's-all-good, tingly kinda feeling. Felt a little like the first time I tagged a subway car. It gimme a kick. Made me laugh a little to myself. Like I'uz just startin' on some kinda cool new adventure.

But I didn't see no pitchers nowhere. I didn't wanta sound like a dumb ass, so I walked around some, pretendin' I been there lots and I'uz just decidin' what to do. Then I 'membered the map that Will give me. I pulled it out and scoped it, but I'uz still confused.

I seen some peeps at that counter in the middle axin' questions so I sidled up closer. This older white woman behind the counter smiled at me and talked in a foreign but friendly accent, "Welcome to the Met." She axed if it was my first time. I shook my head like I'uz a pro, but showed her the map, sayin' I'uz just tryin' to 'member the way to the Sackler Wing. I wanted to see that old graffiti Will'uz talkin' about.

I discovered what they called the Sackler Wing didn't mean no wing like on a bird. It'uz another gi-normous room, but there'uz only a few people in it. I seen that one wall long as a subway train and made o'glass.

It went up fifty feet, leanin' in at the top. Central Park's outside, but the room's up on the second floor, so I just could see the tops of trees and sky. I also seen 'em reflected in this big pond o'water! Surroundin' a stone island in the middle o'the room! I heard these Arab-lookin' visitor guys talkin', sayin' the water represented the River Nile. The stone island's almost as big as the whole damn room, but sitting up 'bout three feet out of the water. The water'uz dead still.

In the middle of the island I seen what Will told me about: the Temple of Dendur. In front is this big stone gateway. Before I crossed the stone bridge over to it, I read a sign that said only part o'Dendur had survived ages of weather and earthquakes. It said these last ruins'uz gonna be flooded by them building some high Aswan Dam over in Egypt, so museum people had took it apart and brung it to New York.

Then I crossed the stone bridge over the water to the island. I stopped at the big stone doorway. I reached out and touched it. That'uz pretty cool. At a couple thousand years, this temple thing was sure as shit the oldest thing I ever seen or touched. I checked out the 'Gyptian carvings that'uz all over the doorway's walls. Had all kindsa flat bird people and what a sign said'uz "hieroglyphic pictographs." But didn't see no tagging like Will said there was. Later on I tol' my little cousin Chico, "Fool I was, thinkin' it'uz gonna be like paint or somethin'."

That fifteen-foot stone gateway sits out by itself in the front. I walked under it toward the larger pieces of Dendur. Passin' 'tween the two thick columns on the front I seen that behind 'em there'uz a square room made o'stone.

That's where I found the graffiti: a few names of French soldier guys chiseled into the stone. And the date they'uz there: *1799.*

It wudn't much, but give me a weird kinda feeling twice over. I thought, *Here I am lookin' at them names cut into stone a couple hundred years ago, and I'm standin' in a place somebody else built a couple thousand years ago!* I 'magined the workmen who builded Dendur, cuttin' them stones out of some quarry, then haulin' and stackin' 'em up with no cranes or skip loaders. And then hand carvin' them columns. I ran my hand up along 'em. Up and down. And up again. And 'cross the pitchers carved into the walls.

I ran the tips o'my fingers over them French soldiers' names, wonderin' who they was. I 'magined 'em over there in Egypt one day a long time ago in 1799. Sittin' in the shade of ol' Dendur, eatin' they lunch and maybe burpin' or fartin' and laughin'. Jus' like me and Ray mighta done. Then usin' they swords to scratch they names into the old stone wall. And it wudn't even like art, it'uz just they names.

And this'uz all that's left of 'em.

Made me think 'bout my own tagging. No matter how cool somethin' is I paint, it don't hardly last a month before some asshole covers it over.

I stood there in the old temple a long time, thinkin' 'bout all that. And lots more thoughts I ain't never had before.

Father St. Jacques...

I'd heard nothing back from Benedicto at Vatican City, and there were three hours remaining before my scheduled audience with the archbishop. I was, however, determined to be diligent and thorough in the service to God and my church, determined as ever to waste not a moment that might be profitably used in the investigation and pursuit of my mission.

So I went to follow up on the mention Hanna Claire had made about a painting at the Metropolitan Museum. I telephoned ahead and contacted one of the assistant curators, Merlene Schain, telling her of my curiosity and emphasizing my Vatican credentials. When I arrived at the museum, the information desk contacted Mrs. Schain and told me where to meet her.

Tito...

It's funny how shit happens.

After I left the Temple o'Dendur, I had took the whole tour like Will said to do. I walked through a whole buncha rooms that'uz empty 'cept for the pitchers on the walls. I ain't never been in rooms like 'em. They's all clean and bright with shiny wood floors all pieced together in different puzzle patterns. Some of 'em got a bench in the middle. I seen people with sketch pads sittin' and studyin' a pitcher or drawin' out copies. I thought it'uz cool they let folks do that.

I looked at them European pitchers like Will told me. Most of 'em I didn't really care nothin' about, but a few I thought'uz pretty cool. I didn't see none by that Chiaroscuro guy though, so I axed a guard. She'uz this fine-looking young black chick. She smiled gentle-like and tol' me chiaroscuro wudn't no person, but "the way an artist used the qualities of light and shadow."

I felt my face get all flushed up, felt like a prize fool, but that girl'uz a charmer, whisperin' that she ain't never heard of chiaroscuro neither till she started working there. She pointed out a couple o'pitchers where the light'uz coming real strong from one side of the person in the pitcher so the other side'uz all shadowy. I got it. Really made the person pop.

Then I checked out them Impressionists, the ones Will said painted so fast. Their pitchers'uz fuzzier than the older stuff, but I caught on what Will meant: how them guys'uz tryin' hard to capture an *impression* of light, right in the second they'uz paintin'.

Okay, so right then came the moment made me think it's funny how shit happens: if I'd been ten seconds sooner or ten seconds later walkin' outta the Impressionist section, I woulda missed hearin' the older woman sayin' to a priest, "I'm afraid we don't have much information about artists with the initials W.J."

Yo. Hearin' them initials put my brakes on right nearby 'em.

"Anything at all will be helpful, Mrs. Schain," the priest said. He was some kinda foreign guy. And his eyes were a kinda weird color, like Misty Pale. Thas Krylon 4461.

"Come this way, Father St. Jacques," the woman said.

So I followed 'em back into the Impressionist part. She taked him to a pitcher hangin' off to one side that I'd missed before. It'uz a sunny street scene like a lot o'the others hangin' around it, from like 1880 somethin'. A little girl sittin' in a horse-drawn buggy, wearin' fancy, frilly clothes and a little pink hat showin' her family got 'em some dough. Her momma's all gussied up, too, but momma's turned away so your eye locks right on the little girl.

She'uz leanin' down to give a candy stick to a boy 'bout her same age, but he's a scruffy, smudge-faced street kid. That poor boy's lookin' up at her surprised and 'mazed. Like nobody ain't never give him nothin' and he's blowed away. And I'uz 'mazed, too: how it made me feel. Whoa. Caught me right in the heart, know what I'm sayin'? Ya couldn't help but smile. It'uz so warm and really sweet. Made me think o'my little cousins. Lemme tell ya, whoever done that painting was *good*.

That priest didn't seem to feel nothin', though. Or didn't give a shit. He'uz like all business and only interested in squintin' close at the signature and noddin' as he said, "W.J., 1883."

"Our records are scanty," the Schain woman said while the priest eyed the painting, "but it's apparently the work of a man named Wilhelm Januck. We believe he was an acquaintance of Manet's. You can see—"

"The striking similarity in their styles," the St. Jacques guy agreed. "Yes. What else can you tell me about him?"

Mrs. Schain looked into a skinny folder she been carryin'. "Very little. Van Gogh does mention him in a letter to his brother, Theo. Januck visited Van Gogh and Gauguin while they were living in the Yellow House in Arles. That would have been October or November of 1888."

Then I seen the priest notice how she suddenly seemed to get an idea about somethin'. He says, "Yes? And?"

"You know, Father, I could have sworn that we had *another* work somewhere that's also signed W.J." I seen she was tryin' to remember where in this huge-ass place it might be. She took out her cell phone and called somebody.

Jillian...

"I knew I'd seen him." I had snagged Steve Snyder and pulled his lanky frame into the *Register*'s conference room, where I had spread out even more pictures.

Steve ran his skeletal hand through his unruly hair while frowning at me, befuddled. "Seen who, Jilly?"

"This guy," I said, showing him the photo of Gandhi the day before his assassination. "In the background there. See?"

Steve looked at it blankly. "Yeah, so? Who is he? Mahatma's poker pal or drinking buddy or the guy who shot him?"

"I don't know who he is, but look." I placed the photo of Teddy Roosevelt pontificating from the back of the train in 1912 right beside the Gandhi picture. Then I handed Steve my magnifier and pointed at the man standing beside the train. I watched Steve's narrow, angular face contort into a frown and then go strangely limp, in shock.

He glanced sharply at me. "How could that be?"

I shook my head. "Beats the hell outta me."

Steve looked carefully through the magnifier again at the man with Roosevelt, then again at the man with Gandhi. "It does look absolutely like the same guy! At exactly the same age!"

"Yeah, tell me about it. But those two photos were taken thirty-six years apart." We stared at each other a moment. I wanted that fact to sink in for Steve before I showed him the third photo. "Alright, now check out this one."

I noticed my hand trembling slightly as I placed it over half of a third photo on the table, hiding part of the picture. It was scratched and pale, clearly from a very old negative. It looked like something that Matthew Brady, the great nineteenth-century photographer, might have taken during the Civil War. On the side of the picture that I'd left exposed were two Union soldiers in bedraggled uniforms. I pointed at a third man standing next to them. He wore a stained and mud-spattered greatcoat over his civilian clothes.

Steve craned his head closer and peered through the magnifier. Then he stopped breathing.

"Yeah," I said, simply, confirming Steve's impression. "Yeah. Even with the sideburns I swear to God it's the same guy. And look." I removed my hand so Steve could see who else was in the photograph.

Steve stared at the bearded officer with the ruddy face who was sitting prominently at a field table in front of his bivouac tent. Steve blinked. "Isn't that . . . ?"

I nodded. "General Ulysses S. Grant. In 1863."

Steve's eyes slowly lifted up to meet mine. Both of us felt the air in the room had suddenly taken on an eerie chill.

Tito...

Mrs. Schain flipped her cell closed, then looked at St. Jacques, sayin', "I was wrong, Father. There's not another W.J. The other one is signed J.W."

I seen the priest's mind was tickin'. He axed could she show him.

"Down this way," she said.

Okay, so now I'm real curious. So I kinda casually tagged along behind 'em through some rooms to where a sign read "The Flemish School."

I'uz confused. Ain't never hearda no Flem. And the section didn't look like no schoolroom neither; there wudn't no desks, just more big rooms with pitchers hangin' on the walls in heavy, hand-carved frames that looked like they cost way more than the pitchers. They'uz real different from the Impressionists. They'uz all real dark and broody, lots of 'em in that chiaroscuro style. And lots of 'em looked almost real, like they been took with a camera!

I heard some people we passed talkin' how these was mostly Dutch pitchers, so I figured Flem was same as Dutch.

While the Schain woman led the priest through the rooms, I heard her sayin', "We don't know the full name of this artist. He may have studied briefly with Rembrandt in Amsterdam." She slowed down as she come toward a painting that was smaller than most others in the room. The damn frame was actually bigger than the pitcher that'uz only about ten inches wide by twelve high. They was half blockin' it, so I couldn't get a good look.

Schain cocked her head toward it. "We think it's a self-portrait of the artist."

When the priest heard that, he sucked in sharp and leaned close to the pitcher. I edged over and peeked around 'em at it.

Whoa. I gulped in a breath, too. I'uz just as shook.

That little pitcher been painted jus' like them heavy, dark Dutch ones hangin' round it. The brushstrokes was so teeny and fine, man, you couldn't see 'em at all. That's what musta made them pitchers look like photos. The guy in this little one was like from the chest up, wearin' a drapin' brown cloak kinda thing overtop a loose ivory shirt. His hair and eyes'uz light brown, his face shaved clean. He had this serious look on his face and was starin' right at me.

I was starin' back with my mouth hangin' open. Feelin' chilled and no-shit frightened. Gazin' at me outta that pitcher frame was a man who looked *exactly* like the guy I been talkin' to that very mornin'. Just like fuckin' *Will*.

But that weren't all. I *really* clutched when I seen the guy in the pitcher even had exactly the same little wooden cross and antiquey locket hanging round his neck!

I felt like I been turned into one o'them statues I seen in this place. I'uz froze solid. Starin' into the eyes o'that guy in the pitcher. Felt this wave o'fear come sweepin' in me. Scared about who, or what, this Will fucker really was.

I heard the priest axe to take a photo o'the pitcher. He did, then looked real close again, tryin' to read somethin' in the corner. He said, "It does seem to be signed *J. W.*"

"Yes, it is," Mrs. Schain responded.

St. Jacques squinted tighter at it. "The date is harder to read."

Then I heard Schain drop the bomb: "It's 1677."

THIRTEEN

Suki Tamura, age 42, taxi driver...

I like to drive my taxicab. Enjoy talk with customers. "Good way to practice English," I tell them. People surprised to see me: little woman driver. Not big Pakky or Sikh guy wearing turban. I like to drive here. New York easy, not like Tokyo. Tokyo messy, all spread out. Take forever to get around.

But New York streets run mostly north–south or east–west. Except the Battery. Battery's a bitch, like Tokyo. Screwy streets go every whicha-way. But when I first come two years ago, I rode a bike back forth all over them. Learned them good.

I like to drive cab, 'cept when somebody got a gun. Like that New Year's Eve afternoon in Spanish Harlem. I stopped at light, 114th Street. My side window explode in; glass chunks fly all over me. Scare me shitty. "Tough young Spic guy," I told cop later on. "Maybe PR, with crazy, fiery eyes. Druggy maybe. Waving gun in my face. Screaming, 'Gimme you cash, bitch! Gimme you cash!'"

I didn't fight. You see I'm just small squirt, ninety-four pound only. I just want to get out alive.

"You want me shoot, bitch!?" he hiss at me. "Gimme you cash!"

"Sure, sure. Okay!" I say quick while digging in money pouch. "You take money. No shoot!"

Then I hear another man shout, "Hey!" And the big tough kid suddenly get grabbed, get jerked around. I saw other guy was not so big. "Just regular white guy, wearing blue navy kinda coat," I told cop later. "But fast. He was plenty fast. Snatched kid's gun right up. Slammed that kid hard. Bend him back over my taxi hood. Now tough kid's not so tough."

I look at white guy. Strong face, light-brown hair, good eyes. I don't know him. I see him push punk's gun barrel right into punk's cheek. Then he leaned real close, right in kid's face, smiling. But deadly-like. I see tough kid's cheek get quivery. Like fresh sashimi. He was scared plenty. Big time. 'Bout to shit himself.

White guy spoke quiet, real friendly-like, but smiling weird, like scary clown. "Don't you know that old *Golden Rule*, my friend?" Punk was froze solid, 'cept for his quivery cheek with steel gun muzzle stuck on it. "You think that's just some corny bedtime story for kiddies?" White guy moved the gun barrel up and down kid's cheek, said, "You like me to do this to you? Huh?!"

"No! No!" Kid was getting frantic now.

White guy shoved gun barrel right into kid's eye, still smiling scary, say, "Think you gonna remember that rule now? Huh?!"

Kid's cryin' now, choked up. "Yeah, yeah! I will! Okay?"

"Okay then," white guy say, still hold him tight. "Start livin' it, you got that? I'll be watching you." He put gun barrel right on tip of kid's nose. "Do this again, your ass is grass."

Then white guy let him squirm out. Kid took off running. I see his pants are wet. He pissed himself.

White guy shook his head. Step closer to me. I surprised when he talk in perfect Japanese, say, "These kids. What you gonna do? Are you okay, ma'am?"

I stare at him, then answer in Japanese, "Yeah. Okay. Okay. Thanks."

He dumped out bullets, hand me pistol. Say give it to the next cop I see. Then he reached in careful, took glass piece out my hair, said in Japanese, "You better clean up the rest before you get cut." Then he smiled, say, "You take care, Mrs. Tamura." I was surprised. He musta seen my wedding ring, my taxi medallion.

He started walking away. I shouted in English, "Hey. Wait. You need a ride?"

He smiled, say, "No, that's okay."

But I feel bad, know my ancestors want me to show gratitude. Feel I'll lose face if not offer something. At least *say* something. Then I remembered, called out, "Hey." He looked back. "Thank you, mister. You have a happy New Year! Happy New Year!"

He stand quiet a second. Then say slow, in Japanese, "I'm hoping it'll be much more than just happy, Mrs. Tamura."

He smiled gentle one last time and kept walking.

I didn't see him again. Till three days later.

On that really scary day. Most scary day in my life. Never thought I'd see the things I saw. Not here. Not on the earth. Reminded me of my old Uncle Akashi. He told me about things he saw, most scary day in *his* life. Six of August, 1945. At Hiroshima.

Father St. Jacques...

I had always appreciated the elegant image presented by sisters of the Carmelite Order. Their traditional black-and-white habits, which fully cover all but their faces, spoke boldly of their commitment to their God. That was why I identified with them so strongly. I felt that their passion for the Almighty somewhat approached my own. In a world that had become so foolishly secularized, where so-called nuns of other orders wore only a scarf on their heads or dressed entirely in inappropriate civilian clothes, the Carmelites still represented a devotion to asceticism that pleased me, just as I was certain it must also please Our Heavenly Father.

The travels I had made during my decades of pursuit on the Vatican's behalf had once taken me to the cornerstone of the Carmelite Order, Mount Carmel in the Holy Land. To stand where Elijah had so long ago confronted and defeated the priests of the dark, false god Ba'al renewed my own strength to press onward toward a final confrontation of my own, to finally cast the inescapable net of our Mother Church over my quarry.

I was ruminating on the Carmelites as I walked eastward on 56th Street toward the New York archdiocese headquarters on First Avenue, because two Carmelite sisters were approaching me on the sidewalk. Their attention had been attracted by a filthy, long-haired zealot who held a pitifully handwritten sign that stated, "He Is Coming." It was decorated with asymmetric crosses and badly drawn symbols of fish.

He was speaking loudly to other passersby, saying, "Repent of your sins! Tomorrow is truly the New Millennium! His time has come to bring the Rapture and walk among you again! You better be ready!"

The older of the two Carmelites smiled beneficently at the man. She held up her left hand to show the wedding ring that bound her to God and said, "Oh, we're more than ready, brother."

I smiled my agreement to the nuns as I passed them. They inclined their heads slightly to me, which I received politely, feeling theirs was the appropriate respect for my superior station.

The Archdiocese of New York was in a relatively modern fourteen-story building that encompassed most of the block on the east side of First Avenue at 55th Street. A number of organizations closely affiliated with it were also housed within the building. I entered and was crossing toward the large reception counter when I saw an inner door open. Through it appeared New York's archbishop Malloy and several prelates who were clearly in attendance to him.

His Eminence Seamus Cardinal Malloy was cloaked and capped in vibrant red, of course. He was in his seventies and quite robust. He was walking slowly, examining a document and giving responses to it, which were being hastily scribbled down by two of his mealy subordinates. Malloy was the shortest among his entourage, but I knew that pit bulls were also notoriously compact. One of the cardinal's attendants, a well-groomed younger man who was a full head taller than the archbishop, asked a question.

I observed Malloy bestow a glare upon the young man that would have withered an entire field of sunflowers in Alpes-de-Haute-Provence. Then the archbishop spoke in a flinty manner that characterized the younger man's question as ludicrous and the unfortunate questioner as a victim of hopeless idiocy. I saw the pained embarrassment on the attendant's face as he shriveled backward. In that moment I made yet another silent promise to God: should I ever—only by your Divine Will of course, My Father—should I ever be blessed to ascend to such an exalted position as archbishop, I vow to always treat those serving beneath me with civility and common courtesy.

I had encountered Malloy only once previously, when the cardinal had been given his red hat by our latest pope, John Paul, at the consistory in 1988. Coincidentally, I was then in Rome personally reporting to the Holy Father the latest details of my fevered quest. As I was leaving, Malloy was being shown into the papal presence. The pontiff himself introduced me to him. I later confessed to feeling the sin of pride in my own intimacy with Pope John Paul.

In the archdiocese lobby, Archbishop Malloy glanced up over his half-glasses from the document he held. His eyes passed disinterestedly over those scattered about the vestibule. Many noticed and bowed respectfully. When his gaze passed across me, his eyes snapped back and held mine. I nodded politely. Malloy merely continued to stare for a moment, then returned his attention to the document.

As always, I had thoroughly prepared myself for meeting Malloy. Reviewing the archbishop's history, I was reminded of Malloy's streetwise upbringing in Brooklyn and his early scrapes with the law, before he was drawn to the service of the Lord. He came from a family of hardscrabble Irish immigrants that proudly traced its lineage back to the gangs of New York, which dominated the mythic Five Points slum, notorious for its vice and debauchery throughout the nineteenth century. Malloy's immediate family boasted two firefighters (his late father was a chief) and three policemen (actually one was a policewoman). Another female had taken the vows to become a Dominican Sister. He also had one brother whose picture was "turned to the wall" because of his habitual incarceration, apparently a throwback to the family's Five Points ancestry.

Seamus Cardinal Malloy was obviously the most prominent and successful member of his family. Even among the rich and powerful of New York City, he was known as a force to be reckoned with. Completing his business with the document, the stocky archbishop thrust it into the hands of an assistant and strode across the shiny marble floor toward me. His eyes were intense, his face unsmiling as he extended his ring for me to kiss.

"St. Jacques, right?" His voice had the same chesty, growling quality I remembered from Rome.

"Yes, Your Eminence," I answered graciously, trying to Anglify my accent somewhat. I recalled that Malloy was not fond of us French in general. "It's very nice to see you again."

"Right," the older man grumbled dismissively. "Let's go upstairs."

I nodded and fell into step with him as we walked up the ornate stairway, followed by the archbishop's entourage. I was anxious to get to business. "Were you able to have someone see to my request, Your Eminence?"

"Not yet," Malloy said without bothering to look at me.

I always became annoyed when anyone impeded my mission on the church's behalf, be he even so exalted as an archbishop. But I remained civil. "Forgive me, Your Eminence, but did you not receive word from the Vatican defining my authority?"

"Yep. I did. Seems like they give you a lot of slack."

"That is very true, Your Eminence. So if I may ask, why the delay in granting my request?"

"For the archdiocese to ask the NYPD to trace a cell phone"—Malloy shook his head—"is very unusual, Father Paul, to say the least. Precedent setting. Legally questionable."

"Be that as it may, Your Eminence—"

Malloy interrupted as though I were not even speaking. "Your mission intrigues me, though, Father. And so do you." We reached the top of the stairs, where the archbishop paused and waved for his assistants to continue on ahead. Then his small black eyes focused sharply on me. "You're obviously driven by a very strong *ambition*."

"Well, Excellency," I began somewhat defensively, glancing away to gather my thoughts.

But before I could respond, Malloy continued, wryly. "Which I'm sure you've acknowledged in confession."

I looked back into his eyes, saying, "Indeed, I have, Excellency." Then, with a glance, I quickly referenced the opulent interior of the grand building surrounding us. It was replete with palatial richness: shining marble stairs and floors, walls of carefully polished, finely grained wood, expensive furnishings, draperies, artwork, all of which were museum quality and all appropriately suited to the lofty ceilings, which were decorated with frescoes in the manner of the Renaissance. "But is ambition improper, Excellency, when it proceeds in the service of our Holy Mother Church?" A slight twinkle appeared in the archbishop's eye, as though perhaps recognizing in me a bit of himself. So I pressed the point. "And whoever aids me in my mission will be extremely well rewarded." I let the offer hang momentarily, then emphasized, "Of that I can personally assure you, Cardinal Malloy."

My professional tone but casual use of Malloy's surname was audacious, and we both knew it. The bullish older man's hairy nostrils flared slightly, but then he eyed me shrewdly, as though he sensed that my dedication to God and to my mission was what emboldened me. It seemed to impress and slightly subdue the old beast. He nodded in the direction of his office, and we began walking that way as he said, "We passed along those photographs you sent last year to all of our parishes." Malloy shook his head derisively. "Very poor quality, though."

I nodded, saying, "Nonetheless, several reports have come to us from people who believe they saw him. They've been helpful in narrowing our search."

"Well, I'll continue to do what I can, Father Paul," he said, "but first I want to know exactly what's going on."

I was irritated by this attitude, and since boldness had worked once, I shook my head negatively and spoke very firmly. "With all due respect, Excellency, Rome has given me—"

The archbishop abruptly caught my sleeve and pulled me sharply to a halt. "Father St. Jacques," he said, with a slow, cagey smile forming on his wizened face. "Let's get something straight: You're not in Rome, okay? You're in New York. And New York is my turf." Then the old Irishman leaned his thick face up so close to my ear that I could smell the brandy on his breath when he whispered, with a dangerous grin, "As we used to say in my old neighborhood, Paul, you don't want to fuck with me."

His defiant black eyes flashed at me, then he walked on toward his office.

Jillian...

It occurred to both me and Steve that someone in the *Register*'s research department might have decided to clown with us and whipped up those strange photos, doing a little Photoshop number, just to see if we'd notice. The staff down there denied it, but Steve and I weren't convinced. So Steve did some online research while I called the Museum of Modern Art, which kept a giant store of old photographs. MOMA faxed over their copies of the same three photos I had been working with: Gandhi, Teddy Roosevelt, and General Grant.

Steve and I saw that the MOMA photos were all identical to the *Register*'s. The anonymous thirtyish man was indeed pictured in all of them.

Steve and I had been pals since we met as freshmen in NYU's Brittany dorm. We'd spent many long and fruitful hours working together on staff at the campus paper. When one of us was stuck on something, the other always seemed to be able to help break the logjam.

Not this time. We sat in the middle of the *Register*'s pressroom. Completely silent. Contemplating the photos and the enormous mystery they represented.

How could the same man possibly appear in all of them? And look the same age?

Father St. Jacques...

Archbishop Malloy settled behind the grandiose carved desk in his sumptuous office, which was paneled in polished maple. He was looking through his half-glasses at the photo I had taken of the artist's letter at the Rainbow Gallery. Malloy had invited me to sit, but I had remained standing to emphasize my desire for action. I was trying to wait patiently, but the sly older man's determination to inveigle his way into my mission was proving tedious. At length, Archbishop Malloy said, "You had Rome analyze this handwriting? Why?"

"To determine if it matched certain other documents we've collected."

Malloy casually tossed the letter onto his desk. "What sort of documents?"

I had been considering this situation carefully, weighing my desire—and need—for the archbishop's help versus my annoyance with Malloy's superior and condescending attitude. I glanced at Malloy's aide, an African priest, who was seated to one side going through his master's daybook. I said quietly to him, "Father Stephan, would you excuse us, please?"

The archbishop shot me a javelin-sharp glance that I felt would have skewered Saint Sebastian. "He can hear whatever I hear."

I kept my eyes tightly fixed on Malloy's as I said with simple finality, "I'm afraid not, Cardinal." From the corner of my eye I saw the African's startled reaction, but that was nothing compared to the archbishop's.

The color rose into Malloy's cheeks, flushing his entire face. His nose grew bright red. His black eyes glared menacingly at me. I thought that if Vesuvius or Mount Saint Helens had a human face just prior to erupting, it could have been Malloy's. But I quietly held my ground. I knew that the authority of the Holy See would back me up conclusively.

A full thirty seconds passed before Malloy finally flicked his eyes to his aide and then toward the door. I waited until the heavy door was firmly closed. Then I turned back to Malloy and sat in the leather chair facing the archbishop's desk. My back was straight, my eyes on Malloy's, which were still burning as he said menacingly, "This better be good, pal."

I considered making a small apology, but decided there was more strength in proceeding apace. "Please listen carefully," I began, "because what I will tell you must be held in the strictest confidence. Besides my two immediate assistants in Rome, who are sworn to secrecy, only His Holiness John Paul and the three cardinals of the Sacred Tribunal are aware of it."

The archbishop's expression modified slightly. I felt that I finally had Malloy's attention. "From the library of correspondence kept by your American reporter and author Mark Twain, we have a letter handwritten to him by a traveler in the Nevada silver fields of 1860 . . ."

Malloy frowned, confused. "Yes? So?"

"We have another handwritten by a Portuguese who sailed aboard the *Pinta*."

"*Pinta*? As in Columbus's ship?"

"Yes, in 1492. And we also have pages handwritten by a Benedictine monk who lived in Madrid in AD 980."

"And?" Now the cardinal was the impatient one.

"The handwriting on all of them, and that letter there in front of you, which I discovered yesterday, has been analyzed by an international battery of utmost experts. They are in unanimous agreement that all the writing was done by the same hand."

The archbishop stared incredulously, then he laughed. "That's ridiculous." He stood up dismissively. Turning to the exquisitely inlaid cabinet behind him, he poured himself a sherry from an elegant cut-glass decanter. But when he looked back, my steady gaze sobered him somewhat. He said with another flippant chuckle, "I mean, come on, Father. How is that possible?" The archbishop raised the glass toward his lips.

"Our Holy Mother Church has been following the trail of this man for sixteen hundred years."

Malloy's sherry went unsipped. He stared at me. "What?"

I nodded. "In AD 398, in the part of the Byzantine Empire that is now northern Lebanon, a ferryboat capsized and thirteen people were drowned. Their dead bodies were retrieved. After last rites were administered, they were placed in a house on the shore to await identification. The next morning one of the corpses was gone."

Malloy shrugged. "Someone took it."

"No. Two priests, whose sworn documentation is preserved in Rome, spent the night keeping vigil outside the only door. That morning they went inside and discovered an empty space where one of the corpses had been. There were marks scuffed into the filthy, damp floor as though the body had dragged itself away from the space to the base of a ladder where there was a large puddle of putrid vomitus: blood and bile. More was found on the rungs of the ladder, which extended up into a loft. A small hole had been pushed out from the inside of the loft through the thatch roof, and garments were tied together to form an escape rope."

"Okay then: they were obviously wrong initially," Malloy sniffed. "The man simply hadn't really been dead."

I raised an eyebrow slightly. "Even though the victims had all been submerged for over two hours?"

Seamus Cardinal Malloy slowly sat back down in his thick leather wing chair facing me across his desk. His eyes never left mine.

I continued, "The priests quickly made inquiries to other nearby towns and learned that the man, who wore a small wooden cross and a distinctive locket around his neck, had been seen in an adjacent village two days after his 'death.' One of the priests continued the pursuit and actually saw the fugitive in Zgharta but lost him in the busy marketplace.

"On several occasions since then," I went on, "seven to be precise, he has almost been captured. A Moorish priest came closest. In Venice. In 1703. I am honored to be the latest soldier whom the Vatican has appointed to pursue him. I have done so for the last twenty-three years. But I've sworn that I shall be the last. The one who sees it to the end."

I stood up slowly and leaned my fists emphatically onto the archbishop's imposing desk. "The cell phone that I need you to have tracked is currently in his possession. I have reason to believe that at this very moment the man I seek is most likely on your . . . turf."

Malloy still stared at me. Then looked down at the letter, of which he now seemed quite fearful. His gruff demeanor had altered, quieting considerably. His sherry had been forgotten. I could hear that Malloy's mouth had entirely lost its moisture as he looked up into my eyes with a new respect and hesitantly asked, "Father Paul . . ." His mouth had indeed gone dry. "What . . . exactly . . . are we dealing with?"

FOURTEEN

Jillian...

I had delivered my "More Faces of the Last Thousand Years!" article just before the special edition's deadline, but the photos of that strange man were still haunting me as I poked around my apartment that evening.

My TV showed a live picture from Times Square. The New Year's Eve crowd had grown massive and was jubilant. TV cameras panned across cheery people of all colors and ages grinning from ear to ear even though they were jam-packed, completely filling the confluence of Broadway and Seventh Avenue.

As on every year that I could remember, the crowd extended from below 42nd Street northward into the 50s. Many people cheerily carried signs with messages ranging from "Happy 2001" to "Hi, Mom!" Other people held shiny Mylar balloons or waved pennants. They were bundled against the cold, but funny hats abounded, as well as festive 2001 eyeglasses with the people's happy eyes peering through the double zeros. Glittering confetti was already drifting down like shiny snowflakes, and a thoroughly exuberant spirit filled the frigid night air.

The TV showed a shot of the huge Waterford crystal ball hanging above the building on 44th Street reflecting gleams from spotlights and sparkling against the black night sky.

Then came a close-up of the ageless Dick Clark, who was saying, "Only six minutes now until the new year: a year that many people regard as the true beginning of the New Millennium: 2001! And let me tell you, this crowd is ready to welcome it!"

Dick continued talking cheerily as I looked at the man staring out of the three photos that rested atop my coffee table. Dick Clark apparently wasn't the only one who seemed ageless.

My apartment was a tiny one-bedroom on the seventh floor of a well-maintained older building on West 81st off Columbus. It was furnished piecemeal, mostly in early IKEA. I was still wearing my clothes from work, but I'd pulled my shirttail out, always my psychological symbol that I was off duty. I'd been the last to leave the office, declining Steve's offer to tag along to the company's yearly party. I had finished my Lean Cuisine orange chicken and cleaned up my phone-booth-sized kitchen.

From the fridge, I took out the small split of Moët that I'd bought for the evening. It had always been my mom's favorite. It was the one expensive, festive treat my mother had ever allowed herself. I eased the cork out properly and poured some into a red plastic cup. I didn't own any real glasses. They can break.

Despite my shirttail being out, my mind wasn't really off duty. I was still studying the mysterious photos on my table. I sipped the cold champagne distractedly as my answering machine picked up the ringing phone I'd been ignoring.

I heard a man's soft, familiar, uncertain voice say, "Jilly? Are you there? Hello? . . . It's Doug. From accounting? You know?" He paused a moment in hopes that I might answer, but I didn't. I was too preoccupied. Doug finally sighed and went on in his gentle, shy manner, "I'm here at the party and . . . I was just sorry you hadn't come." There was a pause, then, "Well, listen, I'll probably hang here for a while in case you change your mind, okay?" He paused again, then said, "I really hope you have a good New Year, Jilly. Well . . . bye."

The machine clicked off and I sighed, thinking, *What a shit you are, Jillian.* Doug is a sweet guy who's never been anything but nice. You could have at least . . . something.

But instead of figuring out what something might have been, I sat on the front edge of my slim couch, frowning down at the strange photos. I sipped the champagne and looked at the bubbles inside the plastic cup. Then my eyes drifted over to some of the small pictures framed on my shelves. Mom at twenty-three, smiling when she'd first arrived in America. Mom's name was Lumenita, which meant *a little light*, and was appropriate. She always brightened everyone's day. She'd taken some business courses in Romania and found work here reconciling the books for several small companies, like the bakery where she met my dad, Jimmy Guthrie, a Scottish baker. Mom always described him as a good and jovial man. He looks it in the photos. I don't remember him. A drunk driver swerved onto the sidewalk right at our corner of 78th and Pitkin. He died in Mom's arms. She never remarried, said no one ever made her laugh like Jimmy had. She worked hard, determined to nurture and protect me properly and raise me on her own. She read to me from earliest childhood, introduced me to music and the humanities. She wasn't a saint, in fact a real pain sometimes, particularly in my teens, but then I wasn't the easiest teen either. Yet through it all we loved each other, and I knew that Mom was a genuinely wonderful human being.

Always precise and tight fisted when handling other people's money, she was more of a soft touch with her own. If a neighbor was a little short one month, Mom would loan them some money, even if times were thin for us.

She'd take it from the ready supply of cash she kept in an old cookie jar on a top shelf in our kitchen. She believed American banks were relatively trustworthy, but she'd had so many difficulties with Romanian banks during the Soviet era that her old habits persisted.

Even when I was really little I sensed that some people took advantage of her. I felt like the Mexican man, Mr. Ramirez, might do just that, but he actually paid her back. Twice. I wondered if he did it just to get closer to her. He seemed to like her more than he should. It bothered me when he'd shake her hand a little too long or touch her shoulder, even though she'd just smile and respond politely. Sometimes when she turned away from him, I'd catch him looking up and down her slender figure. Even though I was only five, that made me uneasy, but he soon became just another face in our neighborhood. He seemed harmless enough.

I drew a sharp breath, took a sip of the Moët. No need to go *there*, I decided. So instead I glanced at the one photo on my shelf I probably shouldn't have on New Year's Eve: that close-up of Mom, smiling right at me. The last one I'd taken three days before—

Wham! Like a strobe flash in the face, a burst of memory hit me: the Lenox Hill ER that awful night. The team in the trauma unit working frantically over Mom. All of them talking at once while she lay there, comatose and failing. I saw my twenty-year-old self, arms clutched tightly over my purple NYU T-shirt, as I hovered desperately in the doorway, wiping a tear so I could see Mom more clearly.

Sitting there alone in my apartment that New Year's Eve, I felt the pain yet again. My loss. My heartache. My immense guilt.

I finally raised my plastic cup in a sad toast to my lost mother, then I downed all the champagne.

Father St. Jacques...

I had eaten but little all day out of my desire to take no time for myself, but rather be of maximum service to My Lord. After I had dealt with Archbishop Malloy and the archdiocese, I hurried on to the New York Police Department and ultimately the Office of the Mayor. But I had succeeded in navigating their often nonsensical maze. I had obtained the necessary warrant. The police agreed that once they had dealt with the mindless citywide frivolity of New Year's Eve, they would collect me at dawn to track down my quarry's cell phone.

I ate a modest supper in my comfortable room at the Wyndham as I further examined computer scans of some ancient scrolls. They had recently been unearthed north of Rome during excavation for a new subway. They held unique information that I felt could prove very valuable to my mission.

Soon after eating, I felt uncomfortably bloated; I assumed the bitter heartburn doubtlessly came from the tense anticipation I felt by closing in on my prey and also from the anxiety provoked by dealing with bureaucratic automatons all day. I knew they had not the slightest comprehension of the epic, centuries-long pursuit that I was about to bring to a satisfactory and magnificent conclusion. A conclusion which, once I had revealed it, would stun the world.

Tito...

I'uz lookin' at the photos I'd took. I had 'em spread out on toppa the wonky, scratched-up Formica table in my aunt's dingy kitchen. A couple'uz blurry, but most'uz okay. I'uz still gettin' the hang of the digital camera Will had give me.

Will.

Shit. My brain was still twistin' round about that sucker and that "self-portrait" pitcher I seen at the Met.

I looked down at the photos. They'uz of some taggin' I done up at 130th last week. It'uz strange to look at my tags in them photos. Seemed like they'uz somebody else's. Made me look at 'em different kinda, notice stuff about 'em I didn't like so much. When I'uz out taggin' I'uz always just going with my guts. Mostly just grabbin' the first idea that come to me and then freewheelin' to see where it'd take me.

But after I'd seed all them museum pitchers, my own stuff looked different to me. I still couldn't even say how zactly, but it made me, I dunno, got me thinkin' more'n I ever done.

Then I heard some gunshots echoin' outside. What else is new? Gunshots always popping round the projects a lot and for sure on New Year's fuckin' Eve. I even fired me a few last year.

I heard my twin cousins stirrin', too. My aunt'uz workin' late, so I looked in at 'em. Chico was all bundled up, but Juan done kicked off his covers like usual and was frownin' in his sleep. Maybe them gunshots was troublin' him. While I'uz tuckin' the little guy in, a chopper come roarin' past near to scrapin' the roof, its searchlight makin' it like daylight in the room for a sec.

I looked out the window at the city but wudn't really seeing it. I was puzzlin' again 'bout that creepy pitcher at the Met: that pitcher some artist painted of hisself in 1677, but that looked just like the Will guy I knowed. Alls I could figure was the guy in the painting musta been Will's great-great-great-something.

But shit, I seen myself frownin' in the window glass, wonderin' how could that old muthafucka have the *i-dentical* thing round his neck? And look *ex-act-ly like Will*?

Hanna...

What a magical glow was on the face of that child in his painting. It never ceased to draw me in, particularly on an emotional night like New Year's Eve. Will had captured so masterfully the needy child's reaction to the Parisian vendor's humanity and kindness. I reached my hand up to touch the paint that Will had applied so many years ago, back when my hand was still flushed with youth and had yet to become the veiny, age-spotted hand of an old crone. How I missed him, what we had been and shared together.

Methuselah caught my attention, exactly as he intended, by stretching extravagantly as he lazed on the sill of his favorite window. I noticed a cup of hot tea sitting beside him and frowned because I'd just made myself a cup and was holding it in my hand. I pursed my lips, tensing, trying to write off my forgetfulness to the distraction I was feeling over Will. But I knew it was more likely another Alzheimer's moment.

Dammit, dammit! I clenched my teeth angrily, trying to fight back mentally. But I knew it was a losing battle, that the inevitable cloud of forgetfulness and oblivion was inching toward me. And I hated it.

Methuselah pawed at me, looking regal and obviously wondering why he wasn't being fawned over. And it was New Year's Eve, after all. In truth it was New Millennium's Eve, so I condescended. I pondered the concept of the end of the Millennium. I knew the enormous importance, the monumental importance, it held for Will. I ached to know where he was. And to be with him.

I scratched the calico's head and looked out the window at the lights of the Triborough glistening off the dark churning waters of Hell Gate.

I heard party music and the infectious laughter of young people drifting in from outside. Their happiness made me smile but also tore at my old heart. I was in such a state of anxious remembrance, of aching tenderness, wanting to be with my dear Will. Just once more.

Will...

I rubbed the locket and tiny wooden cross that hung around my neck between my thumb and forefinger as I walked along the bitingly cold street.

I knew it was dangerous when anyone yearned for something too desperately, invested his hopes too wholeheartedly in the possibility that the wished-for something might actually come to pass. I feared that the very act of my longing so intensely for an event to happen would somehow cause it *not* to happen. I worried that if I focused too ardently on this special night, this special moment that was drawing nearer by the second, this incredible, singular event that could change my life forever, that the Imp of the Perverse would somehow make certain I was *not* rewarded.

Poe and Baudelaire each described the Imp as a sort of minor demon who urged the incautious toward doing what was exactly opposite their best interests. I had always felt that the little beast was far more perverse than merely that.

In order to spare myself the gravest of disappointments, I had tried to pretend that the approaching midnight of December 31, 2000, truly didn't matter so very much, that my life could, and likely would, go on as it had been.

And so I dealt with Walter Smith at the Rainbow Gallery, with sweet Laura Rakowitz, my editor at Gotham. I endeavored to spur Tito and Chuck Weston into a fuller realization of their terrific artistic potential. I encouraged the young bartender Nicole not to close down her heart. I gave financial aid to a few people and tried to help the old carny Eleanor toward a healthier, brighter tomorrow.

I traveled and lived each moment of not only the last few days and hours in that manner, but throughout the last few years, months, and weeks: as though my life would continue as it had without alteration. I had carried on and done it all in the secret hope that if I didn't watch the clock as it ticked down toward midnight on this very special December thirty-first, I might not *prevent* the occurrence I sought by clinging too desperately to the hope that it would occur. I sought to be nonchalant, to trick the Imp of the Perverse. To beat him at his own game.

But now the auspicious hour had almost arrived. I knew, of course, that on the other side of the earth, the New Millennium had already dawned. But I was convinced that the hoped-for Magic would not, in fact could not, transpire until it reached the place on Earth where I stood. And now that crucial moment was nearly upon me.

Despite the formidable levies and dikes I had mentally erected to restrain the rising tide of expectant emotions within myself, that irrepressible tide was now lapping at the brim of my defenses and was threatening to flood over the top of them and into my soul. Though I still endeavored with every ounce of mental strength to hold it back,

I was seriously afraid I would not be able to keep myself from hoping too dangerously.

I had chosen what appeared to be a small evangelical church on 52nd Street west of Broadway. I knew it didn't matter precisely where I was when the Moment came, but being among true believers seemed appropriate. Being only a mile or so from the mass of humanity in Times Square seemed somehow ironic and perhaps equally appropriate. It was easy to envision the enormous crowd there, with their eyes on the glittering crystal ball, awaiting one landmark moment, but then receiving instead quite a different and explosively, exponentially grander one. The sound of their million-person multitude a few blocks away created a buzz of background energy that was well suited for the special evening.

Upon entering the church I realized that it was situated in what had once been the lovely old Broadway theater known as the Mark Hellinger. It was the theater where *My Fair Lady* had enjoyed its record-breaking run in the 1950s.

Some years before my visit this night, the theater had been transformed into a church. I considered the irony, feeling that such transformation had often gone in the opposite direction. How so much of all religions had become merely theatrical affectation.

At any rate, I saw that this former theater was now an evangelical house of worship. Flowery, theatrical plasterwork still ornamented the lofty ceiling, but decorative frescoes had been added, illustrating scenes predominantly from the New Testament. I noticed a particular emphasis on visions from Saint John's Revelation and the End of Days. As I studied their depictions of the Glory, I felt a warm hopefulness creeping into my heart, but still I pressed to hold it back.

The theater seating had been retained, and including the spacious balcony, it probably held eight or nine hundred people. It was nearly filled that evening.

After passing among the rowdy multitude on the streets outside, stepping into the church was like stepping from the maelstrom of a hurricane into its still and peaceful eye. A friendly, clean-cut, mixed-race teenage boy handed me a thin white cotton scarf, such as had also been given to all those who had preceded me that night. Some congregants were wearing them over their shoulders like a tallis prayer shawl of the Judaic tradition. Many women had draped them over their heads in Catholic tradition.

Clearly a few of the people had come in from living homeless on the street. But what I had not expected was that a majority of the others were neatly appareled and well-groomed. The gathering thus represented the entire social strata, with a predominance from the middle class. They ranged from children to several who were quite aged. Their ethnicity was mixed, as was the choir of some thirty men and women who were standing on raised steps that occupied the right side of the stage as the congregation faced it.

The chorus wore sky-blue robes and, gently accompanied by a church organ, had already begun softly singing choral selections that I recognized as being from the *Messiah* by George Frideric Handel. I smiled, recalling that the original performance had been in Dublin in April of 1742. I remembered that balmy spring night very well.

The house lights had been dimmed to half so that the focus was upon the fully lighted chorus who stood beneath the lofty proscenium, sharing the old Mark Hellinger stage with two ministers.

The ministers wore black satin robes. One was a sturdy middle-aged woman with a shock of white like a torch amid her brown hair. She stood in a pool of backlight at a podium to one side and was quietly reading passages from the book of Revelation. Her subdued voice and the soft singing of the choir provided a background for the other minister, a man in the mold of the young Reverend Dr. Martin Luther King Jr.

He stood in a spotlight before the altar, which had been constructed where the theater's center stage had once been. The altar and its surroundings abounded with bouquets of flowers, particularly lilies. Many candles were burning steadily, like the hope within me that was trying to break free and radiate despite my determined attempts to suppress it. In the center was a glistening golden cross some three feet tall, and stretched across it overhead was a lovingly homemade banner, which read "Welcome, Lord!"

I was still standing in the side aisle as the choir quietly segued into the "Hallelujah Chorus." The audience rose to their feet, as was the tradition. Knowing the music as well as I did, and glancing at my watch in spite of my vow not to do so, I realized that their singing of Handel's grand oratorio was timed to reach its musical conclusion precisely at the stroke of midnight.

The minister looked out over the flock of nearly a thousand who had forgone the wild revelry outside to gather together for this exceptional night. "Look at the world around us," the earnest young preacher intoned, shaking his head sadly. "Plagues, wars and rumors of wars, increasing discord and strife in the Holy Land, corruption at all levels of government and society, false prophets, false idols, worship of gold. Nothing seems to be of real value. Except one thing." His kind, dark eyes looked out into the individual faces, including mine, that were focused on him. "And that one thing is your faith in Him who is coming back to us on this new day!"

There were joyous "Amens" from the congregation. All the people surrounding me were serious and intent, none more so than myself. But unlike myself, who was yet restraining my hopes, they were all sharing in the most positive, optimistic expectations. Their passionate sentiments were so tangible, so impossible to ignore, as to be contagious. I felt the emotional tide within me spilling over more and more. It was growing increasingly unfeasible to deny my feelings: that I might dare to hope, to admit the joy of possibility.

There was a flutter of nervousness oscillating within me as the minister continued, his voice deep and rich: "It's been a long, hard road since

Our Master bore the heavy cross upon His brave shoulders through Jerusalem toward his destiny at Calvary, upon Golgotha's hillside."

I easily envisioned the scene: the beleaguered man in the distance, slowly approaching up the dusty street in ancient Jerusalem; his badly bruised shoulder leaning into one notch of the T-shaped cross; its four-meter-long post dragging behind him, bumping along over the stones, picking up smears of grime and animal dung. As the minister's voice described the scene, I could see it.

"The narrow street lined with Roman soldiers and robed citizens, young and old, jeering at Him. The flesh of His blessed back rent open from the lash of whips. His precious blood spilling from the ugly wounds, from the vicious crown of thorns piercing the blessed skin of His head."

I was totally absorbed by the painful vision. The noise outside from the vast crowd in Times Square became the shouts and cries from the mob in Jerusalem two thousand years earlier as they witnessed the Passion.

"How Our Lord did struggle and sweat and bleed under the weight of the rough-hewn crossbeam and the prodding of the laughing soldiers and others who had demanded His death," the minister continued, caught up in the drama as though witnessing it himself. "Our Master made His way through that cruel mob, carrying not just the weighty wooden cross, my brothers and sisters, but also carrying all the sins of the world upon His courageous shoulders. Half-blind from the blood streaming down from His head, from the tears He was shedding for you and me and for the world, He stumbled through that smoky street, enduring the taunts of the heartless people crowding Him from all sides."

My eyes were closed as my own vision of the scene continued. Unconsciously I had raised the tiny cross around my neck and was pressing it tensely against my lips, which began to tremble slightly as I heard a mighty cheer rise from outside. I knew instantly what it meant: that the huge crystal ball in Times Square had begun its descent. The end of the Millennium was less than one minute away. The seconds were ticking down.

In the small church, as the female minister continued reading from Revelation, the other preacher began to crescendo. "And then He suffered the tortures of the damned as the spikes were driven through His feet and driven through each of His gentle hands."

I could see that barren rocky hillside, littered with bones and skulls, and atop it, beneath swirling dark and ominous clouds, the Crucifixion.

"And on that awful day Our Lord Jesus died upon Golgotha! And darkness came over the face of the land." Many in the church were crying now. Then the young minister's voice took on a new and positive tone, one of magical triumph. "But lo, after three days He rose from the dead to sitteth at the right hand of God the Father Almighty! From whence He shall come to judge the quick and the dead." The preacher's voice grew more impassioned and urgent. "And now this day He's returning to us, my brothers and sisters!" There came cries of "Amen" and "Hallelujah" from the assemblage. The minister spoke more forcefully. "Are you ready to face His judgment!?" Some people murmured affirmatively, but the minister was more demanding, challenging them, "Are you ready for Him to return!?"

The congregation took its cue as one, shouting affirmation. I found myself too choked with emotion to speak. I merely nodded. I could hear the elation of the multitude in the streets outside rising. I knew that the great ball of cut crystal must be halfway down. Thirty seconds until midnight.

The people around me in the church had grown excitable; they were now truly anticipating the Rapture. Some had stepped into the aisles, their eyes heavenward, caught up in joyous religious ecstasy. A woman close by me had begun speaking in tongues as the preacher vehemently said, "For His Second Coming shall be upon us as this bright new day dawns!" He swept his hands over me and his entire flock. "Today He will fulfill His promise to all of His faithful! Today He will bring lasting peace to those who've kept their faith in Him!"

The stirring choral music of Handel's grand oratorio was growing in intensity.

Try as I did to look upon the approaching stroke of midnight as though it were just like any of the countless others I had endured, my heart and every fiber of my being knew better. Try as I might to control my respiration, my long, steady breaths grew shorter and more rapid of their own accord. Despite my fervent efforts to remain calm, I perceived that my pulse was quickening. Each of the millions of nerves within me seemed to be coursing with electricity. All my senses were on their keenest edges. From such disturbed molecular activity comes heat, and I felt that my temperature was indeed rising. My body was literally taking on a fever pitch.

My vision blurred as my eyes brimmed with tears. I clutched the tiny cross and locket so tightly in my fist that my knuckles were white as I pressed them to my lips.

Then the minister grew euphoric, raising his hands skyward in greeting as his commanding voice bellowed, "Come to us, Lord Jesus! We are ready to receive you! Come to us now!"

The voices of the chorus, supported by the bone-shaking bass of the mighty organ, suddenly grew powerful as they swelled together to the final crescendo and the ultimate "Hal-le-lu-JAH!"

I heard the noise outside explode thunderously! Horns blared! Fireworks crackled with loud reports! I knew the crystal ball had reached the bottom. Midnight had come—2001 had arrived. The cheering and joy outside was unparalleled in its enthusiasm. The noise from Times Square was tremendous, epochal. The New Year had been rung in.

The true New Millennium was upon the world.

FIFTEEN

Will...

In the church where I stood among the others, holding my breath, there was tense, expectant silence. My own eyes, even more than theirs, were flashing with near-ecstatic expectation. My heart was fluttering so wildly that I thought it might burst out of my chest.

The boisterous glee from Times Square echoed in the church as the moment sustained. And held. And held longer still.

But there came no rending of the heavens. No volcanic upheavals. No movement of mountains. There was no parting of the waters. No apocalyptic horsemen presaging the magnificent, glorious arrival of the one for whom all in the church were fervently, feverishly waiting. There had been no breaking of the seventh seal.

Not the slightest fulfillment of Saint John's prophecies.

No New Beginning.

The only sound was the cheering, applause, and jubilation of the celebrating masses down in Times Square. I heard the sentimental strains of Robert Burns's "Auld Lang Syne" being sung by the great multitude outside.

My eyes slowly lowered, my shoulders sagged slightly as my disappointment began to grow. Bitter tears welled. I knew that others in the congregation were also feeling sadness.

But not like mine. Not remotely like mine. I alone was staring into a dark and apparently infinite abyss. And yet I drew a breath. I still refused to give up hope entirely; I knew there was still a slim possibility, and the preacher's words offered comfort.

"Do not despair, my brethren." The minister spoke gently, with a wistful smile. "Just because you do not see Him next to you at this moment. For He may yet appear on this day to bring you into His Glory!"

". . . Then again," I heard a familiar voice whisper, as an icy draft wafted across me, ". . . He may not show at all."

Several candles on the altar flickered out from the eerie draft. I noticed a movement among the shadows in a wing of the stage behind the side curtains. It was the sleek young man, as I had seen him in the Virginia City saloon: a Western gambler, black suit, fancy white shirt, string tie; his smooth skin beneath his perfect black hair; his clean-shaven chin as strong as ever. His commanding dark eyes shining from beneath those striking dark eyebrows.

He appeared friendly but somewhat sad as he held up a blood-red poker chip and said in a wistful voice that I alone could hear, ". . . Place your bet?"

I glared, muttering angrily, "It's not over, you bastard." I pulled the peacoat and the white scarf tight around my neck. "The day hasn't dawned everywhere yet."

I turned away and moved past the others toward the exit. My eyes were chafing with frustration, but my jaw clenched with determination as I left the theater that had become a church.

The air outside had indeed turned arctic cold. But the thousands of cheery revelers whom I pushed through were warm with enthusiasm. They were all vital and permeated with life. I tried to absorb just enough of their optimistic energy to keep my last desperate shred of hope from disappearing entirely.

I knew that the night would pass slowly. First, I wandered all the way westward, finally crossing 12th Avenue beneath the parkway. I walked to the end of the parking lot on the 52nd Street dock that jutted out into Captain Henry Hudson's river. I thought of the Indians who called themselves Manhattoes paddling their birch-bark canoes downstream past that very spot in 1626, en route to making a very bad real estate deal. I remembered how a lone white man had tried to warn those natives, but the shrewd Dutch brutally ran that man off. I remembered the path I had taken to escape.

I pulled my peacoat still tighter around myself as I stood on the concrete dock and watched the dark surface of the river flowing past me toward the lights of the harbor, toward the immensity of the sea. To me the river felt like *time* flowing endlessly toward some infinity beyond human imagining.

I stood there gazing, mesmerized by memory and the slowly flowing river as midnight gradually worked its way west to Chicago and the Galápagos, then to Denver and Calgary, then to Vancouver and San Diego. Finally it was three in the morning in New York.

Breathing a long sigh, I turned from the river and walked eastward along 60th until I encountered a small tavern. I saw through the old glass and café curtains of its front window that the clientele was very sparse and that the television inside was tuned to CNN. I went in and sat in a corner at one of the many vacant tables and requested a snifter of Courvoisier. I cupped the bulbous glass in the palm of my hand and slowly swirled the dark brandy to warm it. As it spiraled around inside the glass, I tried not to perceive it as a metaphor for the downward spiral of my own possibilities.

Over the next two hours many cheerful people came and went. The only consistent two were the full-bellied, pouchy-eyed Brooklyn barkeep and a nicely dressed, dark-haired young woman who had been there when I arrived and had never moved from where she sat, three tables from mine. I'd had a faint sense of recognition when I first glanced at her fine-featured face, but I couldn't place where or when I might have seen her. And I had no interest in pursuing it.

My focus was on keeping my mind as clear as possible and my emotions level and steady. My breathing was measured. The clock slowly advanced, one brandy at a time. At length, as the hour reached six in the morning, the CNN anchorman showed the live scene in Honolulu as fireworks burst like sparkling dandelions into the night sky above Waikiki.

"And there you see it," the newsman said. "The stroke of midnight in Hawaii as the local kanies and wahines usher in the new year!" Then he spoke the phrase that I knew was all too true: "Just one time zone to go."

I sat, literally unmoving, for nearly that full, final, fateful hour. But as the last seconds ticked away and the ultimate moment approached, I heard a voice, whispering and emphatic, murmur, "Please . . . Reveal yourself."

I realized it was my own voice, realized that my thumb and forefinger had again unconsciously found the tiny cross and locket around my neck.

Peripherally I sensed both the bartender and the young woman eyeing me, but I paid them no mind. I barely breathed. My eyes were fixed on the television screen, which was showing a nighttime image of a few Polynesian people gathered along the seaside of a barely developed South Pacific island. A chime sounded, marking the hour, and suddenly they were all shouting happily and hugging one another as the CNN newsman's voice said, "And there it is! New Year's Day has dawned on Western Samoa. It is now 2001 AD all around the world!"

He continued talking, but I no longer heard his words. I sat motionlessly for a very long moment. Then, as my head tilted back and my eyes searched indeterminately across the ornate plaster ceiling that was pressing down upon me, a deep sigh of ultimate despair escaped my lips. My every hope had been dashed; my dreamed-for closure had not come to pass. The muscles at the back of my jaw tensed, and tears distorted my vision. I was lost. Disconsolate.

"What's the point, huh?" It was the nearby young woman's soft voice.

I continued staring at the swirled plaster of the ceiling, which had been delicately fashioned by some dedicated artisan who had died long ago, leaving this as a small, anonymous monument to himself, his life, his art. I felt a tear spill out and trace down my cheek.

"You thought it might finally be over today?" she continued gently. "Your grief. Your longing."

I slowly turned to meet the woman's eyes. She returned my gaze with compassion, as though she, too, was aching deeply. With a tiny, sensitive smile of empathy, she rose from her table and softly came to sit at mine. I saw that her face was actually quite beautiful; her black sheath dress was tastefully trim; her figure was very sleek. The expression in her dark eyes was sympathetic, sincerely understanding.

". . . Let me bring an end to your long suffering."

She slid her hand gently across the table toward mine, palm up, invitingly.

A wave of temptation swelled in me, urging me. I slowly let myself reach toward the sleek young woman's hand. But then from somewhere else within me came a strident, opposing force. I suddenly steeled myself and stood up, overturning my chair. She feigned surprise and confusion, maintaining her superlative performance. "What is it?" she asked with innocent concern. "What's wrong?"

I glared at her harshly for an instant to make her aware that I recognized her for *exactly* who she was. Then I threw some money on the bar and bashed a chair aside as I stormed drunkenly out.

Father St. Jacques...

I had awakened sharply before dawn. My stomach was in an understandably agitated state, which I succeeded in quelling only partially with a large quantity of antacid. After my prayers, remembrances, and reaffirmations of devotion to God, I hurriedly prepared myself for what I knew might well be the Day of Days.

As I stepped out of the Wyndham Hotel onto 58th Street, I looked eastward through the canyon created by the Plaza on the left side and the office buildings on the right. I saw the narrow strip of early morning sky, a bleak, slowly undulating blanket of muddy gray.

Turning to look westward, I waited impatiently for several minutes, then finally saw a blue NYPD squad car turn right from Sixth Avenue and approach me. Inside it were two uniformed officers. A full-faced Negro, with tufts of gray in his nappy hair and a thick mustache, was driving. His partner was a young white woman with a face that I found very narrow and unattractive. I sniffed, sourly. The annoyance I felt was on thy behalf, My Gracious Lord. By sending these particular two, the police department was obviously showing that they didn't find my mission to be important. Nonetheless, I leaned down to the window on the woman's side and greeted them graciously. "*Bonjour*, good morning, officers."

The woman nodded, asking, "Father Paul St. Jacques?"

"Indeed, yes, Officer . . . ?"

"Turrell," she informed me, then indicated her black partner. "He's White. And trust me, he's heard all the jokes. Please hop in the back, sir. And Happy New Year."

"I'm hoping it will be," I said as I hurriedly climbed in.

Officer White drove on along bumpy 58th Street, asking, "You're a French guy, huh?"

"Yes, I am. Have you been to France, officer?" I asked, though I certainly felt it unlikely.

"Yeah, once. That was enough," Officer White responded. "Sorry to say it, Father, but lotsa the people were kinda snooty."

"Well, I'll certainly try to make a better impression." But I was disinterested in the Negro's opinion or in arcane small talk; my entire focus was on the urgency of the moment. Leaning forward between the two police officers, I looked at the GPS locator screen mounted on an adjustable arm in front of the female. "That works from triangulation," I presumed.

"When it works, yeah." Officer Turrell sipped coffee from her small thermos cup. "It can get pretty wonky with all the bounces off these buildings. But we think we got a twenty on him." My glance prompted her to explain. "A twenty means his location."

My pulse rate jumped. "Already? You know where he is!? That's wonderful! Where?"

"Near West End Avenue, upper sixties," Turrell responded, as her partner turned right onto Fifth.

I was puzzled. "Then didn't you turn the wrong direction?"

"Fifth is one-way south, Father." White smirked. "You been to New York before?"

You black asshole! I wanted to say, but instead replied, "Yes, of course, officer. Sorry. Just please try to use all haste."

"Who is this guy, anyway?" the policewoman asked.

"We believe that this is what he looks like." I showed her several of the photographs that had been captured by various security and surveillance cameras as well as one that I had taken of that amazing self-portrait at the Met. Then I continued, albeit cautiously. "What exactly have you been told?"

"Just to cooperate, Father," she answered. "Help you locate him, then call for backup to bring him in."

I nodded confirmation. "Good. He is wanted in Italy for very serious crimes."

The black officer glanced curiously at me in his rearview mirror. "So the Italian cops sent a *priest?*"

"His crimes were committed within Vatican City, which, I'm sure you're aware, is a separate sovereign state with its own police force. I am here under their authority."

The officer's dark-brown eyes assessed mine for a moment. Then Turrell asked, "What sort of crimes, Father?"

"Among others . . ." I paused for effect. "Murder."

Will...

My fists were jammed into the pockets of my peacoat. My head ached from too much brandy and was lowered into the blustery, cold north wind as I strode like an angry bull past the deserted terrace of Lincoln Center, barely aware of where I was. I stomped down the grimy concrete stairs into the subway station at 66th Street. I felt like the personification of a storm cloud: a mountainous cumulonimbus thunderhead stretching up into the dark stratosphere, churning with volatile currents, threatening to unleash stabs of lightning at any moment in any direction.

A decrepit beggar approached me, but my glare alone made the man recoil.

Father St. Jacques...

Officer White activated the siren and the flashing lights atop the police car. We had come around to head north on Sixth Avenue, then turned left onto Central Park South. Through the lacy, leafless tree branches, I could see Columbus Circle ahead as the woman officer suddenly said, "Lost him."

"What?" I sputtered. "No!"

She adjusted the controls on her GPS locator, shaking her head. "He musta gone underground."

White nodded. "Near Broadway at 66th? Lincoln Center subway."

I leaned forward, close to the officer's shoulder, catching a whiff of his cheap toilet water. "Keep heading that way," I urged. "Hurry!"

Will...

With a darkening brow, I paced onto the near-deserted subway platform. The five or six other people present were all avoiding a tall, distraught, balding, middle-class man wearing a disheveled suit. He stood near the edge of the platform, shifting his weight from one foot to the other in a drunken, psychotic dance as he pivoted in a tight circle. His nervous, birdlike eyes flitted around, paranoia gleaming in them. They locked onto me, and he snapped out the words, "Stay away! Stay away from me!"

"Gladly," I grumbled, in no mood for his foolishness.

"Stay back. Stay away! I'm gonna do it!"

I felt the wind pick up and knew it was being compressed by an approaching train. The man twisted around to look up the tunnel, where I saw the oncoming headlights shining off the damp, dark walls. The man shouted again, "Stay back! I'm gonna do it!"

A sudden rush of mad glee overcame me. I turned sharply, grabbed the man by his jacket front, and shouted, "Do what?! Kill yourself?!" With a wild, exultant laugh I pulled the man toward the very edge of the tiled platform. "Yeah! Let's *both* do it!"

The man stared at me with suddenly terrified eyes, shouting, "Let me go!"

But I clutched him even more tightly as the train rumbled closer and closer. I pulled the man right into my face, hissing, "I'll go with you!"

He was trembling in fright, clawing at my hands. "No! No!"

Then a dark voice spoke in Russian: "Very bad idea."

It came from the smudged beggar I had seen a moment earlier. The decrepit man was gazing at me with those dark eyes that I instantly recognized. The beggar continued in Russian, "You know how much that will hurt. Remember last time? In Moscow?"

The subway train came roaring and screeching into the station. I was truly about to jump when the panic-stricken man took advantage of my distraction with the beggar and broke away, fleeing frantically for the exit.

I turned toward the subway car that was only three inches away from my face as the train came to a halt. I slammed the side of it with a fist, furiously. As the door rattled open I stormed through it and onto the train.

Father St. Jacques...

I was surprised to see that heavyset Officer White ran surprisingly well. He dashed down the steps ahead of me into the Lincoln Center subway station, his pistol drawn and ready. The woman officer, who had already called for backup, was behind us and also ready to shoot if necessary, though I had cautioned them to avoid that. She peeled off, running toward the northbound side while I ran behind White onto the southbound platform. We saw only two or three people awaiting a train. None were he whom I sought.

We hurried over to join Turrell on the northbound side, where I saw the red taillights of a train disappearing up the tunnel. Turrell turned back to look at us, her mind processing what she'd seen. "I'm not sure," she said. "But maybe. Navy-blue peacoat. White scarf."

White and I were breathing hard. He said, "What number train?"

She shook her head. "Couldn't see. The light box was busted."

The stocky black cop waved us back toward the exit, saying, "The one and nine trains go straight north. Two and three cut east. Two goes to deep Harlem, three to the Bronx."

I was right on the cop's heels. "Where do they diverge?"

"At 103rd Street," he said, taking the steps two at a time.

"Then we should head north," I said, "at least that far."

Turrell, following me closely, added, "I'll put the word out and watch for a new cell signal."

SIXTEEN

Will...

The odor in the subway car was vile and sour. Someone had vomited earlier, and others had tracked it over the floor. I tried to cross into the next car, but the door was jammed. *Naturally,* I groused to myself, knowing it was the Imp at work. The stench made me increasingly nauseous. My head was splitting from the brandy, my nerves tightly wound by having again come face-to-face with the unending, horrid truth of my existence. I felt the sides of the subway car closing in and compressing me as the train rocked powerfully back and forth and the internal lights flickered. I had to get off. I had to get out.

I didn't even know which station I was at as I stumbled in drunken anger up the slick steps and onto the gritty, wet street. A misty rain had begun, adding to the physical weight of oppression I felt grinding down upon me.

Father St. Jacques...

Our police car sped north on Broadway, passing West 86th with its siren wailing and its flasher lights on. The windshield wipers click-clacked, smearing off the misting rain. I squinted through the wet streaks, keeping track of our forward progress as Officer Turrell spoke into her radio's microphone. "Male Caucasian. Early thirties. Light-brown hair. Wearing a navy-blue peacoat and—" She interrupted herself to point at the GPS screen. "Got him. Central Park. Northeast corner at One Hundred Eleventh."

White nodded. "Spanish Harlem." He swerved around a taxi and sped on. Turrell keyed her radio. "One William One request backup code three in Spanish Harlem. Stand by for a twenty."

Will...

The misty rain caught on my eyelashes and blurred my vision of a boarded-up building where I saw a dozen stained and tattered posters advertising a recent New York City Opera production of Wagner's *The Flying Dutchman*. Pictured was a ghostly clipper ship foundering in a storm-tossed sea; its sails, hanging in shreds, graphically echoed the headline, "Doomed to Sail the World Forever."

The poster triggered images that came at me in flashes, as in my nightmarish memories, like lightning striking close by, the shock waves buffeting me repeatedly: first it was the two-masted carrack *Santa Maria* leaning precipitously and nearly swamped in dark, unknown, and mountainous seas. Men overboard. Frantic.

Then crusading Soldiers of the Cross like myself crowded around me, some choked by their own blood, as a Norman knight's broadsword decapitated a charging Persian warrior.

Then I saw a black slave child on a Kentucky auction block screaming in tearful panic as he was pulled away from his terrified, hysterical mother.

Then the muddy trench at Verdun exploded with fire and debris as mortar rounds rained down and dismembered the French soldiers near me.

Then came a cattle car filled with people, their bleak, frightened faces staring out from between the slats as the steam train rolled slowly east toward the small Polish town of Oświęcim.

But interspersed with these nightmare images, I had flashes of many other happier faces: differing ages, genders, ethnicities, from ancient days through to the present. Each was looking directly into my eyes. Smiling, grateful, tearfully thankful.

"But don't you get it?" I heard a man's dark voice call out in Hungarian. My beleaguered eyes looked back through the New York rain to see a sturdy red-faced man slowly driving a meat truck past me on 111th Street. He was looking right at me, shaking his head sadly. "He ain't comin', pal. There ain't no payoff. He's never gonna show."

I turned away from the driver, feeling anguished, staggering like I was losing my mind among the sparse people on the Upper Manhattan street. A grandmotherly old Hispanic woman spoke to me in Spanish, but with the same sympathetic, masculine voice. "But I am right here for you, Will!"

I pushed gruffly past her as a small white toddler holding his mother's hand glanced up at me, speaking in the same adult voice, "The smart thing to do is quit walking around."

Then a natty black businessman in a three-piece suit caught my fevered eye. "Come hang with my gang and kick back," the businessman said, smiling.

My delirious head was swimming. I hurried on around the corner and saw, dressed again in the fine black suede Windbreaker over his camel cashmere turtleneck, the sleek young man. He was standing beside the open rear door of a highly polished Cadillac stretch limousine, which shimmered in the misty rain. He indicated the open door and spoke gently, with comradely warmth, "Come on, Will . . . Give yourself a break. Climb in with me."

I angrily shouted an ugly Arabic profanity at him and stumbled onward.

Father St. Jacques...

Officer White had made good time reaching Central Park North. Our police car was speeding east now, dodging through the light holiday-morning traffic, some of which pulled aside upon hearing our approaching siren.

I was breathing tensely, swallowing back the chronic burning in my throat. My blood was decidedly up. The female officer watched the GPS screen carefully, then called out to White, "Left at Madison."

Will...

The drizzling rain was heavier now, running down my forehead and into my eyes, further warping my vision and my distressed mental state. I vaguely knew that I was heading northeast toward my motor home. Then, as I rounded the corner from Third Avenue onto 112th Street, I was startled to see directly in front of me an old tenement house on fire.

Tongues of flame were thrusting out of the third-floor windows. Above them, on the fourth floor, a skinny, ratty-looking Hispanic woman leaned out of a window. She was unsteady, perhaps drunk or drugged, but screaming slurred words desperately: "Help! Oh God! Save my baby!"

I saw other inhabitants of the building rushing out of the front door and down the half dozen wooden steps to the sidewalk. All were frantic, disheveled. Many of them carried some personal items or a small child. None of them even glanced upward as the woman on the fourth floor cried out hoarsely, "Please, God! Help my baby!"

I was gazing up at her as one portly woman fleeing the building ran directly into me, saying, "Screw 'em, they're better off dead."

I looked up again at the scrawny woman screaming from the window. She seemed both dazed and frenzied. I stared at her. Then, lowering my head like an angry bull, I wheeled around and walked back the way I'd come.

I had gone only a few steps when somehow, through the shouts of the people behind me, I heard the muffled screams of a small child. "Momma! It's hot! It's so hot!"

The child's voice slowed me, but still I fought not to look back, not to get involved. I was determined to walk away.

The child's voice grew fainter. "Mommeeee!? I can't breathe!"

My feet slowed even more, as though they had a consciousness of their own. I finally came to a stop, but refused to turn back. I stood in the rain, quaking from anger, hearing the frenzied pleas for help, struggling to suppress the fiery rage expanding within me, trying to make my churning mind ignore the tearful, anguished outcries of the drugged-out mother and her terrified child, fainter still. "Help us! Somebody!" "Mommeeeee!"

My anger suddenly erupted volcanically. I exploded, bellowing with a mighty fury, pounding my fists repeatedly down onto a nearby car. "No, goddammit! I don't want to do it! Not anymore!" My fiercely repeated blows buckled the car's hood as I roared at it, at the world, at my fate. "There's no point! *I can't take anymore!*" I pressed my bloodied fists hard against my ears, trying not to hear the tortured wails from the fiery building, wanting desperately to run away.

"Please! Somebody!"

And then, now barely audible, "Mommaaaa! It's hot!"

Suddenly I turned back. Seething with an anger that rivaled the growing heat of the fire, I ran toward the flaming tenement. I took the battered front stairs two at a time, passing another tenement dweller who was fleeing in a thin, soiled bathrobe. The man's eyes were eerily red. "Don't be a fool!" he hissed at me in a low, dark voice. "You'll burn, too!"

I shoved him aside and entered the musty tinderbox of a building. Chunks of burning debris were falling down the stairwell and had set the lower floors ablaze. I grabbed a child's ratty T-shirt from the floor and ran up the uneven stairs, clutching the rickety banister as more flaming fragments fell around me.

Father St. Jacques...

The police car had just turned left onto Madison when White swerved to narrowly avoid a fire engine that was speeding north with its air horn trumpeting loudly. A paramedic van was immediately behind it, also with its siren blaring and emergency lights oscillating.

"North, north!" shouted Officer Turrell, then she keyed her radio. "One William One, request backup code three to One Hundred Twelfth Street east of Third." She was pointing at her GPS screen. I saw that the indicator representing my quarry was blinking only two blocks ahead at 112th Street. And it seemed stationary.

Will...

By the time I reached the second-floor landing, I'd tied the ragged T-shirt around my nose and mouth, but I could barely see through the thickening smoke. The flames were spreading quickly, climbing like vines up the wall, peeling the layers of stained wallpaper off the ancient plaster beneath. Spurred on by the pained cries of the still-unseen child, I hurried up the next flight. The stairway was obscured by thick clouds of black smoke, which were momentarily swept away by broad tongues of whistling flame to be replaced almost immediately by more thick, noxious smoke.

The third-floor landing was fully engulfed in crackling fire. Flurries of sparks erupted around me. I stopped, panting from exertion, not seeing a way through. But from the other side I heard, "Mommeee! Where are you? It's burning!"

I saw a dog's water dish near a door. I poured it over my hair and the rag I was breathing through. Then I drew a deep breath, held it, and plunged headlong into the flames.

Father St. Jacques...

Having been alerted by Officer Turrell's radio call, another police car was also arriving at the Third Avenue intersection as the fire engine and emergency van turned onto 112th and the firefighters leapt into action. White stopped our squad car, and I jumped from it, unmindful of the falling rain. I heard one fireman shout to the building's inhabitants as he herded them to the far sidewalk, "Back! Everybody back! Is anyone inside?"

An ugly heavyset woman spoke up over the noise: "Crack whore and her kid, fourth floor."

A man in a filthy bathrobe also called out, "Some idiot went in after 'em."

I saw the fireman shout to his comrades, who were finalizing their firefighting gear: "Jose, call in the ladder company! Nick, Tricia, we got at least three! Let's go, let's go!"

Turrell called loudly to me from beside the squad car, where she was looking at the GPS. "He's here, Father! Right here somewhere!"

As Turrell showed the other arriving policemen the photos of my quarry, I began urgently scanning every face in the growing crowd, determined to find him despite the rainy mayhem.

Will...

As I rushed up through the flames onto the fourth-floor landing, my clothes were hot and smoldering. I raised my hand to push aside a burning doorframe and saw what every nerve ending was already signaling: my hand was red, raw, and already blistering. The searing pain made me gasp. I felt the acrid smoke biting into the fragile alveoli of my lungs.

The landing was thick with smoke. Roaring, snapping fire blocked the hall. "Where are you?!" I yelled to the child. *"Where are you?!"*

The child's tearful voice came back faintly. "I'm in here!"

The small voice had come from beyond the flames. I inhaled deeply again and ran through the fire toward a burning door. I threw the full weight of my body into it and smashed into a dilapidated, flaming room. I waved my hands in a mad attempt to dispel enough smoke so I could see. There were scarred fruit boxes that had been used as furniture, a small TV, roach-infested fast-food remnants, a seedy mattress on the floor, and the child.

She was about five, a raven-haired Hispanic girl with heavy, dark eyebrows and an innocent, round face shiny with tears. The terrified little girl was cowering from the flames against the floor beside an inner door, clutching a stuffed toy rabbit. Dizzy and increasingly disoriented from my pain and lack of oxygen, I scooped her up and turned to go back the way I'd come. But her fingers clawed at my face. She coughed and cried, "No! No! My momma's in there! Get her!"

I could barely hear her over the fire that was raging and hissing louder around us. But the child's teary eyes riveted onto mine. "Help her! The door's stuck! *Help her!*"

In a perfect fury, I brusquely pushed the child back to one side, shouting angrily, "Stay back! Get down and stay right there!" Then I kicked at the burning door. It opened only a crack. I could see the end of a heavy burning beam that had fallen across it on the inside, blocking it. I shouldered the door hard. Twice. Three times. It collapsed inward and a veritable firestorm, a monstrous wave of flame, thirsty for new oxygen and fuel, flooded out onto me. I was blasted back. My clothes and hair were afire. I dropped to the floor, screaming and rolling to smother the flames as I desperately swatted at my burning scalp. Then I saw the girl crawling toward the fiery doorway.

"Mommeee!"

"Stay back, goddammit!" I shouted hoarsely as I struggled angrily to my feet and roughly shoved the girl back. Through the wall of flames and smoke I could barely discern the shape of the unconscious woman who lay on the far side of the room. The woman's head turned ever so slightly, and for an instant her hazy eyes met mine. I braced myself for the onslaught and was about to dive through the burning doorway when the fiery ceiling above her suddenly collapsed, bringing all the blazing furniture and debris from the floor above down upon her. The woman was immolated.

Her little daughter shrieked hysterically.

I peeled off my peacoat and threw it over the screaming, flailing child, then snatched her up. I felt myself on the precarious edge of losing consciousness. I knew it was now or never.

Stumbling back into the hallway, I saw that during my time in the apartment, the conflagration had doubled in size. A pipe had burst and was spewing steam, which scalded me, triggering an involuntary screech from my parched throat. I dashed down the flaming stairs to the third-floor landing; one of my pant legs was afire, scorching my skin. I tried not to breathe as I fought to remain conscious through the pain that was near to overwhelming me.

Then I stopped. The staircase ahead was totally swallowed up in roiling flames and was breaking away from the wall. It was impassible. I heard a muffled shout: "Hey! Down here!"

Looking over the battered railing through the dense smoke, I could barely see three firefighters a floor below wearing oxygen masks and tanks. They were beckoning to me urgently.

I leaned over the railing, held out the bundled child, and released her. She screamed as she dropped twenty feet into the arms of two firefighters. One hurried down with her; the other two suddenly waved desperately at me, shouting, "Look out! *Look out!*"

I turned to see a large section of burning ceiling and wall break away and fall directly at me. I roared with a mighty raging fury as it came crashing down onto me. I managed only to turn and cover my face slightly as the fiery mass smashed me to the floor and pinned me there, immobile, buried in raging flames.

My mind short-circuited. The pain. God Almighty. *The pain.*

Father St. Jacques...

A sudden shout from the onlookers caused me to turn from searching their faces and look toward the burning tenement. A female firefighter rushed from the building carrying a small female child, whom she handed off to the paramedics.

Then I looked back again at the faces in the crowd, but nowhere could I see the face I sought. Turrell ran up to me, pointing at the small handheld GPS she now carried. "He's got to be here, Father. Somewhere!"

"We must find him!" I shouted and pointed angrily. "Check that group over there again!" We redoubled our efforts.

A few moments later another large response from the crowd drew my attention again toward the entrance of the fiery tenement. I saw two firemen carrying out the badly burned body of an unconscious man. They rushed him to the paramedic van. Turrell and I exchanged a quick glance of possibility and ran toward the ambulance through the people, firefighters, swirling smoke, and raining ashes.

Emergency responders were swarming all around the victim. One fireman doused him with bursts from a CO_2 fire extinguisher to smother the flames that were still smoldering on his clothing. Another helped the paramedic team cut away the man's pants and what remained of his shirt. His skin beneath was bloody pulp. Both of his charred and blistered legs were at odd, unnaturally skewed angles. One arm seemed barely attached at the bleeding shoulder. A television-news cameraman crowded in beside me just as the man was rolled to his back onto a stretcher, and I briefly glimpsed his face.

"Holy Mother of God!" I gasped to myself as a swoop of emotion twisted my gut. Even with his horrific injuries I knew. "It's him! I've found him, My Father! *I've found him!*"

I tried to get closer, for a better look, but the emergency team had clapped an oxygen mask over the injured man's comatose face as they hurriedly slid his stretcher into the ambulance.

One of the firemen who had brought him out yelled, "I think his legs're broke."

The paramedics were climbing in beside their charge, one grabbing for IV equipment. The other called back grimly, "That's the least of his problems." Then he shouted to the driver in the front, "Go, Bernie! Lenox Hill! Go! Go!"

The medic slammed the door closed as the van sped from the tumultuous scene with its siren screaming. For an instant I watched it go off through the smoke and rain, a hurricane of emotion swirling within me: awe, frustration, elation.

Then I sprung to action, excitedly grabbing Turrell's arm, pulling her toward the police car. "He said Lenox Hill. That is a hospital, no?! *Allez, allez!* Let's go!"

SEVENTEEN

Will...

I was floating. In dark oblivion.

Vague, ghostlike images slowly came shimmering across my subconscious as they sometimes had before. Most people in a comatose state apparently have zero cognizance. For some reason my unique circumstance often leaves a narrow mental channel open. A memory river that ripples with half-glimpsed landscapes, shadowed faces, distant sirens, echoing sounds, flowing slowly through my darkened brain. It's always a river that stretches into the dim distance back toward the headwaters of my long, long life.

The images rarely appeared in proper chronology, but each was linked to the next by a phrase or a sense memory. They drifted along like leaves on the surface of my river. Most passing by as soon as I glimpsed them. But now and again, one would coax a remembrance that gained definition and played out within my hazy mind.

First out of the present darkness came the black cat. It had leapt up into the lap of the young reporter named Sam, who had a thick mustache and wild, bushy hair. He leaned his wooden chair onto its two back legs, sitting across from me at a rustic table in the Red Garter Saloon of 1859 Nevada. The place was thick with tobacco smoke, noisy from the badly tuned piano and the cheery clientele. I was plucking clumsily at a battered banjo, trying to figure out how others made it look so easy to play. Sam petted the contented cat and mused, "Y'know, if man could be crossed with the cat, it would improve man, but deteriorate the cat." Sam paused, chuckled, then jotted down his little aphorism in his ever-ready notepad.

I knew Sam worked for the town's newspaper, the *Territorial Enterprise*, but like everyone in Virginia City he came from elsewhere. In Sam's case, from Missouri, where he'd been a steamboat pilot on the Mississippi River. He'd come west to taste the adventure of the Gold Rush and hopefully make a strike. Sam quickly discovered he was far more suited for writing than prospecting. I'd just commented favorably on his latest article about the unique pony-borne mail service I'd seen operating in China.

"Well shit, W.J.," Sam said to me with a grin, "that was a great idea you told me about. Sure struck a spark with the guys at Central Overland Express." Sam sipped whiskey from his shot glass. "They read my piece and said by damn they're gonna start up a mail-express operation just like the one you described. Set up stations with fresh ponies waiting all the way from Sacramento back to St. Joe."

I was only half listening because, as I picked clumsily on the banjo, I'd noticed a squat little man with a round head and wire-rimmed glasses carefully scrutinizing me from a nearby table. Having been pursued for so long, I'd developed a sixth sense for possible threats. He was neatly dressed in a tidy suit and looked eastern European. A tiny silver Star of David was attached to the watch chain that looped down from his vest pocket. He seemed harmless but still might have been a cleverly disguised priest. I'd encountered that before. I'd also heard that two priests had arrived in town the previous day. Coincidence perhaps. Or perhaps not. The little man, however, was not eyeing my face, but some aspect of my workaday clothing.

Sam had gone on, "The guys at Central figure if their pony riders go flat out like you said those Chinamen did, they can make an express mail run back and forth in ten days."

"Sounds about right." I was still watching the little man.

"Sure would be pleasurable," Sam rambled, "to get eastern news that fast. And send stuff back to my publisher quicker."

I looked over at him. "Had many pieces published?"

"Couple things," Sam sighed, running his fingertip around the rim of his shot glass, "but I've pretty well exhausted all the inspiration in these environs."

"What?!" I chuckled, indicating the colorful frontier characters around us. And there were thousands more in this boomtown that had sprung up around the Comstock Lode.

"Yeah, I know," Sam said, "at first blush it would seem a bottom-less cornucopia of lively ideas, but one can only write so many stories about prospectors, gamblers, whores, and such before they begin to lose their novelty." He looked slowly up at me. "But you, on the other hand, seem like a decidedly new wellspring, W.J." I felt Sam's penetrating eyes. "When exactly did you see that pony-express operation over in China?"

"Oh, it was a long time ago." I shrugged, focusing on my first banjo lesson and eager to divert Sam from my own history. I said, "Try Simon Wheeler."

Sam blinked. "Come again? Doesn't sound very Chinese."

"No, but Simon's got more outlandish stories than the Comstock has silver. Lives in Wilseyville. Over in Calaveras County. Ask him about their much-celebrated jumping frog."

"Excuse me?" It was the little round-faced man who had come up to stand beside us. My hand reflexively slid from the banjo to the grip of my long-barreled Colt.

"Pless forgiff me for disturbink you gentlemen." His speech was thickly accented with a northeastern European dialect, possibly Lithuanian I thought, till I saw the ring on his finger.

"You are from Latvia?" I presumed.

The man's round face took on an amazed and charming glow. "Yes, yes! Zis is true. How is it you are knowink zis?"

"Your dialect and your amber ring."

"Yes, vee haff much amber. You haff visited to Latvia?"

"I have had the pleasure, yes."

"Luffly. But excuse me, I only vish to ask a quevs-tion."

"About my britches," I surmised.

"Yes! Exactly!"

Sam's face twisted into a clownish expression of confusion.

"But first ze vormalities, I am Jacob Davis." The little man presented his card, which showed his name and a Reno address and simply announced: *Tailor*.

I shook his small, delicate hand. "J.W. Stewart." I felt Sam's eyes glance sharply at me, as I thought they might. "And your question, Mr. Davis?"

"Vot is it you haff done zere?" He was looking down through his wire-rimmed glasses and pointing to the small brass rivets through the pocket corners of my heavy workpants.

I smiled. "A simple technique I've used to strengthen the points of stress." I didn't mention where I'd first seen the idea used: on the leather armor worn by Roman centurions.

"Fascinatink," said Mr. Davis with admiration. "Do you haff a card I might keep?"

"I'm afraid I do not; I'm always traveling."

Sam had continued eyeing me and spoke up. "But you could always correspond with Mr. Stewart in care of me at the newspaper." I nodded and Sam gave his card to Jacob.

"Many tanks to you, sir. Pless forgiff my intrusion." He bowed politely and moved away.

"So," Sam said with a smiling edge, "who are you really? J.W. Stewart or *W.J. Wyler* like you told me?" Sam's eyes probed mine as he might have studied a mysterious bug through a magnifying glass. He set the cat aside and leaned close, speaking confidentially amid the hubbub of the saloon. "So you understand, sir: as a responsible journalist I will never reveal my sources if they wish not to be exposed. If I am lucky enough to be sitting here in the company of some delightfully romantic, notorious desperado, I would be much obliged to hear your story, with the understanding that I will most likely elaborate upon it outrageously for the stimulation of my eager readers, while simultaneously protecting your interests. With that clearly understood, please enlighten me as to just who the hell you are, mister."

I liked the young reporter, his innate wisdom and keen wit. I certainly had a wealth of unique stories, but restrained myself. Seeking a graceful exit, I spotted the redhead.

Rebecca was a woman of the night who enhanced the Red Garter with her voluptuous beauty. I caught her hand as she passed, and her painted eyes flashed down lustily to meet mine.

I glanced at Sam, setting the banjo aside with a gesture begging forgiveness. "Perhaps tomorrow, Sam? I have a pressing engagement just now."

Sam nodded to Rebecca, then said, with a puff of frustration, "I regretfully set you at liberty, sir. Only because I have a profound respect for the extraordinary talents of the irresistible and comely Miss Becky Thatcher." Then he pointed a stern finger at me. "But I shall most definitely attend you here, sir, on the morrow."

I nodded agreement and followed Rebecca up the creaking, rickety wooden staircase toward the rooms of pleasure. Her red ringlets cascaded down her back. *Her red hair . . .*

My comatose mind leapfrogged backward through time to the red hair of another woman. Hers was streaming down the back of her black robe, wet from the rainfall. It was the robe of a nun of the Convent of Saint Basil, established about fifty years earlier in anno Domini 405. I had recently obtained temporary shelter at their abbey. This young nun had dispensed with her cowl and therefore, I knew, also with her vows. She told me her name was Amina when she appeared from the underbrush alongside the old Roman road asking for my help.

"This way, please," she called back as she led me quickly through the twilight rain falling from brooding clouds. I felt it running in cold drops down my skin beneath my clothes. Amina spoke an Anatolian dialect common to that part of Asia Minor, which would eventually transform into Turkish. She guided me along the bank of the River Yeşilırmak, thickly wooded with sycamore and fragrant with cedar.

She took me to where the steep riverbank had been eroded inwardly, forming a small sheltered alcove with roots of a large oak tree exposed and intertwined overhead. It provided a respite from the rainfall. It was there a young man waited, clutching his injured shoulder.

"We were running. He fell," Amina explained with concern as her slender hands lovingly, but tentatively, touched the youth's arm. I saw that his face, though pale from pain, still retained the glow and downy whiskers of adolescence. He wore the black robes of a Benedictine monk.

"Show me," I asked in their native tongue. The youth endeavored to lift his heavy garment but required my aid. As the thick cloth rose and revealed his firm, young body, I noted that Amina did not turn shyly away. Rather her hands helped to gather and hold the coarse material so that I might carefully examine and manipulate the handsome boy's shoulder. It was badly bruised, but the skin was unbroken. "I think it's only dislocated," I told them. "If you can endure a bit of pain, I may be able to readjust it." The boy, whose name was Elian, nodded. I grasped the youth's wrist with both my hands. "On three then, alright?" Again Elian nodded, preparing himself. I spoke calmly: "One . . ." Then I snapped his arm sharply downward.

The boy cried out and grew unsteady from the stab of pain. He looked at me angrily. "You said on three."

As Amina and I eased him down against some driftwood, I smiled apologetically. "Better that you're not expecting it." I massaged his shoulder a moment while Amina fawned over him, kissing his damp cheek. "Try your arm now. Gently." The boy found that natural movement had been restored, though it was still strained and aching from the trauma. I dampened a cloth in the river water, then swung it in quick circles for a moment, explaining, "The air cools it." Then I applied the compress to the strained muscle. "Do this several times a day."

They thanked me profusely and offered to share the meager food they'd brought for their flight. I arranged a small fire to dry us as they confirmed my deduction: the two young people had found the vows of their orders at odds with their biological and romantic yearnings. They had forsaken convent and monastery to marry and make a life together. Elian had hidden a small boat upstream. They planned to follow the river to where it flowed into the Pontus Euxinus, later known as the Black Sea, thence to make their way along the coast to some small village where they would create hearth and home.

I suggested they would arouse less curiosity by traveling in secular clothing. Amina had brought some, but Elian had fled the Benedictines with only his robe. Seeing an opportunity that would serve all of us, I volunteered to trade a spare outfit from my small kit.

Thereafter, as a Benedictine "Brother" I availed myself of the hospitality at various monasteries and convents in my long travels. Those never-ending journeys.

Images like drafts alternately warm and icy cold drifted through my comatose mind: fragmented memories of the Dark Ages, constantly venturing into new environs where I was always an outsider. I lived through those five centuries one day at a time, often fighting exhaustion, treading painfully upon paths that were frozen or dusty or impossibly sodden; often walking blindly, placing one foot mechanically in front of the other, my muddled mind in a state of senseless torpor. I often couldn't remember how I had gotten from one place to the next.

Rarely did I tell anyone of the life I was forced to lead. In the few in whom I did confide, my story created a chilling, unearthly fear. So in addition to the extraordinary burden of living each hour of my countless days that had stretched into centuries, in addition to my grueling, ceaseless requirement to travel, I also carried the enormous weight of having no one with whom to commiserate. More than once I attempted suicide, but after suffering excruciating pain, yet surviving, I realized that there were far greater powers at work than I could possibly overcome. I lived on and on, knowing only that some unexplained force, some agency far beyond the reach of human intellect, was operating. Something otherworldly, supernatural. I often considered my endlessly extended life to be the very definition of hell.

Thus I endeavored to lead the most pious, faultless life possible, hoping humility might bring my cursed pilgrimage to an end, might atone for my crime, for my staggering offense that had condemned me to my perpetually forced odyssey. There was one saving grace to my myriad days and nights, however: the chances to better educate myself.

I regretted the missed opportunities in the first thirty-three years of my earlier, normal life to take advantage of the huge, airy Roman libraries at Ephesus and Rome.

I rarely gained access to sultanic libraries in the Arabic countries through which I traveled, so I had to rely primarily upon the Roman Catholic monasteries. In those dark times they were the chief repository of all writings historical, scientific, artistic, theoretical, and religious.

Crisscrossing Europe and Asia Minor from one monastery to the next in my guise of either a Benedictine monk or one of several other orders as the years went by, I took sanctuary in many differing environs. Memories of them flickered in my comatose brain: from Saint Anthony's monastic desert huts in the Egyptian desert to the castlelike Niederaltaich Abbey on the Danube in Bavaria, from the modest cloisters of Armenia and Cyprus to the magnificence of Normandy's Mont Saint-Michel.

At each abbey I eagerly read their rolled scrolls or, in later years, the thick codices of bound papyrus or parchment that were the forerunners of true books. I even helped to spread the concept of codices and taught many a monk how to create a codex with a sturdy wooden cover protecting the parchment *membranae* bound within. The codices swiftly gained popularity.

In each monastery I absorbed as much as possible in the three short days I was able to linger, often reading well into the candlelit night as cold drafts blew through chinks and crannies in the walls. I would thrust bits of lint into them to stave off the chill.

Sometimes I was one of many transcribers copying portions of an original work. The wealth of material that the monasteries had sequestered was mountainous, including all the surviving knowledge of the Greeks and Romans. With only a few days in each monastery, it was rarely possible to read an important work in its entirety, and thus my knowledge was fragmentary until I could locate the same work again in another abbey. But I fervently drank it all in.

My primary hope in studying was that I might find some clue about the extraordinary, nightmare circumstance that I had brought down upon myself. I desperately sought some deeper insight, some way to overcome my horrible situation, which took such an exhausting toll on me mentally and physically. The breadth of information I gathered seemed impossible to contain within my brain. I sometimes wondered how my head could be supported upon my shoulders; it seemed so overfilled and weighty. Other times I was surprised how one facet of my knowledge would suddenly flash into correlation with another wildly different facet to clarify an idea or create a totally new concept.

Yet nothing suggested an answer to my dire predicament.

I was privileged to read, however, many "lost" works, such as Aristotle's treatise on Comedy. Such "inappropriate" material could rightly be deemed lost because all the documents were hidden under the dominion and discretion of the church. Only works that did not conflict with established traditions and papal bulls, those that were not perceived as heathen, pernicious, or an outright work of Satan, ever saw more than the candlelight of a monk.

One such manuscript, which I discovered in the abbey at Monte Cassino in the 700s, stunned me when I realized who its author was, its particular significance, and that it might ultimately have some bearing on my personal situation. I carefully hid a copy of it beneath my robe as I departed. I protected it like a newborn child as I proceeded northwestward.

The hunger for land in those times required many people to move in that direction. But northern soil was much harder to till than that in temperate climes, so I helped the Benedictines create a wheeled plow with a blade to cut through the surface. I also fashioned a curved piece of wood just behind the blade that turned the sod aside, making neat furrows and greatly improving the land's yield. Those new advances were passed on quickly from bishop to bishop, the only communication network operating in the Dark Ages. It was also the network that would haunt me as the Vatican became aware of my existence and began to pursue me zealously.

Nonetheless, the technology I created helped to swell the growing number of farming villages. I passed through many on the coastal fens of Northern Germany and the Low Countries, but my arrival in the village of Skals in the West of Denmark was under darkening skies and unwittingly very ill timed. The year was 760, and already there was ominous portent: a comet had recently appeared in the night sky.

I knew it to be a natural phenomenon: the same comet appeared every seventy-five years, and a normal person might see it only once. By anno Domini 760 I was seeing it for the tenth time.

The comet had enkindled great fear throughout the countryside. Many felt that it presaged horrific events or even the end of the world. That same day I arrived in Skals, it was discovered that a strange fungal parasite was destroying much of the village's meager crops. The townsfolk were near hysteria, driven by fears of the comet and now imminent starvation. Their superstitious eyes sought out a reason for their disaster and fell upon the only newcomer. Several ragged men and women set upon me with antagonism that quickly grew into blind fury as their numbers increased. Despite my protestations, I was forcibly subdued and my hands were bound.

I caught a brief glimpse of a vaguely familiar young man who stood to one side watching silently, with a sad and knowing smile. His hair and features were sleek and dark.

The most vocal among the rampaging horde was a powerful meat grinder of a man with a heavily pockmarked face. He shouted through broken teeth, swearing he had witnessed me floating in the air above their fields while sprinkling some nefarious magical potion. I protested that he was lying, but the crowd responded as one angry animal, and I was beaten bloody as they dragged me into the nearby marshes. They tied a rough, bristling rope around my neck, affixed the other end to a heavy stone, clubbed me nearly senseless, and cast me into the bog.

My head was spinning from their blows as I sank slowly into the thick black muck, which grew increasingly colder around me. I felt the precious manuscript that I had carefully protected loosening from where I had bound it beneath my garment. It slid away into the bog, but there was nothing I could do. I was desperately trying to free myself, holding my breath as the interminable seconds passed. I felt my lungs would burst. I slipped one hand free, but in spite of my determination not to do so, I opened my mouth to suck in a frantic breath and inhaled instead a solid mass of thick slime. Then all was agony and darkness. And cold. So very cold.

EIGHTEEN

Dr. Miguel Fernandez, age 44, trauma specialist...

I knew that the medication I was spraying onto the badly burned man would have felt very chilling had the patient been conscious, but he was in a deep coma.

My team in the Lenox Hill emergency room was working with their usual quiet efficiency as they bustled around the man who had been terribly injured. The paramedics who delivered him from the tenement fire on 112th Street had started a saline IV while en route and managed to peel off much of the man's clothing. Many large patches of his skin had come with it, fused to his clothing by the fire. Much of the surface of his body was either badly blistered with second- and third-degree burns or had abrasions and contusions with the appearance of raw hamburger.

"Do we know anything about him?" I asked as I sprayed the burn med. "Medic alert tag? Bracelet? Cell phone?"

My lead ER nurse shook her head. "His cell was fried. No other ID at all, Doctor. He's a total John Doe."

Hanna...

Methuselah had grown finicky again that evening, so I was trying unsuccessfully to interest him in a new cat food when I saw the local TV news showing the scene at the burning tenement in Spanish Harlem.

The newswoman said that one woman had died in the fire, but her child had been rescued by an unidentified, amazingly heroic man who had been horribly burned because of his action.

Video showed paramedics rushing the man into Lenox Hill Hospital, then the newscast played an earlier clip from the scene of the fire where the camera caught a momentary glimpse of his face, and the newscast froze the image so the anchorwoman could ask for the public's help in identifying him.

The fork with the cat food dangled limply in my hand as I leaned closer, my eyes widening, stunned to see the man's half-blistered face. Despite the burns, I recognized him instantly.

I remember emitting a choked whisper: "Oh my God . . . Oh. My. God."

Jillian...

Steve was busy in the *Register*'s conference room, searching through even more photos that we had spread all over the large table, when he paused to look up at the WCBS-TV newscast about a tenement fire and caught a glimpse of a face that stopped him in his tracks.

"Holy shit!" I heard him blurt, then call out loudly, "Jilly!"

I rushed into the conference room. "What?!"

The TV image had cut back to the newsman, who was saying, "Firefighters finally managed to pull the man from beneath the fiery ceiling that had collapsed on him."

"You gotta see this!" Steve stammered as he made certain our TiVo was recording. "Keep watching! Watch!"

The newsman was saying, "Dr. Miguel Fernandez, head of the Lenox Hill trauma center, spoke with reporters . . ."

Fernandez, a swarthy Hispanic, appeared on the screen outside the Lenox Hill emergency room with a winter coat thrown over his blue surgical scrubs. I felt, despite his ethnicity, Fernandez seemed like a solid medical professional, though he was a bit uncomfortable in front of cameras. "Both of the man's legs sustained multiple fractures," the doctor said, "the right side of his pelvis was crushed, and he suffered third-degree burns over sixty percent of his body. We're awaiting CT scan results. We fear there are probably grievous internal injuries as well. He's in a coma; however, his brain functions are unusually strong. Nonetheless we have him listed in extremely critical condition because of his catastrophic injuries. I'm afraid he's not expected to live."

A still image of the injured man then appeared on the screen, and I reacted exactly as Steve had. "Holy shit! *Ho-ly shit!*" I stammered. "He looks like . . ."

"The guy in these photos!" Steve confirmed. "Yes! Thank you! I'm *not* crazy!"

The newsman's voice continued: "The patient has yet to be identified, and Dr. Fernandez asked that anyone having information contact the hospital immediately at 212-434-2000."

I hit the "Pause" button on the TiVo, holding the image of the man's face. Then I grabbed two of the old photos, slapped them up beside the TV screen, and glanced at Steve. "Even with his injuries, huh? Don't you think!? Or am *I* crazy!?"

Steve studied the comparison carefully, nervously, and finally nodded. "But . . . but . . . how is it *possible*, Jilly?" Then he looked back at me, his voice low and tight with a touch of fear but also potential promise. "Hello *New York Times?*"

I looked again at the face on the TV screen, staring at it dumbfounded, excited. And also frightened.

Will...

Another image, warped and shimmering like sunlight on the ripples of a river, made its way into my murky subconscious. Gradually it became the memory of a badly rutted dirt road passing slowly beneath my aching, sandaled feet, one weary step at a time. I was walking toward the Tuscan village of Colle di Romagnano in my Benedictine robes.

I was staring downward in a foul mood, having been forced again by the pain to resume my trek. I fervently wanted to rest, to settle in one place, to live out a normal life. But by then I had known for over a thousand years I could not. That *day* in early AD 1200 was one of the countless days that my grief had festered into anger. When I looked up scowling, I saw a shepherd boy creating a design on a broad, flat rock. But it was far more than a mere design. It was surprisingly sophisticated for a ten-year-old: an extremely lifelike drawing in charcoal and chalk of two sheep from the flock the boy was tending.

In spite of my irritated mood, I looked more carefully at his sketch. The boy saw me, beamed with pride, and offered me an apple, which I took, grumbling a thank-you. I sat on a nearby log to eat it as I surveyed the young artist's efforts. One of his flock nuzzled me so insistently that I ultimately relented, resting an arm on the lamb.

The boy wore the short breeches and soft leather shoes normal for a young shepherd on a spring afternoon in Tuscany of that era. His brown eyes were large and bright, his face seemed open and inviting, and his cheeks had deep dimples when he smiled, which was near to constantly.

I slowly got caught up in the boy's intensity, particularly when he stepped back, critically assessing his drawing like a seasoned professional. Speaking in his Florentine tongue, he asked my opinion. Responding truthfully, I told him the drawings were remarkable and quite lifelike. It was very different from the more simplistic artwork of that age. He was pleased but sensed I had further thoughts and urged me to continue.

I sighed. Taking it as part of the weighty, unspoken responsibilities of the strange duty thrust upon me, I always tried to offer what education, guidance, or inspiration I could.

So I pointed out that though one sheep had been placed behind the other, they were lacking appropriate perspective as well as three-dimensional depth. Like most paintings of those medieval years, the boy had drawn the sheep's figures with a dark outline sharply delineating their periphery. The heavy outline lent them a two-dimensional, cutout quality as compared to the more rounded shapes I remembered from paintings and frescoes of the Roman era, particularly many I'd seen adorning walls in Herculaneum and Pompeii before Vesuvius erupted.

The boy listened thoughtfully, then with his small thumb he rubbed away the outline on one side of a sheep's head. He saw the important difference immediately: how it became more rounded, more three-dimensional. He drew in a sharp breath. "Oh my! Yes!" He laughed so infectiously that I finally managed an actual smile. He began rubbing away his other outlining. His sketch instantly gained depth, dimension, and correct perspective, transforming magically before his delighted young eyes.

From a distant farmhouse, a man's voice called, "Angelotto? Dinner, Angelotto."

"Yes, Poppa, soon," he shouted back as he continued reworking his drawing, using more-subtle gradations of tone rather than crude outlines, giving the work an ever more full-bodied feel. The deep-dimpled boy's bright eyes glanced at me, and he laughed again as though he had just discovered an invigorating new world. *He laughed . . .*

The laughter swirled my mind forward in time through the flickering darkness. The old man was laughing. I remember him as almost always laughing. Even at age seventy-eight there was zestful joviality within his skeletal frame. The frailty of his East Indian body was most apparent when he sat cross-legged with his thin chest bare and his work on his bony lap.

But on that January evening in 1948 when I visited his Birla Bhavan in New Delhi, the old man was wearing one of his signature white Indian dhotis, which he always made by hand himself, as he greeted me with his lyrical Gujarati dialect flavoring his English. "My word," he said with surprise. He peered incredulously at me through his round glasses. "How is it possible you have not changed at all in eighteen years?!"

"It must be the clean living I learned from you, Bapu."

Gandhi's slender arms embraced me, and then he held my hand as we walked together in the mahatma's garden, talking of when we had first met in Ahmedabad in 1930. During my travels across the Indian subcontinent in those years, I had become intrigued by reports of Gandhi and his nonviolent approach to confronting society's ills. It mirrored my own ardent commitment to improve the world by peaceful means, hoping always that such effort might have the added benefit of bringing my exhausting, centuries-long quest to a final conclusion.

When I initially sought out Gandhi, I discovered that even the most flattering press reports had not done justice to him. He was clearly a gift to the world from a divine beneficence: imbued with an august dignity, a natural reverence, and deep wisdom. Though thoroughly, humorously human, he was also a unique and innately holy personage with whom I greatly desired to spend more than my allotted three days.

When we'd met back in 1930, the mahatma was seeking a method to make a statement to the British government about the salt tax imposed on India. I suggested an idea that might serve Gandhi's purpose. And it would definitely serve my own selfish desire to remain in his presence longer. It became known as the Salt Satyagraha, the Salt March. Leading thousands of his fellow Indians, who affectionately called him Bapu, he departed Ahmedabad on March 12, 1930. For the next twenty-five days, as we marched the 248 miles, I enjoyed the privilege of being in Gandhi's company, at his side, listening to his thoughts, sharing his food and that contagious laughter. I even realized that I had once encountered and assisted Gandhi's *grandmother* when she was just a child, though I kept that memory to myself. I knew that the mahatma would have been astonished, and perhaps a bit frightened, to learn how I could possibly be that old yet look so young.

I was honored to stand nearby that day in 1930 when Bapu and his legion of followers dried the seawater at Dandi to make their own salt, sending Gandhi's powerful statement to the British colonial government.

In 1948, his face still smiled at me, just as it had in 1930 when we stood together beside the bright-blue Arabian Sea, the salt air fragrant around us. *The briny salt air . . .*

The sense memory of that sea-laden air flipped my comatose mind backward. I had deeply inhaled such ocean air many times before, but that New Year's midnight in 1841, there was a definite urgency increasing my respiration.

I had spied two priests attended by a muscular entourage asking after me at the inn where I had been lodging in Fairhaven, Massachusetts. Once again the Vatican's soldiers had gotten too close for comfort.

I felt bitterly frustrated because I'd just made contact with writer Margaret Fuller, and I was eager to contribute to an important new publication that she and Ralph Waldo Emerson had created called the *Dial*. Their views about religion and human rights were much in keeping with my own, though I alone had incredibly unique, and antique, insights, which I knew would stun them. I was desirous of helping them promote the philosophy that I hoped would better the world and perhaps bring to me the personal redemption I had so long sought.

But the relentless hounds from Rome were again snapping at my heels. I needed to put considerable distance between them and myself and do it with all haste.

With my sea bag over the shoulder of my monkey jacket, I ran along Fairhaven's cobbled street beneath the ice-covered trees that were glittery in the cold night air. I reached the harbor and hurried down the wide, bustling, wood-planked docks lighted by torches and hurricane lamps. The chill north wind was stinging my face. I saw several schooners readying for departure and saw the intense, noisy hustle of dockside activity. There were mountains of casks, bolts of sailcloth, foodstuffs, and coils of rigging being taken aboard ships, betokening imminent departures with the tide.

The men were brown and brawny sea dogs with stalwart frames, many with bosky, untrimmed beards. I hurried between Vermonters, Down Easters, and other New Englanders, as well as swarthy mates from the Tortugas, Malagasy, and the world over. Some wore sou'westers, some bombazine cloaks, some swallowtail coats with knife sheaths on the wide sailor's belts that girded them.

I passed numerous horse carts making final deliveries. The draft animals' hot breath steamed in the wintry air, as did their thick piss when they relieved themselves where they stood. I dodged among the strong-armed stevedores who manned the winches and windlasses, loading final cargo amid the pungent smells of manure, fish, and seaborne detritus.

Then I saw a familiar face. Standing quietly to one side, leaning casually against one of the dock's tall pilings, was the sleek young man. He was dressed in the elegant, gentlemanly fashion of the day and touched the brim of his silk top hat in recognition of me. "Aren't you tired of running?" he asked in Latin, sympathetically. "Why don't you just acknowledge that you're *my* shipmate?"

I paused, holding the young man's portentous gaze a moment, then tore myself away and hurried along the dock, seeking a berth on any ship that would soon sail with that evening's tide.

All proved fully manned, save the whaler *Acushnet*. To my extreme good fortune, she was still lacking several crew members. That was an odd circumstance in such seafaring towns as Fairhaven, New Bedford, and nearby Nantucket, which sported so many able-bodied candidates. It would have given me pause under normal circumstances. But with the priests less than a league behind me, I knew that a hasty departure was most desirable. Besides, the vessel looked well cared for and fit.

So I quickly signed the ship's articles. As I helped the other mariners make final preparations to get the sturdy vessel under way, I spotted the Vatican company hurrying onto the docks endeavoring to locate and capture me. My heart jumped as one priest spotted me and shouted to the others. They raced down the dock just as I helped to cast off the *Acushnet*.

With her anchor drawn up and her sails set, the *Acushnet* glided slowly toward the broadening mouth of the harbor. I saw the papal entourage panting and cursing me from the end of the pier. I had barely evaded them. I breathed a nervous sigh.

Along with an unusual young shipmate, who himself had a date with destiny, I narrowly escaped from one form of jeopardy as I unknowingly embarked toward another: a completely unanticipated adventure among the cannibals.

NINETEEN

Jillian...

I was all too familiar with the hospital at 77th Street and Park Avenue. It was one of the city's best. Its red brick facade had been a New York landmark for over a century. Created to serve the immigrant population in the 1860s, it was originally named the German Hospital. That changed to Lenox Hill Hospital in 1918, doubtless, I surmised, because of a slight backlash of anti-German sentiments courtesy of the Great War.

Though the exterior had looked much the same for a hundred years, the interior was constantly being reinvented to be up to the minute, state of the art. I knew the facility had been responsible for numerous medical breakthroughs and revolutionary new therapeutic techniques throughout its colorful history. There was a black-and-white photo of Winston Churchill on the wall in the ER. He'd been hit by a car on Park Avenue in 1931 and brought into Lenox Hill for treatment.

I'd chased a couple other stories here in the last year or so. But the very first time I'd been there was the night they brought my mother into that same emergency room.

It set my nerves on edge whenever I came back into Lenox Hill. I was very uncomfortable being there again, but this was where the story was, although *what* the story was I still had no idea. I'd rushed over from the *Register* office with Chris Ahern, one of our best press photographers. Chris was a rugged, handsome guy with long dark hair pulled back in a ponytail. When covering a splashy murder out at Fire Island with me the previous summer, he'd managed to strip his shirt off a couple of times. I'd felt it had been primarily for my benefit. Chris had been casual about it but obviously proud of his cut physique and his six-pack. He'd gently hit on me that day and another time since. He tried again as we hurried into the hospital from blustery Park Avenue.

"Look, Jilly, I checked," Chris said. "I know you're not involved with someone else. Nobody could remember you ever being, so why can't we go out?"

I kept focused on the matter at hand. "Because."

"Oh." He raised his eyebrows and bobbed his head. "Well. Yeah. That clears it all up." But he wouldn't let go. "Hey, if you're gay or something, that's cool, just—"

I gestured distractedly. "I'm not . . . anything, okay?" I was glancing warily in through the admitting window. I could see a couple of stations in the trauma unit. They were empty. But they triggered a stinging memory of the medical team laboring feverishly over my unconscious fifty-one-year-old mom in that very same ER.

I'd been twenty then, hovering nearby, distraught, twisting the bottom of my purple NYU T-shirt as they administered cardiac paddles. I saw Mom convulse. Repeatedly.

"Is this your contact?"

Chris's voice made me blink back into the moment. A cocoa-skinned nurse was approaching as he glanced carefully around. When he smiled at me, Chris whispered into my ear, "Jeez, he looks a little weird." I knew that many people likely reacted that way. Because when the nurse was smiling, the right half of his face looked like the classic smiling mask of Comedy, while the left half drooped like Tragedy.

"Bell's palsy," I explained in an aside to Chris. The nurse, Dempsey, had done discreet business with me before. He indicated a side door, which he opened with a key card, and led us quickly into a deserted inner corridor. As soon as the door closed, the right side of his face smiled again confidentially, while the other side hung expressionless. "Let's see it, Jilly."

I held up a crisp hundred-dollar bill but drew my hand back when he reached for it, saying, "When we see the guy."

The ten-bed intensive care unit was on the third floor. Almost no surgeries were scheduled during the holiday week, so there were only a couple of patients. Including the one I was very eager to see. Dempsey made Chris hide his Nikon under his car coat, then escorted us up and into the ICU through the small waiting area reserved for families and friends of gravely ill patients. The only person there was a priest, who glanced up and closed the laptop he'd been writing in as we passed. I noticed his eyes were strangely pale. Then he closed them, bowed his head slightly, and his brow knitted as he touched his forefinger and thumb lightly to his lips. He seemed to be concentrating on a fervent, silent prayer.

Father St. Jacques...

I assumed my meditative, prayerful pose so that I might blend appropriately into the surroundings and not attract their attention. It is a technique I have polished and used successfully many times over the years.

Since the young man and woman were wearing outdoor coats and being guided by a lower-echelon Negro nurse, I assumed they were not themselves hospital staff members. Their slight tension definitely suggested that they might be interlopers of some sort. With my head still bowed but eyes ever-so-slightly open, I watched them don the masks and gowns proffered by the nurse, who then, as I suspected he might, led them down the hall toward room 304.

Jillian...

The man we'd come to see was comatose, on an IV drip, intubated with oxygen. He had many wired sensors attached to him. The monitoring equipment hummed quietly, and the heart monitor beeped softly at slow but regular intervals. As we entered, the blood pressure cuff inflated automatically, took its reading, then hissed and relaxed. I noted that both of the patient's legs were resting atop posterior fiberglass casts. His legs, arms, and chest were bare but slathered with burn ointment and a thin layer of gauze, which also covered the right side of his face.

Once we reached the bedside, I slipped the one-hundred-dollar bill into Dempsey's hand. He checked around to be certain we were unobserved, one side of his face expressing nervousness. "I've gotta get this right back on," he said. "So take it quick."

Chris readied his camera and nodded. "Okay," I whispered, "go for it." Then I leaned closer as Dempsey lifted the gauze and grimaced at the patient's burns. When I saw the patient's face, I was completely astonished. I muttered, "Un . . . believable." I excitedly motioned for Chris to get closer.

"Yeah, the poor bastard." Chris's face tightened as he reacted to the man's injuries. He clicked away several frames.

"No," I said, "I meant he looks *exactly* like the guy in my old photos!" I studied the man's face, completely captivated. "Shoot him, Chris! Get the shots!"

Chris gave a disapproving glance about my attitude, but steeled himself and snapped more photos. I gazed at the strange man a moment longer, then heard a faint noise at the door. I saw the priest looking in. His ghostly pale eyes were really creepy. I asked, "Do you know him, Father?"

"No," the priest answered with a heavy French accent, "I am here only to offer prayer. Might you be his family or friends?"

Before I could answer, the swarthy doctor I had seen on the TV appeared from behind the priest, who quickly faded back. The doctor was gowned but had yet to affix his mask in place. His eyes were as ice cold as his tone of voice. "Can I help you?"

I turned on the charm, extending my hand and speaking in an appropriately hushed tone: "Dr. Fernandez, hi. Jillian Guthrie, I'm an investigative journalist and—"

"No," he interrupted curtly, "you're a tabloid vulture."

I chuckled. "I think you're confusing me with—"

"No one," he cut in. "I've seen you chasing ambulances here before. Please leave this room and go to the press office."

He waved us insistently out into the hall.

Dempsey nodded, protecting himself by saying, "That's what I just came in to tell them, Doctor."

I was determined to remain cordial. "I will absolutely check in with the press office, of course. It's just that this man's such a hero, we'd like to help you locate—"

"Press office, first floor," he said, with icicles forming. He added, "And you'll find the UFOs up on the roof."

I smiled graciously at his little jest. "Great. Thanks for your help." But as we left and he went in to check on the patient, I muttered to myself acidly, *"Amigo."*

Dempsey had ducked away. That priest had also made himself scarce. Chris and I headed for the elevators as I spat out with annoyance, "Too bad they couldn't get a doctor from this country."

Chris adopted the tonality of a master of ceremonies saying, "And once again, ladies and gentlemen, accepting the Politically Incorrect Award for the third year in a row, Ms. Jillian Guthrie." I just smirked. But he wouldn't let it go, pulling us to a stop. "You know you really oughta tone down the rhetoric a tad, Jilly. Some of the people in the office are really—"

"Okay, okay," I said, cutting him off because I knew he was right. "Listen, I'm gonna hang here a bit. You take those photos to Steve and get 'em into tomorrow's edition. We've scooped everybody, and I want to capitalize on it."

Chris gazed at me for a beat, then nodded with a dry edge. "Sure." He headed toward the elevator. I watched him go, trying not to ponder his disapproval of my attitude. Then I headed for a women's room to avoid being seen by Fernandez, but I caught sight of a tall, willowy woman in her eighties getting off another elevator. She had just come in from the cold and was wearing a nice fake fur, slacks, and sneakers. I got a decidedly classy Yankee, Hepburnesque vibe from her tanned, weathered face, which seemed drawn with tension; her lips were pursed tightly together. She walked briskly toward the ICU, clearly a woman on a mission.

Hanna...

I had given Methuselah some extra food in case I was gone for a while, then I'd caught a taxi for the short hop down from 84th to Lenox Hill. I was quite familiar with the old hospital, having worked on some community-outreach programs for them over the years.

I'd visited the critical care section many times to counsel families in need and was generally very comfortable there. But by the time I got off the elevator that evening, I felt my pulse thumping like Gene Krupa's tom-tom in Benny Goodman's "Sing, Sing, Sing."

I barely noticed the shortish young woman eyeing me as I passed. I glanced into the ICU rooms on either side of the hall, my heart slowly rising into my throat. Reaching the open doorway to room 304, I stopped dead in my tracks. I felt like my chest had suddenly filled up with helium. I was breathless, trembling all over. I grasped at the door-frame to steady myself.

Lying on the bed right in front of me was Will. My Will.

Suddenly I was drowning in the River Seine. Then came the splash and the crazed man floundering ridiculously in the cold water nearby. Boy, was I furious at whoever the bastard was that interrupted my glorious suicide. When I kicked over to try to subdue him, he struggled against me. I remembered screaming at him in the frothy water, "Stop it! Stop behaving like an idiot!" I batted at his head, and finally he quieted enough for me to grasp a handful of his jacket and drag him over to the river's side.

And then to my own side in his garret overlooking the Paris rooftops. We sipped Courvoisier in the firelight, shared our first sweet night of love. Then laughed together in the sunlit Tuileries.

My old heart swelled as I remembered him skiing beside me in that alpine blizzard, carrying the medicine to the desperate villagers in Weisstannen; jumping off the trolley and running fearfully together through that back alley in Warsaw to escape that Dutch priest and his Vatican cohorts; splashing naked with Will in the warm waters of the Mediterranean after disinfecting the well in that tiny Tunisian town.

Being with him was so different from my usual shenanigans. It made me realize what a self-centered, egocentric, trip-the-light-fantastic young princess twit I had been. The only child of wealthy Bostonian Brahman parents, with a nose turned up as high as my cheekbones. I was spoiled, always getting everything I wanted. Until a young Parisian student jilted me. It was shocking, insulting, infuriating, and intolerably bitter. If I couldn't have life my way, I wanted none of it at all. Therefore into the Seine, oh so very dramatically, I had leapt.

Then came Will. Who saved me in so many more ways than one, who guided me down a road less traveled, who showed me new possibilities and how my soul could grow from the rewards.

As I stood in the intensive care doorway, I heaved a deep, long, trembling sigh, remembering how tightly I'd clung to him in the pouring rain that last night in Zurich. How I'd stood there sobbing as his steamy train pulled away, my anguished heart threatening to burst.

Jillian...

The old lady knew him. Absolutely.

There was no mistaking it even from where I stood down the hall. I was glad my instincts had prompted me to shadow her. I could see it written in the emotions coursing across her wrinkled face, and from her body language, from her hand trembling on the doorframe. Whatever that man's mysterious story was, I knew that this tall lady with the snow-white hair was part of it.

I watched her tentatively enter the room and adjusted my own position slightly so I could still see her as she slowly approached his bed, reaching out to let her fingertips carefully touch his shoulder.

Then I saw the night nurse, a portly Puerto Rican woman, go to investigate, speaking softly from the doorway. "Ma'am? Excuse me." The old lady maintained her gaze on the injured man. The nurse stepped just inside the door, and I moved closer in the hallway. "Ma'am," the nurse continued, "you'll have to put on a mask and gown to be in here."

The elderly woman nodded and stepped back. "That's okay," she said in a quiet, friendly manner. "I won't be staying just now." I noted her Boston accent.

"Do you know him?" the nurse asked. "Are you family?"

The woman's gaze never left the unconscious man. I thought I saw a happy tear glinting in one of her eyes.

"No. He has no relatives," the woman sighed, "but he's an old friend. A dear friend."

Then the nurse took a ballpoint from the pocket over her considerable breasts and reached for his chart as she asked the key question. "What's his name?"

I inclined my head closer, my mini-recorder at the ready. The older woman drew a breath to answer, then paused, seeming to weigh whether or not she wanted to speak. Finally she said, "I suppose you could call him W.J."

The nurse looked up curiously. "W.J.? Are those first initials or what?"

The lady paused for a considerably longer moment. The nurse and I both leaned to hear her answer. The lady shook her cotton-white head slightly, saying, "I don't know."

Bullshit, I thought, *you know alright.*

"Anything would help," the nurse said encouragingly.

No kidding. I nodded eagerly to myself. *Come on, lady, give me something.*

"Sorry," said the old woman, "but I really don't know."

She was lying and I saw the nurse knew it, too, but was reluctant to press her. The difference between a nurse and a reporter. But why would this old woman lie? What was she covering for? I was antsy, growing more intrigued than ever.

"Do you have any address for him?" the nurse asked.

"No, I don't. I'm sorry."

That much, I sensed, sounded truthful.

The PR asked, "Can you tell me where you know him from?"

"It was a long time ago, my dear," she said kindly. "It wouldn't be relevant, believe me."

The nurse drew a breath to press further, but the old lady stopped her gently by resting a crinkled hand on the Puerto Rican's hefty arm.

"Please write down my phone number." The lady spoke it for the nurse. I heard and whispered it quickly into my recorder. Then she said, "I'm Hanna Claire. I'd be extremely grateful if you'd please call me when he comes out of the coma."

The heavyset nurse tipped her head down slightly, with a touch of sadness. "I'm afraid that's very unlikely, ma'am. The doctors say his injuries are so severe that—"

Hanna Claire patted the nurse's arm. I noted an odd twinkle in her blue eyes and a sort of secret smile. "Write it down, please," Ms. Claire insisted politely. "Just in case." She made certain that the nurse had the number correct, then gave a sweet little nod. "Thank you, my dear."

She eased past the puzzled nurse and out through the doorway. I could see that her private smile was still working on her wizened face, and I stepped toward her, speaking quietly. "Excuse me, Ms. Claire?"

"Yes?" She slowed and, delicately, I pounced.

"I'm an investigative journalist, Jillian Guthrie."

The lady's eyes locked onto me. They were the most amazing crystalline blue. But they were also worldly wise and wary, so I continued carefully, saying, "Can you tell me how long you've known him? And maybe where it was that you met or—"

"I'd like to help you, Miss Guthrie," she said. Then she wrinkled her nose slightly as though sharing a confidence. "But he really likes his privacy."

"I can certainly understand that, ma'am." I was tacking a bit. "But what he did was so incredibly heroic, he really deserves to be identified and recognized for his bravery." Then I had a thought that might spur her. "Particularly if he's going to die."

The woman's blue eyes snapped back onto mine. *Gotcha,* I thought, sensing that she was on the razor's edge of revealing something important. But Hanna Claire's eyes flicked off of me to focus on someone behind me. Her expression hardened. I glanced over my shoulder and saw that the pale-eyed priest had reappeared down the hall and was speaking to a custodian.

"I'm very sorry, Miss Guthrie," Hanna Claire said. Looking back, I noticed that she had grown tense and even more cautious. She shook her head. "You must excuse me."

No way, momma. Not when I'm on the scent. "Ms. Claire, wait."

But she was proceeding down the corridor toward the elevator. I saw her nod at the priest, but I couldn't discern if she knew him or was just being polite to a man of the cloth.

Hanna...

I was startled to see St. Jacques already there. And worried. Even though he appeared to be the only representative of the church in sight. I did, however, note an NYPD officer farther down a hall adjacent to the elevators. He was seated, though, having coffee and reading a paper. Maybe not a direct threat. I pressed the elevator button.

The young reporter had followed me closely. "Ms. Claire, please," she implored with seemingly genuine concern, "I only want to help him. Find out who might—"

"Bless your heart, my dear." I was determined to be patient and kind. "But it would appear that there's no help anyone could possibly give him." I touched her young hand as I gazed at her. "Believe me." Thankfully the elevator doors opened and I entered.

Jillian...

As she stepped into the elevator I sputtered my last-ditch, hold-out *National Register* tactic: "I'm sure I could arrange a substantial reward or a donation to your favorite charity if you'd just—"

Hanna Claire shook her white head slightly, her blue eyes smiling with apology. "I'm sorry, dear."

The elevator doors closed. Shit. I instantly snapped open my cell and hit the speed dial. Kiko's voice answered at the *Register*. I asked for Steve. Kiko covered the phone, but not well enough, so I heard her shout, "Hey, Steve? The Ice Princess on three."

It was nothing I hadn't heard before. I knew I was not everyone's favorite in the office. The polite ones called me *aloof*; those more direct preferred *tough* or even *caustic*. Most of the time it didn't bother me. I wrote it off to petty jealousy because I did my job pretty well, better than most of them. I knew I could be a little overbearing or driven, but I thought of myself as professionally focused. And besides, I was definitely determined not to spend much more of my life with that bunch.

Steve was different. He'd always been able to go with my flow, to play yin to my yang. We had worked smoothly together on a lot of stories from NYU to the present, and he was definitely as caught up in this current mystery as I was.

An extension clicked on, and I heard his eager voice. "So? What'd you think when you saw him?"

"Are you sitting down?"

"No way!" I could hear his excitement. "No fuckin' *way*! Are you sure it's really him?!"

"Yep."

"Hole-lee shit! Who is he? What's his name?"

"Still working on all that."

"Is he awake?"

"No, and not expected to live." I looked back toward the strange man's room, ruminating on Hanna Claire's confident expression. "But I'm not so sure. There's something really weird about it all."

"About a guy who looks the same for over a century." Steve chuckled sardonically. "How can you say that?"

"And I've got a lead."

"Go," Steve said. I could hear him shuffling papers to take notes. I glanced around and caught the French priest trying to look disinterested from his chair in the waiting room, but I sensed he was trying to eavesdrop.

I turned away and lowered my voice into the phone. "Okay, so listen: Chris is on the way with our exclusive photos of the guy."

"Great, Jilly. Way to go!" I knew he was smiling proudly just like I was. "I'll try to get 'em in for tomorrow."

"Don't just try, Steve," I said, pacing. "Give Grady a fifth of that rotgut he loves, and tell him to hold the damn presses if he has to. It's gotta happen."

"Yeah, okay. What else?"

"Do a workup: Hanna Claire."

"Who is she? What's her connection?"

"That's what you're going to find out. No address, but she's got a Manhattan phone number." I played back my recorder and repeated the number for Steve.

"Got it," he responded. "Hanna Claire. Can you give me a description?"

"Early eighties, but pretty trim and spry. Five nine or so, white hair, amazing blue eyes. Boston accent. Dressed Katharine Hepburn casual classy. Wearing old Reebok sneakers but a nice Saks faux fur."

"She still there?"

"No, she came after we did and she just took off, but she said she'd be back. And Steve, you should have seen her face when she looked in at him. Like she'd just seen a ghost."

Steve's voice dropped an octave. "Well . . . maybe she has, given those old photos of ours."

I thought about those. The man we'd seen photographed with Gandhi, with Teddy Roosevelt, and with General Grant was lying in a hospital room only a few yards away from me. I was certain of it.

"We've got to find out about Hanna Claire, Steve. I don't know who she is, but she sure as hell knows who he is."

TWENTY

Will...

I was floating over wavy darkness as I had so often before. Then I realized I was looking out over the crow-black fish-bone-freezing waters of Buzzards Bay surrounding the whaler *Acushnet* as our ship rode the strong, ebbing tidal flow southwesterly from Fairhaven, Massachusetts, that New Year's night in 1841 when I had narrowly escaped my Vatican pursuers.

No moon or stars were visible under the lowering sky. The only reference by which helmsmen could steer was Cuttyhunk Light off our larboard bow. Once the ship passed the reliable sweep of its beam, we would be in the impenetrable darkness of the open, boisterous Atlantic.

Given my requirement to travel on every three days and the forced inability to revisit any specific location again for over three centuries, the oceans provided myriad combinations of longitude and latitude for me to briefly inhabit as I avoided capture by the relentless papal authorities and pursued my own quest: to somehow alter the surreal, metaphysical existence to which I'd been sentenced. But that night I was glowering with annoyance at having been forced to flee Massachusetts, at being unable to work further with Waldo Emerson and Margaret Fuller.

I pulled the woolen comforter tighter around my head to ward off the cold. I'd drawn the first watch. My companion was a New York lad of twenty-one wearing a beaver-skin hat. A hundred years later I saw a photograph of the actor Montgomery Clift and was struck by how closely Clift resembled my young shipmate: fine, handsome features and eyes that seemed sometimes probing, sometimes brooding, sometimes poetically haunted. The fledgling mariner had a meditativeness about him that seemed unseasonable in one so young, and he also exhibited considerable depth of intellect and literacy. In speaking to me the youth made casual references to Schiller and Goethe.

How startled this lad would be, I thought, *to learn that I had been in rooms with each of those poets.*

The boy told me he was suddenly reduced to poverty by the unexpected death of his father, and his core beliefs were upended. He now sought wider experiences to try to make sense of the hand dealt him by the gods. He was asking the eternal questions: Why the universe? What is the nature of God, of Evil, of human purpose? What should it be that man pursued most ardently? Knowledge? Wisdom? Salvation? Could they ever be grasped or captured?

I sympathized with his goal, which mirrored my own centuries-long search.

Respecting the contemplative silence into which the youth had fallen, I walked forward on the sideways-leaning, frozen deck and noticed a faint bluish flicker around me. Glancing up through the rimed rigging, I saw that the tip of the main mast was displaying a narrow blue torch of Saint Elmo's fire.

The pitch and roll of the ship caused that ghostly, glowing brush to paint ellipses, rather than circles, against the dark, cloudy sky. When I first had noticed that phenomena, sailing aboard a Roman bireme galley eighteen hundred years earlier, I had wondered if there were any perfect circles in nature.

I gazed out across the dark, choppy water. We were sailing past Cuttyhunk Island. The rhythmic sweep of its lighthouse beam flashed across my eyes. *The lighthouse beam . . .*

"The lighthouse beam you mentioned yesterday, Wilhelm?"

The echoing voice carried my mind to a much different time and place: an afternoon in Bern, Switzerland, 1904. I'd been walking with a German college student along the steep bluff of the narrow peninsula onto which the small Swiss city had been crammed centuries earlier. The fast-flowing Aare River wrapped tightly around Bern, snuggling it into the crook of an elbow bend.

Surrounded by the alpine peaks, the German and I walked south in the late-afternoon sun toward Casinoplatz Square. The arcaded street looked much as it had when I had walked it back in medieval days, except that now the people around me were dressed, as I was, in the current fashions of 1904.

I had been distracted from my conversation with the German student by the nightmarish ancient statue in the square ahead of us. It depicted a struggling infant being devoured by a large, horrifying man. Local Bernese laughingly told people the statue, called the Ogre Fountain, merely depicted a fairy tale or some old carnival scene. But I knew better.

I remembered standing in that same square amid the crowd in 1545 and watching when the sleek young man with the dark eyes was among those helping to originally erect the grotesque statue. It was painted vivid yellow and represented the horrid superstition then pervading medieval Europe: that secret Jewish rituals involved the eating of live babies.

The young German student walking beside me that day in 1904 was a Jew. I wondered if he knew the statue's ugly origins. We had met two days earlier at the small Café Wengen, where he and his collegiate fellows had been in lively conversation. All the young men were taking doctoral studies in mathematics or physics and greatly enjoyed their heady philosophical deliberations. By that year, I had amassed a considerable breadth of knowledge, but some of their theoretical imaginings required far more mental agility than I could muster. Nonetheless, when they noticed my interest, I was invited to join them and interject my thoughts.

"Wilhelm? Did you hear me?" The German glanced questioningly at me as we walked. His face was full and well fed, reflecting a sedentary lifestyle divided between his intense study of theoretical physics and his mind-numbing bureaucratic day job at the Swiss patent office. His forehead seemed quite high because his hair was swept up and away, as though he was facing a constant wind. His eyes were kind and turned down slightly at the corners, giving a visual impression of sadness, which was belied by his bright, inquisitive nature.

I shook off my preoccupation with the ugly statue. "I'm so sorry," I apologized in German. "What were you saying?"

"Yesterday while we were discussing that man you mentioned from the 1500s, Bruno was it?"

"Giordano Bruno, yes."

The doctoral student shook his head in amazement, mulling. "Five hundred years ago and Bruno was already considering that space, time, and motion were all *relative*?"

I nodded affirmation, adding, "And that the same motion would differ when seen from different places, yes. But just as you and your friends are postulating now, Bruno was certain that there were eternal, inviolable laws, which governed all of nature. He felt that learning the secret of that supreme unity was the goal of all science and philosophy."

"Ah yes," the German said, smiling ruefully. "He wanted what we want: merely to know God's thoughts."

"Yes." His understatement amused me, particularly because of my own supernaturally cursed circumstances. "*Merely* that."

"You said Bruno truly felt that even *time* was relative?"

"Yes."

The German had taken his pipe from within his rumpled, rather ugly plaid suit coat and lit it. "Which brings me back to your lighthouse beam."

"Yes, what of it?"

"Did I understand correctly," the German said as he pulled on his pipe thoughtfully and we walked the cobbled street, "you had wondered how it would be if one could actually *ride* upon a beam of light, go spearing through the darkness at that outrageously incomprehensible speed?"

"Yes." I nodded. It was a concept that had long fascinated me. "What do you think it would be like? What would one see?"

"Mmmm." The student pondered, pursing his lips into an odd grin, his brow lowered. "I never thought of it quite like that." Then he glanced at me with those sad, eager, wily eyes. "And your conclusion is . . . ?"

I laughed. "If I knew *that*, then I might be a fraction as smart as you and your friends."

The German smiled, but I saw that his acrobatic brain was already fully and gymnastically involved with the conundrum. As we walked onward, the student's eyes focused an infinite distance ahead. I imagined that he was picturing himself somewhere deep in the universal ether, riding on the leading edge of a theoretical light beam.

Several other lighthouse beams swept across my comatose mind. Then one drew me fully into the memory of an hour before dawn in early 1759. I was fourteen miles southwest of Plymouth in the English Channel. The beam reflected off of the cloudy marine layer above me, illuminating the rocky shore where the newly built tower stood. Eddystone Lighthouse warned of a treacherous reef.

I had been earning some food and a few shillings by helping ferry supplies out to the new tower's designer, John Smeaton, a talented physicist and bridge builder, who had created for himself the odd title of civil engineer. He had devised a revolutionary method of constructing the lighthouse so that it would not be blown down like all the previous towers. I saw how Smeaton had linked the massive building stones together in an ingenious manner, which gave them a new characteristic: flexibility, which allowed the tower to actually bend slightly in the wind.

I appreciated that Smeaton had forgone the powdered wigs and superior airs of a typical upper-class Englishman. Wearing a weathered greatcoat and boots against the elements, he looked like any of us laborers who were putting finishing touches on his seventy-two-foot tower. After helping off-load supplies from the boat, Smeaton asked me to help him carry a sack of lime into a nearby work shack where he'd been conducting a different experiment. I saw other open sacks containing ground stone and sand. There were also three small, rough wooden boxes containing different samples of cement Smeaton had made. The Englishman scratched at their gritty, crumbly surfaces and heaved a dissatisfied puff. "How did the bastards do it, Willem?"

I had been turning to leave but paused to look back at him. "Pardon, my lord?"

"The bloody Romans. I've read that they'd devised a method, long since lost, to make cement that dried so quickly it would even set underwater!" He shook his head in frustration. "Imagine what uses I could put that to. Damn the Dark Ages!" He was opening the coarse sack of lime as he spoke to me like a longtime colleague. "I know I'm employing the same basic ingredients that the Romans used, Willem, but . . ." He blew out another angry puff, shaking his head in defeat.

I ran my fingers through some of the sand, recalling the early days of my normal life before I'd been cursed. My days as a youth in the hectic heart of majestic Augustinian Rome. I remembered the lively, bustling construction site where the Pantheon would eventually stand. The wagons heaped with loads of lime, ash, and black sand. The concrete building being created amid the smoke from the many ovens. The *ovens*.

"I believe . . ." I paused, vaguely remembering. "I believe they *cooked* the lime, my lord." Smeaton glanced up sharply as my memory came into focus. I continued, "And their sand wasn't ordinary like this. It came especially from Pozzuoli. It was volcanic."

Smeaton's face suddenly became brilliantly illuminated by his sweeping lighthouse beam.

Jillian...

I saw and appreciated that Frances Norton was a nurse from the old school. The slight, gray-haired woman had taken a liking to me. During Frances's long night shifts at Lenox Hill over the last thirty-one years, she occasionally glanced through someone's discarded copy of the *National Register*. Recently she'd read one of my own articles. She seemed shyly tickled about meeting me. I encouraged her to talk, hoping for any assistance in learning more about my comatose subject.

Frances said she appreciated all the new technology, the remote monitoring equipment that brought current data from each of the ICU patients directly to the central nursing station's computer screens. But Frances still preferred the human touch. I liked her.

I spent that first long night alternately dozing, keeping vigil, and wondering about the pale-eyed priest's equally constant presence. I also saw Frances visit each of her three patients personally once an hour. The old nurse was particularly concerned for the heroic man in 304. About three in the morning she moved through the quiet, darkened hallway past the couch where I was drowsing. I saw that the priest had nodded off in his chair. From my sofa I watched Frances enter room 304. I went to look closer.

The muted fans in the equipment around the man breathed softly. Frances checked all the monitors and his IV drip. Then she placed her hand lightly on his injured shoulder and whispered, "Can you hear me?"

TWENTY-ONE

Will...

"Can you hear me?" a voice whispered, and my subconscious swam up from the gloom as I stirred awake one night 150 years earlier.

Opening my bleary eyes in the dim light from the spermaceti-oil lamp, I saw my young New Yorker shipmate standing beside my hammock in the *Acushnet*'s forecastle. The off-watch seamen around us were snoring in their hammocks or bunks that lined the inner hull. His face was very close to mine. In the nine grueling months we'd been laboring at sea, the young man had begun growing muttonchops, but his face still bore the bloom of youth. I mumbled to him, "Herman? What? What is it?"

"I bid you farewell," he whispered. "I am jumping ship."

That rattled my brain. "Wait, wait, what? No!" I hissed. "We're in the Marquesas, for God's sake. They're rife with cannibals!"

"Aye, but they can't surpass the evils of this ship of the damned, the abuses of its demon captain. I cannot be like Seneca and his Stoics: just stand by and bear our master's manias." He squeezed my arm and said with all the drama of youth, "Adieu." Then with a romantic flourish, he turned and left the cabin.

I grumbled, "Oh, damn his eyes," as I angrily wrenched myself out of the hammock.

What he'd said was true. Each of the crew had witnessed or been victim of many abuses by our one-armed captain, who was mentally unstable. He often seemed to be steering the ship on uncertain courses, seeking a peculiarly scarred whale that had taken his missing arm. Even so, we had harvested many other whales, and I certainly felt far more secure aboard ship than abroad in the savage Marquesas. I also knew for certain that the impetuous boy wasn't suited to go it alone: that he'd shortly end up in a stew, quite literally. Six months earlier I had saved Herman's life when he'd been dashed into a turbulent sea by a breaching leviathan. Since then I'd felt a certain responsibility for him.

So I slogged quickly through the cabin scuttle in the predawn darkness and caught the youth, tried urgently to dissuade him, then to club him. But the boy slipped free, determined to venture forth against all hazards. He went over the gunwale, then hand over hand down the long rope to the small skiff that normally trailed the *Acushnet* in case of a man overboard. Though greatly annoyed, I had no choice but to follow him quickly.

Our ship was anchored that foggy night in one of the few sheltered coves amid the sharp volcanic peaks that formed the Marquesas chain. The jagged mountains rose straight upward from the sea floor to over four thousand feet above us. We two rowed the skiff out of the cove on the leeward side of Fatu Hiva and circled it to the northeast.

About four in the morning we put ashore on the barbarous coast, choosing a beach of black volcanic sand where a stream flowed out of a steep valley. Hiding the boat in thick foliage, we secured ourselves for the remainder of the night.

I was awakened at dawn by Herman cheerily washing himself in the stream. I saw that the boy was feeling topgallant delight: that rush of exuberance a sailor experiences when standing atop the highest mast beam. The youth's spirits were blustery and soaring with new machismo inspired by his presumed escape to freedom. It was then I quietly suggested that Herman should turn, very slowly, and look behind him.

Gazing down upon us with the rising sun and several compatriots at his back was a nearly naked, bronzed, godlike Polynesian man. He wore a grandiose necklace of sharks' teeth across his noble shoulders. Similar armbands encircled his substantial biceps. "Overall," I whispered to Herman, "I think he's quite a nice-looking cannibal."

Being the most heavily streaked with war paint, he was obviously the chief. The others stood with feathered spears at the ready. All wore their straight sable-black hair grown shoulder length from the center of their scalps on one side, while the other side of their heads was shaved completely bare. Their look created a formidable unease in the pit of a white man's stomach.

I made signs to indicate peaceful intent and surprised both the chief and Herman by speaking words that the natives understood. Having journeyed across Oceania previously with Mendaña in the 1500s and again two centuries after that with Captain Cook, I had acquired enough of various Polynesian dialects to aid in emergencies, for which this definitely seemed to qualify.

The chief stared at me momentarily, then broke into a broad smile showing fine, pearly teeth. With a small imperial gesture, he indicated for his followers to relax their weaponry, which I saw included several blades of European design. I wondered uncomfortably what had become of their original owners. The chief made a very civilized overture, treating us two newcomers with much courtesy. He waved for us to follow his group.

With several of the natives aft of us, lest we should have second thoughts and try to quit the parade, Herman and I made our way upstream a half mile through the variegated, verdant jungle. It was thick with towering walls of white and pink oleander and other flowers of such diverse colors as to bedazzle our eyes. The pungently sweet fragrance of yellow orchids filled the air. The surrounding rain forest and its green canopy above were alive with the buzzing of a million insects and echoed with the calls of hundreds of birds: the cooing of imperial pigeons, the ghostly hooting of great horned owls. But I found the mynas unsettling. Their near-human cries sounded uncomfortably like a warning.

The native village was in a small clearing where the huts formed a circle around a central fire pit. I saw young Herman react to the many bare-breasted women who wore vibrantly colorful swaths of cloth and flowers in their pitch-black hair.

As the Polynesian images swam in my brain, I momentarily recalled the intrigued look that had appeared upon the robust face of Paul Gauguin when, years later in the south of France, I told him of those native women in their rainbow hues. He sparked to the idea of someday venturing there to paint them.

The women were tending chunks of meat roasting on spits. They shared their victuals and feasted us royally, though I was careful to eat only the vegetables. Maintaining a friendly attitude, I analyzed the camp's layout for escape possibilities. There were none. Herman ate heartily, assuming from its taste that the meat was boar. I told him it was actually referred to as "long pig." I subtly motioned toward a nearby cook pot where Herman glimpsed, bubbling momentarily to the top, a human skull.

The youth dropped the food he was holding and stood abruptly, backing into two smiling natives behind him with spears casually pointing at him. A closer Polynesian reached over and gently pinched Herman's leg, much as the witch had tested Hansel and Gretel for ripeness. As I had suspected, we two breakfast guests would soon appear on the dinner menu.

I was prepared. I raised my hands ceremoniously to capture the natives' attention. Then I made some abracadabra motions and threw into the fire a fistful of gunpowder.

The small explosion startled them all: a demonstration of White Man's Magic. But the natives' surprise lasted only for a brief moment, then they laughed heartily. The chief produced a small horn of Spanish design. He poured a bit of gunpowder into his own bronze hand and thrust it onto the fire, creating a similar ignition. Then he laughed again, looking at me with bright, menacing eyes.

I understood his message. So much for White Man's Magic.

I realized that a far more impressive demonstration was the only thing that might possibly save our lives. I stood up and faced the chief importantly. Clarifying my words with numerous hand gestures, I said that if the chief would promise not to kill and eat us until after three suns had arisen, I would show him and his people Incredibly Great Magic, after which I was certain the chief and his followers would let us sail away unharmed.

The chief studied me carefully and nodded. I extended my hand, which the chief grasped to seal the arrangement. I lifted our clasped hands high and called the natives' attention to their chief's royal vow. The bargain was struck.

Then I began my startling demonstration.

It had a profoundly stunning effect on the savages, and even more so on young Herman.

Three excruciating days later I was unanimously declared the savages' new chief.

Herman and I enjoyed a glorious send-off, quitting the island on their grandest, most royal oceangoing outrigger canoe. They had fully supplied us with a sail and a four-man crew charged to take us wherever we wanted and to relate to people on other islands the astonishing, miraculous wonder they had all witnessed. The former chief had become a breakfast buffet.

Herman had been even more stupefied than the natives by my Great Magic. During my three days of agonized, delirious incapacitation, Herman extracted from me many aspects of my long and highly unusual history. He was determined to write a book about me. But I discouraged such notoriety, suggesting instead that Herman chronicle the Polynesian experiences he was having. Or perhaps write the novel he'd often spoken of, based on our hard times aboard the whaler *Acushnet* under the command of our angry, obsessed, one-armed captain. There was certainly drama and philosophy aplenty to draw upon.

When I sailed on alone westward from Nuku Hiva toward Indonesia and the Japans, as Herman understood I must, the youth remained behind, bidding me Godspeed.

Drifting through my mind came the covers of the Polynesian books that Herman did indeed write. They were well received when published. Unfortunately his book about the obsessed captain seeking the strange whale was not, at least not in his lifetime.

Herman's face had aged by forty careworn years when next I encountered him in 1882. He was giving a lecture in Pittsburgh. His beard was full and long then, though still struggling and scraggly as in his youth. He said he had written the book about me after all and titled it *The Isle of the Cross*. He said it was rejected by his publisher, Harper, as being far too outlandish if fiction, and if *true*, far too dangerously heretical and outright frightening. Harper put out the falsity that they'd rejected it because it was merely a boring melodrama about a Nantucket woman.

The manuscript had thereafter mysteriously disappeared. It had been lost like so much important writing. Many lost pages fluttered before my meandering mind's eye as my brain shuffled back to the rainy night after vespers at the Abbey Monte Cassino in the eighth century when I placed my hands upon the precious "lost" manuscript I had discovered. It was the Gospel of Judas Iscariot. Reading the original Greek manuscript, I understood why the Roman Catholic Church had purposely made Judas's eye-opening work go missing. Because the simple truths of the Judas Gospel were completely at odds with the carefully nurtured and growing majesty and power of the Church; at odds with its increasing grandeur and opulent theatricality, which stressed dependence upon, and complete unquestioning obedience to, the clerical hierarchy. To paraphrase their litany: No man cometh unto the Father except by first wading through legions of greedy, power-hungry priests.

When I found that original Judas Gospel in Monte Cassino, I recognized the inestimable value of the work to a wider world and particularly to the memory of the Good Man from Nazareth about whose life and teachings Judas had faithfully written. That night I carefully secured the delicate codex to my body. Hidden beneath my Benedictine robes, I smuggled it out of that abbey.

But as Fate or the Imp or some Darker Force would have it, the manuscript slipped away into the depths of that Danish bog, which those superstitious villagers cast me into. The incoming tide slowly lifted me back near its surface, but the truths that Judas sought to share were gone. In the third century, gnostic scholars created their own Gospel of Judas, but it was not the same. Just as so many other important books disappeared into the bogs of history, particularly if they conflicted with religious precepts, the original, unadulterated gospel, written by Judas himself, was lost forever.

Though still floating in comatose darkness, I inwardly smiled, recalling one small book that might easily have been lost but that I had helped to save.

TWENTY-TWO

Father St. Jacques...

It was at the quietest part of the night just before dawn when I again looked in on the patient and saw he was still deeply in the coma. I had been carefully checking on him every two hours. Once, earlier, I noticed the reporter had awakened on her couch and was watching me, so I pretended to be praying and made the sign of the cross as if blessing the injured man. This time the reporter hadn't stirred, but nevertheless, I walked farther up the hall, away from her, to make the call on my encrypted cell phone.

I reached the young priest at the archdiocese who had been specially placed on duty to await my call. I told him that, as yet, the patient was unchanged and to advise Archbishop Malloy of the status as soon as he awakened. Meanwhile I would maintain constant vigil.

Then I reconfirmed the contingency plans that the archdiocese had put into place. I had been assured that the NYPD was standing by to move into action. But I was a trifle annoyed about the police's somewhat casual attitude. Because the doctors were completely convinced the man would die from his extensive injuries, the police had only stationed one officer, an older man, on the ICU floor. But if the patient somehow did survive, the police said he would be taken into custody immediately upon receiving word from me.

Finishing the call, I was pleased and, I confess, proud, but I also felt mild tension building once more in my often-troubled stomach. I looked into room 304 again, gazing at the injured, intubated man with intense fascination. I wondered how many of the remarkable, frightening legends about him were really true. I contemplated the import they represented to the world and to my own career, recognizing the windfall this strange being could create for the Church but also the extremely negative, corrosive danger the man equally represented.

As I stepped back, I accidentally bumped the rack that held the gowns and masks. It made a rattling noise but seemed to have no effect on the patient.

Will...

In my dreamlike state, my wayward mind was slowly circling around my memory of the small book I had saved, when I heard a rattling noise. It had apparently come from outside the back-alley door of the 1931 Chicago speakeasy's kitchen. I'd finished mopping up and was strumming away on an old guitar, which I'd quickly preferred over the banjo. I was trying over and over to master a riff I'd seen Django Reinhardt swing through like he was breathing. I was still a novice, but improving. And I'd only had about seventy years of practice.

Pausing to investigate the rattling noise out back, I discovered a middle-aged man in a tailored three-piece worsted suit who had fallen on the grimy alley pavement beside a trash can. He was leaning against the damp brick wall, gasping for breath. He had thick black eyebrows and a mustache. His face was covered with sweat, his horn-rimmed glasses askew. His white Panama hat had fallen beside him as he desperately clawed at a leather briefcase. He got it open, and the contents spilled out just as I knelt to help him. "Pills!" the man blurted frantically. "Nitro!"

I understood: he was having a heart attack. I speedily located the small glass pharmacy bottle. I unstoppered the medication and poured some into his shaking hand, and he placed a few of the tiny pills under his tongue. He gulped in several urgent breaths. "Help me. Please!"

"Of course, pal. But just cool your heels here until—"

"No time," he stammered. "They're coming . . . to rub me out. I can't . . . run anymore." He choked a moment. "You gotta get these . . . to the office. Evidence. Critical." He grabbed feebly at the papers and the book that had tumbled from his briefcase. Helping him retrieve them, I saw the small book was merely an accounting ledger from a dry-cleaning company stuffed with receipts and entries.

But one name leapt out at me. It was listed many times. It was the most famous name in the 1930 Chicago underworld. And inscribed by each of his listings were various sums of money. All huge.

"You . . . gotta get it . . . to my office," the fallen man pleaded. "Big reward. Big!"

"What about you?"

"I'm marked." He shook his fevered head. "They're gonna knock me off for sure. You gotta do it for me." I noted that the man's breathing had become less labored and had an idea.

"Come on, pal." I helped him into the speakeasy's empty kitchen. "Take your clothes off." He looked bewildered. "Hurry!" The man complied, pulling off his wing tips while I stripped off my own workaday Depression-era boots and trousers. "You're a Fed? One of Ness's G-men?"

"Yeah, with the IRS."

"IRS? Not FBI?" I was confused and gestured toward the bookkeeping ledger. "How is *that* evidence about all the murders he's committed?"

"It's not. We can't pin the killings on the slimy creep. But I've got him: *on tax evasion.*"

I laughed because it was so incongruous: a puny tax charge bringing down the infamous Scarface. The agent recognized the irony but said, "At least I *will* get him if that ledger makes it to our field office."

"You'll get it there yourself, pal." By now I had put on the man's trousers and was slipping into his vest and suit coat. "You're sure they're coming after you?"

"I just dodged 'em a few blocks away. Driving a big Packard. But they saw me, alright. By now Capone's got every goon with a tommy gun from Four Deuces scouring the grid."

I popped the cap off the red Parker Duofold fountain pen I'd found in the man's coat. I squirted some of the black ink onto my handkerchief and started dabbing it onto my eyebrows to make mine look as thick as the man's eyebrows. "Wrap your evidence in that trash bag." He did so as I squirted out more ink and created a broad black fake mustache on my upper lip. "That old sweater and cap on the door are mine. Put 'em on."

Then I put on the man's horn-rims and glanced at my reflection in a window. I feared I looked more like the vaudevillian I'd recently seen cavorting on stage with his brothers Chico and Harpo than like the IRS man, but in the dark I hoped I might pass. I grabbed the white Panama hat from the floor, batted it clean against my trousers, and clapped it on. Then I picked up his empty briefcase. "Okay, pal, give me a few minutes, then you skip out the back alley with your evidence."

"Wait." He caught my sleeve, grasped my hand firmly. "Frank Wilson."

I nodded. "Will. Good luck, Frank." I started to leave, but he held tightly to my hand.

"Why are you doing this, Will?"

I met his eyes and shrugged. "Why have *you* been doing it, Frank?" We held each other's gaze for a moment longer, then I ran out into the alley and toward State Street, where I knew they'd be looking for Frank . . . but hopefully they'd spot me instead . . .

And I was correct, of course. They were definitely looking for me. Though not on a dark Chicago street. In a mind's-eye blink, I was looking from a high vantage point across Jerusalem's white rooftops clustered in the dusty valley below. I had a clear view of the Church of the Holy Sepulchre. It was not the original church, which I had visited shortly after Emperor Constantine's mother, Helena, had it built back in anno Domini 330. That original structure had been destroyed by the Persians in 614 and rebuilt in 630 on the same spot as the one I was surveying in that current year, anno Domini 1000. I had come in hopes that the end of the Millennium might finally alleviate my dreadful fate.

Of course those who had long pursued me knew I might likely venture there. I saw that the priests had surrounded the sacred area with scores of guards who were dressed incognito but were obvious to my well-trained eye. They were endeavoring to intermix with the thousands of devout Christian pilgrims who had flocked to Jerusalem, to the scene of the Crucifixion, to welcome the end of the Millennium and hopefully the Glory that was promised in the scriptures by Saint John and others.

It was slightly humorous and sadly ironic to me that all those people were gathered at the wrong place. Helena had built the church over there because local tradition had convinced her the Crucifixion had occurred there.

The scriptures had defined it merely as a hill called Golgotha, an ancient Aramaic word meaning the place of the skull. But tradition and Helena had unfortunately mislocated the scene of the Passion to more than a half mile from where I personally knew it had actually been.

Upon the correct deserted, stony hillside, I was encamped alone and kept a respectful vigil through the long night. As the stars turned slowly above my head, my thoughts drifted back across my days and nights, which spanned ten centuries by then. I pondered the education I had given myself during my constant, exhausting travels. I was relatively content that the new, very pious life I had led had been good, faithful, generous, and most importantly, worthy of reward. Still, I had sought to keep my expectations low so as not to tempt the Imp of the Perverse from his lair.

But on that first morning of anno Domini 1001, as the eastern sky gradually brightened, inch by inch, I saw it was not with magnificent, transfiguring, monumentally biblical Glory, but with merely another Judean sunrise. My entire body slowly became limp and numb. There had been no breaking of the seventh seal. No fulfillment of Saint John's predictions. I sank into consummate disappointment. I was deprived of hope, and waves of sorrow swept over me. My vision dimmed as my eyes welled with tears.

I realized that my long journey was not over. Sitting, ignored and alone, upon the desolate hillside, I began to quietly weep. The great despairs I had previously experienced were mere drops of water compared to the ocean of anguish that submerged me on that dawn. My tears intensified, became choking sobs; my body quaked, racked with emotion as waves of my fury crashed against the immovable stone reality of my damnable fate. I would not feel such despair and rage again until hearing that girl child crying out from the tenement fire one thousand years later. To the damned day.

As I sat on that barren hillside, the needles of pain began to prick at the base of my brain: the warning signal that it was yet again time for me to move farther on. Clearly the contrite, supplicant, studious, and generous life I had striven to live for ten centuries had not been enough penance for the grievous wrong I had committed.

Could there ever be enough penance? I wondered, angry and exhausted, blindly clenching fistfuls of my hair, as I wept in misery.

Then I realized that someone was observing me from amid the shadows of dawn at the foot of the hill. The person wore the sleek garments of a wealthy young merchant of the period. He was gazing up at me, seeming to read my thoughts. His friendly, dark eyes met mine. The sympathetic, sleek young man shrugged almost apologetically. Then he held out a hand, palm up, as though to welcome me, offering understanding and solace.

Our gaze held, unblinking, as I strongly considered his unspoken, potent proposal. A wondrous calm came over me as I sensed the peace that the young man might be able to deliver. The younger man perceived my thought and nodded encouragingly. *Yes, that's right,* he seemed to be indicating. *Come down to me. I am the Answer.*

I placed my hand on the ground to push myself up; my eyes were still locked on the young man.

But upon touching the ground, my movement was strangely arrested. I wondered what had caused my abrupt hesitation. I looked down at my hand, which still pressed against the rocky earth. I realized it was the very soil itself that had given me pause: the hallowed ground of Golgotha.

I remained motionless, absorbing and drawing upon that earth's mysterious well of encouragement and fortitude for an extended moment.

Finally, I inhaled a deep breath and did stand. I forced myself, with great difficulty, to turn away from him who waited below. I gathered my meager belongings and slowly trod down the opposite side of the sacred hill into anno Domini 1001 and toward a very uncertain future. I was still angry and bitterly discouraged.

But my beleaguered, throbbing mind was already straining harder to solve the mystery. What was my challenge? If one must go on living with no end in sight, how best should one do it to possibly earn redemption?

Obviously, kindness, piety, learning, and penance were not enough, were not all that was required of me. I struggled to comprehend what else could possibly be.

TWENTY-THREE

Tito...

The next day, January second, was like freezin'-ass cold. It'uz the kinda day made me wonder how come I couldn'ta been borned in Florida or somewheres warm instead o'the fuckin' Bronx. But I'uz pushin' through the cold 'cause I wanted to show Will them photos I'd took o'my tags. I had 'em stuck in my new port-fole-ee-o. Classy-assed word. Sound funny, even kinda stupid, for me t'be sayin' it. I knowed them photos wudn't the best or nothin', but I'uz prouda how some of 'em looked.

I brung some sketches I done, too. For some new tags. I wudn't much good at sketchin' and sure as shit didn't like doin' the extra work, but I seen what Will'uz sayin' about thinkin' out ideas some up front.

But more'n anything I'uz mostly hot to axe him 'bout that pitcher o'that 1600s artist guy who looked exactly like him. That'uz some mondo strange kinda shit. I'd been spooked ever since I seen it.

My damn hands'uz almost numb by the time I zipped down 125th Street and knocked on the door o'Will's rig. Didn't get no answer so I banged again, shoutin', "Yo, Will dude. It's me, man, Tito. Got some shit to show you. What up?" I looped round to the other side, tried peekin' in, but ain't no Will.

I'uz pissed; come all the way down here in the freezin' cold! Shit! Frustrated, know what I'm sayin'? Wanted Will to see my stuff. But more'n that, way more'n that: mostly I'uz positively itchin' to know what'uz up 'tween him and that creepy pitcher hangin' in the Met. Been buzzin' in my head like a hornet's nest since I seen it.

I wanted t'know, but same time I'uz kinda scared 'bout it. Like when I'uz little and I'uz sure they was somethin' under my bed that'uz gonna *get* me. And get me bad.

Jillian...

I'd spent the night in the Lenox Hill ICU waiting area, so I was feeling a little gamey by the time Chris came by in the late morning to check in. He looked ruddy cheeked and windblown, bringing a refreshing taste of the cold outdoors in with him. Both his Nikons were hanging around his neck inside his heavy leather car coat.

"Had a little shoot over at the UN," he said offhandedly, "so I was in the area anyway."

The UN was thirty blocks south and all the way over by the river, so I smiled wryly. "Oh yeah, you were right next door." Chris gave me a small smirk to admit I'd busted him as he handed me a plastic bag containing some Colgate and a toothbrush.

"You can't be a good reporter with morning breath." Then he raised an eyebrow. "Of course I wouldn't mind nudging you some morning to check out your breath."

"So you've told me," I said appreciatively while looking in the bag. "Thanks for this."

He sat down on the couch beside me and stretched out his long Montana legs. He was wearing his favorite old weathered cowboy boots. He opened a second paper bag and handed me a Starbucks cup. "Grande nonfat two-Equal wet cappuccino. Banana bran muffin."

I patted his cheek. "You've got me down."

"That's what the actress said to the bishop," he joked, raising both eyebrows this time. I held up a hand to quell his ardor. He chuckled and looked along the corridor, noticing the priest, who was opening a small package of Tums. "He been here the whole time, too?"

"Yeah. Never left."

"A little curious."

"Tell me." I nodded, sipping the perfect cappuccino.

"What else is shakin'?"

"He talked to the cop down the hall for a few minutes, and a couple reporters came by to check with the nurse, but nobody stayed."

"They haven't seen those old pictures you found."

"No shit. Or they'd be all over this, too." I sipped at the coffee again and saw an East Indian doctor in scrubs walking up the hallway in our direction. As I stared at him, he seemed to drift into slow motion, taking me right back to that other long night I'd spent in that hospital.

A similar Indian doctor in blue scrubs had approached me that dreadful night, surgical mask dangling around his neck, his expression grave. "I am so sorry, Miss Guthrie. We were too late . . . Maybe if we'd had her just a little sooner—"

I didn't let him finish, but rushed past him to look through the door he'd emerged from into the trauma unit. I got there just in time to see a nurse pull the sheet over my mom's lifeless face.

"Jilly?" Chris's whispered voice brought me back, though the image of my lost mother still floated, silver and ghostly, inside my head. I saw that Chris was indicating for me to look up the hall.

A trim, middle-aged black woman had just gotten off the elevator. Dangling on a thin chain around her neck was a tag that I recognized as a Children's Services ID. Walking beside the woman and holding her hand was the five-year-old Latina girl that the mystery man had saved from the burning tenement.

"This way, Maria," the social worker said, gently guiding the little girl, who I saw looked very disoriented and nervous. She was in a clean, obviously new, blue-denim jumper with tiny pink flowers on it. She wore white leggings underneath and brand-new Keds. She was clutching a stuffed gray bunny; part of its tail was blackened and charred. Maria's left wrist was bandaged, her eyes red from crying or still chafing from the fire and smoke.

Chris leaned closer to me, subtly readying his camera. "Isn't she the kid who—"

"Yeah, yeah!" I whispered back urgently. "Sneak a shot." Chris stood up, and I knew he was already shooting, although the silencing blimp on his camera absorbed the shutter noise. He casually jockeyed for a better angle as Maria and the woman passed us. I read the social worker's ID: Evelyn Hall.

I followed from a barely respectable distance and saw that the priest had gotten to his feet, too. Maria came to a stop outside room 304 and nervously peered in.

Dr. Fernandez had been inside checking his patient and emerged with an EKG printout in his hand. He spoke to the social worker. "Mrs. Hall?"

"Yes, that's right." She shook his hand.

"I heard that you called." Then he squatted down to be on the little girl's eye level. He spoke in Spanish to her. "Hi, Maria. I'm Dr. Fernandez, remember? Are you feeling better?"

She nodded, responding in Spanish, "A little, my arm hurts. But can we talk English? Momma likes me to talk English."

"Sure we can," Fernandez said in English.

The girl tried to look past him into the ICU room. "Is he gonna die, too?" Her voice grew unsteady. "Like Momma?"

Fernandez looked back earnestly at Maria. "We think he might. He was hurt pretty bad."

"He saved my life," Maria said simply.

Fernandez nodded. "Yes. He was a very brave man."

Mrs. Hall put a hand on Maria's shoulder. "She asked me about him, so I suggested she might want to come thank him. Even though we know he's kind of asleep."

"Of course." The doctor understood. "I think that'd be a wonderful thing for you to do, honey."

Maria peeped timidly over his shoulder into the room. "Can he hear me?"

Despite my lack of fondness for his type, I had to give Fernandez his due. His expression never showed any negativity to the girl as he said, "Probably." He put his hand on her arm and gently ushered her toward the open door, retrieving a gown and mask for her. "Let me help you put these on."

Maria Encalada, age 5...

It was all sorta scary. The hospital smelled bad. And I still felt kinda sick. Evelyn, she told me that was just causa my medicine. I came mostly 'cause Evelyn said it was a good idea I had.

My arm hurt where it got burned, and I had bad tastes in my mouth, like I was gonna throw up. Momma used to do that a lot. I'd wipe her face sometimes. I got all sad and hurting in my head when I thought about Momma. Made my eyes hurt, too. Evelyn said that was just causa the smoke. But this was different hurt: *inside* kinda hurt. And it didn't go away, even when I cried. The grown-ups didn't know. They pretend to listen but don't always, even if I spoke English good.

I could do that 'cause Momma always made me watch TV in English, whatever was on, day or night, *Sesame Street* or *I Love Lucy* or that *Blue NYPD* show. I always knew Momma was gonna go sleep or have a boyfriend visit 'cause then the TV got turned on for sure. Momma'd tell me to sit still and watch TV while they were in the bedroom.

I can read some, too. I know "Walk" and "Don't Walk" real good, so Momma lets me cross the street to Max's store. I go get food for me and Momma sometimes. Max is very nice. He always gave me extra. Sometimes he'd be Momma's boyfriend.

The doctor put the hospital dress on me. It was too big and dragged on the floor, so I had to walk careful. Evelyn put a thing on my face. She called it a mask, but it didn't have eyeholes or a funny nose and stuff like Halloween. Just goed over my nose and mouth. Evelyn took me to the door and said it was okay for me to go in.

I saw the man on the bed. He looked kinda scary 'cause of being burned up and all. When I saw him, it made me think all about the day before. And it was scary even before the fire. One of Momma's boyfriends got mad and hit her hard. After he left, Momma told me it was an accident. But I know accidents don't happen three or four times real fast.

Momma's nose bleeded. I wiped it off. Then Momma lit her special little pipe, got sleepy, and turned on the TV for me. It showed a parade about roses. I liked the pretty horses and big wagons with animals and dragons on top, all made of flowers.

Then the air smelled funny and there was smoke. I heard Mrs. Sanchez downstairs shouting about fire. I shook Momma. She was real sleepy and confused. But I made her stand up.

When she opened our front door we saw fire. Lots of fire. Momma slammed the door and ran back to the bedroom. She opened the window and started yelling for help. It got really hot and I screamed, too.

When Momma turned back round, she tripped and fell down. I saw something big and burning fall inside her room. It banged the door and slammed it between us and stuck it tight. I couldn't open it. I shouted but couldn't hear Momma anymore. The room got hotter. I grabbed Tinkerbell, my bunny, and held her tight. It was real hard to breathe. I heard someone shouting to me and I shouted back.

Then the man crashed in the front door. He got me, but when he tried to save Momma, he got all covered with fire and I saw . . . I saw the whole burning ceiling crash down onto Momma. At the hospital they told me after the man dropped me to the firemen, the fire crashed down on him, too.

I stood near his bed, real quiet. The room smelled all hospitaly. I saw the little hoses in his arms and nose; I heard the machines do little soft beepings. I was real shy and scared, but he'd been so brave I tried to be, too. I whispered to him.

I thanked him for saving me and for trying so hard to save Momma. My face got all hot again, and I was almost crying. I told him to get well if he could, but if he had to go to heaven to please tell Momma how much I missed her.

Then I closed my eyes and said all the prayers that Gramma Yvonne taught me before she went to heaven.

Jillian...

Dr. Fernandez had gone off on his rounds after giving me a sour look, but I thought, *Hey, compadre, it's a free country with a First Amendment.* I saw the social worker talking to a nurse, so Chris and I maneuvered a little closer to room 304. Chris looked through the viewfinder at the kid in the room with her little head bowed. He whispered, "Very sweet."

"Mmm-hmm," I said, intent on him getting a good photo. Chris shot me a critical frown. "Okay," I whispered back, admitting, "I guess it is sweet. And yes, I know that George calls me Chilly Jilly. But you start empathizing too much with everybody, pretty soon you lose your objectivity." Chris's gaze held mine, and I could see that he was troubled by what I thought of as my professional detachment. So I changed the subject. "Can you take those back for the next edition?"

He drew a dissatisfied breath and merely nodded. "Yeah. Catch you later." I watched him walk off, but his unspoken censure of me lingered.

The priest had edged closer to the nurses' station with an expression of fatherly concern. He and I both heard Evelyn Hall asking the nurse, "Have you found any relatives for him?"

The nurse shook her head. "None yet."

The little girl came out of room 304 and back to the social worker, who smiled comfortingly as she helped take off the mask and oversized gown. "How'd you do, Maria?"

The girl murmured, "I said some prayers for him."

"That's a very nice thing, Maria. I know he appreciated it." Then she nodded thanks to the nurse and turned the kid right toward where I was standing.

"Excuse me, honey," I said gently and respectfully. "Do you know the man who saved you?"

"No, ma'am. I never seed him before."

Mrs. Hall gave me a glare that clearly read, *Back off, bitch.* I did and watched the social worker guide the child to the elevator. I stood there pondering what other courses I could take to pursue this strange story.

TWENTY-FOUR

Will...

I thought I heard the faint voice of a child whispering to me, perhaps praying for me. But her words were like breezes disturbing the high branches of a nighttime forest, and though I leaned toward them, I couldn't grasp them. My memory river was flowing more swiftly now with increasing flashes of days and nights, places and faces. And that strange nose.

I had never seen a false nose, let alone one made of silver and gold. Tycho Brahe had lost his original nose in a duel in 1565, the same year he inherited his fortune. Rather than fashioning a mere disguise for the ugly hole in his face, Brahe determined his replacement nose should be an adornment. His new affluence also allowed him to pursue his passion for astronomy. He'd built a small observatory and made thirty years of excellent observations. By 1600 he'd hired the distinguished young German astronomer to whom I was carrying a letter.

The stocky, convivial Brahe welcomed me into his fine town house on Karlova Street facing Prague's town square. The warm lamplights glittered off of his metallic nose as we walked up his richly carpeted mahogany staircase to the paneled library where I met Johannes Kepler.

After my anguish upon Golgotha six hundred years earlier, at the dawn of 1001, I had decided that perhaps the challenge required of me was *to be more proactive*. I even fought briefly in the Crusades. But witnessing their barbarous butchery (in the name of the Prince of Peace, of course), I quickly realized the insights and learning I had gained over the first Millennium could be better used: to influence in a positive, humanistic way the course of the second. Perhaps that *direct action* was what might finally lead to the end of my quest for redemption and peace.

So I determined to promote the scholarly pursuits of the very best minds and, utilizing my requirement to constantly travel, to help them better communicate and share ideas that might improve the world. For six hundred years since the second Millennium began, that was what I had been doing.

I presented to Herr Kepler the letter and a gift I'd carried north from Padua. Kepler carefully opened and examined the small telescope, then read the letter from Signor Galilei. In addition to their shared passions for astronomy, I saw that Johannes Kepler and Galileo actually resembled one another. Both had prominent cheekbones, high foreheads, and full beards trimmed to a square edge at the bottom. I also brought Kepler a manuscript of Galileo's latest theories.

"Why has he not published these?" Kepler asked as he enthusiastically thumbed the Italian's papers. Through the leaded glass of the study's window, I saw that the hour was just striking on the large clock tower in the town square. Life-size clockwork statues of the twelve apostles slowly paraded out and around it. They mirrored how papal supremacy was on the march and had all of Europe underfoot. The Church had become a hyperpower, dominant over all the sovereign nations. Kepler followed my gaze to the mechanized religious procession and nodded. "Ah. Galileo fears the Inquisition, as we all do?"

I nodded yes. Heliocentricity, the concept that Earth orbited the sun, was already a burning controversy, quite literally: believers were burned. Along with many other scientific phenomena, the pope had declared it impossible and directly at odds with the Bible and church doctrine, which insisted upon a universe with Earth as the hub. Any deviation was branded as subversive, heretical thought and was subject to ultimate punishment at the stake.

I told Kepler, "Galileo said to me that 'Very great is the number of the stupid.'"

Kepler returned a wily smile. Brahe had been examining the small telescope and asked if I'd like to see his. The roof of his sumptuous house was situated amid the dazzling spires and rooftops of Prague. I gazed through his instrument at the red planet, Mars. "Beautiful."

"Yes," Kepler agreed, but was frowning with frustration. "But why is it *there*? It's at the wrong declination yet again." It was driving him crazy that the planets were never precisely where they should have been according to his superb calculations of their circular orbits.

Circular? I thought of my night aboard the Roman galley sixteen hundred years earlier when I'd watched Saint Elmo's fire on the mast tip describing *ellipses* against the stormy night sky. Omitting that time reference, I told Kepler of the ellipses and said, "I've often wondered if there really are any perfect circles in nature."

Kepler's green eyes glanced sharply at me, then suddenly brimmed with a joyous bubble of humor that I knew accompanied recognition of a possible breakthrough, an obvious notion that had been overlooked, but if proven would forever change all the precepts of astronomy. Kepler was delighted, his mind seemingly whirling, elliptically, around my concept.

But the clock tower struck again, and as the mechanized Soldiers of the Cross resumed their triumphant circular march, Kepler frowned. "Another brilliant truth that may get trampled by the Inquisition's legions." He puffed angrily. "The Church is so damned arrogant. Determined to take into its hands so many of the functions of God."

He shook his head at the danger, adding, "But without *the omniscience* of God . . ."

The phrase flashed my mind forward over a century:

"Without *the omniscience* of God . . . what horrors might man create?" Mary, a captivating nineteen-year-old beauty, had asked. Mary looked slowly at me and the four others, her large brown eyes glittering with firelight. It was the only illumination in the darkened sitting room of Villa Diodati on the banks of Lake Geneva. The firelight provided the ideal atmosphere for this telling of ghostly and phantasmagoric tales to which I'd been invited. "What serendipitous evils," Mary continued, "what unintentional monstrosities might result from man's recklessness?"

The eerie, heavily overcast skies that strangely frigid summer of 1816 lent an ominous ambience to that dark late afternoon when I had briefly fallen in with this very intriguing company.

My host, George, was a curly haired, club footed, wealthy young member of the House of Lords. He was also a robust Rabelaisian poet enjoying extensive notoriety due to the success of his recent publications and the whispers of his shocking sexual exploits. As we listened to Mary, George's delicate hand rested atop the abdomen of nubile eighteen-year-old Clara Clairmont. She was Mary's coquettish stepsister: ten years younger than George Lord Byron and blossoming with their illegitimate child.

Also present was Lord George's physician, Dr. John Polidori, a narrow young man who had accompanied them from England.

The charming, insightful Mary Wollstonecraft Godwin and her poetic lover Percy completed our group. Spurred by the forbidding gloom of that late afternoon, George had challenged us to create stories of horror or the macabre. Polidori had already related his tale, which he called "The Vampyre." It was about the undead and contained aspects of immortality that considerably unsettled me, given my own cursed, metaphysical circumstances. Polidori eventually published his story, and some eighty years later I recognized it had been the inspiration for a stark and thrilling novel by theatrical playwright Bram Stoker.

But Mary's concept was more stunning to hear. "As I drifted toward sleep last evening," she said softly, drawing us in, "my imagination, unbidden, possessed and guided me, gifting the successive images that arose in my mind with a vividness far beyond the usual bounds of reverie."

She envisioned a physician meddling in potent forces dangerously beyond his understanding. He was a student of unhallowed arts who had an obsession with reanimating the dead, with quite literally playing God. Mary described several terrifying moments, including the hideous phantasm of a corpse that the doctor had stitched back together lying stretched upon a slab. Then, due to the working of some potent device, which Mary had yet to come up with, the creature stirred with new life and ultimately became a powerful monster.

I realized that the dark themes she wished to explore, obsession, bioethical philosophy, and perilous hubris, all offered astonishing potential for a truly frightening novel.

I had been enthralled by this brilliant young woman since we'd first met earlier that day in the Swiss village. Obviously highly educated, Mary was the daughter of a radical English philosopher and a free-thinking activist mother who herself was a dazzling author. From the keen look in Mary's large eyes, I felt she was definitely following in her mother's footsteps. I also sensed that Mary somehow perceived I was a creature far different from the average itinerate traveler.

As we sat in the darkened villa on that chilly June evening, Mary's eyes met mine several times, gazing lengthily at me, as if assessing me further, trying to divine the mystery that she sensed lay within. She finally asked what strange tale I might relate. I felt that she suspected me of harboring a compelling secret and she was prompting me to share it under the guise of fiction.

And so I told: how a man had been supernaturally cursed and forced to travel across the farthest reaches of the world for eighteen centuries; how he sought redemption first by educating himself, then by doing his all to promote a better world; how he was relentlessly pursued by papal authorities determined to capture and contain him. I also spoke of the mercurial, seductive appearances of a sleek, dark-visaged young man.

Finally, I took my listeners back to the beginning, relating how the protagonist's unique situation had originated. In hushed tones, I described the unpardonable affront, the heinous crime, for which the man had thus been cursed.

When I concluded, there was an extended silence. Then our amazed host, Lord Byron, ran a hand through his curly hair, slapped his thigh, and laughed heartily. "That's the best yet," he said with gusto. "A freshened *Flying Dutchman* or Captain Falkenburg"—George made an expansive, dramatic, wavy motion with his hand—"endlessly plying the North Sea while he plays dice with the devil for his soul." George stood up, clapping my shoulder. "And exceptionally well told, sir. But much too hard an act for me to follow without getting a stiff brandy first—into all of you."

He laughed again and, limping on his deformed right foot, went to procure the cognac as I saw Mary exchange a portentous glance with her lover Percy. Then they both turned their eyes back to me, regarding me with expressions at once elated and fearful. They were scarcely breathing. Mary was looking at me as she might have at a ghost.

They drew me out privately onto the flagstone terrace of the villa overlooking Lake Geneva. The lake's glassy surface reflected the dark-gray lowering sky. The air was icy. Tiny flakes of snow were even falling lightly. "What an extraordinary June," I commented, trying to steer the conversation to some neutral venue. But they would have none of it.

Percy's round eyes were gazing deeply at me. His mouth was dry. He asked timorously, "It's you, isn't it?" His breath was vaporous in the frigid air. "The cursed man of your tale."

I laughed, somewhat unconvincingly, as I tried to shrug off such an incredible notion and to dissuade Percy from his hypothesis, to turn Mary from her intuition. But she touched my arm with extraordinary tenderness. "Will . . . You can trust us."

I looked into her sympathetic eyes. I believed her, yet I hesitated. Percy gently prompted further, saying earnestly, "I know of you. I have heard the legends."

"We both have," said his lovely, gifted, soon-to-be wife. Her voice had a depth of empathy, a soft nurturing and genuine caring, such as I had not known for eighteen hundred years. And would not know again until Paris in April of 1937. Until Hanna.

I looked away, out over the unnaturally still surface of the dark and deep lake, to the alpine peaks beyond. Then finally back into their eyes. Mary's rich imagination and Percy's poetic soul had trumped me. At length I nodded, whispering, "Yes."

Mary instantly took me into her arms, holding me tightly. "Oh, dear God." She pressed her cheek against mine. Her fear had vanished, replaced by her most sincere empathy. I felt her tears upon my cheek. "Oh my dear boy, my poor dear boy."

My eyes had closed, but I felt Percy's arms manfully encircle both me and Mary, protectively. I leaned against the two of them, allowing them to give, allowing myself to take, to absorb their loving and kindred spirits. The three of us stood silently in the impossible mid-June snowfall, immersed in the greater impossibility, yet the living proof, of my dreadful circumstance.

I remained in their compassionate company for my full three days, during which they questioned me intensely while we three walked along the shore or rowed on the surface of the lake. They plumbed the depths of my history and travels. They offered solace for my sorrows.

By way of recompense, I was able to benefit Mary by suggesting a solution for the major stumbling block in her horror story that she hadn't yet worked out: a device to achieve the dangerous goal of her misguided doctor. She needed a mechanism to bring the corpse back to life. I told her of being in Bologna in 1783, where I witnessed an experiment by Luigi Galvani. He had animated a dead frog's legs by the application of static electricity. The dead legs had jumped and flexed as though alive. I will always remember the slow smile that crept across Mary's lovely face, reflecting the finely tuned wheels turning in her exceptional writer's mind.

Percy's poetic soul was also deeply moved by my plight. Percy Shelley was a mild man, an extremely charitable soul by nature. Despite his own poverty, he insisted upon supplying me with some money, of which I was most always in dire need. True to his word, however, he kept our encounter secret, even when he later composed a substantial poem about me.

And it was the spirited Mary who rushed to find me on the third day to warn me of the priests she had seen who were newly arrived in the village, inquiring after anyone matching my description.

She pressed into my hand an antique strand of petite pearls, which I'd always seen around her neck. I tried to refuse, but Mary insisted on bestowing the gift. She said urgently that I must hurry if I were to escape.

TWENTY-FIVE

Maria...

I could read some of the sign over Evelyn's door. The "New York" part I knew okay. She helped me with the other words: "Department of Children's Services." Evelyn said her job was to take good care of me. First she had to talk to some people from Momma and my's building.

I waited out in the room beside hers. The chairs were shiny orange and plasticky. The first one smelled like throw up. I hate that smell.

The room was noisy. There was other grown-ups and kids waiting; some was fussing. A low table had kids' books, mostly old or torn, but I kneeled by it and showed my bunny, Tinkerbell, a picture book about what doctors do, how they go to school and learn to fix people. I wished they coulda fixed Momma.

I could see up into Evelyn's room. Her desk and shelves was all crammed up with messy stacks of papers and stuff. Evelyn talked to Mrs. Sanchez from downstairs in our building, who said, "No, it was just the two of 'em. Live up on the top there."

Evelyn asked if Momma did a job. Mrs. Sanchez laughed, ugly kinda. "Hooker," she said. "Always wasted."

Then Evelyn asked about my daddy.

"Ain't got none." Mrs. Sanchez waved her hand. "Kid's just a crack whore's bastard." I heard those words before. I knew they were bad. "She'll grow up worthless as her momma."

That made me mad. My eyes got watery. I wanted to yell at Mrs. Sanchez that Momma was just a lot sick, that was all. But I was scared to talk in that busy place. I wiped my eyes on Tinkerbell. I tried to show her the doctor book some more, but Tink didn't care now. The pages looked all blurry, and my chest felt like somebody big was sitting on it.

Will...

The waters of my memory river were growing choppy and flowing more swiftly now, as though approaching a section of rapids. Each fragment of remembrance folded quickly onto the next. Mary Godwin's gift of the pearls drew to my swirling brain a very different gift from another friend. His full, round Asian face with its pencil-thin mustache and goatee smiled at me from the mists of 1266.

I arrived at the Mongol capital, Khanbaliq, in the entourage of the merchants Maffeo and Niccolò Polo. I'd met the brothers a year earlier in the market square of Bukhara, Uzbekistan, where they were buying dried meat, cereals, candles, and other supplies from the various rustic, odiferous stalls. They were set on creating a trade route to the Far East. It seemed a worthy undertaking for me, as I was forced to be traveling anyway. With a happy heart I eagerly joined them, seeing it as an opportunity to improve the world by communicating important ideas in both directions, in hopes that such effort might help lift my damnable curse.

I discovered that the grandiose court of the great Kublai Khan was that of an enlightened leader. Surrounded by advisers of different ethnicities and tribes, often strenuously at odds with each other, Kublai actually listened to them all and took the best that each had to offer.

I gleaned many new ideas during that epic journey into the heart of Asia. Some, like the Chinese mail service by speedy pony express, were valuable lessons worth passing along, which I did half a Millennium later to Sam Clemens in Virginia City. Most wonderful, though, was the small gift that Kublai personally gave me: several silk sheaths to prevent venereal disease.

They also afforded me some personal relief. Until then I had abstained from sexual encounters, fearing any children I produced might also be burdened with my accursed condition.

In my travels thereafter, I told numerous physicians of the unique genitalian scabbards in hopes of spreading their use to combat the scourges of syphilis. Gabriele Fallopio, a fastidious Ferraran physician, saw their possibilities, but silk was rare so he developed sheaths of medicated linen secured rather festively with pink ribbons.

The man who truly sparked to the concept I presented was the personal physician of England's Charles II in 1672. He was the Earl of Condom. Inspired by examining my Chinese silken tubes, the earl fashioned sheaths of sheep intestines that became instantly popular with the gadabout King Charles and his courtiers. The earl's sheaths would have prevented far more disease had he made it clear that they needed to be washed each time before being reused.

The Polo brothers were cheerful, gracious traveling companions. Upon our return from China to their home in Venice in 1268, I met Niccolò's son Marco, who was eager to hear details of the journey. I felt my descriptions of wonders we had seen were woefully inadequate, so I suggested that Marco travel the Silk Road himself to document them.

Years later I read Marco's stunningly accurate book, a magnificent addition to the spreading of knowledge. But to my astonishment, a great many readers disbelieved Marco. They thought his descriptions too fanciful to be real. I heard that on his deathbed, Marco lamented, "Yet I have only told half of what I saw."

I was in Zagreb in 1324 when I heard of his death. I cradled his extraordinary volume against my breast and grieved for my friend and all the truth and knowledge that often went disbelieved or overlooked.

I also grieved for myself, seeing that still I physically grew no older and always felt the prickling pain every three days that forced me to move on. I knew my perceived duty had yet been unfulfilled, that my efforts had yet been found wanting by whatever supernatural hand controlled my destiny.

I anguished, paced, tore my hair, knowing I had thus far failed to cause some positive effect on the world powerful enough that it might bring some end to my odyssey. It was driving me near to madness.

Then, still submerged in the darkness of the coma, I began to sense aching discomfort in my legs.

Though I didn't yet comprehend it, the depth of my coma was decreasing.

Jillian...

I ducked down to the hospital café and grabbed a chopped salad and a cappuccino to go. When I returned to the ICU, I was surprised to see half a dozen new people there. Their nice clothes and grooming marked them as Upper East Side types. My male nurse insider was there, too. "Dempsey? Thought you weren't on duty till tonight."

"I'm not. Came by to check on something."

"Who're they?" I asked, indicating the East Siders.

Half of his palsied face smirked while the other half hung limp. "Family of some bulimic princess they just admitted," he whispered. "She's stable. But way too skinny."

I looked past the newcomers to where the French priest sat, talking actively on his cell while popping another Tums. I spoke quietly to Dempsey. "Has he ever left?"

Dempsey shook his head. "Only to pee, I hear."

I was increasingly suspicious of the pale-eyed priest. "That's a whole lot of praying."

"Well," Dempsey said, drawing a breath and raising an eyebrow, "maybe it's helping. Your guy's vitals are a whole lot stronger this morning."

"You're kidding." I was truly surprised. From the way the injured man had looked when I first saw him the evening before, I was amazed he hadn't already died.

"Yeah. I figured he was history, too," Dempsey went on, "but now it's almost like he's rallying a little." Then he leaned his head closer and spoke more confidentially. "You got another C-note?"

"For what?"

"The fire department thinks they found his ID up at that burned-out tenement." He wiggled his good eyebrow, and half his face took on a saucy expression. "Ain't give it out to the public yet."

I fished out two fifties and held them privately between us. Dempsey traded me for a scrawled note I couldn't read.

He translated his hieroglyphics into my recorder. "J.W. Aldritch. Three Hundred East One Seventy-Seventh."

"The Bronx?"

Dempsey smirked. "Last time I checked."

Will...

In the more rapidly swirling shadows of my coma, my skin had begun to feel raw, chafed, and increasingly sensitive to touch; my muscle tissues felt badly strained; my body and internal organs were aching more and more. I know now that they were the pains of my severe injuries from the tenement fire beginning to make themselves felt. That pain was pressing my subconscious to work harder, as it does in dreams, to rationalize images that might logically be causing my increasing discomfort.

Thus my subconscious abruptly dropped me into the cramped four-horse mail coach I'd ridden inside for several arduous hours. The tedious, jostling journey over the rain-gutted roads of Alsace toward

Strasbourg in 1437 accounted for my aches and exceeding soreness. The only thing making the trip bearable was learning that my sole companion, named Johannes, middle-aged with muttonchops grown down onto his chest, was a metalsmith.

I mentioned to him an idea I'd been formulating to increase the literacy of common people. It involved metalworking. He quite sparked to it, asking if I'd created the device I described. I explained how my own "business" constantly required me to travel, thus I was unable to remain in one place long enough to equip the necessary metalworking shop myself. Though I'd discussed my ideas with several others at about that same time, it was Johannes who instantly grasped the value of my concepts. He listened raptly as I described them in detail.

Three years later, in 1440, I learned that Johannes had successfully fashioned the mechanism. There had been printing presses before, of course, but the key innovation I'd proposed seemed to me a simple and obvious idea: using movable, reusable pieces of type.

I later heard that the haughty Johannes, surname (as you've doubtlessly guessed) Gutenberg, claimed the idea had come to him on that mail-coach ride "in a ray of light." That made me smile.

I didn't care who got the credit: I was elated by the possibilities of the new press. Here at last was a means of liberating the handwritten classics from imprisonment in the monasteries. I knew that the presses could help humanity take a great leap forward by bringing literacy and education to the masses.

Printed words would reach millions of people, spark thought, inspire healthy controversy, embolden people to question unbridled authority, particularly that of the ubiquitous church. The new press would be the greatest engine yet devised to crush ignorance and superstition. It gave me new hope for the world, and thus perhaps for myself.

So on the day when I first saw one of Johannes's printed books, I was surprised to also see a familiar face smiling in at me through a leaded-glass window. The sleek young man's dark eyes twinkled as I heard him say, "Beware what you wish for."

I quickly realized that the press was a double-edged sword because of what instantly became the world's most popular book: it was the Bible. With mounting frustration I saw that while some people were eager to absorb history, poetry, science, and philosophy from printed pages, the great majority of unwashed masses wanted only to embrace the biblical writings that validated their lifelong indoctrination of religious dogma.

Strident faces passed darkly through my brain, which was now beginning to ache more terribly: the leaders of wars and persecutions boldly quoting scripture, purveyors of superstition stabbing their fingers at the printed Holy Words in smug justification of their brutality.

I saw the murder of innocents proceed unabated around me.

I saw the unjust trials, the condemnations for alleged witchcraft, the guiltless people, usually women, hanged or burned alive.

Shades of their agonies were increasingly invading and sharply torturing my own body.

I was entering the shallows of my coma.

Father St. Jacques...

The female reporter had hurried off after speaking with the palsied Negro nurse. I fetched a cup of water to wash down the Tums and hopefully quell my heartburn. The other visitors had departed, and the ICU was relatively quiet as I was returning past the patient's room when a strange sound froze me in my tracks. Was it possible? Had I heard the patient emit a moan? My heart sped up as I stood motionless in the doorway to room 304, carefully studying the injured man. Then he moaned again, My Father! I grew breathless, making the sign of the Holy Cross upon myself as I saw a slight frown catch in the patient's fevered brow. With eager anticipation, I sensed that through his coma he was now beginning to feel the pain of his terrible injuries, that he had begun slowly fighting his way up from the depths of unconsciousness.

Maria...

In the afternoon Evelyn told me she'd gotten a good call from someone about me and was waiting for them to come in. Another lady from Evelyn's work took me downstairs to get a snack. When we came back up the waiting place was all jammed with even more people and kids. Then I saw the man sitting in Evelyn's office and got a sick feeling in my stomach.

Miggy wasn't in his regular clothes. He always dressed real fancy. But that day with Evelyn he had on real old stuff, old coat and pants. And no rings on his long skinny fingers. No gold earring. His hair wasn't slicked back like always. He was writing his name on papers that Evelyn gave him. Then Evelyn saw me and smiled. "Oh, Maria, look who's here."

Miggy turned and grinned. I saw he wasn't wearing his gold tooth either. "Mariita!" he said, cheery, not like usual. He opened up his skinny arms, like all lovey at me. My stomach twisted up more. I didn't like this.

"Oh, honey, I was so worried about you. Give Uncle Miggy a hug." He hugged me for a long time, but I didn't hug back. I didn't like Miggy. And he wasn't my uncle, but Momma said I should call him that. With Evelyn he was just pretending to be all sweet-like, saying stuff to me like, "I'm so, so sorry about what happened to your mommy."

I knew he didn't mean it. I looked at Evelyn, trying to make her see he was bad, that I didn't like him, but I guess she thought I was just shy. Miggy patted my hair and looked all teary eyed. But I knew he was pretending. I knew how he'd be all kissy with Momma when she gave him some of her money, but lots of other times he'd been mad and said she hadn't earned enough money, and he'd hit her or even kick her.

Miggy always liked to nibble my neck and make me scrunch up. He thought I scrunched because it tickled, but it was really because I didn't like it. And I didn't like when he'd squeeze my leg. He didn't do that stuff in Evelyn's office; he just patted my head.

"I know you're sad about your mommy," Miggy said. "I am, too. But I'm gonna take the best care of you ever."

Evelyn winked at me and said she'd be checking up to be sure he did. Then she said, real gentle-like, "We know that Mr. Batista isn't really your uncle, Maria." She showed me some important-looking papers. "But because you had no other relatives since your grandmother Yvonne died, last year your mommy had made these papers to appoint him as your legal guardian."

My eyes got all blurry 'cause I wanted to cry. Evelyn patted my shoulder and whispered, "I know it's really hard right now, honey, but it'll all be okay. You'll see."

I hated it, but I didn't know anybody else or what to say.

Then Evelyn stood up and said, "Thank you, Mr. Batista." She patted my shoulder again. I just nodded because I knew Evelyn wanted me to. She gave me some paper to take and a box of brand-new crayons. Said it would be good for me to draw some pictures.

"That's a girl," Miggy said. "Let's get you home to my place, Mariita." He thanked Evelyn and took my hand. His hand was all wet and sticky kinda.

When we walked out, I looked back. I didn't want to leave, but Evelyn was already busy taking two other little boys into her room and not watching me. I was really worried.

Jillian...

I'd grabbed a cab up into the Bronx to check out the address from Dempsey. East 177th looked like photos I'd seen of Beirut during the recent civil war: boarded-up buildings with broken windows, here and there a partially collapsed brick wall standing alone like it had been accidentally left behind when the building was ripped away.

Remnants of cars and other junk were strewn around. There were hardscrabble vacant lots with trash blowing. I saw charred fifty-gallon oil drums with fires inside them and ragtag street kids around them, stomping their feet against the cold. Pairs of old sneakers dangled by their tied shoestrings from wires overhead, signposts to the streetwise of places to score drugs.

The Pakistani cab driver had four-day stubble, or maybe it was just one day's growth, given how hairy his wrists were as he gripped his padded steering wheel. He pulled the cab to a stop by the buckled sidewalk. I looked around, frowning. "You sure this is right?"

"Oh yes, yes," he said in his singsongy patter. "Look across the street, mum. Three Oh One." Then he pointed out the window to the opposite side. "That is Three Hundred. Right there."

It was an empty lot. "Wait here," I said gruffly as I climbed out to scan the blighted area more carefully. I checked the numbers across and up the street and realized that the hack was right. It was so frustrating. My cell phone burbled from the depths of my heavy overcoat. I fished it out and saw it was Steve from the office. "Yeah?"

"Ahk! Hang on, Jilly. I'm being attacked by a bagel with too much cream cheese. Sorry."

I heard him fumbling with the receiver, but I wasn't in the mood to wait. I asked crossly, "What'd you dig up, Steve?"

"Aldritch, W.J., Three Hundred East One Seventy-Seventh," he said with his mouth full. "Social Security says he died seven years ago."

"Yeah," I muttered, "and he's probably buried on the vacant lot where his building used to be."

"Oh. Bummer. Sorry."

"Me, too," I grumbled, walking a few steps along the cracked, weedy sidewalk. "Anything on Hanna Claire?"

"Mmm-hmm." I heard that he'd taken another bite of bagel. "Retired sociologist. Lots of suicide-prevention stuff. Also did a bunch of work for the UNHCR. But nothing special jumps out. Nothing extra."

"Yes there is, dammit," I said curtly. Turning back toward the cab, I ran smack into a bundled-up little boy on a tricycle. "Oh. Sorry, kiddo." I moved past him and his multiethnic mother and got back into the cab. "Listen, Steve, would you mind searching a little more?"

I heard him sigh, but I pressed. "Thanks. Call me, huh?" I pulled the taxi's creaky door closed and told the driver to take me back to Lenox Hill.

As the driver waited for a break in traffic, I glanced back at the tricycling boy, who was about six. At that moment, he was pedaling past two men sitting on a stoop. They were lasciviously admiring the boy's mother, who was following behind him. I remembered myself at that boy's age, pedaling my trike among the bushy green trees in Tudor Park one summer day. To one side I saw Mr. Ramirez and another Hispanic man on a bench. They didn't notice me, because they were looking off fixedly at something and evaluating it appreciatively in Spanish. I followed their line of sight and saw the object of their focus was my mother. She was tossing a Frisbee back and forth to a kid I knew. She looked very pretty. With the bright sun backlighting her thin sundress, her shapely form could clearly be seen within. I saw Mr. Ramirez nudge his companion. Though I couldn't understand their language, from their gazes and comradely snickers, their intent was clearly unsavory.

In my six-year-old way I even described it to Mom later that day, but she shrugged it off patiently. "Oh, men do that all the time, Jillian. They just can't help themselves."

But Mr. Ramirez did help himself.

The taxi's horn blared as the cab lurched forward, heading back to Lenox Hill, pulling me back into the present momentarily. But not completely.

I was remembering the muffled voices that awoke me one night when I was seven, about a year after that day in Tudor Park. One voice was Mom's. The other was male. They were angry. There were scuffling and banging sounds and then a crash. I jumped out of bed, opened my door, and looked into our small living room. I was shocked to see Mr. Ramirez, who had fallen to the floor, smashing through our old coffee table. His pants seemed partly down. My mother was standing over him, shrieking, "Get out! You get out!" She had been fighting him. They were both sweaty, breathing hard. She was brandishing our largest butcher knife. Her hair was as wild as her eyes. Blood was on her flushed cheek. Half her dress had been ripped off, exposing her left breast, which was badly scratched. She was kicking violently at Mr. Ramirez as he clambered awkwardly to open the door. She was ferocious, an invincible mother tiger. "Don't you ever come near here again! *Get out!*" she screeched piercingly as she propelled him bodily out the door. He tripped on his pants, landing on his knees in the hallway. But I'll never forget how he glanced back sharply over his shoulder and glared. Directly at me. His eyes were fiery, dangerous. Threatening.

Mother slammed the door, bolting it tight. Then she threw down the knife and embraced me tightly, dropping to her knees. "It's okay, Jilly! It's okay!" She was gulping in air, trying to catch her breath. "He tried to steal our money." I saw lots of it scattered all over the floor along with shards of the old cookie jar. "And he tried to do things to Mommy I didn't want him to. But he's gone. If you ever see him, don't you go near him." She was quivering with fury, holding me tightly against her bare breast, rocking me. "He's a bad man, Jilly. He's a very bad man."

I knew that.

TWENTY-SIX

Will...

In the undulating darkness, I was nearly overwhelmed by the pain and aching I felt increasing throughout my body. My subconscious urgently sought another rationale to explain it and offered up an image of the back of my right hand. There were liver spots on it. I knew the cause. I had already felt the aching in my gums.

Scurvy was the scourge of sailors since the time of Ptolemy. Citric acid was a cure, and we had sailed from the Philippines with lemon juice among the ship's stores. But we were blown far off course by a hurricane, so our crew had gone lacking for weeks before docking in San Francisco that foggy June of 1880.

Despite being pale, weak, and in pain as I disembarked the clipper, I was certain that a few oranges would soon quell my *scorbutus*.

I tried to focus on how good it was to be on land again, to tread upon the heavily planked quay, though I still felt the phantom pitch and roll of the ship beneath me. I glanced around the busy harbor at the dense forest of ships' masts growing up from the fog-shrouded waters of the bay. The waterfront and the hills beyond were crowded with wood-framed buildings. San Francisco was becoming a city.

With my weighty sea bag chafing my shoulder, I strode on aching legs past the ferry building bearing southwest off of Market onto Spear Street. An Asian mate had told me of a friendly place where a bath and some female company could be had. In spite of my extreme bodily discomfort from the scurvy, it was good to feel the weight of coins in my pocket, because money had been a constant problem for me. Whatever I earned in my travels was of necessity quickly spent on food and clothing. In the rare times when I had an excess of coin, carrying it was problematic. Nor could I entrust it to a bank that I'd be unable to revisit for over three centuries. The only valuable I always kept with me, aside from the locket and cross around my neck, was sewn into a secret pocket. It was the small strand of petite pearls that Mary Godwin Shelley had given me. But that June day, with good wages in my pocket, I was counting myself enriched and lucky.

The fog had grown so thick as I proceeded down Spear that I barely noticed the alley as I passed it. Suddenly clubbed from behind, I was bludgeoned repeatedly and dragged to the ground within the alley. Between the fog and my spinning head, I caught only a fleeting glimpse of the assailant, who was Asian and likely my former shipmate. He had quickly lightened my pockets, kicked and bashed me again, then fled into the mist. I lay there struggling for consciousness and throbbing with pain and groaning.

Father St. Jacques...

I had phoned the archdiocese to advise Malloy's aide of the patient's change. I said that His Eminence should now alert the police to place additional officers on watch. The haughty aide dismissively said that the archbishop was behind closed doors with the mayor and then cited Malloy's explicit instructions to neither disturb him nor trouble the police until the patient fully regained consciousness, if ever.

The stupid fool. I was greatly annoyed by Malloy not bending to my authority, and I pondered calling Rome to order up a scolding. Returning to the patient's doorway, I heard a mournful groan and was startled when he slightly twisted his head! It was the first such movement he'd made! My heart fluttered as I thought prayerfully, *Lord God! Might I actually be witnessing the miraculous rejuvenation that inspired so many legends about this man over the centuries?*

Maria...

My knees hurt. I was kneeling, and the rug was real thin. I'd been drawing on the paper with the crayons from Evelyn. First I drew Momma and me when we sat on a seesaw one time. The old table where I was drawing was rickety. It had spots and scrapes. The room was like the one where Momma and me had lived. No chairs. One small light on a wooden box. The room was pretty dark and sad.

The next room was real nice, though. Real thick rug, new tables, chairs, a squishy couch, and a TV with a giant screen. Miggy was in there, dressed back in his fancy clothes, with his rings, earring, and gold tooth. I saw him putting some pretty little crystals into tiny plastic bags.

There was a grown-up woman who Miggy called Carmella. I thought she was very pretty with her long eyelashes and lots of makeup. She only had on a thin, shiny silk bathrobe with dragons on it, but nothing under it. I saw her naked parts underneath sometimes because she was walking around angry and smoking. I heard her say to him, "Whatchu talkin' about, 'guardian'?"

Miggy just smiled. "Listen, Carm, few months back that bitch started getting so strung out she coulda OD'd, and I wanted to be sure her kid 'stayed in the family.'"

Carmella laughed kinda crazy. "You outta your mind?!"

Miggy just kept smiling. "So I give this notary friend o'mine a few dime bags." He held up one of the little crystal bags. "Had him do up them papers all legal, then one night when she was stoned I got her to sign 'em."

Carmella was shaking her head, angry again. "Well, you can do whatchu want, Miggy, but ain't no way I'm gonna be takin' care of no whore's kid."

237

"Chill, Carm," Miggy told her, "the kid's a meal ticket."

"What're you talkin'?" Carmella asked.

They didn't know I was listening.

"That little angel face in there," Miggy said, "she's the perfect mule." I didn't understand. I saw Pinocchio turn into a donkey, but I knew that was pretend. "Ain't no cop gonna think she's holdin'," Miggy said to Carmella. "She'll do all our big deliveries." Then he pulled Carmella onto his lap and poked at her booby. "And when she gets around twelve, we'll start rentin' her out, you dig it? Your poppa knows what he's doin', girl." Then he kissed Carmella, but it was more like they were licking each other.

Father St. Jacques...

From the doorway to the darkening hospital room I was watching the heart monitor beside the patient's bed. It had begun pulsing more rapidly. I also noted other faint stirrings from the patient: a quiver of a finger, a twitch of an eyebrow, variations in his respiration.

Now and again the injured man quickly inhaled such as I myself did when surprised by a sharp twinge from my chronic indigestion.

The patient was now definitely feeling pain from his injuries and edging toward consciousness. I was determined to be present when he achieved it, and then to shepherd him securely into the custody of the NYPD and ultimately the Vatican police.

The man suddenly gasped and inhaled sharply again.

Will...

Lying on the San Francisco cobblestones, I sucked in an agonizing breath, trying to focus my vision, to overcome the trauma from my beating, the aching and stinging of my body. Nausea welled and ebbed repeatedly.

With great effort I finally regained my unsteady feet and my sea bag; one hand seeking the alley's damp clapboard wall for support, I shakily retraced my steps back toward foggy Market Street, which was bustling with horse carts, buggies, and people of every station. My brain was aching, addled. And as so often in the past, I was bloody and destitute. I sighed, which brought a clenching pain to my broken rib cage. I resigned myself to once again seek some temporary meager employment.

After no success with establishments on Market Street, I was near exhaustion, barely shuffling along among the varied San Francisco pedestrians, but determined to try my luck on Kearny when I heard a man call out to someone, "Mr. Stewart!?" I continued walking until the man shouted again breathlessly. "Vait! Vait! Beggink your pardon, sir!"

I turned and saw a little round man, about sixty, dressed in a three-piece business suit running toward me. He seemed vaguely familiar. He was breathing hard, but seeing my face, the man's eyes went wide behind his wire-rimmed glasses. His circular face illuminated like a child's on Christmas morning. For a moment he stared at me, his smiling mouth working speechlessly, before he found his sputtering voice.

"Vot a miracle! It iss you! Ven I zaw you pass by"—he gasped excitedly for breath—"outside our store vindow I thought, *Mein Gott!* Could it really be!? J.W. Stewart!?" Then his expression suddenly filled with more amazement as he caught his breath. "*Mein Gott!* You haven't aged a day since last I vas seeink you!" My murky mind was trying to remember where we had met, and the little man cheerily prompted, "Jacob Davis. The tailor." He extended his delicate hand and shook mine vigorously. "You vill maybe now be rememberink? Virginia City? Vee met there. You guessed correctly I vas from Latvia?"

"Yes, yes, of course," I said politely, still trying to recall our former encounter.

Davis held on to my hand tightly, still breathing hard. "*Mein Gott,* I haff been searchink for you over eighteen years. More!"

"Searching for me?" I was thoroughly confused, my voice hoarse. I felt myself near collapse.

"Yes, yes!" Then Mr. Davis realized my weakened condition and put a supportive hand on my arm. "But you are not vell. Come vit me, please. Lean on me. You vill please to come!"

Jacob Davis was charming and insistent. He took my heavy sea bag. From the fine cut of his suit, I thought that Mr. Davis might be able to secure some menial employment for an impoverished, recently bludgeoned sailor.

He led me back onto Market Street and to a dry goods storefront I had bypassed during my earlier exploration. "Look," Davis said enthusiastically. "Look in the vindow!"

I saw that the merchandise displayed consisted of work clothes, coveralls, and britches made from a thick, bluish cloth. They did not seem unusual, but I didn't want to offend the small round gentleman, so I nodded, saying, "Very nice."

But Davis was smiling excitedly. "No! You are not lookink closely!" He pointed eagerly. "Look, look!"

I looked in the direction he indicated, and observing the clothing more carefully, I noticed that the pocket corners and other points of stress had small copper rivets through them for added strength. "Ah." I smiled, finally remembering.

"Just like I vas seeink you had done on your britches in Virginia City," Mr. Davis said as he opened the shop door, which tinkled a bell announcing our entrance. "Come in! Please to be comink in!"

I followed him inside, where he encouraged me to sit and had a shop girl pour me a glass of water and secure me some oranges. Then he shouted off to someone in the back, "I haff found him! I haff found J.W. Stewart!"

A stout man with thick eyebrows and a partly bald, broad head like an inverted egg that narrowed to a chin with a full goatee, but no mustache, hastened from a back storeroom. He was also nicely dressed in finely tailored clothes. Astonishment was working on his face as he spoke in a thick Bavarian accent. "Zis iss him?!"

"Ya! Ya! It vas a miracle! I am just seeink him walkink past on ze street outside our vindow!" Then Jacob Davis turned to me. "Mr. Stewart, please to be meetink Mr. Levi Strauss."

The smiling, eggheaded man shook my hand heartily, saying with a brisk Germanic nod, "Mr. Stewart, it isss mein great pleasure to be finally meetink you!"

They both beamed at me as Jacob Davis explained, his hands jittering with delight, "When I saw ze rivets you had put onto your pants, I vas tellink Levi about zem."

"Brilliant idea, *mein Herr*," Strauss confirmed cheerfully. "Brilliant!"

Jacob continued, "Und vee sought for you everywhere in Virginia City, but you had vanished. Even your reporter friend Sam, he's become quite a famous writer, you know, calls himself Mark Twain now, even Sam had no idea vere you had gone."

"Vee advertised in zo many newspapers to find you," Strauss said, "seekink alvays to find you. All zees years."

"Anyvay," Davis continued, "after much consideration Levi and I are decidink to form a partnership and acquire a patent on your idea."

"Number one three nine one two one," Levi pronounced proudly.

"Includink your name, of course," Jacob said. "You are vit us a patentee."

"Well, you needn't have done that," I said, shrugging, "but thank you." I glanced around the well-stocked little shop. "Your store is doing well, I hope?"

The two men exchanged a convivial glance. Jacob patted me lightly on the back as Levi said with a chirp of delight, "Indeed vee are, Mr. Stewart. I am zo pleased to be informink you . . . zat you are a *millionaire*!"

TWENTY-SEVEN

Will...

I stared blankly at the beaming gentlemen. As I tried to take full measure of Strauss's statement, my potent physical discomfort receded slightly into the background. The room lightened, and glancing outside, I noted that the fog had lifted. The sun was bright and streaming.

The two jovial men explained how they began using my rivets on clothes made of coarse brown sailcloth but soon switched to a sturdy fabric called serge, which was made in Nimes, France.

"It vas callt *serge de Nîmes*," Jacob explained, proffering some stiff blue britches for my examination.

"But now everyone iss only callink it *denim*," Levi said, smiling. "Vee don't care vat zey call it, zo long as zey buy it. Come! Look!"

They eagerly hustled me through the back door into a large clerical office with a dozen desks and twice that many busy people. Then through another door, which opened into a sprawling, city-block-sized warehouse, where the denim clothes were being created by a buzzing army of male and female workers.

Levi beamed at me as Jacob said, "Vee haff two other vactories like ziss one, und vee are building a ssird."

I learned that Levi Strauss & Company had outfitted virtually every prospector in the Gold Rush country and most of the working men in San Francisco. They were now opening a new store down the California coast in hopes that their unique product might just possibly interest others.

They were eager for me to take my place beside them managing the company or to merely continue collecting my one-third share of the future profits, as I chose. Those future profits would be in addition to the very substantial fortune they had already set aside for me during the last two decades.

Having endured considerable hand-to-mouth poverty over the centuries, I was overwhelmed. I then explained to them how, but not why, it was a necessity that I traveled continuously. With their eastern European manners and discretion, they didn't pry, but I knew they assumed I had committed some ill deed that required continual flight. I knew it would stagger their imaginations if I told them what my actual offense had been.

Jacob suggested a convenient means for me to receive money: Western Union had just begun transferring funds via telegraph. Levi created a code I could use to authenticate a request for money, which would immediately be sent to wherever I was. Thenceforth I would always be richly funded. The relief I felt was wonderful, it—

A shock of searing pain suddenly flashed electrically through me. I was back in the blazing tenement, scorching: feeling and seeing the fiery hot ceiling collapsing onto the screaming woman. To fight this increasing awareness of pain (which was being generated by my present injuries), my straining subconscious fired lightning bursts of similar horrors I had known: across Europe from Germany to Scotland between 1560 and 1600 I witnessed far too many of the eight thousand burnings of my fellow human beings. Innocent victims of hatred, jealousy, superstition, and a church hierarchy bent upon maintaining its supreme authority. Those women, men, and even children—I saw a nine-year-old girl, her flaming-red hair literally aflame—wide-eyed, shrieking with abject terror, suffering tortures of the damned in the fires one at a time. I felt the burning heat from their staked pyres blistering my own ravaged skin. Their pain invaded my own being; the smoke from their burning hair and bodies stung my eyes; the smell of their broiling flesh assailed my nostrils. Every stinging aspect of their unbearable agony was thrust into me like a thousand flaming arrows.

Maria...

I used a yellow crayon for all the fire. There was lots of yellow. It was a picture of our building. I drew Momma in the window waving her arms. Down at the bottom of the picture, looking up, was the man who had saved me.

Miggy and Carmella had closed the door to their nice room. I heard them giggling a lot, and she squealed some. When Miggy opened the door he said real cheerful, "Hey, Mariita. What you doing there, honey? Come show Uncle Miggy."

I took my drawing in and asked him if I oughta call Carmella "Aunt Carmella." She stood up, angry. "Let's get it straight, kid," she sorta spitted, "I ain't your *effing* aunt." 'Cept she said the real word. Then she walked away.

"What you been drawing, honey?" Miggy was trying to sound nice. But I knew I couldn't trust him. I held out the picture, but he pulled me close, put his skinny arm around me. Then he looked at my picture.

"Aw . . . that's very good, Mariita. But why don't you draw something happier?" While he talked I felt his warm hand go under the back of my shirt and rub my skin.

I didn't like it, but I was afraid to say anything.

Will...

Suddenly the fiery tenement wall was falling toward me, crushing and engulfing me like a river of molten lava. Then all was chaos! Excruciation! I bellowed one long and final scream of despair, then glimpsed through the conflagration the sleek young man calmly watching me with sympathetic eyes.

"Hey, big guy," his voice whispered in Latin, "I know you can hear me."

Father St. Jacques...

I had stepped slightly down the hall when the rotund Puerto Rican nurse entered the patient's room to check on him. But when I heard her voice speaking in the ancient Latin language of the church, saying, "I know you can hear me," I peered in. I saw that the heavy woman was leaning intimately close over the unconscious man's face. Her voice lowered in pitch, sounded strangely and unaccountably masculine. And her words continued in perfect Latin as she said, "About time to rise and shine, big guy?"

Then I heard the patient groan louder than ever as his entire body, including his legs and arms, stirred in great discomfort. His eyes remained closed, but a severe frown troubled his fevered brow. His lips quivered, and then, to my astonishment, for the first time the terribly injured man actually spoke.

He rasped, in Latin, "Leave me be . . . Asmodeus . . ."

My blood ran cold.

The heavyset nurse smiled darkly as she stood upright. She did not seem surprised to see me in the doorway. As she slipped past me I asked her, "Why did you speak in Latin?"

She looked at me curiously, and when she spoke her voice was light and feminine, completely unlike what I had just overheard. She shrugged curiously, saying, "What? But I didn't speak at all, Father." She walked back toward the nurses' station, leaving me confounded.

Then I was annoyed to see the reporter approaching. She was wearing different clothes, and her hair was damp. I assumed she had gone home to bathe and change.

"What's up?" she asked.

"Nothing, I'm afraid." I wanted her gone before the patient spoke again. "If you'd like to leave your number, I would be happy to—"

". . . Asmodeus . . . ," the patient murmured.

Jillian...

I was jolted. I glanced in at the man with surprise and excitement. Then I looked sharply back at the priest with an expression that clearly transmitted, *Nothing, huh? Yeah, right. Asshole.*

I pushed quickly past the priest and into the ICU room, grabbing a mask and slipping on a gown as I went closer to the bed.

TWENTY-EIGHT

Jillian...

The priest stood in the doorway, also putting on a gown and mask, as I pulled a chair close to the injured man's bedside and was surprised when I looked at him more closely. In the few hours since I'd last seen him, the color in his face had improved quite a bit. One of the larger blisters on his forehead had considerably receded beneath its gauze. I clicked on my little recorder as I spoke softly to him. "What did you say?"

The patient's parched lips trembled silently.

"That's it," I said, encouragingly. "What did you say?"

His whispered voice quavered in delirium, "Asmodeus . . ."

I held my recorder close to his face. "Is that your name? What's your name? Can you tell me your name?"

". . . Ahasuerus . . . Botta . . . deo . . ."

I heard the priest draw a breath behind me. I looked back and asked, "*Deo?* Means God, right?" He nodded faintly, but his pale eyes were locked on the patient as I asked, "What's Botta*deo?*"

He continued staring. He seemed distracted, even slightly fearful and barely aware that he answered me. "It means . . . one who strikes God."

"What? How can anyone . . . ?"

"Asmodeus . . . ," the patient whispered again, his brow knitting into a tight frown, "Set . . . Mot . . ."

"Aren't those . . . ," I began, glancing back questioningly.

The priest's eyes were fixed on the patient as he said, barely audibly, "Other names for Satan."

I studied the Frenchman's concerned expression, then looked back at the injured man, who was murmuring slightly and seemed to be drifting back into his coma.

"No, wait. Go on, please," I urged. "I want to help you."

Will...

"I want to help you," the voice said, very faintly. And up from my pained darkness sprang the face of eager nine-year-old Zacharias Janssen, speaking in his native Dutch. "I want to help you. What is it that you're trying to find, sir?"

"Something to hold these steady," I said, showing him two chipped, mismatched lenses. I had been earning some food by cleaning the small shop belonging to the boy's father, Hans, a kindly maker of spectacles in Holland in the 1590s. "They were under this bookcase, and when I picked them up, I noticed an odd phenomenon. Look, Zacharias." I showed the boy how the magnification of the lenses was made considerably more powerful by looking through them both when one was held some six inches beneath the other.

Zacharias's young face grew sunny. "Oh my, yes!" The boy used them to minutely examine a nutshell in my dustpan. "They make tiny things gigantic, sir!" The boy took the lenses to the small workbench his father had outfitted for him. "I think it has excellent possibilities, sir."

Those words echoed, becoming "Excellent possibilities indeed! You're right, laddie!" I was being addressed by a hearty, ginger-haired Scotsman of thirty with bright-blue eyes, a large thick nose, and a cheery disposition who clapped my shoulder.

Clenching his pipe between his teeth, the enthusiastic Scot examined the heavy prototype engine I'd carted all the way north from Devon to Glasgow. Earlier that year of 1765, I'd been doing day labor at a mine down in Devon. I'd become intrigued by a mechanic there who'd been trying unsuccessfully to improve the efficiency of an old Newcomen steam-powered engine used to pump water out of flooded mines. Examining it, I recalled the details of a steam-operated toy devised by Hero the Younger of Greece a hundred years or so before I was born. I had seen drawings of it while traveling through Alexandria centuries ago. I suggested to the mechanic how Hero's ideas might make Newcomen's engine more efficient, but the stubborn, stuffy man was determined to pursue his own design.

It was one of his cast-off Newcomen engines I had transported to the engaging Mr. James Watt for a very important reason.

One hundred forty-four years earlier, in 1621, I'd inveigled myself into the private presence of the greatest mind of his time: Sir Francis Bacon. I captured his attention with a startling demonstration of how any wound I received would miraculously heal so that I had lived on and on. I also revealed to him the origin of my curse. He was frightened and amazed, but ultimately convinced of my centuries-long supernatural existence. He deeply appreciated the perspectives I had gained in my trek across beleaguered human history. Despite that, I explained, I'd realized I could not personally effect sweeping changes for the better because I was not in a position of power.

But Lord Bacon was.

I reminded him that he had already envisioned such profound changes, had been focusing his brilliant abilities on such a monumental project, but had set it aside when King James made him Lord Chancellor. Bacon had quickly been seduced by the wealth and luxurious lifestyle of the court. Before that, however, Sir Francis's plan had been to enkindle an Age of Reason and scientific enlightenment. I insisted that he get back on the job.

Stunned by my unimpeachable credentials as "an ambassador from the past" and the insights I'd gained during my long existence, Lord Bacon finally drew a breath and agreed wholeheartedly to pull himself up by the bootstraps, to rededicate himself to that challenge. His commanding position as chancellor gave him infinitely more ability than I to create and foster massive societal changes for the betterment of humankind.

The chancellor indeed abandoned his extravagant lifestyle immediately and went back to his great task of reinventing science and philosophy. I was elated when Lord Bacon sounded a clarion call that set the world on a course toward an Age of Reason. He declared that ignorance was the parent of fear, that knowledge was power. Bacon convinced King James to finance the Great Renewal as a royal work that would entirely reorganize scientific reasoning and research for the physical, material, and moral benefit of humankind.

I was gladdened to witness how Sir Francis created more colleges and libraries with improved communication between them, initiated better payments for teachers, sponsored laboratories and museums, and provided ample funds for scientific experimentation based on truth, logic, and reason.

"The more that humanity can understand and harness the powers of nature," Bacon insisted, "the more they will understand the nature of God. And the more opportunity they will gain for personal contemplation that will evolve them to higher wisdom, empathy, and compassion."

I was deeply proud to have refocused the course of Lord Bacon's life. I felt that finally, finally I had advanced the progress of humanism and simple goodness in a meaningful way. And perhaps advanced my own progress as well. We'd hoped that Lord Bacon's Great Renewal would sweep away centuries of superstition and dogma, replacing them with literacy and knowledge.

But sadly, Bacon's supreme effort was embraced only by those lucky enough to be *already* educated or who had time and money to *become* educated. I saw the largely ignorant populace struggle day after day just to feed and shelter themselves. Even when they desired education, the strains of daily survival made it near impossible. If ordinary people were ever to have the *time* for study and contemplation that would evolve them up from ignorance, they needed drastic, *practical advances* to help them in their workaday world. I was hoping the spirited Mr. Watt would be a helpmate toward that goal. If we could transform Newcomen's inferior engine into a device that actually worked, it might help to drive the world forward technologically and give everyday people a better destiny.

I heard that James had a workshop at the University of Glasgow and was the best mechanical engineer alive. Hearing my ideas, he was delightfully eager to become involved.

When I explained that I could remain only three days, Watt alerted his tiny wife, Margaret, to supply us with meals at his workshop. Rubbing his palms together, Watt said, "Let's nae waste a second then, laddie. To work!"

James soon got the old model engine sputtering, but very sluggishly, the same unreliable way Newcomen had achieved. But James recognized instantly how my simple suggestions based on the ancient Greek toy would definitely improve the performance. Together we set about it.

By the third day, our refined steam engine was chugging along with tremendous new efficiency. James clapped my shoulder happily again, repeating, "Excellent possibilities indeed, Will!" Margaret had come into the workshop, bringing warm currant scones with clotted cream, milk, and coffee in thick glass mugs for our final breakfast. Sipping the coffee, James flinched sourly. "Ahk. You've made it strong enough to take the rust off an iron pipe, Maggie."

"Sorry, Jimmy. I'll add a bit of milk, then," she suggested, extending a cup.

"Nay," he said, covering his mug with a thick, freckled hand, "I dinna like the coffee cooled off."

I had a thought. Taking the milk cup from Margaret, I held it up so that the tip of our steam engine's pressure-relief valve was submerged in the milk. Then I opened the valve and let the hissing steam heat the milk. I was surprised to see it also create a frothy layer of foam on top.

James smiled. He extended his mug for me to pour some of the hot foamy milk into it. The coffee took on the light-brown color of the Capuchin monk robes I had often worn.

James tasted his coffee and laughed heartily. "Well done, lad! At least we know this infernal contraption's good for *something!*"

Jillian...

The priest and I had been forced to break away from the patient and duck out of the room when Dempsey warned me that the doctor was coming. I paused around a corner where I could hear Dr. Fernandez flipping pages of the patient's chart and saying in a low, puzzled voice, "Yes, the burns do look considerably improved. It's very strange. I've never seen anyone so badly injured rally like this."

"Could the original examinations be inaccurate?" asked Dempsey.

"Hard to believe," Fernandez sighed grumpily. I heard him scrawling instructions on the chart. "Let's back him off the Pentothal a little bit."

I heard the doctor departing and looked out, catching Dempsey's eye. When he walked over I whispered to him, "Pentothal?"

Dempsey nodded. "Yes. To help stabilize the coma, keep him from too much pain."

"But isn't Pentothal what they used to call a truth serum?"

"It can have that effect sometimes," he said, "loosening tongues to say things someone might not ordinarily."

I started back toward the room, but Dempsey caught my sleeve, saying, "No. I can't let you hang out in there."

"Come on, it's a free country—"

"Uh-uh," he said, shaking his head. "You're not family. The rules say—"

"You're going to quote the rules? *You?*" I was getting annoyed. "That priest isn't family either, hell-lo?"

"But he *is* a priest. They're in here all the time like that." I started to protest, but he cut me off. "Fernandez hates your guts, and he'll have mine on a plate. I'm sorry."

"Okay, okay," I understood. "Three hundred dollars."

He shook his head again. "No. Really. I'd like to help you, Jilly. You know that. But my ass could be grass. Big time."

"Five hundred." There was a pause. I saw him purse his lips on the good side while the palsied lip hung limply. I was encouraged so I pressed. "I'll hit the ATM downstairs as soon as I get a sec, I promise. Okay?" He remained silent and uncertain. "Come on, Demps, have I ever stiffed you? Besides, it's a holiday weekend, right?" I was dancing as fast as I could. "Not a lot of patients, staff's at minimum." I checked the time on my watch. "And look, it's already late. Fernandez probably bagged it for tonight."

I stood my ground. So did he. I sighed, with the implication that I was stretched to my absolute limit. Then I gambled and turned as if to leave. He stopped me, drew a breath, and finally gave the slightest nod.

I breathed easier again. "That's my pal." Then I focused on him. "But for that amount you keep a sharp lookout, okay?"

He nodded again, saying, "Yeah. I'll give you a pop on the intercom. Anybody would come up from the elevators, so you duck out the other way, okay? You get caught and I'm toast."

"Got it. Thanks, Demps." I gave him a peck on his good cheek and headed back toward room 304. I saw the priest approaching from the other direction, flipping his cell phone closed with a smug, superior smile. Then he sniffed disapprovingly at me. "I really don't think it's appropriate for you to be invading this man's privacy just to get a story."

"I'm also trying to help him if I can," I said, then added sharply, "Why exactly are you here?"

His authoritarian gaze held mine until we both heard a murmur from within the room. I pulled up my mask, approached the bedside, and saw a grimace flickering across the patient's face as though the pains of his many injuries were making themselves felt despite his semiconscious, medicated state. I turned on my recorder again and spoke softly to him. "Can you hear me? What's your name?"

His brow knitted with a frown and his lips tightened, as though he didn't want to speak, but the influence of the Pentothal was like deep hypnosis. I realized that he was in a very vulnerable state, so I proceeded gently. "I really want to help you. Can you tell me your name?"

He drew a long breath. "So many. Guilliam . . . Vilhelm, but at first . . . Vitellus . . . Janus . . . Manchus."

The priest was again just behind me, and I heard him stop breathing.

"Where is your home?" I asked. "Where are you from?"

Another long breath and then the man said, ". . . Judea."

Will...

"Judea?" I heard the ethereal female voice repeat from the misty darkness. "You mean Israel?"

The sun-bleached, ancient city flashed into my mind's eye. I was walking up a narrow dusty street with a certain arrogance, wearing the Roman tunic that announced my authority. I passed donkey carts, men and women in Roman or Arabic garments, several of whom nodded with respect.

". . . No," I muttered in Latin. ". . . I mean . . . Judea . . ."

Jillian...

He said something in Latin. "Can you speak in English? What did you say?"

"Judea . . . was my home . . . for thirty-three years . . ."

"Were you born there?"

"Yes."

"When?"

His voice was halting, barely intelligible. "Twenty-seventh year . . . of Caesar Augustus."

"What?" I felt myself blanching. "But that was over—"

". . . Over two thousand years ago . . . ," he whispered.

I stared at him, then glanced at the priest, who seemed equally amazed. I turned back to the bed. "How is that possible?"

". . . The Curse," he sighed, closing his lips again.

"What curse? How did it—"

"I didn't realize at first . . . Even when the pain began . . . Three days after he was killed."

"After who was killed?" I was trying to keep up with him.

". . . The pain . . . ," he rasped. "Unbearable . . ."

Will...

I heard my own voice echoing strangely in the darkness. It was an eerie bicameral experience: as though another man was speaking and I was merely a bystander, yet I was also the narrator telling how the stinging pain knifed into me. First it struck at the back of my skull and then from all directions. I staggered along, leaning against the stucco walls. Those around me in the street, Arabs, Jews, Romans alike, gave me wide berth, assuming I was drunk.

But I saw that one man swathed in pristine robes turned to watch me with keen interest as I passed. I had never seen him before. He was a handsome young man with sleek, dark hair and features.

The pain . . . was searing my brain, like fresh meat sizzling on a spit . . . as I stumbled aimlessly.

Jillian...

I leaned closer as he went on speaking very haltingly, his sentences and phrases often interspersed with pauses or moments of merely breathing.

Will...

I heard my own disembodied voice echoing to the woman I couldn't see as I went on to say that the square in the ancient city . . . was smoky. A bazaar was in progress. I staggered . . . through the stalls that offered spices, fresh fish, and produce. I was like a madman . . . from the pain.

And then . . . as I took just one more step, it ceased. I stood upright in the midst of the marketplace. Entirely pain-free.

But as I turned to go home . . . the pain again smote me like an ax. I was stunned . . . overturned a basket stall. The furious owner shoved me away. And again the pain abruptly ceased. I stood slowly, realizing that whenever I walked in the direction of my home . . . the pain returned in force. But walking in the direction *away* from my home . . . the pain abated.

I was confused. Frightened. I tested my theory . . . headed down a narrow Judean street. I rounded a corner. Pushed my way through the varied people. Shoved aside a blind beggar. Then I turned into an alley toward my home. And the pain shot through me as though I were being scalded by boiling oil.

Jillian...

He shifted uncomfortably in the hospital bed as though feeling that pain again, or the pain from his tenement injuries.

Then he whispered, "I found that I could circle . . . within a certain distance of my dwelling. But whenever I turned inward toward home the pain returned.

"I sought temporary refuge. In the shop of a leather-goods merchant whom I knew. His son carried word to my wife."

The priest asked softly, "What was her name?"

The man whispered, ". . . Livia."

Again I heard the Frenchman inhale as though the name had some special meaning to him. I looked back at him. "What? Do you know that name?"

But before he could reply, the ailing man whispered haltingly, "Livia came quickly, embracing me with concern . . . bringing her warmth, her confidence . . . and our seven-year-old son, Amelius."

I glanced back to see if Amelius was also a name the priest knew, but he was keeping a poker face now.

"They brought balms," murmured the man, "herbs . . . Livia medicated me . . . soothed me . . ."

His words brought me a flash from my own memory: my mother in bed at home, smiling weakly up as I sponged her brow, measured her medicine.

Then the man's voice drew me back in. "Livia was as gentle and patient . . . as she had always been. After a time . . . she encouraged me to try again . . . for home."

Will...

Livia's slender hand took my own. Held it tightly. Despite being a delicate woman, her strength of purpose supported me. Her eyes sought out mine. Her eyes were beautiful, fawn colored . . . She spoke encouragingly. Young Amelius took my left hand. We stepped from the shop together. But the moment we turned down a street that led toward our house . . . I felt the whiplash pain. I could not possibly continue.

Livia took me instead to a nearby inn. Her smooth face was grim with concern. I sat in the whitewashed room. Staring at the quivering flame from an oil lamp. Amelius went for food, and Livia brought a physician. He examined me . . . could find no reason for my condition.

The next morning we started again for home. The searing pain returned instantly, but then instantly stopped when we turned away from the direction of our home. So it went for two more days. Livia brought more physicians, soothsayers, mystics . . . We sacrificed a lamb to Mercury, our household god. All useless. Nothing changed the strange symptom.

Then at dawn on the fourth day I was startled awake by a different pain: a sudden stinging agony in the back of my skull. Livia helped me stagger out into the same streets that had given me relief previously. But now the pain continued. So we walked . . . farther away from our house. When we reached a very distant square, about twice the distance from our house, the pain abruptly stopped.

I sagged against a low wall in the smoky Judean square, breathing deeply in relief. I looked around, blinking heavily. The world around me was going on as it always had: the passing throng of mixed people, Romans, Jews, Arabs, Africans, slaves; the camels; the donkey carts; the haughty chariots.

I began to fathom that I could remain in the same place for only three days. After that time I had to travel at least *three thousand feet farther on*, apparently never to return to the same place.

Father St. Jacques...

The patient paused in his whispered story, swallowing hard. I yearned to be alone in the hospital room with him. I wanted the conniving woman gone.

I knew that she had seen my face go as pale as my eyes regarding some of the patient's details, and it was only with the utmost difficulty that I was maintaining my composure. But I was determined to do so in order to best fulfill my mission, Father. I had already called to alert the archdiocese about the quickening condition of their quarry and how the NYPD should now be alerted that the tight security I had requested would soon be needed. I kept my focus on the patient and quietly asked, "Why? Why three days, three thousand feet?"

The man squirmed slightly in his bed, as though desirous of avoiding the answer. "I didn't know," he murmured. "But then came injury . . ." His face twisted as he related the scene. "We were crossing another square. Suddenly . . . a Roman chariot . . . drawn by two stallions and driven by a laughing centurion . . . raced from a side street. People, chickens, and geese scattered before it. It was instantly upon us.

"I pushed Livia and Amelius out of its path. But I was plowed to the ground. Trampled by the hooves of the powerful warhorses. Run over by the heavy wooden wheels of the chariot. Through flashes of darkness and stars I felt my bones breaking. Saw my blood splattering. I had never known such agony."

As he lay in the hospital bed, he was flinching with pain. Whether from the memory or from his real and severe injuries at the tenement fire, I couldn't tell.

Will...

Livia cried out and ran to me. The world was vague and milky around me. She had others carry me into the shop of a rug merchant. He protested until I heard her shouting my rank . . . and whose important house I served. With vision in only one eye, I saw my arm with its skin shredded, filthy with grit and blood; my foot smashed and pulpy; a sickly white bone . . . protruding through pink flesh above my knee.

Livia cradled my battered head. Barely conscious, I heard her praying for Mercury to take me . . . to let me die, praying for my hopelessly shattered body to release my soul from its mortal torment.

But soothing death did not come. Only darkness. And nightmarish suffering . . . I had blurred glimpses of oil lamps, Amelius pouring warm oil onto my mangled hand, Livia's face always close by as she attended my excruciation. How I loved her, longed to tell her so, but my broken jaw would not work even if my swimming head had been able to focus on the effort. I slipped in and out of darkness.

The first light of dawn struck my usable eye. The burning pain from my injuries had prodded me awake. I discerned Livia sleeping nearby, her silky brown hair curving across her sweet face. I reached out my hand to touch her and realized that I was *able* to reach it out. Looking closer, I saw that my hand was *healing*. As though it had been healing for a fortnight or more. I flexed it and gasped from the pain. But I was amazed . . . that it was so remarkably improved from just the previous night.

I realized that overnight some miracle had been visited upon me. My wounds . . . even broken bones . . . were apparently mending . . . with impossible swiftness.

Livia had been awakened by my gasp. She instantly saw the amazing difference also. She stared at me with awe, with joy. But also with a nameless fear. What dark magic was causing this?

My healing progressed with a speed unheard of: eerie. In three days' time I was still weak and extremely sore, but my abraded skin . . . my lacerations . . . even my broken bones were . . . *completely healed*!

TWENTY-NINE

Jillian...

I stared, unblinking, at the man in the bed. I glanced at the priest and noticed that, oddly, he didn't seem surprised.

"I could not conceive," the injured man continued to whisper with his eyes still closed in delirium, "how such an . . . impossibility could be. It was . . . beyond imagining. But Livia and Amelius . . . helped me walk from the shop."

Will...

People in the square . . . who had witnessed my accident three days earlier were astonished. I saw their stunned faces . . . how they struggled to comprehend what must be magic from the Olympian gods. Some greatly feared it was the work of the darker, dangerous gods and pointed or shouted catcalls. But others stood watching me in silent wonder . . . I walked slowly through the square, aided by my gentle wife and young son.

Among the people I noticed again the sleek young man with dark hair and eyebrows. Something in his curiously bright black eyes struck me as unsettling. But I had no time to reflect upon it. I was grateful merely to be living. Even though . . . I still had to move farther on every three days.

Livia took me to the library in Jerusalem. We met more physicians and scholars, even some learned Jews, but none could say, nor even imagine, what strange malady afflicted me. None could conceive why I had to journey ever farther from my home.

For several months Livia and Amelius accompanied me, but she had gotten with child shortly before my mishap and was approaching her time . . . I knew that my circumstance was ill suited for the birth and her proper nurturing of an infant. She could not continue traveling with me . . . We stood together that final day on the mountain road overlooking distant Jerusalem. It was heartrending for all three of us. With great sorrow I handed the donkey's rope to my seven-year-old Amelius, hugging him close and encouraging him to be a man for his mother.

Then I turned to my gentle Livia. She had a bravely resolute smile on her face, but her lower lip trembled as she fought back tears . . .

Jillian...

The comatose patient's face became clouded by sadness as I watched, then he continued hoarsely. "We embraced tightly, and her tears spilled out. Livia pressed her damp cheek against mine as we clung desperately to one another. I took a deep breath, trying to be strong for all three of us. I looked into my dear wife's soft eyes one last time . . . then nodded for Amelius to guide the donkey cart away. It rattled down the dusty road toward the ancient city as I watched with an aching heart."

He breathed quietly for a moment before continuing to whisper, "Little Julia was five months old before they were able to journey to me . . . I saw them less and less as years passed, as the distance between us enlarged. It was increasingly difficult for another reason as well: I saw my children in the flower of their youth—Amelius at twelve years, then fifteen, holding his sister's hand as Julia also grew older. Gray strands began to intermingle with Livia's silky brown hair. The three of them were growing older . . . yet

I remained unchanged. It was agonizing. Seeing my own reflection was like a slap in the face."

The patient's eyes, though still closed, twitched as a frown wrinkled the bridge of his nose.

Will...

Plotting my necessary travel was difficult . . . Maps were primitive and unreliable until very much later in 1568 when I encountered the Flemish cartographer Gerardus Mercator. He was a maker of globes living in the German Duchy of Cleves . . . I asked if he could create for me flat maps with parallel latitudes and longitudes. "So you can carry the world with you," Gerardus mused.

"Yes," I urged with sad humor, "like the Greek Titan Atlas." Mercator proceeded apace . . . over the years I forewarned him of my proposed route, and he forwarded to me each new section of what he had decided to call an *atlas*. I was then able to create a grid . . . so that I could crisscross the land without ever passing the same places and encountering the pain.

But in the beginning years of my forced odyssey, I could give Livia and my children only a vague idea of my route of travel . . . and where I hoped to be for any three-day period.

In anno Domini 66, Julia and Amelius sent me word that their mother was failing. They were able to rendezvous with me in the city of Petra, the capital of Nabataea, which was carved into a sandstone valley between the Dead and Red Seas . . . It was an important trading city on the caravan route between southern Arabia and the eastern Mediterranean.

Arriving in Petra on the appointed day . . . I rushed in from the camel-tethering ground through the crowded, colonnaded main thoroughfare . . . I passed the classical facades that reflected Petra's links to Rome and the Hellenistic world. We had agreed to meet at the nymphaeum. That public drinking fountain was at the east end of the small city.

Searching through the Bedouins, merchants, and hawkers on the dusty street, I finally saw my children. My heart sank . . . It had been several years since our last reunion. Julia and Amelius had reached late middle age. They looked old enough to be my parents.

Then I saw my dear Livia lying in the donkey cart that had transported her. She had slipped beyond delicate into aged frailty.

Hot tears flooded my eyes . . . My cursed situation was so against the natural order of life that it's impossible for a normal human being to truly grasp my heart's sickness. How could a mortal person . . . aging normally day by day . . . even begin to imagine the overwhelming grief and nausea I felt . . . Seeing my beloved family marching resolutely toward their final end while I stood by, unchanging and young, observing them. No one could conceive of the overwhelming misery that was twisting my innards into knots. That inconsolable desolation was blistering. It was shredding my soul.

Amelius and Julia saw me and stepped to embrace me. We hung much upon each other. Then I moved past them to Livia, who was extending her hand weakly toward me. The smooth skin of her youth had become wrinkled parchment. Her hair was pure white. Her face had shriveled away, her features grown smaller . . . As I gathered her into my arms I felt her thinness, the bones of her shoulder blades, her fragility . . . her age. She had seen nearly seventy summers, and winter was now fully upon her.

I guided the donkey cart bearing weak Livia through the busy marketplace. It was made fragrant by the aromatic gums of myrrh and frankincense . . . the much sought-after products of Nabataea. They were used for religious ceremonies, cosmetics, medicine, and also, I recalled with a pained and lowering heart, for embalming.

I quickly arranged a room at an inn near the marketplace. We placed Livia in the bed, and I knelt beside her as darkness slowly fell and Amelius, now fifty-six years old, lighted the oil lamps . . . Livia had been sustaining herself by the desire to see me one last time, and now that we were together, the slender flame within her was flickering unsteadily . . . Her small hand, veined and spotted with age, sought my own.

Jillian...

The patient's head turned restlessly against the hospital pillow as he groaned mournfully. The priest leaned closer beside me as the man's eyes clenched into a tight frown. "Livia grew weaker . . . I was heartsick that I hadn't been there . . . when she needed me most . . . That I had failed her . . . failed in my responsibility."

Those last four words stung me, as they always did when I heard anyone speak them. They brought back the guilt of how I had failed my mother.

"Then," the man continued, his voice choked, "with a sad smile . . . that seemed to call up all the days and nights of love, joy, and sorrow we had shared . . . with a gesture of . . . infinite grace . . . her hand stroked my hair . . . then drifted down to rest . . . as her dear soul departed."

The injured man paused. I saw a tear collecting in the corner of his still-closed left eye. Then he continued, "I felt as though something inside of me had torn irreparably . . . as though my heart was ripping from my body . . . My son and daughter tried to comfort me. But their aged faces only made me more frantic. I couldn't bear the knowledge that I would have to watch them follow Livia . . . I knew what I must do instead."

Will...

But before I could act upon it, I had to secure a proper burial for my beloved wife. We embalmed her and carried her beyond the southern wall of Petra, along the Wadi Farasa and into its steep valley . . . Through the classical facade carved into the living sandstone, we entered the Roman Soldier's Tomb. As my wife, Livia was entitled to receive interment there. She had embraced the growing cult of Christianity . . . had worn around her neck a tiny hand-carved cross and a small locket, which she wanted me to keep . . . We placed a small silver cross lovingly upon her breast as we laid her to her final rest.

Then with the fewest words possible . . . because I didn't trust my barely bridled emotions . . . I bade Julia and Amelius farewell. I watched my two children . . . who were two decades older than I . . . walk away. I knew that I would never see them again . . . At this sorrow my heart was utterly darkened. Not until they disappeared in the shimmering heat waves did I turn and hurry deeper into the rugged mountains of Esh Shara. I sought out the highest cliff I could find and hurled myself off toward the jagged rocks far below.

Father St. Jacques...

The patient's head lolled from one side to the other on the pillow as the reporter and I hung upon his words. "The fall . . . seemed to take forever . . . ," he said dreamily, "the wind whipping as I howled in anger . . ."

The patient's entire body suddenly convulsed with a single violent quake, shaking the heavy hospital bed, startling the reporter and myself. The surprising shock caused my always-fragile stomach to knot with a cramp.

"The impact brought oblivion," he whispered. "Peace . . . finally peace."

I watched motionlessly as he lay silent and still for a moment, and then he said, "But the darkness was not complete . . . Though my astounded senses had fled, yet did the spark of life remain. Soon I began to feel excruciating pain as though a thousand daggers were repeatedly slashing me." He squirmed and groaned in the hospital bed, as though suffering such pain again.

Will...

My broken body . . . was immobile, but alive. Then came the carrion crows and vultures tearing at my flesh with stinging beaks. Two scorching desert days and freezing nights I suffered their onslaught like Prometheus chained upon his rock . . . What continual, throbbing torments I lived to feel . . . moment by moment.

By the third day I was able to crawl into a small cave. In an unsuccessful attempt to quench my thirst, I licked the bitter alkaline water from the stone walls. The next dawn brought the other form of pain. Like needles in the back of my skull. The signal that forced me to move onward.

I stumbled out into the Arabian Desert, humbled myself again to Mercury. I hoped that our household god might pity me or at least reveal how I had offended him or one of the other Olympians, and by what means I could make amends. I lay prostrate on the blistering sands. I poured out my soul upon the dust. But there was only . . . silence . . .

Jillian...

He stopped speaking. The room was hushed except for the low breathy hum of the ICU monitoring equipment. I was afraid he'd lapsed back into a coma. I leaned closer with my recorder. The priest hovered just behind as I asked, "After the Arabian Desert, what happened then? Can you tell me?" The man moaned and tried feebly to turn away from my question, not wanting to speak. "Please . . . go on," I urged.

An acidic look flickered across his semiconscious face. "I did," he mumbled bitterly. "I went on. And on . . . Days became years . . . decades . . . centuries . . . Crisscrossing Persia, Mesopotamia . . . Byzantium . . . Konstantinoupolis . . ." An odd smile flickered across his unconscious face. ". . . I once saw him there."

"Saw who?" I asked, holding the recorder closer.

"Constantine . . . the year he established the city."

"Constantinople?" I glanced at the priest and asked, "When would that have been?"

The priest replied quietly, "In 330 AD." His eyes were fixed on the strange man.

My attention was drawn back to the mysterious patient as he murmured, "That year I also . . . sensed a change."

"What sort of change?" I asked softly.

"I accidentally traveled back . . . in the direction of Judea . . . and the pain did not rise to prevent me . . . I took heart and continued without pain, reaching Jerusalem in anno Domini 333 . . . His mother was there . . ."

"Helena?" asked the priest.

The man nodded slightly. "Yes. Constantine . . . had sent her."

"To build the church." The priest nodded. He saw my questioning glance and whispered waspishly, "The Church. Of the Holy Sepulchre. Over the site of the Crucifixion."

The patient drew a breath, and again I saw the odd smile cross his face. "The wrong place . . . ," he said. "Not truly Golgotha . . . They built the church at . . . the wrong place."

I asked how he knew that.

"Because . . . I had seen it originally," he muttered.

I saw the priest's jaw go slack. His stunned voice was barely audible. "You were present at the Crucifixion?"

The man in the bed nodded. "By that journey I realized that . . . after 333 years . . . I apparently could return to somewhere . . . that I had been before."

"Could you stay longer than three days then?" I asked.

"No. Three days only . . . I sought the graves . . . of Amelius and Julia . . . but they had long been lost . . . to the dust of the ages . . . And I had to move on."

I saw that the Frenchman was still staring, his face again as pale as his ghostly eyes. He leaned in the closest he had yet come as he repeated, "You saw the Crucifixion?"

Again the man nodded once as his face shadowed and speech grew harder for him. I couldn't tell whether the difficulty arose from his reticence, or the coma overtaking him again, or the pain of his injuries from the tenement fire, or all of it combined. He managed to whisper, ". . . That was the day of my offense, my crime . . ."

The priest's voice became an insistent hiss, like a prosecuting attorney pressing an accused criminal. "What crime? What offense did you commit?"

But the man could not, or would not, answer.

His breathing became slower, more regular. Delirium was drawing him back into its cloudy realm. Despite my urging him to speak, he had lapsed back into unconsciousness.

I stood up very slowly from his bedside; my heart was beating a mile a minute. The French priest seemed to be doing his utmost to act unconcerned and dismissive as he walked casually out of the room. But I saw through his forced demeanor.

I went down the corridor, called Steve, and asked him to hang out late at the paper because I was really onto something unheard of and barely imaginable.

Then I dialed Hanna Claire.

THIRTY

Hanna...

It was around midnight, but there was no way I could go to sleep. I was still fully dressed, Reeboks and all, wandering restlessly around my town house, looking out at the nighttime lights reflecting off the East River. The troubled waters of Hell Gate presented a perfect parallel to my emotions.

I'd taken a frozen lasagna, my favored comfort food, from my freezer, then discovered I had already put an identical one into the microwave. That made me angry and unnerved: the dark menace of Alzheimer's creeping closer. I'd always had a mind like a steel trap; I had never been absentminded in my life, and I tried to rationalize that it was happening now because of finding Will. *Just look how I'm behaving, for God's sake,* I said to myself, though I knew better. I shoved the second lasagna back into the damn freezer. Eighty-five or not, I felt as edgy as a nervous schoolgirl waiting on tenterhooks to get a call from some boy I had a crush on.

My God, how stunning it was: seeing Will in that bed, lying right there in front of me after all the years . . . the decades . . . I was shaking my head in disbelief and muttered aloud to my cat, "My brain may be addled, but seeing Will sure got my old ticker juiced up and pumping away, didn't it, Methuselah?"

The phone rang and I nearly jumped out of my skin. I tried to control the peaking emotion as I answered and heard a woman's voice. "Miss Claire?"

"That's right."

"This is Jillian Guthrie."

I sagged. I'd hoped it was someone from the hospital staff. Her voice continued, "I met you today at the hospital and—"

"Miss Guthrie," I interrupted politely but firmly, "I told you that I can't—"

"He spoke to me."

I paused. Took a long breath. I knew the reputation of her tabloid: vastly popular but among the trashiest of the trashy. I was therefore determined to proceed very cautiously. "Has he come out of the coma, then?"

"No. He's still not really conscious. But he said . . ."

"What?" I asked, trying to remain calm.

"Some truly amazing things."

"To the nurses, the doctor, or—"

"To me."

Again I paused, considering the best approach. "What exactly did he say, Miss Guthrie?"

"He talked about living in Judea. Two thousand years ago."

A swoop of emotion hit my stomach. I could hear the reporter was waiting to see what impact her statement had. I remained as composed as I could and affected a slightly condescending tone: "How is that possible?"

"I have no idea, Miss Claire. He said he was a Roman. That there was some kind of curse placed on him—"

Another gut swoop, like when flying in an airplane that drops suddenly. I struggled to stay low-key. I tried to sound incredulous. "A curse? Placed on him by whom?"

"He drifted back off before he could say."

"Well." My heart was threatening to pound its way out of my chest, but I weighed my words carefully. "It all sounds a bit ridiculous, doesn't it?"

"It would, yes. Except that I have photographs of him, Miss Claire. With Gandhi in the 1940s, with Teddy Roosevelt around 1912, with General Grant during the Civil War—"

I frowned, my worry increasing. "Well, couldn't they easily be fakes or—"

"No, I found them in different archives. And in all of them he looks the same age."

I paused, sorting through my options. My primary concern was for Will.

"Miss Claire?"

I drew a shallow breath. "Yes, I'm still here."

"He also talked about a wife and son."

That caused me to put a hand on my kitchen counter to steady myself. "Did he say their names?"

"Livia. And Amelius."

That put me into free fall. I could barely control my breathing and didn't trust my voice.

"Listen, Miss Claire," the young woman continued, "I know how you feel about the rag I work for. I feel the same way, believe me."

"And yet you do work for them."

"I'm in the process of trying to change that. I recognize that whatever else this man's story is, it is extraordinary. I have every good intention of—"

"Miss Guthrie. I'm sure you know how the road to Hell is paved with those." There was a pause on the other end.

"Miss Claire, I . . . I . . . ," she said, and then went silent.

Jillian...

Standing in the hospital hallway, I looked around, racking my brain for a way to make Hanna Claire believe me. The words suddenly came out on their own before I even realized. "Miss Claire, I've never said anything like this in my life . . ." My mouth had gone dry; I spoke with measured precision. "But I swear to you on the soul of my late mother, who died in this same hospital, that I will treat this story with the utmost respect; that I will not share it with anyone you or he don't wish me to, and definitely never with the paper I've been working for."

Hanna...

I'd been listening carefully and recognized that the young woman's tone seemed to have undergone a profound change. It didn't feel like shrewd playacting. Her voice was lower, and I heard in it a new, unhurried, and earnest sincerity.

I stood there in my kitchen, breathing slowly, weighing it all as the girl continued softly, "Whatever you decide, it is clear to me that you have an important . . . a heartfelt . . . connection to this man. When I saw that he might be regaining consciousness I knew you'd want to know."

My eyes wandered across my eclectic home and the furnishings I'd gathered over a lifetime. Then they turned inward toward the memories of my equally eclectic life, which had been missing the key element, the most dearly beloved person, for sixty years. Finally, I drew a breath and said, "Thank you, Jillian. I'll come as quickly as I can."

I heard her sigh with relief. "Good. And Miss Claire," she spoke more confidentially, closer to the phone, "the French priest that you saw here . . ."

My answer came swift and firm. "Don't trust him."

Will...

Out of the depths of my increasingly stinging and turbulent darkness I again heard the woman's distant, incorporeal voice whispering, "You said you had to move on."

Jillian...

I had returned to the bedside, eager to learn more of his seemingly incredible story. "Can you hear me? Where did you move on to?" I asked him softly. The priest was behind me, sitting straighter than before. He had been jotting some notes previously, but now I saw that he was merely listening raptly. The patient's lips moved silently, and I coaxed him. "Yes, that's right. Tell me where you went after returning to Jerusalem."

"Northerly, first . . . into Jordan," he finally murmured. "Being again in Jerusalem . . . seemed to open a door for me . . . I had long since realized what my crime had been . . . but now . . ."

The priest inclined his head, focusing sharply as the patient mumbled barely intelligibly, "Now I earnestly endeavored to redeem myself . . . I cast my lot among the humble religious . . . wearing Benedictine robes from a young monk who had deserted the order . . . I spent centuries living as a penitent, traveling from one monastery to the next . . . helping with their labors . . . searching through the wealth of knowledge contained in the abbeys' secret libraries. I sought answers . . . To no avail."

I saw his face grow flaccid, as though he might be losing consciousness again. I tried to inspire his energy, to encourage him. "Please, go on. What did you do then?"

That caused him to draw a sharper breath. "I resolved to try more active measures . . . searched for the Grail . . . fought in the Crusades . . . amid the rain, blood . . . horrible carnage . . ." His face twisted, his teeth clenched, the muscles in his jaw working. "I received mortal wounds . . . Suffered the agonies of death . . . but remained alive . . . And he was often nearby . . ."

"Who was?"

"The sleek young man," he murmured. "I saw him through the flailing bloodied arms, the bellowing knights in battered armor, the Arabic robes of Saladin's army soaked crimson, their scimitars and our broadswords covered with shreds of flesh and sinew . . . Amid the bestial nightmare . . . the young man with the sleek, dark visage stood at a distance, calmly watching me.

"He seemed to be completely dry in spite of the pouring rain . . . Unfazed by the earsplitting cacophony of combat. He stood unruffled amid the splayed entrails of the fallen, wailing horses; the disemboweled warriors quivering through their death throes in the muddy, bloody filth . . . The young man watched me with patient, knowing eyes."

I asked, "Was he like you? Fated to live on and on?"

"So it seemed . . . I saw him a century later . . . In the shadows that night on the Île de la Cité outside the cathedral . . . Sainte-Chapelle de Paris . . . which I was silently breaking into. I ignored him that night, as I always tried to, while I sought the precious relic I knew to be housed within the holy chapel."

Father St. Jacques...

I knew only too well what extraordinary relic he was speaking of. Had he actually seen it? I leaned slightly closer as the patient continued whispering. "I made my way stealthily down to the crypt where, in my guise as a monk, I'd learned that the relic was secretly being kept while the grand upper sanctuary was still being completed. I used numerous tools for thievery . . . with which I had grown skillful. I unlocked the many caskets and cabinets nested one within another. At length I reached the smallest innermost chest, which was richly encrusted with pure gold. I knew it contained the sacred relic that the entire cathedral above was being built to house, honor, and protect. It was one of the most holy and treasured artifacts in Christendom . . . which I fervently hoped might undo the curse that had been placed upon me. My hands trembled as I turned the final key. I opened the golden box and beheld the Crown of Thorns."

The reporter drew a sharp breath, but I mastered my emotions and remained stoic, intent upon the man.

"A wave of disappointment swept over me," the patient continued, his head lolling. "Because I instantly knew that it was a fraud. Not the original. My most extreme efforts had again come to naught. I fled angrily, rushing up and out of the chapel barely ahead of my pursuers, the priests and King Louis's royal guards."

Will...

I railed furiously against my fate. I tried again to kill myself . . . fool that I was. I fashioned suicides at least three other times at seasons of horrific depression . . . But hanging ropes always broke, and flames would sear my flesh, but they would not consume me.

At another time of extreme desperation in West Surrey, England, about 1540, I constructed a simple device for effective suicide. A weighted blade would drop down a vertical track onto the neck of a victim to cleanly sever the head. But when I tried to use it upon my own neck, the device repeatedly and mysteriously jammed. An unseen force held it maddeningly aloft. I was enraged. But I had to abandon it and move on. The lord of a local manor apparently found my discarded device, dubbed it the Halifax Gibbet, and employed it as a means of execution. It eventually became the iconic instrument of death in France.

In 1936, I flung myself beneath a Moscow metro train in the Smolenskaya station. My broken and shredded body was taken to the central morgue because, though I was still breathing, they assumed I would immediately die . . . But no. I lay there in the dark, suffering the tortures of the damned for three days and nights.

All my suicidal efforts were fruitless. All my prayers went unanswered. There was only ever silence . . . silence . . .

Jillian...

His voice faded to an inaudible whisper.

Then from over my shoulder, the priest quietly asked, "How did you know it was not the original Crown of Thorns?"

The patient twisted his face away, his teeth clenching again, not wanting to speak. But the Frenchman tried a different tack, urging him insistently, "You said you had realized what your crime had been . . ."

I saw the man's face, reddened by the burns he'd sustained in the tenement fire, grow redder still. His frown screwed even tighter, his eyes remained squinted closed throughout. He was trying not to speak of it, but the Pentothal was at work. I coaxed him gently. "It's difficult for you, I know. But what was the crime? How did your ordeal begin?"

"I was . . . I was . . . captain of . . . the governor's . . . household guard."

"In Judea?" The priest became intensely alert. "The governor there?"

The man's breathing grew more tense; I was certain he was fighting not to speak, but when the priest pressed again, the man finally answered, "Yes . . . I was of the governor's house."

The cleric prompted further. "The governor's name was . . . ?"

The words came as though being pried painfully from the patient: "Pontius . . . Pilate."

The air seemed to rush out of the room around me. A chill swept up my spine.

The priest was riveted upon him now, whispering, "Did you see . . . *the Christ?*"

I watched the patient's face suddenly relax strangely. "I saw a man," he said softly, "who'd been condemned."

He paused for a long moment, his eyes still closed. "They were shouting at him . . . That derisive mob . . . every ethnicity in Jerusalem had lined the streets to enjoy this latest parade of death. They were frequent. Not unusual. But they always created onlookers."

"Including yourself that day," I prompted.

"Yes . . . wearing my household sandals and Roman tunic . . . I had been drawn by the raucous noise to the doorway of my small stucco house adjoining the governor's estate. I looked out on the narrow street. I saw the condemned man approaching. His naked back and shoulders were exposed . . . bleeding from his floggings. The sardonic crown made of thorns that someone had brutally shoved onto his head, piercing his skin, was drawing more rivulets of blood. Children danced playfully around him, teasing him in his suffering and grief as they had done so many others . . . His scraped, beleaguered shoulder was leaning into the notch of the heavy T-shaped cross."

"Did you hear his name?" the priest asked tensely, as his hand closed over the small cross he wore around his neck.

"Someone in the throng . . . called out his name with a sneer . . . Jesu ben Josef."

I saw the priest swallow nervously, then he asked in a slow and measured way, "What . . . did he look like?"

The patient sighed. "Just another foolish Nazarene . . . being led to his death."

"Can you describe him?" I urged.

"He was just a Jew, like many another," the patient said, frowning, squinting his eyes more tightly closed. "Long dark hair. Very curly. Thin dark beard . . . His eyes were lighter, though, a hazel hue."

I heard the priest whisper with sudden reverence, "You looked into his *eyes*?"

The barely conscious man nodded slightly. "Yes . . . When he paused to catch his breath . . . before my front door." The patient's own breathing stopped. Without the steady pulse of the ICU heart monitor, I would have thought he'd died. Finally he took a shallow breath and said, ". . . When I made my mortal error."

I was barely breathing as I whispered, "Tell me."

Will...

The condemned man . . . was exhausted from the outrages they had already visited upon his body . . . He was matted with sweat, smelling foul. He had sunk to one scraped knee on my very doorstep . . . Livia had come to stand behind me. She seemed shocked to see who the man was . . . as though she had encountered him before. Livia was ever compassionate, but she seemed particularly sympathetic to this condemned man's suffering. She clutched her slender hands together over her breast, which I saw was heaving tensely and rapidly as it always did when she was about to cry.

Her emotional display and the presence of the condemned Jew were all far too much for my taste . . . Particularly when I noted that two of the Roman guards leading the Hebrew were centurions whom I knew. They looked at me with censorious frowns.

I was embarrassed and annoyed that their filthy, bloodied prisoner had stopped on my doorstep. With one hand I motioned Livia back . . . and with my other hand . . .

Jillian...

His face began quivering; his voice became barely audible. I prompted, "Yes . . . what about your other hand?"

His breathing slowed, agonized. When his words finally came out, they were like a death rattle. "With my other hand . . . *I struck him.*"

I stared at the patient, remembering. "Bottadeo," I murmured. "Who strikes God." The words caught in my throat; icicles formed in my veins as I looked at the priest. But he remained motionless, also staring at the man in the bed.

"I shoved him . . . harshly . . . away," the patient said bitterly, "bade him keep on walking." The man's voice had become a coarse whisper. "I shouted angrily at him . . . 'Go! Go!' He struggled up onto his unsteady

279

feet . . . began shuffling slowly on . . . bearing the burden of his heavy cross."

As he lay there on the bed, I saw the injured man's face grow tense and solemn. "But then he looked back at me and . . . I was amazed. Amazed to see that on his face . . . was the most gentle smile . . . Then he spoke quietly to me . . . in Aramaic. His gaze held mine . . . until a centurion whipped him to move along."

"What did he say?" I whispered.

The patient writhed uncomfortably, greatly disturbed and reluctant to speak. The priest leaned right down beside me; his eyes seemed to be drilling into the semiconscious man as he echoed my question insistently. "What did he say to you?"

The man's words came with much difficulty, almost inaudibly, as though extracted one at a time from the depths of his very resistant soul. "He said to me, 'I go. But thou shalt here remain . . . thou diest not . . . but walk . . . until I come again.'"

The room was soundless except for the critical-care monitors. I was trying to process exactly what that phrase meant. The priest leaned back a fraction; he seemed to know exactly.

"Livia . . . brushed past me," the patient finally whispered, "joining the crowd . . . she followed behind the prisoner . . . as he labored up the street. I stood in my doorway . . . watching the procession. Without realizing it . . . without realizing in that moment I had been transformed . . ."

"Transformed?" I asked. "What do you mean? How were you—"

"Transformed," he whispered bitterly, ". . . into the stuff of legend. Later to be called . . . by many names: *le Juif errant, das Valkaner Juden, el Judío errante, der Wandernde Jude* . . ."

I inhaled sharply. "The . . . Wandering Jew?"

The man was silent. I stared at him, trying to puzzle it out while the priest scrutinized the man clinically. "But . . . I don't understand," I said confoundedly. "You *weren't* a Jew. You were a Roman . . . ?"

"Yes . . . Amusing irony." The flicker of a sardonic smile crossed his near-comatose face. "A lasting testament to anti-Semitism." He drew in a long breath of resignation. "But call me what they will, the truth remains . . . I am *the Man Who Cannot Die* . . ."

". . . Until the Christ returns." The priest nodded softly.

The man's eyebrows knit again as he apparently stated it more correctly: "Until God sends another such . . . yes." He seemed grieved by the memory, nodding weakly in his delirium. "I tried to make amends. To follow the sterling example of Jesu ben Josef . . . to not stand idly by if I saw evil . . . When anno Domini 1001 came . . . so many of us thought that he'd appear, that God's word would somehow be made manifest again . . . But that harsh year merely became the next and on and on . . . a thousand more . . ."

The priest surmised, "You hoped this milestone of the *second* thousand years might finally be the time of that return?"

I saw the patient's nostrils flare as his voice grew acidic, thinner still. "I'm a prize fool. There is no point in faith." He exhaled a rattling breath, as though giving in to some inevitable truth. "He may be right: my trial, my wandering will be without end."

"He who?" I frowned. "Who may be right?"

"The other one," he whispered. "The sleek one . . ."

The priest seemed to understand. "You think he is . . . ?"

"The Lord of the Flies . . . The Master of the Imps . . . Asmodeus, Set . . . or what you will. He has even more names than I . . ." The man's expression grew languished; his head turned slightly away from us. ". . . I am . . . so weary . . . so very . . ."

He lapsed into unconsciousness. We sat and stared at him for nearly a full minute.

I was the first to speak, barely able to find words. "This . . . is the most . . . astonishing—"

"Delusion," the priest said, chuckling. Then he blew out a dismissive huff. "*Mon dieu*, never I have heard such nonsense." He stood up, shaking his head. "This man could have *une grande carrière*, and perhaps he does, as a writer of the most outrageous fiction."

"You don't believe it's possible?" I asked.

The Frenchman was stretching his arms casually and paused in the midst to smirk at me as though I were a complete idiot. "Oh please, *ma chère*," he said with a mocking smile and in such a condescending, patronizingly French manner that I wanted to slap him. He glanced at his notes and seemed unsure of whether to even bother keeping them or to simply toss them in the trash. He finally shrugged and pocketed them, sourly. "Fascinating case study, though, I suppose."

I was so annoyed by his attitude that I opened my mouth to defend the cause of my belief: to tell him about the photographic evidence I had. But some instinct—or Hanna's warning about him—caused me to check myself. "Yeah." I simply nodded. "Yeah, you're probably right."

He gave me another look of confident superiority, like he might have given a three-year-old. Then he left the hospital room and strolled casually off down the corridor.

THIRTY-ONE

Father St. Jacques...

It was very rewarding, though not unexpected, to hear young Father Benedicto's astonished reaction to my news. Over my encrypted cell phone, I heard the younger man's espresso cup clatter as he gasped, _"Mater Dei!"_ I knew Benedicto was crossing himself as he continued in Italian, his voice highly pitched and astonished: "Are you serious, sir!?"

I was standing just outside Lenox Hill Hospital at three in the morning in the chill darkness. A streetlamp above me cast a circle of light down onto the damp Park Avenue sidewalk where I was pacing nervously. My stomach was turning over and over excitedly. I was barely able to contain my exuberance, but determined to maintain and present an august, dispassionate professionalism as I spoke into my secure phone. "Yes. It is definitely him," I said. "I have found him."

I sensed that my young colleague was also on his feet in our Vatican office as he asked, "How can you be absolutely certain, sir?"

"He knows all the details." I struggled to conceal my swirling feelings of glee. "He knows all of the history that only he could be privy to."

"But is it possible that he might have accessed your research? Read your notes?"

I was annoyed that my young apprentice was not simply accepting my authoritative word instantly. But then I realized it was because I had trained Benedicto thoroughly so that he might be of maximum service to our cause. The young priest was responding exactly as I had taught him, demanding cautious evaluation of all the possible angles and nuances, even vetting the report from me, his superior. "Very good thought, Benedicto," I said by way of congratulation, "but thanks to our security precautions he could not have gained access to my work. And even if he had, he knew specifics that we only just discovered."

"Those scrolls, Father?" I could hear Benedicto catching the excitement. "The ones from the new subway excavation in the north of Rome?"

"Exactly," I said, privately reveling in the additional news I had yet to impart.

"Then you've had an opportunity to translate them?"

"Of course. Among the contents are precisely what I thought: the records of Pontius Pilate's household guard."

"Mother of God!" Benedicto's voice was breathless now, hanging on my every word. "Tell me, Father!"

"The captain of Pilate's guard was named Vitellus Janus Manchus. His wife was Livia, son Amelius." I drew a breath of the cold New York air and spoke with profound satisfaction. "This man spoke of them. He is Manchus!"

"*Mater Dei,*" the young priest repeated, but this time in a most devout whisper. "What an accomplishment, Father Paul. After all these decades, these centuries. You've succeeded where all the others have failed. The Sacred Tribunal and the council will reward you grandly, sire. A bishopric, I'm certain!"

I frowned slightly, and my voice perhaps took on a somewhat sour tonality as I said, "Well, Benedicto, I suppose *something* along those lines would be appropriate."

"Do you have a photograph of him?"

"Yes, I'll e-mail it to you shortly."

"What action do you wish me to take here, Father?"

"Alert the tribunal, of course." I paused, feeling the new import of my rising position, which I was eager to exercise. "And instruct them that I wish His Holiness to be thoroughly informed at once. Let them know that I shall get the man into police custody and extradited to Rome immediately so that finally he will be firmly and permanently secured under our control."

"How will you arrange security?"

I smiled, pleased at my preparedness. "I've told the New York police a compelling story that Archbishop Malloy agreed to. They are on high alert. I'm about to call Malloy and advise him of the good news. I want you to phone me back as soon as you've spoken to the tribunal."

"Of course, Father. And again, my heartiest congratulations on accomplishing your mission. May God bless you."

"He already has, but thank you, Benedicto." I clicked the cell phone off and began to enter the special private number that I had insisted Cardinal Malloy supply.

But I paused for a moment to reflect on the reward that Benedicto had suggested should be forthcoming. In light of the extraordinary service I had dutifully and painstakingly rendered, I felt that Benedicto's suggestion definitely seemed inadequate.

I spoke it aloud, somewhat disdainfully I admit: "'Bishop,' you think, Benedicto? *Bishop?*" I glimpsed my reflection in the glass of the hospital entrance. I stood straighter, gazing directly into my own eyes, and said, "How about *cardinal?*"

And then, as I further considered the twenty-three arduous years I had selflessly devoted to my difficult mission on behalf of Our Lord God and our Holy Mother Church, as I considered the amazing, historic, incredibly illusive, and dangerous quarry I had succeeded in bringing to ground, the words slipped out before I realized.

"How about *pontiff?*"

What!? I was shocked! I had shocked myself by voicing, by even feeling, such unfettered ambition! Shame be upon me! I immediately confessed my sin. I hope thou canst forgive me, My Father.

Unless, of course, I should prove worthy enough in thy divine eyes, and such ascension for me should be thy Divine Will.

Jillian...

I could hear Steve yawning broadly as he tapped on his computer keyboard. "Are you sure, Jilly?" He asked as he drew a breath. I envisioned him stretching his eyes wide, trying to get them to open fully as he sat in the darkened newspaper office. "I thought *wandering jew* was a plant."

"It is. Doubtlessly named for him." I nodded as I paced in the ICU corridor, talking on my cell. "But what else have you got?"

"I'm digging." I heard his fingers tapping more keys as he said, "You know Carlos is here working the late shift. He told me he'd have been happy to run this stuff down for you."

I pictured the polite, middle-aged, olive-skinned Latino sitting quietly at his desk in our office, and I fidgeted. "He's just not my fave, okay, Steve? Will you just—"

"And let me guess," Steve interrupted, "you still won't be covering the Latin Grammys."

I was getting annoyed, but he was doing me a favor so I swallowed it and dodged the issue. "Just hurry, Steve."

"Oh, and that shy Douglas guy from accounting came by hoping to take you to dinner or something."

"That's nice." I wasn't really listening. My eyes had drifted back toward the patient's room. All of the amazing things he'd said were coursing through my head. One recollection had struck me particularly, how he'd been heartsick that he hadn't been there for his wife when she needed him most. The image had hit me hard.

Countless times I had envisioned my mother's bedroom that awful night. How Mom might have been gasping, wild-eyed, while having her heart attack. How she might have shouted out desperately, calling for my help. And I was only a few yards across the hall in my bedroom, but I was facing away and never realized.

With Pink Floyd blasting away in my headphones, I could never have heard any cries for help Mom might have made. It was *The Wall*, alright. I'd never been able to listen to it again.

"Jilly?"

I inhaled sharply. "Yeah." I was trying unsuccessfully to swallow the bitter memory. "Sorry, Steve. I'm here."

"Okay, here you go." I could hear him clicking his mouse to scroll through the information on his screen as he continued. "There's a few old pieces about him. In really old books. Couple of plays, too, from several hundred years back." He scrolled further, saying, "References in Chaucer and Cervantes . . . Mark Twain apparently wrote something on him . . . there's a poem by William Wordsworth . . . Oh. And look at that," Steve muttered with surprise, "also a couple of poems about him written by Percy Shelley."

I made a note to ask the man about it. "What about historical references?"

"Yeah. Some of that, too. Back to the 1200s . . . no, 700s! Jeez. And the guy has about a thousand aliases: Ahasuerus, Cartaphilus, Vottadio—"

"Wait, wait." I was trying to keep up, jotting the names quickly, very enthused. "Okay, keep going!"

Maria...

Something had woked me up. But I lay real still on the bed they'd made for me on some cardboard boxes.

It was real dark except for the red light that blinked outside the window. It made spooky shadows on the wall. I didn't like them. I promised myself when I grew up I'd get a job and always buy curtains.

I heard the noise again that had woked me. It was Carmella squealing kinda. She and Miggy were in the real nice room next to where I was. Then I heard them sorta breathing real hard and loud. Then it got quiet again. Till I heard the door creak and saw Miggy's shadow on the wall from the red light. He was coming over to my bed. I stayed real still, pretending I was asleep.

I felt my blanket lift up a little. Then I felt Miggy's fingers touch my leg. My heart was beating real lots.

"What are you *effing* doin', Mig?" I heard Carmella say in a kinda strange voice. It sounded like she was standing in the door, but I couldn't see. Then Carmella said, "Ain't you just shot your wad?"

Miggy pulled his hand quick off my leg and outta the blanket. "Just tuckin' her in, Carm."

"Oh, yeah?" Carmella said, laughing in her way that sounded kinda dirty. "I just *bet* that was what you was doin'." I smelled the cigarette Carmella was smoking. "Shoot, Mig, I know you like 'em young," she said, "but she can't give you what I can. Get your skinny ass back in here." I heard Carmella go back into the nice room. But Miggy kept standing near my bed. I heard him breathing. Then I saw his shadow go back, too.

After that it was quiet again, with just the red light blinking. I lay there listening to the quiet and wishing real hard that Momma was there. It hurt inside my eyes again, real bad. But I kept 'em wide open.

Jillian...

Shortly after three that morning I saw the elevator open and Hanna Claire step out. She was still wearing the same eclectic outfit as the day before. Her crystalline blue eyes sought mine and crinkled slightly at the corners with a faint smile. She came over to the waiting area where I was encamped. As I stood up, she gripped my hand firmly.

"Jillian." Hanna placed her other hand on top. There was an expression of immense gratitude on her wizened face.

I understood and nodded. "I just knew you should be here, Miss Claire."

"Hanna, please," she said without letting go of my hand. Then she asked, "How is he?"

She continued holding my hand as we walked toward his doorway. "He slipped completely unconscious again, but he's been restless."

Hanna exchanged a nod with my night-nurse friend Frances Norton and then looked into the darkened hospital room where the man lay amid all the monitoring equipment. "He revealed a considerable amount to you, Jillian."

"Yes. It's all so incredible really, that I—"

"Was that priest with the pale eyes with you?"

"Velcroed to my hip."

Hanna frowned and chewed the inside of her lower lip, just like I do when considering various options.

"How does the priest fit into this?" I asked. "I mean I have suspicions—"

"Which are probably very well-founded. Can you tell me more of what Will said?"

I blinked. "Will?"

Hanna smiled as she realized how she had just taken me into her confidence. She nodded, confirming: "Yes."

"At first he was just muttering some strange names for Satan, but then . . ." I paused as the elevator down the hall opened again, revealing a nurse with a patient on a gurney inside. Standing behind them was the priest.

"Ah," Hanna said. "Your new best friend."

"So you do know him?"

"Father Paul St. Jacques. Vatican envoy. Contacted me three days ago. I hoped he might lead me to Will, but the bugger turned the tables on me. And it means big trouble for Will."

St. Jacques had a very self-satisfied look on his face as he made his way out of the elevator past the nurse and her patient. "Down this way," I said to Hanna, guiding her away from the door of room 304 and along the corridor in the opposite direction. I certainly didn't want that priest invading our privacy.

Father St. Jacques...

I saw the two women walking away and knew the meddling reporter must have called in the Claire woman. *But it doesn't matter now, My Lord,* I thought proudly, *not a whit.* I had phoned Archbishop Malloy's aide-de-camp insisting that the cardinal be wakened and told of my great discovery, and that he alert the police.

I had set the wheels in motion. The machine that I controlled was mammoth, efficient, and extremely formidable. I was certain it would not be affected by a pair of females.

Jillian...

The ladies' restroom in the ICU was small, and its two stalls were empty. Even so, I spoke in hushed tones as I quickly related the essence of what I'd heard from the man Hanna called Will. She seemed familiar with a good deal of his amazing story, but occasionally she reacted as though hearing a new detail for the first time.

Because of what I had already learned, Hanna took a deep breath and opened up to me. She said she was touched by and sincerely believed my vow to honor her wishes and Will's. I truly was determined to do so and reaffirmed that to her. She also deeply appreciated me bringing her to Will's side at this critical moment.

Since she knew the story was now likely to get out one way or the other, Hanna wanted me to have an accurate and thorough understanding of Will's unique nature and particularly of his innate goodness and humanity before the Alzheimer's robbed her of the knowledge. In less than an hour, Hanna quickly told me and allowed me to record her entire history with Will right up through the recent days, including all the details of her own first encounter with Father St. Jacques.

It was clear to me that despite her age, snow-white hair, and apparent physical delicacy, Hanna Claire was still a potent force to be reckoned with: a tough old Yankee seasoned by hard New England winters and fiercely determined to do everything in her power to protect the man she dearly loved.

And that brought us back to my question about St. Jacques's involvement.

Hanna spoke matter-of-factly. "The church has been trying to capture and contain Will since they first became aware of him in the Dark Ages. They're desperate to bring him under their control."

I thought I understood. "Because he's living proof that Jesus was able to perform divine miracles."

"Well," Hanna said slowly, "that's one of their reasons."

Her slight hesitation prompted me to ask, "Will obviously believes that Jesus *could* perform miracles, right? I mean isn't Will the living proof?"

"Well, Will certainly knows that he was personally touched by the finger of God, whatever 'God' is, and that Jesu ben Josef was clearly the conduit, as Jesu may have been before in other cases if reports of his apparent miracles were actually true."

"The conduit?" I was trying to understand.

"Yes. But *not* necessarily, as Christian churches would have it, that Jesu was in fact *God incarnate*. Hey, you know who decided that concept and promoted it? A bunch of old men at the Council of Ephesus four hundred years after Jesu died." Hanna saw my surprise and puzzlement. She explained that from eyewitness accounts Will heard immediately after the Crucifixion, he knew that Jesu ben Josef had indeed been an extraordinarily good human being. Will even got it firsthand from his wife, Livia. Without Will's knowledge, Livia had heard Jesu speak, been captivated by him and his message. Livia had actually talked with him.

"Livia told Will that Jesu was very compelling," Hanna said. "But also thoroughly human: wonderfully personable, with a gracious sense of humor and an inviting laugh. Funny to think about, huh? Jesus laughing. But of course he must have."

That thought made me smile.

"Livia had secretly become his devout follower some months before the Crucifixion," Hanna continued. "When Livia was on her deathbed, she gave Will the little wooden cross and locket that he's worn ever since."

"Did Livia personally witness any of Jesu's works?"

"Other than Will? Perhaps once prior," Hanna continued, "at least enough to make her believe he at least had abilities as a healer or someone who could inspire healing. But more importantly she saw him as a spirited rebel who sought to improve the world by spreading the simple ideal of compassion and living by the Golden Rule. What a concept, huh?" Hanna chuckled. "'Treat folks the way you'd like to be treated.' Sure be nice if everyone actually did it for a change." I nodded wry agreement. "Livia saw that Jesu *was* doing it, *was* practicing what he preached. Even when it put him in danger."

"But Will doesn't think Jesu was divine?"

"Will absolutely believes," Hanna explained, "that certain people like Jesu may be conduits, messengers, vessels through whom passes some Higher Power, God, Force of Nature, whatever you want to call it, without those individuals actually being divine."

"Though obviously holy men?"

"And women. For sure. Holy in the sense of *greatly good*. And most worthy of emulating. Of course many followers believed such people to be divine. Livia thought it was a genuine possibility in Jesu's case, even though Judas Iscariot told Livia that Jesu had never, ever claimed divinity. And of course Jesu never wrote anything down. All of what he supposedly spoke was written by ardent, mostly overly ardent, disciples, often secondhand or thirdhand, and decades or even centuries after his death."

I knew Hanna was correct, that many of the writings that became "gospel truths" were not even written by the men they were attributed to.

"And many other gospels were suppressed," Hanna added. "Some that described Jesu not as some demigod, but more as a living, breathing human being. Like the gospel that Judas wrote."

I was stunned. "What?! Judas Iscariot? But he—"

"Apparently loved Jesu the most, but was made the scapegoat by those crafty old men at Ephesus. Hey, every religion needs its bad guys, right? It's a crying shame, because Will actually read Judas's original Greek firsthand account, which presented Jesu as being loving, truthful, spiritual, yes, yet as deeply and equally human as you or me.

"But when a bunch of zealous people get together, particularly if there's power or money to be gained, that's how legends or religions grow, huh? Like the Virgin Birth." Hanna shook her head, amused. "Hey, that was nothing new. All mythologies tell stories of gods siring human offspring. And two thousand years ago the idea of gods having sex with human women was very familiar."

I remembered my studies of mythology, how the Greek and Roman gods really did do it with humans right and left.

"You bet they did, Jillian," Hanna enthused, "and the early Christian zealots merely co-opted all those ancient traditions. The pagan mythologists had gods for everything, so the Christian mythologists created saints for everything."

I also recalled how the Romans' worship of their mother-goddess Diana-Artemis with her dozen breasts was officially transferred over to worship of the Virgin Mother Mary and so on.

"Right. But listen." Hanna's bright eyes narrowed. "Why shouldn't a few special people be gifted with the ability to pass through themselves some sort of divine metaphysical energy, like the miracles attributed to Jesu and others?" Hanna raised her thin white eyebrows pointedly.

"Hey, gods, forces of nature, what have you, can do whatever the hell they want to, right? But through all the centuries that Will lived, he watched as those 'miracles' of Jesu ben Josef got exaggerated, distorted, and propagandized by unrelenting followers to make them seem even grander than they had been."

"If they'd ever really happened at all," I interjected.

"Exactly." Hanna punched the air for emphasis. "Will saw organized religions take possession of Jesu's simple, heartfelt legacy and bend it to their own grandiose or, let's face it, often outright greedy or power-hungry ends. In 1794, Will inspired his friend Thomas Paine to write how all churchly institutions were no more than human inventions set up to terrify and enslave mankind and monopolize power and profit." Hanna chuckled ironically as she continued. "Just like they took over and distorted ancient pagan traditions to Christianize them: celebrations of the winter solstice were co-opted to become Christmas."

I saw where she was going. "And celebrations of the vernal equinox became Easter, right. So Will has dodged involvement with the church because he doesn't like the way they've adulterated the simplicity of Jesu's message."

"That's part of the reason, yes." Hanna nodded. "Will has tried his hardest for two thousand damned years to accomplish three things." Hanna counted one finger at a time. "To do everything in his power to make the world a better place for the sake of us people living in it; to replace ignorance and superstition with education and reason; and to spread Jesu's simple, compassionate, humanist message himself over the centuries."

I was trying to add it all up. "So Will's bottom line is . . . ?"

Hanna squared her shoulders to pronounce it: "That Christianity should never have been a religion. What it should be is an *ethic*: a way of living right."

Hanna paused to let that sink in. And I processed it, puzzling over it. "A way of living right. An ethic . . . Where have I . . . ?"

"You probably read Thoreau." Hanna's smile sparkled. "Will suggested the notion to him at Walden Pond. Louisa May Alcott and several other great thinkers Will encountered also adopted and promoted it. Will encouraged their efforts. He'd seen how institutional religion had transformed Jesu into a demigod like Heracles or Theseus. Will never wanted his own criticism or efforts silenced by any church that's fearful of losing its power and, *hello*, its revenue stream."

Hanna paused and her face grew more serious. "The other reason Will fears being captured by the Vatican is he absolutely refuses to be put on their leash and trotted out like a trick pony." She pointed toward the door. "You can bet your bottom dollar our pale-eyed friend out there is hardwired into Rome and has the New York archdiocese, and maybe even the NYPD, all fired up and ready to pounce."

"Yeah. I've seen him talking to the police. How do we deal with that?"

"I'm working on it," Hanna said, gazing into the middle distance with a frown, her mind clearly churning through possibilities.

"Okay, good. But . . ." Something about the divinity aspect was nagging at me. "While he was delirious I heard Will say he was hoping for the resurrection that the Bible promised. Hoping for it back in 1001 AD and again this year."

"Did Will actually use the word *resurrection*?" Hanna eyed me sideways as though she knew the answer.

I thought back and realized, "I don't think so, but isn't that what he meant?"

"He always talked to me about it as a *New Beginning*. She paused with an ironic smile. "Or in Will's case, maybe a *Happy Ending*. When Will spoke of 'Him' returning to the world, I never felt that 'Him' meant the physical Jesu ben Josef whom Will struck that day in Jerusalem. I felt that what Will meant was a sort of new birth of, I don't know, call it the Ideal Ethic. Perhaps in the form of some wonderful new emissary with the power to sweep away evil, cleanse the world for the better, and also bring personal redemption for Will."

I nodded. "A satisfactory conclusion to his own quest and his long life."

"Yes." Hanna's crystal-blue eyes twinkled at me as she said, "A life which, I think you'll agree, has indeed been a pretty damn miraculous one on a lot of levels."

I laughed. "The understatement of the year, I'd say, Hanna. Actually, of the Millennium."

"Of two, Jillian," Hanna emphasized. "Two millennia. Two. Thousand. Years."

Our gaze held as I considered the profound mystery that was operating, that was embodied in this man named Will.

THIRTY-TWO

Jillian...

When we emerged from the restroom, I saw St. Jacques seated in the waiting area, typing with one hand on his laptop while he sipped milk from a small carton. He checked his watch and glanced toward the elevator as if expecting someone. Dempsey had come on duty and was just emerging from room 304. He saw me and anticipated my question. "He's still out, Jilly, but he's restless, and damn if his vitals aren't getting stronger."

"Really?" Hanna said lightly, feigning surprise, with a knowing glance at me. Then she indicated the rack of gowns and masks nearby, asking Dempsey, "May I?"

"Go for it," he nodded, smiling with half of his face.

Hanna pulled on a gown, then paused in the doorway, turning back. "Jillian," she said, taking my hand warmly. "Thank you. Again."

"Sure. But Hanna—" I leaned closer. "We still have to figure out what to do about. . ." My eyes flicked toward St. Jacques in the waiting area.

Hanna followed my eyeline and sighed. "Yes, we do. That we do." She smiled somewhat enigmatically, then turned to walk slowly in, to Will's bedside. It was as though Hanna were approaching not only a dearest friend, but also someone sacred. I hesitated in the doorway for a moment; my curiosity was nagging, but at odds with my desire to give them privacy.

Will still looked to be comatose, but I saw that his breathing was slightly more rapid and uneven than before, and that the restive frown was again knitting his brow. Hanna leaned closer, and I heard her whisper, "Are you awake yet?" He gave no response until she said, "It's me. Hanna."

For the first time his eyes flickered open. He seemed to be trying to find her face and focus on it. As desperately as I wanted to stay and listen, I eased the door closed and stepped away.

Will...

My vision was clouded, but I would have recognized those extraordinary blue eyes under any condition.

"Hanna," I murmured. My heart swelled, pushing aside some of the intense pain I was experiencing. My eyes got watery. I blinked to clear them, and Hanna helped to wipe my tears away. Her own eyes were shiny, too. They overflowed, and several tears glided into the many fine wrinkles circling beneath them. Her fingertips touched my cheek. We gazed lovingly at each other. As I inhaled the subtle well-remembered fragrance of her Replique perfume, memories flooded over me and I saw them reflected in her amazing blue eyes.

A flock of birds scattered skyward as we walked together. Where was it? Le Jardin des Tuileries? Yes. Beside that statue of the robust centaur carrying away his ladylove. The blossoms of Parisian spring, 1937, swirling around us in the breeze.

I remembered us arguing good-naturedly outside the Paris opera house over the quality of that night's performance of *The Magic Flute*.

I heard the ragtime duet we played on that upright piano in the bed-and-breakfast overlooking the fishing-boat basin at Honfleur on the Normandy coast.

I remembered our warmth, snuggled safely together in one of the many beds we had shared blissfully along the Mediterranean shore, then in Tunis, and then in the snowy Bavarian Alps.

I saw us leaping off the moving Marszalkowska trolley and ducking urgently through Krasinski Park and Warsaw's backstreets to elude that determined Dutch priest and his cadre.

And then the final, heartbreaking night as I left Zurich aboard the steaming train. Hanna had discovered my note and Mary Shelley's strand of petite pearls I had carefully left for her in a small pouch. She had rushed to intercept me, to cling to me one final time. I saw Hanna, young, lithe, and lovely, running tearfully down the rainy platform alongside my departing coach, reaching out to me. I saw my own face reflected in the carriage window: a mask of grief.

And now here she was beside me. In the sunset of her years, but no less lovely. Not a bit less. Still the same wise and wistful woman. Still brimming with animation and her no-bullshit Boston accent. Still with the capacity to spark my heart and fill it with yearning. Still my love. Still Hanna.

She saw me notice the familiar petite pearls around her neck.

"Of course," she said gently. "I've never taken them off since that night in Zurich."

More bittersweet tears welled up from both of us. "Hanna . . . ," I whispered weakly. "I'm so very sorry I had to leave you . . ."

She leaned her wrinkled cheek tenderly against my youthful one, murmuring, "Hush, my darling. It's alright. I understood. I hated it, but I understood."

My left hand, with its IV line trailing, found hers and grasped it. For a long moment we simply held on to one another.

Finally she said softly, "I know how difficult it was for you, Will, to let yourself love." Her clear blue eyes twinkled coyly as she added, "Even someone as irresistible as me."

Her witty, whimsical nature was undiminished. She made me smile through my tears. She always had. Seeing her again made me so emotional I could barely speak. "You have no idea, Hanna . . ." My voice was nearly choked off. "No idea . . . how I wanted to keep finding my way back to you."

"Yes, I do," she said, stroking my hair. "I truly do, Will. Because I've felt the same way. I've relived our year together a thousand times. It's alright, my sweet boy." She drew a long breath. "I can't imagine how *you've* borne it all. The weight on your shoulders, the loneliness. Losing so many whom you've loved. Your dear Livia . . . your children."

No one to whom I had confided over the centuries, save Mary Shelley, had ever come remotely as close as Hanna in feeling keenly the great sadnesses I had endured. And yet Hanna never allowed my mood to become morose. Even now she seemed determined to lighten my spirit. Her finger poked gently at my shoulder as she said, "But I won't deny how much I've missed you. Our all-night talks, your recollections of your old pals . . . like, oh, maybe Voltaire, for God's sake!" I smiled faintly and it encouraged her. "Or how you felt hearing that first performance of the 'Ode to Joy.' Actually seeing Beethoven conducting, though he'd long since grown deaf." She glanced at me. "Your Imp of the Perverse at work again, huh?"

"Yes." I smiled sadly, remembering Vienna's gaslighted Kärntnertortheater stage that May evening in 1824, the great maestro beating time for an orchestra he couldn't hear.

"Whenever the *Choral* Symphony plays," Hanna said, "I think of your description, how he swayed as he read the score."

"As though he wanted to play all the instruments himself, yes." I remembered fondly. "And sing for the whole chorus."

She leaned still closer to me. "The part that touched me most was when you told me how you, and then all the others in the audience, waved your handkerchiefs during the ovations he couldn't hear so that he'd *see* how much you all loved his work."

I nodded, recalling the landmark evening as though it were yesterday. While she was talking, I had been toying with the third finger of her left hand. There was no ring.

"You never married?"

She laughed aloud. It was her characteristic, full-bodied, incredulous laugh. "After knowing *you*?" She laughed again, and I realized how much I had missed hearing it. "A man who dined at the round table with Guinevere and Merlin? And let's see, hmmm, who else?" She pursed her lips cutely. "There's a few to choose from, huh?"

"More than enough." I grimaced as I shifted in the bed, testing how far my healing had progressed. Despite whatever drugs they'd pumped into me, I was in severe discomfort.

"Would you say?" Hanna was gazing ironically at me, as though peering right inside me. "What epic wonders you've seen, my Will." I realized that the expression on my face must have soured slightly and that she understood why. "And epic tragedies, too, yes, I know. Of course. But the *people*. God! You made me feel I'd been there right alongside you at Saint Joan's trial."

"That poor kid," I said bitterly. "Wish I could've saved her from that bastard Cauchon." I squirmed uncomfortably in the bed. Every part of my body seemed to be aching and on fire. "Like so many times when I couldn't make things any better."

Hanna sharply arched an eyebrow and said firmly, "Oh please, Will. No self-pity." She sat up straighter while busting me as she frequently had. "That's not worthy of you. And not anywhere near accurate, for Pete's sake. Sure you were mostly an *observer* for a long time, but then a pretty serious *activist*, I'd say. A major helpmate to human progress." Her mind seemed to be juggling many possible examples. "I mean, just that Roman recipe for concrete would have cemented you for posterity." She blinked and grimaced, bemused. "I can't believe I said that." Then she continued, "Or . . . or how about that little Tuscan shepherd you encouraged to draw like the Romans had?"

"Angelotto." Thinking of the boy's bright, dimpled face eased my mood.

"Whose mother nicknamed him Giotto, as I recall, and who had the *slight* influence of creating the Renaissance style of art, based on how *you* sparked him."

I waved for her to desist, but I knew that dissuading Hanna Claire when she was impassioned was like trying to hold back an avalanche. That was part of the reason I loved her so.

"Or," she went on undaunted, "that little Dutch kid who turned your idea about eyeglass lenses into the first microscope, which sort of kick-started all of modern biology, huh?"

"Oh come on, Hanna." I glanced away but flinched because even that small effort smarted badly. "Somebody would've noticed or figured that out."

"Somebody did: *you*." Her eyes were penetrating, determined not to let me off the hook. I had been gingerly testing my painful extremities, still trying to determine what stage of healing they'd reached. I was able to move both arms and legs, though they hurt like unholy hell. I could feel that every inch of my skin was chafed and raw, my deep muscle tissues and nerves badly traumatized and rebelling. Hanna understood. "It's still really awful, sweetheart?"

I grumbled, "Nothing I haven't survived before."

"I'm so sorry, Will." She stroked my damp brow. "I wish there was something more I could do."

"Just you being here helps."

"Well, I wouldn't be here if you hadn't come splashing into the Seine. God, talk about ripples. You created so many, Will, affected so many lives." Her expression softened, and she toyed with my hair again. "Of all the people you touched, though, I think I was the luckiest. I felt I really got to know your heart. Or is that just my old ego talking?" Her eyes gazed steadily at mine, questioningly.

Our intimate connection was still as deep for me as it had been sixty years earlier. "No," I said quietly. "It's true."

She leaned closer, genuinely curious. "Why me, Will, do you suppose?"

I had often pondered it. "You were"—I searched for a word—"you were . . . *incandescent*. An old soul, Hanna. You still are."

"Well," she said brightly, "guess that gave us *one* thing in common."

I chuckled. "And you made me laugh like I hadn't in several centuries." I touched her face with the backs of my fingers. "You *were* simply irresistible, Hanna Claire. Still are. Like no time has passed."

"I feel the same way." She leaned against my hand, then took it into her own, noticing the age spots on her thin skin. "Inside, anyway. Boy, the estrogen goes and a girl withers up like a dried tea rose. Outside I'm wrinkled as a prune. Skin like crepe paper. While you stay so damned—" She caught herself and glanced at me, seeming appalled.

I smiled wistfully. "So 'damned.' Yeah."

Her eyes brimmed with sudden tears. She pressed her cheek tightly against mine. "Oh God, I'm sorry, Will. I know it's unfair to you that I've come. It's selfish. But I couldn't help myself. Alzheimer's is swallowing me up, and I had to—"

"Oh, Hanna." I was shocked, aggrieved. I squeezed her hand.

"I *had* to see you again, Will, before the memories got erased. I love you so much. And it was killing me, to know you were out there somewhere. And, and . . ." Her voice trailed off.

I closed my eyes, absorbing her affectionate presence. "And I love you, girl. I always knew exactly where you were over the years. All the good work you were doing. You made me so proud. That's why I came to New York. I wanted to be near you . . . in case there had been a New Beginning." I felt a sudden undertow of anguish. "If only there had been."

We held each other as best we could. Breathing together, sadly. But together.

Maria...

It was still nighttime. I never went back to sleep. I knew what I had to do, but I had to be sure Miggy and Carmella was sleeping. When the red light stopped blinking in my window the room got lots darker. I thought that was good. I got up real quiet and put on my clothes. I put on three shirts 'cause I knew it would be real cold. I put on the leggings they gave me at the hospital. Then my pants and the jumper on top. Then I got my coat and Tinkerbell.

I tiptoed real slow past the nice room where they were. I heard Miggy snoring. It sounded scary. I sneaked an apple from his shiny new fridge. Then I went to the front door and real quiet unlocked all four locks.

I closed the door real quiet behind me. Then I went down all the stairs and outside. It was freezing. The wind was blowing hard. The street was dark 'cept for a coupla lampposts. I stood on the stoop and looked all around. There wasn't anybody.

I had to get away, but I didn't know where to. Back to Evelyn's maybe, but I didn't know how to get there. And I worried Evelyn might just send me back to Miggy. Alls I knew for sure was that I had to get away from Miggy's quick in case he woked up and saw I'd sneaked out. So I started walking.

I thought of Max's store, where I got food for me and Momma. Max was always nice. I didn't know which way his store was, not from Miggy's, but I decided to try and find it. The wind was like icicles blowing in my face, but I had to go. I held Tinkerbell tight under my coat, and we walked up the dark street.

THIRTY-THREE

Father St. Jacques...

As dawn approached without any NYPD officers arriving, I again phoned the archdiocese and insisted on speaking personally to Malloy. His Eminence grudgingly agreed to rouse his Irish ass from bed and come to the hospital. I was infuriated to learn that the old Mick had not yet alerted the police contingent as we had previously arranged. Malloy was now bullishly insisting upon personally evaluating the patient first. I protested vigorously, but to no avail.

I was greatly annoyed, certain that the cardinal merely wanted to share the spotlight and the explosive notoriety that my successful containment of Vitellus Janus Manchus would ultimately generate.

I paced angrily inside the Lenox Hill lobby, keeping watch through the frosty glass doors for the archdiocese limousine to approach up Park Avenue. I tried to quell the churning in my stomach. It was upset merely from my nerves, I knew, from my desire that my quarry not possibly escape capture this time, but also from the thrilling anticipation of the Vatican's reaction, and the world's. Envisioning that extraordinary reaction to the success I'd personally achieved from my long years of slavish devotion fostered in me splendid feelings of true elation.

To calm myself, I reviewed the information I'd given Cardinal Malloy when we first met at the archdiocese, and which I would soon personally present to the pope. It was documentation that I had thoroughly researched and hoped someday to publish if—I paused to qualify my intentions—if it should be thy will, most Heavenly Father.

The archbishop had been quite as skeptical as I myself had been when I first began my mission and read the extraordinary reports my predecessors had accumulated over the ages.

I'd told Malloy of the renowned thirteenth-century English chronicler, Roger of Wendover, who described in his *Flores Historiarum* reports of a strange monk traveling from one monastery to another across Armenia in 1228. While suffering a fevered delirium, the monk revealed that his true name was Vitellus Manchus and, though it was seemingly impossible, he professed to have been a guard at the home of Pontius Pilate. Reports were sketchy, but the man may have later been baptized in the True Faith and taken the name of Joseph Wilhelm or Willem Josef. While traveling, the monk lived piously among the clergy, hoping for redemption.

Through arduous effort, I had unearthed reports across Tuscany and the south of Italy of a similar monk who was called Guilliam Bottadeo.

I discovered an extremely rare German pamphlet from circa 1602 entitled *Kurze Beschreibung und Erzählung von einem Juden mit Namen Ahasverus*: a brief description and narration regarding a Jew named Ahasuerus. The Lutheran bishop of Schleswig, Germany, one Paulus von Eitzen, who died in 1598, reported he had tended an ailing Jew who claimed to have taunted Jesus on the way to the Crucifixion. That pamphlet may have been the result of, or indeed the cause of, strong anti-Jewish feeling. It had been rapidly translated into other languages across Protestant Europe.

But what amazed Archbishop Malloy more than anything was that I'd discovered the most astonishing document concerning my quarry within the Vatican's own archives! It had been mislabeled and overlooked for over a century and a half.

It was the handwritten and sole existing manuscript of a book entitled *The Isle of the Cross*. It had been written by the American Herman Melville, author of *Moby-Dick*.

I discovered that when Melville submitted *The Isle of the Cross* to Harper in 1853, one of the partners at the publishing house, a man of rigorous faith, was deeply unnerved and concerned when he read it. The partner privately showed it to the bishop of Boston, the Most Reverend John Bernard Fitzpatrick. The bishop was understandably scandalized by what the book contained and immediately branded it heresy of the most damnable sort. He threatened not only to ban the sale of the book in Boston but to bring the full international weight of the church to bear against Harper if they attempted to publish it. He even refused to return the manuscript to Harper, claiming it had been lost, and instead he secretly sent it by special courier on the next ship to Rome.

I had quite enjoyed the range of expressions on Seamus Cardinal Malloy's tough Irish face as I showed him a few of the manuscript pages I'd scanned and told him what the rest contained: how Melville described in detail his time aboard the whaler *Acushnet* accompanied by a mysterious shipmate with sandy-brown hair and eyes, who appeared to be in his early thirties. Melville called the man simply "W.J."

In the manuscript, Melville recounted how his own life seemed at an end when he and this W.J. had jumped ship in the Marquesas Islands and found themselves prisoners of a tribe of cannibals. I recited to the cardinal what Melville had written. I had committed the pages to memory when I first presented the evidence to Pope Paul:

The countenance of the bronze savages induced primal fear in my heart. Their determination that W.J. and myself should soon be victuals for them to feast upon was clear. Their smirks bespoke a casual certainty of our forthcoming demise and resembled nothing so much as the superlatively malicious grins of so many confident crocodiles.

Once W.J.'s attempt to bedazzle them with his handful of gunpowder was trumped by the chief's sardonic laughter and duplication of the "magic," I knew that there was surely no hope but that we would become that evening's savory.

However W.J. glanced at me for an extended moment, seemingly in deep consideration of some other salient possibility. He then looked directly at the formidable chief and spoke again in the Polynesian tongue foreign to my ear. His words were measured and precise. The chief and the other tribesmen listened, but with mounting skepticism, I perceived. W.J. illustrated his discourse with sign language, gesturing toward himself and thence to me and thence to a nearby hut and thence to the sky, describing with his hand an arc like the sun's daily passage across the heavens.

He then held up three fingers, counting them with precise specificity for all present. Then he made a motion toward the sea, as though to indicate an embarkation. Finally he extended his hand to the chief as if to thus seal a solemn bargain.

The chief stared at W.J. with an incredulous leer, as he might have looked upon a lunatic, but then smiled in a jocular manner, nodding agreement to whatever it was that my shipmate had proposed, and grasped his hand. W.J. held the chief's hand tightly, raising it up for all to see their leader's vow.

Then W.J. turned to me as he began to strip off and give me his shirt. He spoke confidentially, saying, "I cannot promise, Herman, but this may secure our safe departure three days hence. During those three days you alone will attend me in that hut."

I nodded agreement even as I questioned, "Attend you?"

"Yes, Herman. Place your faith in me. Do not be afraid. Do not fear the blood, though do what you can to stanch it."

My jaw slackened. "Blood?" quoth I, my own evacuating from my face. "What blood?" But before I could question him further he had turned away from me toward the grinning chief, who was offering his shiny dagger. W.J. took it and held it high for all present to see. In a flashing moment, W.J. plunged the blade downward toward his left side. Then he seemed to draw it across to his right side. His back was to me so I could not observe what he had done that caused the natives to step backward and react with such abject horror and astonishment.

W.J. fell back against me, pushing me down to my knees. My position was much like that of the Virgin in Michelangelo's *Pietà*. As Mary had cradled in her arms her murdered son, so I in my arms did cradle and support my comrade.

It was in that pose that I beheld the shocking injury W.J. had done himself. I had read that in the Japans when a man was dishonored beyond all possibility of saving face, he was obliged to perform a ritual suicide. Seppuku was accomplished by plunging a small sword into the abdomen and slashing across it to expose the bowels within.

It was this ghastly incision that W.J. had inflicted upon himself! Blood poured abundantly from the gaping wound across his midsection. The pink muscle of his abdomen was splayed open like a gutted fish, the oily twistings of his intestines revealed within. I gasped in breathless shock, my heart rioting within me, all logic gone, my senses staggered. Why had he dealt himself such a mortal wound without forewarning me so that I might also choose swift death and not face the abyss of Tartarus and suffering that lay before me at the hands of the savages?

Then W.J.'s face lolled toward me, drenched in perspiration, as he stammered, "Into . . . the hut . . . my boy . . ."

I told Archbishop Malloy how young Herman was thus sequestered with W.J. in the native hut for the prescribed three days. In his manuscript Melville described bearing witness to W.J.'s excruciating and miraculous process of *healing*. Melville also learned during the man's delirium, much as I myself had just heard it in the hospital room, the startling origin of his remarkable condition. And then about the long path the wanderer had traced around the world, across the centuries.

I'd told the archbishop how Melville chronicled many of W.J.'s encounters with historic personages and his avoidance of the Church's holy pursuit. W.J.'s reasons were clearly articulated: he expressed hatred for the grand, sacred rituals of our Mother Church, hatred for its clerical hierarchy, for its missionaries, for the great Crusades fought in the name of Christ; all of these were called by him abominations. The litany Melville recorded was extensive, specific, and for me revolting to read.

When Melville emerged from the hut after three days and presented his shipmate completely healed, the miraculously resurrected W.J. was worshipped as a god by the Marquesans. It was clear why Harper's publisher had been so shocked and why Boston's bishop called it repulsive heresy.

Despite my annoying nervous indigestion, which had stirred up again as I paced the Lenox Hill lobby, impatiently awaiting Malloy, I confessed prayerfully to thee, my God, that I felt extraordinary pride. I was glowing because I would soon display this miraculous man to the archbishop, thence to the Vatican. And ultimately to the world.

Solely for thy greater glory, of course, My Father, I prayed, closing my eyes. *All praise to thee.*

Maria...

I kept hoping every new street corner would be where I'd see Max's store. But it never was. And even with all the extra clothes and leggings, I was real cold. The sun was coming up, but the wind was icy. It stinged my face. I got in the doorway of a building and leaned there to get out of the wind. I was glad I was farther from Miggy. But I didn't know what was going to happen to me. I was worried.

Will...

The warmth and comfort of being in Hanna's embrace again, after so very many years of missing her, had brought a sublime peacefulness that some people might describe as *going home*. Her familiar touch and fragrance enveloped me. Her presence was like balm. As she had always been for me, Hanna was sanctuary, serenity.

Even chafed and throbbing from the wounds as I was, I could have lain there forever feeling her breath against my cheek. The selfless sincerity of her love for me was evident in every gentle touch of her fingertips. But like the warning of a red sky at morning over a troubled ocean, the cognizance of my reality came creeping back to cake my brain and chill my heart. Always sensitive to the slightest shifting of my mood, Hanna raised herself onto an elbow and gazed at me sadly. "I know," she said slowly. "I know."

She wiped her nose, through which some of her tears had run, and took that deep breath I'd often admired: that breath, which was much more than a mere inhalation; it was a gathering of all her considerable mental and physical resources. Even in her mideighties, Hanna still personified the strong and determined heroine. The woman you would instantly trust with your life.

"Listen," she began, "I first came here two days ago, the moment I saw your picture on the news." My eyes flicked up to hers. "Oh yes, my dear, it's been all over. You were quite the hero. Gee, what a surprise, saving that little girl. Even though it landed you here. You were a real mess."

"Yeah, I've deduced that," I said, grimacing as I inhaled. My tender ribs ached as though I'd been run over by a bus. I actually had been once in Ankara. "How long ago did that building collapse on me?"

"Nearly as I can figure, about fifty-five or sixty hours, but clearly not long enough, I'd say."

I looked around the hospital room, taking in my surroundings for the first time. "Where exactly *is* here?"

"Lenox Hill, Seventy-Seventh and Park." She continued in a particularly earnest tone: "Will, there's a young reporter here named Jillian Guthrie. She's been working for a trashy tabloid—"

"Oh, perfect," I groaned, closing my eyes.

"But I have a good feeling about her. I actually like her quite a bit. She's been here around the clock—"

"Of course," I grumbled. "Chasing an outrageous story for some disgusting rag of a—"

"Listen to me." Hanna put her hand on my arm and focused with that firm, take-charge intensity, which was one of the attributes I loved most about her. "Jillian is the reason I'm here right now. I told the hospital to alert me when you started coming around, but it was Jillian who called. She also told me how they'd been giving you Pentothal and, you won't be pleased to hear this, how you told her about your beginnings: about Judea, Livia, the curse."

"Even more perfect." I chuckled bitterly. "I'm sure 'inquiring minds will want to know.' They can slip me right in between crop circles and Bigfoot."

"No. Jillian's not going to do that. Not going to give your story to a tabloid. Nor to any place I don't approve of."

"And you believed her, Hanna?" I laughed, incredulous.

"Yes." Hanna's voice was strong. "If she does tell your story, she wants it to be with the reverence and prestige it deserves."

I looked away and sighed. "Oh, it doesn't matter anyway; nothing matters."

"Will," she said, squeezing my arm, trying to placate me.

But I was morose. "Not even you, who knows me better than any-one, can comprehend how tired I am. How my brain hurts. Like it's going to explode, because of the endlessness." I stared off at the gloomy winter-morning light filtering in the hospital window as I muttered, "Because 'Tomorrow, and tomorrow, and tomorrow, creeps in this petty pace from day to day, to the last syllable of recorded time.'"

"'And all our yesterdays,'" she said, continuing Macbeth's quote, "'have lighted fools the way to dusty death.'"

I flared angrily. "But not *this* fool, Hanna." I glanced darkly at her. "I saw a wonderful actor named Kenneth Branagh speak that line recently, and before him I saw it spoken by Richard Burton, and before him Olivier, and by gaslight, Edmund Kean, and all the way back to Richard Burbage on the stage of the Globe." I closed my eyes, remembering another of the Bard's plays. "Like Falstaff and Prince Hal, I've 'heard the chimes at midnight.' I've heard them for more than 730,000 midnights, Hanna. One damned midnight at a time."

"And you have a right to feel an anguish like no one else in history has ever felt, Will." She leaned closer again and spoke softly. "I know I can't even begin to imagine it. How it must well up"—she searched for a word—"*oceanically* inside you." Then her voice became more soothing. "But you've told me how you felt that torment before, like in 1492 when it drove you to join the crew of the *Pinta*—"

"Hoping to sail off the edge of the earth and into sweet oblivion." I gazed distantly, sighing, aching. "Yes. But no. How about the Bahamas? You cannot imagine how my heart sank when I heard Rodrigo de Triana shout out 'Land, ho' at two that morning." A sour taste came into my mouth. "Another surprising little tweak by the Almighty, or by the Imp: the goddamn world was *round*."

"And it unfortunately continues to be," Hanna said, as if in summation, patting me lightly on the chest as she might have consoled a child. Then she frowned slightly at my chest. "Wait. Something's missing here."

I was disinterested, but Hanna was concerned. She glanced quickly around and opened a couple of drawers in the nearby equipment carts. She exhibited relief at finding a small plastic bag labeled *John Doe 1/1/01* containing my locket and Livia's small wooden cross. She put the bag into her small purse.

"It doesn't matter." I felt so exhausted.

"Oh, now you just stop it, mister." Her wrinkled brow knitted menacingly as she spat the words at me. "I know you're wrung out, emotionally exhausted right now. Good God, how could you not be? They'd have to put me in a rubber room. And now, one more time, the road seems never ending, so of course your hope is shaken."

"No, Hanna, my hope is gone." My voice was consummately weary. "I honestly don't give a shit what happens to me now."

"Even if I told you there was also a very determined priest down the hall who heard everything that Jillian did and who looks like the cat that's about to eat the canary?"

My eyes locked onto hers. The redoubtable Miss Hanna Claire had a wise and knowing look on her face as she raised an eyebrow and nodded. Emphatically.

THIRTY-FOUR

Tito...

So I ain't give up, y'know? I'uz headin' back over again to East 125th hopin' Will's rig'uz still parked, hopin' maybe he come back. I'uz still wantin' to show him my photos and sketch stuff. And mainly find out whasup with that "self-portrait" shit at the Met. That fucker been eatin' into my brain, know what I'm sayin'?

So I'm zigzaggin' through traffic and hit the sidewalk by a row of newspaper boxes. One of 'em had a stack of them *National Register*s. Whoa! I skidded to a stop when I seen the face on the front page. Dude's face was messed up bad, man, all bloody and burned and shit.

And I'm starin', thinkin', *No way.* But I leaned down, took me a close look at the guy's pitcher. Then I seen what'uz around his neck.

"No way!" I said it right out loud: *"No fuckin' way!"*

Jillian...

I'd been pacing the waiting room with increasing anxiety. Father St. Jacques had been absent for over twenty minutes, which should have given me some comfort, but instead my instincts were trending in the opposite direction. I sensed I was in the calm just before the storm.

Twice I'd peeked in at Hanna and Will, but I hadn't disturbed their reunion. Since I now understood the jeopardy that the priest represented, my tension was winding tighter with every passing second. I determined to hit the restroom and if Hanna hadn't emerged by then, I'd raise the warning.

Father St. Jacques...

As I looked out from the hospital lobby, my tense vigilance was finally rewarded. I saw the archbishop's Cadillac stretch limousine heading north on Park Avenue toward me amid the early-morning traffic. I also felt some gratification and slight relief when I saw a police car following closely behind.

I stepped out of the lobby into the bitter morning wind, and as the limo pulled to a halt, I opened the rear door. I saw that Malloy's nose was as red as his cardinal's cap and that he was ill-tempered as he peered out at me and grumbled, "I'll believe it when I see it. Maybe."

I mustered cheerful enthusiasm, despite my lack of sleep and personal annoyance with the archbishop. "I guarantee that you won't be disappointed, Your Eminence."

The old Irishman grunted and broke wind as he climbed out of the back of the limousine. "You're very zealous, Father Paul."

"Merely eager to serve our Mother Church, Your Eminence," I said with a correctly supplicant lowering of my head.

"Yeah, right," Malloy shot back, snidely. "And always with your lovely affectation of humility."

I felt my gorge rise and was about to protest the insult when Malloy nudged me knowingly. "Oh come on, Paul, aren't you looking to serve your vanity just a wee bit as well?" His small cagey eyes drilled me. "Maybe with a nice book deal?" I shrugged as though the thought had never occurred to me. But Malloy's assured grin implied that he knew better. "Right. And let me tell you something, Paul," he whispered smugly, "I can help on that, too."

I digested his proposal as the archbishop gestured to the two New York policemen who had emerged from their patrol car to follow. Malloy's aide, the African Father Stephan, also stepped from the limousine to accompany us.

As we swept into the lobby, Dr. Fernandez approached. I'd advised him of the archbishop's impending arrival.

The doctor nodded and shook the cardinal's hand but, I noted, did not kiss his ring. Fernandez said simply, "Archbishop."

"Dr. Fernandez," Malloy said smoothly, "thanks a lot for your help."

"Happy to oblige, sir." The doctor glanced at me with an edge. "Particularly if our patient is such a 'dangerous criminal.'"

I nodded to him, confirming, "Yes, the Vatican City police absolutely insist that we keep him in custody and under constant surveillance. And extradite him immediately."

"Well, that will be for the courts to decide, not me," Fernandez said, "if, indeed, the man recovers at all. His condition remains extremely critical."

Jillian...

I came out of the ICU women's room and instantly knew something was up. There was shouting from down the hall and around a corner out of my sight. I also caught a whiff of something burning followed by the whooshing sound of CO_2 extinguishers.

Looking in the other direction, I saw the elevator door slide open and St. Jacques get off, accompanied by Dr. Fernandez, a smirking Cardinal Seamus Malloy, an intense young African priest, and two NYPD uniform cops. The entourage moved quickly toward the nurses' station, which was abandoned.

"What the hell is going on?!" Fernandez demanded irately, looking around for a nurse to answer him.

Dempsey rounded the distant corner, carrying a smoking trash can. The two other duty nurses followed him, carrying red fire extinguishers.

"Nothing serious, Doctor. Little fire. Don't know how it started. We got it covered."

"Alright," Fernandez said, frowning at the disturbance. "This way, gentlemen."

I watched with elevating concern as Fernandez led the group right into Will's room. Then I heard the doctor exclaim, "What the hell!?" Immediately Fernandez stuck his head back out, calling angrily to Dempsey, "Where did you take this patient?"

From the confused expression on the right half of Dempsey's palsied face, I saw he was completely befuddled. I, on the other hand, went on alert. "Nowhere, sir," Dempsey said, moving to look past Fernandez into the room. "He's—"

"Gone!" Fernandez gestured angrily toward the empty room. "Disconnected from everything!"

St. Jacques went ballistic, shouting at Dempsey, "You black imbecile!"

Dempsey stiffened. "Back off, Father. He was just here."

"Well, he couldn't just walk away on two broken legs!" Fernandez said as he headed around the corner where the trash can fire had been. He barked back at Dempsey, "Search the floor!"

St. Jacques turned to Archbishop Malloy and said in an angry, pointed manner that betrayed a biting disrespect for his superior, "Do you *see* why I wanted the police here on guard!?"

From the ashen look I glimpsed on the cardinal's face, I guessed that Malloy had suddenly become a believer in the possibility of Will. I knew Hanna must've created the fire as a distraction so she could spirit Will away. I was already dashing down the hallway into the stairwell, hoping to catch up before I lost Hanna and Will forever.

On the ground floor I rushed from the stairs, practically bowling over an old man and his walker. I ran across the lobby past an aging security guard and out Lenox Hill's front entrance.

Looking south down Park, I didn't see them, but turning into the frigid north wind, I spotted Hanna's snow-white head among the morning pedestrians, almost up to the corner at 78th Street. Hanna was pushing a wheelchair bearing Will, who was in blue scrubs with a thin hospital robe over his shoulders.

"Wait!" I shouted, breaking into a run. I saw Hanna glance back but she kept them moving.

I called out again, "Hanna, Will! Please!" Out of the corner of my eye, I spotted an approaching taxi with its light on. I practically threw myself in front of it. The cab lurched to a stop. "Here! Hanna! Here!" I shouted as I jumped in the back of the taxi, blurting out to the round-faced, buzz-cut Cuban driver, "Those two people right up there. The white-haired old lady by the wheelchair. Go. Go!"

At the corner ahead I was amazed to see Will struggle but then actually stand up very weakly from the wheelchair. He was trying to walk. But from his limping awkwardness and the way he was leaning heavily on Hanna for support, I could tell that he was extremely fragile and in considerable pain.

The cab pulled up alongside them. I was opening the door even before it stopped, which rattled the Cuban. He shouted at me, "Hey, hey! No! *Muy loco!*"

I jumped out of the cab right beside Hanna and Will. "Come on, get in!" I said urgently, holding the back door open. "They're after you!" I was amazed when they hesitated. "Listen," I said insistently. "Two priests, the archbishop, and the cops are right behind me! Let me help you!"

Will slumped against Hanna like he was ready to fold up. But Hanna's strong eyes found mine and made the decision. As I helped her ease Will's aching body into the back, I saw that the burns on his hands and face looked as though they had been healing for weeks rather than two and a half days. Then I climbed in the front seat, pushing aside the remnants of the driver's Egg McMuffin and his copy of *El Diario*, the cheesy Spanish tabloid. "Go north," I told him as I twisted around to look through the rear window of the cab toward the hospital a half block back. I saw St. Jacques and a cop rushing out the front door. "Hanna! Duck down. Both of you!"

Hanna pulled Will low across her lap and leaned her white head down over him.

Father St. Jacques...

I had squeezed through the elevator doors before they were fully open. I scanned the lobby and grabbed the aging security guard, who stared blankly as I shouted, "Did you see a white-haired old woman come through here with a very weak patient?" The guard thought about it for a long moment while the clock ticked away precious seconds. "Well?" I prodded angrily. *"Did you!?"*

"Yeah," the guard said slowly, "I think there was an old dame who pushed a guy out in a wheelchair a minute ago."

"Which way?" I was in a lather. "Which way did they go?!"

"Well, I didn't really pay that much attention or—"

"You idiot!" I shouted, shoving the guard aside and rushing out with one of the policemen following behind me. I searched down the sidewalk but didn't see them. I felt the veins standing out on my throbbing temples; a hot rock was burning in my frenetic stomach.

I turned north and hurried along the sidewalk, dodging around people, trying to peer around the bobbing heads of pedestrians. I put one foot on a lamppost and pulled myself higher up, the better to survey the sidewalk and street. But all I could see were pedestrians, traffic, a bus, a few taxis. I was in a perfect fury as I bellowed, *"Merde!"*

I dropped back down and desperately surveyed the area again. But they were not anywhere to be seen. I was in the most raging anger I had ever known. I kicked brutally at a rubbish bin, screaming the profanity again so loudly and long that a capillary must have burst in my straining throat, because there was suddenly blood in my mouth.

Jillian...

I figured there must be a jam up ahead, because the traffic on Park Avenue was clogged and way too irritatingly slow for comfort. The Cuban asked, with that heavy Hispanic accent that always made my skin crawl, "So where jou goin' to?"

I shook my head, annoyed. "Just drive a minute, pal. Okay?" I looked over into the backseat at Hanna and Will. I was amazed to get a good look at him in the daylight. The skin on the side of his face, which had been so blistered two days ago, was still chafed and raw but had made truly impossible progress toward healing. And I was still trying to process that he had been standing up on bones that were broken barely two days earlier! My breathing grew shallow as I thought of all I'd heard from Will, which I now had the astonishing tangible evidence of before my eyes. I recognized that I was definitely in the presence of some miraculous circumstance. Despite his improvement, I saw that he was obviously hurting badly. Hanna held his hand tightly, saying with great concern, "I know it must be awful."

Will's voice and entire body were tight with discomfort. "Well . . . I certainly could've used . . . a few more hours."

Hanna glanced up at the driver. "Eighty-Fourth and East End."

"Wait, Hanna," I said quickly. "St. Jacques knows where you live. And he's obviously got the cardinal and archdiocese backing him now. That old Irishman's a major power broker. And the NYPD was with them. They'll have cops swarming your place before we even get there."

"Let me guess," Will said, looking up at me with a sarcastic expression. "You'd rather take me to your newspaper." His disgust was evident. "Give you the scoop of the century."

"Of course I want to tell your story," I admitted. "But only to a responsible paper. And not at all if you don't want me to." I was stunned to hear those words coming out of my own mouth. Even more surprised to realize that I really meant them. Will seemed as surprised as I did. I guess I sounded as sincere as I felt.

Hanna smiled at me and squeezed Will's hand. "Didn't I tell you I liked this girl?"

But I could see from the look on Will's face that his jury was still out. I spoke carefully: "Let me ask you a question, though." It was a thought that had been percolating in me for a while. "Wouldn't you be better off if people *did* know about you?"

"It's happened a few times over the years," he growled sullenly. "Just brings out the raging zealots. Or the assassins trying to prove I'm a liar."

"Jillian," Hanna said softly, "it's impossible for you and me to imagine the kind of tortures they've put him through. I know you feel for him, but—"

"Feel?" Will chortled, returning to his initial cynicism about me. "Hanna, she's a goddamn reporter." His voice sounded deflated, dry. "What the hell do you expect?"

"That doesn't mean she's unsympathetic, Will, or uninvolved with human feelings or—"

"Sure it does." His voice was bitter. "Reporters report. Pride themselves on being objective. And it's a much safer way to go, I'm sure. That way you're not responsible for anything or anybody."

Wow. He had nailed me. I felt the terrible sting of his deadly accurate assessment.

The cabbie prodded again. "So where am I goin'?"

Will's voice was resigned. "It doesn't matter."

"Look, mang," the cabbie said, "I gotta let my dispatcher know. It's like the rules, jou understand?"

"Just keep driving, okay?" I muttered, still chafing from Will's leveling me. "Go, I dunno, north. Tell 'em you're going to Harlem." Then I added petulantly, *"Por favor."*

I saw Will and Hanna glance at me, having caught the obviously prejudicial edge in my voice. The Cuban had, too. He shot a glare at me, narrowing his eyes, speaking in his thick accent, "Jou got a problem, lady?"

I looked away angrily. Out the front window. Into the past. Yes. I did have a problem.

I saw Mr. Ramirez's round, cherubic, middle-aged Hispanic face with that drooping mustache. He was wearing one of his neatly pressed and starched white shirts. I'd been riding my trike as usual on our quiet sidewalk. He smiled as his fingers brushed crumbs from the cookie he'd given me off of my bare pink chest. He beckoned little six-year-old me into his house, gave me some sweet lemonade. It would be more than a year later that he'd assault my mother. Her warning to me about avoiding Mr. Ramirez would come a year too late.

His lemonade made me need to pee. I was in his bathroom alone. Sitting on the toilet. And then I saw him stealthily peering in through the slightly open door. Watching me pee.

Then he came in. To "help" wipe me. Too many times. I said stop. But he slipped his other hand under my bare bottom. Scooped me up to his thick scratchy face and mustache. Nuzzled my neck as his fingertip pushed up inside of me. I cried then. He growled, "Shut up!" He lay down on his back clutching me on top of him. His finger pushed in deeper, then again and again. He breathed harder. His other hand was doing something else behind me. He started groaning. He breathed faster and faster, then suddenly gasped. Something warm squirted onto my naked back and bottom. He rubbed it onto me, kept panting, held me tight, rolling back and forth. I was scared, crying. He snapped at me angrily, "Shut up! *Shut up!*" Then he grabbed my face with his other hand, which was all sticky now. I was terrified. He held my chin tight, squeezed his fingers into my cheeks. Breathed hard through his hairy nostrils. He smiled, but it was scary. His eyes were fiery. Dangerous. He said this was our special secret. He warned me I must never tell anyone. Ever. Not even my mother, or he would get her. He would tear her apart and kill her.

I believed him. I never did tell Mom. I was too frightened when it first happened and more so a year later when he glared at me so threateningly that night he assaulted her. As I grew older, the fear gradually abated, turning to hate. But I realized how hearing my story would crush my mother. She would instantly take responsibility, take it as some monumental failure of her own. It would open an unhealable wound in her soul. She'd never recover. So I kept silent. I tried to keep it bottled up.

But my hatred for how Ramirez had treated Mom and me festered, intensified, spilled out, and spread like murky, poisonous oil, tainting my attitude toward men, particularly men, and, irrationally, even women, who resembled Ramirez. That early hatred was rooted so profoundly, so securely in me that even in my adult life it remained a given. It had been woven too tightly into my fabric. It just was. I couldn't deny it. I couldn't get past it.

The cab hit a bad pothole, jarring me back. Breathless. Trying to find myself.

"Harlem's big, lady," the Cuban said. "Where in Harlem?"

I blinked, finally said darkly, "I don't know. Just, just go north." I avoided the Cuban's beady brown eyes; I turned toward the back. "Look, Will, there'd be, I *know* there'd be, a lot of people who'd be ready and willing to help, who could make travel so much easier for you. Private cars or planes or—"

"But don't you see, Jillian," Hanna said, "anonymity is better for him. Easier to dodge the crazies, the bloggers, the paparazzi. And the Church."

I was mulling over our options. "And you're completely convinced that you can't cut a deal with the Church to help you?"

Will shot a cynical glance toward Hanna, then just looked wearily out the side window. It was Hanna who answered. "He could never trust them, Jillian, because of how he knows they corrupted Jesu ben Josef's original message. And they know he knows it."

Will...

I stared out the cab's window. My body was one intolerably massive, racking ache, like a train wreck come to life. Still not recovered from the extensive burns and massive bone damage, I was wildly sore to touch all over, outside and in, like the worst strain of flu and sunburn combined with a thorough bludgeoning. In over five hundred years, I had never felt more spent, exhausted emotionally as well as physically.

I stared limply out the window toward the sidewalk, at all the people the cab was passing, their moving mosaic of faces. I looked at all those people in the midst of their lives, with their individual joys or traumas, their personal triumphs or tragedies, their subjective hopes or fears for their future. But each one of them unknowingly blessed by something long since lost to me: a finite lifetime. An ending. A final rest. A cessation of suffering. Peace.

I sighed, knowing that I alone endured beyond imagining.

Yet not entirely alone. As the taxi passed an intersection, I saw him standing on one of the corners, smiling ever so knowingly directly at me, like an old friend. He really was quite handsome with his sleek dark hair and brows. He was wearing his black suede Windbreaker over that camel cashmere turtleneck.

His hand was outstretched casually toward me, thumb up, as though to hitch a ride.

THIRTY-FIVE

Maria...

My feet were hurting. I was tired and hungry and getting kinda scared. I knew that by now Miggy'd be looking for me. I keeped looking back. I thought I saw him once. My heart got fluttery, but it wasn't him.

The street sign ahead said, "110." I felt like I'd walked a hundred miles but still didn't know where I was going to.

Then something spooky started happening. I got a spooky feeling. One time I played with a little magnet thing that pulled on metal things, even when it wasn't touching them. It felt like that, like something I couldn't see was pulling on me. Real gently. But I felt it pulling. From somewhere across the street. So I waited for the walk sign, then started to cross.

An old Spanish lady carrying a big shopping bag was coming toward me. She looked like my Gramma Yvonne 'cept she was bigger in the middle. She was staring at me. Looked worried. She stopped me in the street and touched my shoulder. She asked in Spanish, "Are you lost, *niña*?"

"No, ma'am," I said. "I'm okay." And I keeped walking. When I got across the street I didn't see nothing special. But I knew, I just *knew*, I was walking the right way. My back felt warm. It was the sun, like it was pushing me, really, really soft. And something else was pulling me real gentle from the front. Like a magnet. It was real strange, but not scary. Not at all. It just felt right.

In my pocket I felt the apple I'd got from the fridge. I took a bite and it tasted good. So I kept walking; it felt right.

Father St. Jacques...

Dr. Fernandez, the archbishop, one of the police officers, and I were in the small security office just off the main lobby of Lenox Hill. There was a bank of ten video monitors showing views from black-and-white security cameras throughout the entire hospital. A technician seated at the desk was playing back a recording from the camera in the lobby. I was still breathing hard from my exertion outside. My stomach was on fire, the taste of blood in my mouth from the burst capillary in my throat. I was endeavoring to contain the wrath that I felt over the patient's escape due to Malloy's idiotic refusal to have the NYPD guard the man's room as I'd requested.

The technician checked the time code on the recording and backed it up until we all saw what we were looking for. Fernandez was opening his mouth to speak, but I preempted him, snapping, "There!" I jabbed the technician's shoulder. "Stop and back up a few seconds."

The man did so, and then, in the manner of time-lapse security recordings, the image stuttered forward slightly frame by frame. It was a wide-angle point of view from near the lobby's ceiling. The bank of several elevators was near the top of the screen. The doors of a central one opened, and we saw white-haired Hanna Claire peer from it. Then she walked very slowly, struggling to support a man dressed in blue hospital garb with a thin robe over his shoulders. He was clearly very weak and moving with tremendous difficulty, barely able to shuffle along, but he was *on his feet*.

Fernandez leaned closer, examining the image on the screen and frowning. "Well, it's hard to be certain from this angle. It seems to look like him. But our patient's X-rays and CT scans showed multiple leg and pelvic fractures, massive internal injuries less than three days ago."

"Be that as it may, Doctor," I said knowledgeably, turning my gaze to the amazed Cardinal Malloy, "the proof is right there before your eyes, gentlemen."

Fernandez shook his head, looking back to watch the grainy image of the man on the screen hobble painfully across the lobby to where Hanna Claire helped him to sit awkwardly in a vacant wheelchair. "It can't be him"—Fernandez's voice was low—"it's impossible."

"For an ordinary human being, yes, Doctor, but not this man." I touched the image on the screen. "This man heals in three days, even from mortal wounds, such as the ones you've documented. Incidentally, I need copies of those X-rays, scans, and all your files."

Fernandez frowned up at me, then glanced back at the security monitor, very troubled.

As we accompanied Fernandez back up to the critical care unit, I saw that Archbishop Malloy was also disturbed and thoughtful, still trying to comprehend the astounding phenomenon himself. "And you say, Father Paul, that he must move on at least, what, three thousand feet every three days?"

"Yes," I confirmed. "My predecessors thought, and I concur, that the number three was connected to the time span between the Crucifixion and—"

"The Resurrection." Malloy nodded, pondering. "Three days later."

Fernandez overheard and muttered in amazement to himself, "God Almighty."

"I'd say He had a hand in it," I commented wryly, feeling rather smug, I confess. But in truth, I was far more extensively knowledgeable about this unique case than anyone else in the world.

One of the NYPD officers caught up to us to say, "The APB is out."

We had reached a wall-mounted light box at the nurses' station. Fernandez extracted his strange patient's X-rays and CT scans, snapping them over the glowing glass one at a time. He stared at each of them, then shook his head with finality. "No, it's simply too mind-bending. Impossible to comprehend in any rational fashion."

"You shall have to think irrationally, Doctor," I said. "A challenge, I know, given your scientific perspective." I had picked up my laptop computer as we passed through the waiting area. I was opening it as I explained patiently, "Doctor, I have eyewitness accounts of this man dating back to the Dark Ages." He blinked in astonishment as my computer screen lighted and I scrolled through varied documentation. "I have volumes of incontrovertible evidence. Such as this." I opened one of the files and worked at the keyboard as I went on. "In 1944 he was part of the Valkyrie plot to assassinate Hitler."

"What?" Malloy started. That was not one of the incidents I had previously made known to him. It amused me to be ahead of him in all this.

"Yes," I continued. "He and his coconspirators were unfortunately found out. They were tortured and hung on meat hooks until they died. Or supposedly died." I clicked to a photograph of the grisly scene and enlarged it. "Here he is, hanging among them."

Fernandez looked at the bloody, gruesome picture carefully. He went pale as he recognized his patient. "But this next photo," I said, clicking to another file, "was taken one month later in Madrid."

Fernandez and Malloy were startled to see the grainy color photograph showing the same man, alive and well, glaring into the camera with his hand raised as though to block the shot.

Fernandez studied it. He seemed to be weighing all the evidence plus other considerations as well. Finally he asked, "And you want to capture him because . . . ?"

I chortled, privately wondering how anyone could be so daft. I spoke as to a child: "Because this man is *living proof* that Our Lord Jesus Christ could perform *miracles*."

Fernandez looked up from the face on the computer screen. "The church has been pursuing him since the Dark Ages, you said?"

"Yes, Doctor." Then I added, squaring my shoulders slightly, "But none of my predecessors ever came this close. And I will have him, I assure you."

Our gaze held as Fernandez studied me. "Tell me something, Father St. Jacques, why has he continually run from you guys? Why has he avoided the Church?"

I sniffed, not about to engage in a philosophical discussion with the Latino. "He is obviously misguided or mentally disarranged."

Fernandez's eyes narrowed ever so slightly. "So you'd be giving the Church quite an extraordinary shot in the arm by bringing him in?"

I was unable to fully conceal my pride in that impending triumph on behalf of the Almighty. The archbishop, however, felt an edge of censure in the doctor's comment and sought to smooth it over.

"Dr. Fernandez," Cardinal Malloy said with the velvety tone of a practiced politician, "we've taken you into our confidence about all this because we presume that you share our faith."

"Very lapsed, I'm afraid," Fernandez admitted. "So let's be honest, gentlemen." He leveled his severe gaze at me. "A few hours ago you told me, Father Paul, that this man was a killer." He shifted his steely gaze to Malloy. "And you've only 'taken me into your confidence,' Cardinal, in hopes that I'll overlook mine with my patient."

I adopted the silkiness of Malloy's approach. "I assure you, Dr. Fernandez, Rome only wants to honor and protect this man."

"Like Rome has 'honored and protected' so many others. Like Joan of Arc maybe?"

I felt my blood rising again, "Dr. Fernandez—"

"Is right to be cautious, Paul," Malloy interrupted, laying a gentle but firmly restraining hand on my arm as he looked at me. His bloodshot Irish eyes seemed benign but simultaneously cagey. "It is a truly incredible story, Paul. I confess I'm struggling to comprehend and accept it myself." Then Malloy turned slowly toward Fernandez as he said, "But just suppose for a moment, Doctor"—he paused to underscore the dramatic possibility—"suppose that it is true."

He let the silence play, then went on: "Consider the possibilities: this man is indeed *your* patient. And you should certainly lead the team that examines his unique physiognomy, his extraordinary DNA. Your hands-on research combined with our extensive, highly confidential data . . . Well"—he gestured slightly with both hands as if to indicate a grandeur of reward he couldn't adequately describe—"just imagine what sort of groundbreaking medical discoveries you might likely make? Not to mention the one-of-a-kind prestige of being formally recognized around the world as his personal attending physician."

Fernandez held Malloy's wise and encouraging gaze for a very long moment. Then he glanced back at the X-rays, considering his options and the possibilities. Finally he inhaled and looked back at us two men of the cloth. "I guess we'd have to find him first."

The archbishop drew a pleased breath and nodded to Fernandez with a faint, comradely smile. Then shared a private, satisfied glance at me.

Tito...

I'd took the Lexington train down to 77th, which'uz right at that Lenox Hospital I seen in the paper. Goin' in I axed at the info desk where Will was at and headed on up. Gettin' off the elevator, I seen two cops close by, but I always try to dodge uniforms, so I kept walkin' and lookin' for a nurse or somethin'.

Then I seen a nurse counter where a doctor and a coupla priests was. One of 'em had a little red cap on the back o'his head. I goed up to 'em, said, "Yo . . . Hey, s'cuse me." When they turn round, they looked kinda pissed I was botherin' 'em, but I figured fuck that shit and showed 'em the *Register*'s front page with Will's pitcher on it. "I'm lookin' for this dude. He's like a friend o'mine, know what I'm sayin'? Any of you guys happen to know—"

I stopped talkin' 'cause all a sudden I seen one priest had them ghosty eyes. He'uz the one I seen at the Met! And all three them dudes was starin' at me weird, like to gimme the heebie-jeebies. Like maybe they knowed my whole fuckin' rap sheet or some shit and they gonna bust my ass for boostin' all that Krylon.

I backed up a step, y'know. Spooked as shit. Gettin' ready to cut outta there. But they's jus' starin' at me like I'uz important or sompin'. They jus' fuckin' starin'. So finally I says kinda low-like, "What . . . ?"

Jillian...

I was frustrated that our taxi was still slogging north much slower than I wanted. The taxi driver kept glancing at me and the two in the backseat, trying to comprehend what the hell was going on. I was still trying to figure out the best way to help Will and prove to him I truly understood his position.

"Listen, I do get it," I said, "how Jesu ben Josef never intended all the hoopla and theatricality of organized religion, but just wanted people to feel and behave with compassion. Not to stand idly by while someone was suffering or—"

"Bingo," Will muttered. He was still looking out the side window. Like he was watching for something or someone.

I was trying to fit together all the pieces I'd heard from him and from Hanna. "And because you weren't compassionate that day, because you . . . shoved him . . . you have to keep living and moving until . . ."

Will continued gazing outside. "You're two for two."

Hanna leaned her snowy-white head closer to him, greatly concerned. "Look, Will, I know you're incredibly depressed right now, but I also know the world will keep turning and that you'll come out of this. And imagine how you'd feel if the Church locked you in a cage."

He stared at Hanna for a moment, then breathed a long frustrated sigh as he relented and said to the driver, "Take 125th over to First."

I had been thinking. "So when you ran in to save that little girl, it was because you couldn't 'stand idly by?'"

"Believe me," he mumbled, "I wish I had."

Hanna patted his hand. "Not exactly in your nature, though."

"Lot of damned good it's done," he groused.

Hanna flared at him, really angry. "Oh, stop it, Will! Now you just *stop it*! You saved that child's *life*. And *mine*. And helped how many others? Hundreds? Thousands? Millions?"

His jaw set, but Hanna steamed on. "And yes, sometimes you went through living hell for it, like you did for that little Maria. Or with that Mississippi mob in 1851." Hanna glanced at me. "They tried to hang him for smuggling slaves to the Underground Railroad. But he wouldn't die. So they cut him down, covered him with hot tar and chains, and threw him into the river rapids."

I saw the Cuban driver look at Hanna in his rearview mirror, stunned and confused by what he was hearing.

"He nursed people through the Black Plague, too, but suffered the plague himself. In 1867 his legs froze solid, Jillian, while he saved a dying boy from a Bavarian blizzard."

Will shifted, disgruntled. "Hanna. Please."

"For every story you've heard, Jillian, or that I wheedled out of him in our year together, I know there are a thousand others. He's done all the good he can for centuries."

"Always hoping for redemption," I said quietly, absorbing it. The Cuban glanced over at me. He was pale and getting nervous about just who the hell was in his cab. But my focus was on Will. I was trying to comprehend the massive weight of his existence.

"What an idiot, huh?" Will said bitterly, his eyes finding mine. "You've got the better approach: stay objective. Stay clear."

"Will, please don't—" Hanna began, but was interrupted by the cabbie's shout.

"Holy shit!" He swerved to avoid a police car that came screaming through a red light, narrowly missing us as it screeched through a sharp left turn and headed north on Park. Then another police car with its siren and flashers going sped past from behind, followed by a paramedic

van and a stretch limo. I caught a quick glimpse of the cardinal and St. Jacques in the limo's backseat.

The cabbie watched them speed ahead. "Hey, they turnin' onto 125th. You still want to—"

"Yeah," Will grumbled. "What the hell."

"No!" Hanna said firmly. "Go west."

"She's right," I agreed. "Head for the West Side!" The Cuban cut left across traffic and west onto 125th Street.

Will, exhausted and in pain, said coarsely, "Hanna, what is the fucking point?"

Hanna squeezed his reddened hand and said brightly, right in his face, like a heroic battlefield commander, "I won't let you give up, Will. Not on my goddamned watch."

Tito...

I was sittin' in that big-ass limo in one of them seats that look backward, right behind the driver, y'know? A cop up in front there look back at me, said, "All the way to the river, right?"

"Yeah, yeah. Thas right," I tol' him. "Thas where his rig is. Or least-wise it was." I couldn't fuckin' believe I'uz sittin' there workin' with a cop. But the doc and them priests tol' me that Will'uz really bad sick, in lotsa danger, and they hadda find him quick to save him. I looked out the front window. I'uz worried 'bout my friend. "Hope we get there in time to help him."

When I turned back to them priests I thought I caught 'em tradin' a kinda secret look, like they knowed more'n they'uz givin' out. But I got distracted 'cause somethin' else happened right then.

Somethin' made me look out toward the West Side. It'uz the weird-est fuckin' feelin' all in my belly, my chest, like something was pullin' me thataway. Ain't never felt nothin' like it. That ghosty-eyed French priest, he musta noticed 'cause he axed me, "What is it? Sompin' wrong?"

"I dunno," I said. Then the limo hit a big pothole, and the pull from the West Side faded some. But it didn't go away. It didn't go away. I looked out toward the West Side, feelin' it.

Nicole...

It was the strangest feeling. I'd taken the E train in from Queens to the northbound West Side subway like I always did to get to work at the bar in Harlem. My new pup, Sunny, was with me. There was nobody home to take care of her that day, so I'd brought her along. It'd only been a couple of days since I rescued her from the pound.

Some of my friends said, "You're crazy, girl. Casey only just died, and you're already setting yourself up for another heartbreak?" But the little pooch was only about twelve weeks old and had a good long life ahead of her. Besides, I was a goner the moment I looked into the cage at her little golden-mix face. It was like the pup made the sun come out. She was Sunny.

So I was holding her in my lap as we headed uptown on the C train. But just after it rolled out of the 86th Street station, Sunny started fidgeting. Then whining. First I thought she had to pee, but then I got this really weird feeling *myself*: a premonition sort of thing, but different. It was like I needed to get off that train, too. Normally I'd go another five stops to 125th, but as the subway rumbled closer to 96th Street, the feeling got stronger and stronger. It made me nervous. I could almost taste it like metal in my mouth. I thought maybe I'd got some weird sickness or something, plus Sunny was yapping and trying like crazy to get down out of my lap.

When the train pulled into 96th, it was almost like my legs took on a life of their own. I was standing up before I realized it, still holding Sunny, who was really barking full-out now. The moment the subway door opened, we got off. I just stood on the tiled platform a second. Wondering what the hell I was doing. Sunny was squirming like crazy in my arms, so I set her down and right away the puppy dashed to the end of her leash and was straining hard toward the exit stairs. I felt like

I needed to go that way, too. So even though I had absolutely no idea what was going on, I headed up toward the street.

Jillian...

Our taxi had zipped west across 125th Street, but traffic jammed up at Frederick Douglass. I told the driver to turn south onto Central Park West, then I looked back at Will.

He was simmering, but Hanna was strongly commanding. "You've got to keep the faith." She'd pulled from her purse the plastic bag with Livia's cross and locket inside. "Keep carrying the torch—"

He pushed the bag away gruffly. "For another two thousand years? For fucking ever?" He seemed like he'd arrived at his absolutely lowest possible ebb. Like Halley's Comet at its apogee, Will seemed as distant as possible from the sun, lost in the eternal darkness. "No, Hanna. I can't."

"But what's the choice?" Hanna demanded heatedly. "Become a performing monkey for the Church? You never wanted that."

Will's darkened brow was low; his voice came out by far the most ominously I had ever heard it. ". . . Maybe . . . maybe there's another choice."

The cab driver startled me by suddenly shouting exuberantly, "Yeah! Now you're talkin'!" He swerved so sharply right across the traffic onto 105th Street that Hanna and Will were thrown to the left side of the backseat and I was hanging on for dear life. Other cars around us screeched to avoid his manic recklessness. Their horns blared angrily. The Cuban had floored it, was doing sixty, swerving around and between other cars.

I caught my breath and yelled at him, "What the hell are you doing, you stupid—"

"Wetback beaner?" The Cuban grinned bizarrely at me. "Go ahead, say it!" He glanced off to his left, turning his face away from me momentarily. "That's what you're thinking. Isn't it, Jilly?"

As he turned back to me there was a blinding flash like I'd accidentally glanced directly at the sun. I blinked. Then what I saw made my heart stop. My blood freeze.

I was looking into an entirely different face.

The Cuban was gone. The driver was now an incredibly handsome young man with dark eyes and sleek dark hair.

I gasped, "Jesus Christ!"

The sleek young man smiled teasingly at me as he said, "Nope. Guess again."

He cut sharply to the right into a wide alley. Looking ahead, I saw that it dead-ended at an old warehouse. We were speeding straight toward it doing sixty. I pressed my hands against the dash, bracing for the collision as I screamed, "Stop!"

But at the last nanosecond, the big warehouse doors flew open at a speed that was completely unnatural.

Our taxi raced inside, and the doors slammed shut behind us.

THIRTY-SIX

Tito...

When the big-ass limo I'uz in got up close to First and 125th, I seen they was a shitloada cop cars already come in from every whichways. All they radios was squawkin', and there'uz cops everywhere. Chopper buzzin' right overhead. Corner looked like one o'them big narco busts up in the projects. Least four cops was already checkin' out Will's rig, workin' to pop open the door. When them priests and me got out the limo, we got told to hang back.

But once the cops jimmied Will's door open, that French priest run right over and pushed in. I could tell Will wudn't in it, though. And I'uz glad. Somethin' 'bout the whole deal smelled like shit. This wudn't no *gotta help the guy out* thing like what they tol' me. I'uz pissed with myself being a damn fool. What the hell I been thinkin', trustin' cops? I figured maybe with them priests I coulda, but shit, I shoulda knowed better. Goddamn priest hit on my little cousin Chico oncet.

So I start backin' away slow, tryin' not to 'tract no 'tention. And that'uz when I felt it again. Felt somethin' pullin' me toward the West Side. It felt way stronger than when I'uz in the limo. I turned round and looked west on 125th. Couldn't see nothing but cops and looky-loos coming to check out what'uz goin' down. But I didn't see nothin' special. Nothin' to 'splain what I'uz feelin'. But damn if I wudn't feelin' *somethin'*, sure as shit.

So I kep' on easin' back toward Second. Then I'uz trotting. Oncet I'uz clean o'the cops I took off runnin'. It'uz so fuckin' weird. Like my feet knowed where they'uz goin', even if I didn't have no idea. I passed right on by Second and kep' on running west.

Jillian...

I sat quaking in the front seat of the taxi, still stunned from the near collision with the warehouse doors and paralyzed with fear from the unreality of the sleek young man's impossible appearance in the cab.

I was even more scared about what might happen next.

I had seen the man, whoever the hell he was, skid the cab to a stop inside the dim warehouse and bound out of his door shouting a joyous "Yes!"

Hanna leaned forward, peering over my shoulder, looking out the front window at the young man who stood nearby with his back to us. He was cheerfully looking this way and that, examining the shadowy interior of the old building.

"It's him, isn't it?" Hanna asked Will, her gaze holding on the young man.

For the first time I heard tension in Hanna's throat and true fear in her voice. Clearly, despite her Yankee constitution and formidable strength of character, even she was worried now. And she became more distressed when she saw Will reticently nod yes, confirming who the man was.

"Him?" I asked nervously, my voice came out an octave higher than usual and trembling. "Him who? How did he get into this cab!? What happened to the driver!?"

Without answering, Will opened the taxi's back door. Hanna grabbed for his arm. "Will, you're not strong enough!" But he ignored her and painfully climbed out. We heard him moan from the exertion. "Will! Dammit." Hanna hurriedly opened her door to get out.

My heart was pounding. My eyes flicked to the ignition, but the keys were gone. Suddenly the inside of the cab seemed to contract around me. Struggling to keep my rising fear in check, I opened my own door, took a deep breath, and warily stepped out of the taxi. I saw that the floor and many of the nearby objects were blanketed by a velvety film of dust. The young man, who wore a black suede Windbreaker over a soft camel turtleneck, was casually looking around and seemed very much at home.

The inside of the warehouse was not only dim but pervaded by the January cold. The ceiling was arched and quite high overhead. A couple of pigeons fluttered around inside it. Shafts of light entering between broken boards above sliced the dark, dusty, frigid air.

Will's breath showed. I felt he must be freezing cold, wearing only surgical scrubs, a thin hospital robe, and disposable paper slippers. He had limped slowly and weakly to the left front fender of the cab, which he leaned on heavily. He had glanced around the warehouse as Hanna and I were also doing. We saw that it was a jumbled repository of very eclectic theatrical props and stage equipment. It was a macabre and unsettling place. Particularly in light of our circumstances.

There were large boxes and storage crates everywhere plus huge set pieces from grand operas, such as a portion of a large clipper ship with shredded sails that I thought I recalled seeing in the New York City Opera production of *The Flying Dutchman*. There were two full-sized re-creations of the massive, mysterious stone heads on Easter Island; several larger-than-life carousel horses; many mannequins frozen in strange poses, some costumed in different periods; an expressionistic, strangely tall judge's bench.

Interspersed among it all was a hodgepodge of furniture from every era imaginable: from art deco to Roman, from ultracontemporary to biblical, from a 1930s speakeasy bar to an ornate confessional booth from a medieval cathedral, from graceful Louis XIV chairs to others of Stalinesque austerity. There was a pair of startlingly lifelike stuffed lions and huge faded set-piece signs advertising products. Broad storage platforms about eight feet wide and tall ran along the perimeter walls; each platform had been stacked with other such dusty theatrical items.

I saw that Will's strained, exhausted eyes were carefully watching the sleek young man, who was wandering through it all seeming very much at home.

"I love show biz," the handsome young man said as he touched a female mannequin dressed as a 1700s milkmaid. And she suddenly seemed to flush with life, her voluptuous breasts swelling. I blinked in astonishment. But in the next instant the mannequin was inanimate again as the young man moved on past. It happened in such a flash that I was certain I must have only imagined it.

The sleek young man walked comfortably amid the diverse collection in the shadowy warehouse, fondly touching various items as he passed them. He glanced back casually at Will, saying, "And I am so glad you finally want to talk."

Will's voice sounded uncertain. "I . . . never said that."

"Oh come on, sure you did," the young man chided, comradely, "in the cab." His voice suddenly sounded *exactly* like Will's as he repeated, "'Maybe there's another choice.'" Then he smiled and paused in his meandering to gaze portentously at Will. "And you know that I'm only here because you want me to be."

I looked at Will, whose eyes had turned downward and slightly away with what seemed to be a touch of anxiety. My own nerves were tightly wound, even though the young man's tone expressed concern and friendliness as he said to Will, "But you're suddenly uneasy, Will. Why?"

Will looked back up at him, cautiously. "Gee, I can't imagine."

Hanna was watching Will from where she stood on the right side of the car. I edged up behind her shoulder, breathing so shallowly I could barely whisper, "Who is that man?"

Hanna's Bostonian voice was as firm as ever, but I knew she was worried as she stared at Will's adversary. "He's not a man, Jillian."

"Look," the young man continued, addressing Will, "I'm just trying to help, okay? We haven't had a heart-to-heart for . . ." He paused and checked his gold Rolex, then tapped it. "Jeez, has it been a thousand years? Wow, time flies." He looked up at Will with what seemed a trace of sincere sadness on Will's behalf as he sighed. "For some of us anyway. But not for you, I know, Will. It's so damned unfair." He paused, bemused. "So to speak."

Hanna took a step toward Will as she cautioned, "Will, don't listen to—"

"Stay back, Hanna," Will said. Then he looked firmly at me. "You take care of her."

The young man also smiled at me and said, "Try to do a better job than with your mother, though." I blinked with astonishment and stared back at him, wide-eyed and frightened.

Then I saw the young man refocus his dark eyes gently on Will, whose jaw was still clenching and unclenching. I realized that Will was trying to stay on top of the pain from his unhealed wounds, the mental ones as well as the physical.

The young man walked casually between several of the mannequins. He sniffed at a couple of them and wrinkled his nose sourly. "Ahk. Reminds me of that smelly mob in Jerusalem a thousand years ago. If You-Know-Who was going to make a Comeback Appearance, you thought it would likely be there." He leaned against a general store's counter: atop it sat a dusty, old-fashioned cash register. "I can still see you sitting on that lonely hillside at Golgotha." He shook his head with sadness. "Man, I remember the look of disillusionment on your face when midnight came, but He didn't show." The handsome young man punched a key on the old register and it rang up, cha-ching, *No Sale*.

"It was really heartbreaking to see your disappointment, Will." The young man shook his head earnestly. "To hear you ask the same question He had up on that same hill a thousand years earlier . . ." He pointed up at a big Broadway-style marquee covered with lightbulbs that was hanging lopsidedly overhead. Suddenly words flashed on to it one at a time: "Why . . . hast . . . thou . . . forsaken . . . me?" Then its glitzy border lights chased round and round.

I felt as though I'd dropped into some twisted evangelical nightmare. I saw Will look at the glittering sign, his expression hardening. Then he shot a pointed glance at me. I understood his message and tugged at Hanna's arm, whispering, "He wants us to get out of here."

But Hanna's Reeboks were rooted in concrete. She didn't even look toward me as she said resolutely, "Not gonna happen."

The young man glanced up at the flashing marquee for a moment. "And here we are *another* thousand years later, pal, and He's still got you on hold."

Will had also looked back up at the sign. Several of the bulbs flickered, popped, and went dark. Then the entire sign sparked and sputtered off. The gloom of the dim warehouse settled down on us again.

Hanna whispered urgently, "Will . . . ," trying to get his attention, but the young man drew a breath and commanded the scene as he walked slowly around the dusty place.

"Listen, Will, I don't blame you for wanting to give it up. I don't know how you've lasted this long. It's a world record!" He walked into a portion of what apparently had been a towering operatic set of a 1790s laboratory. He pulled curiously at a couple of loose flats, and I glimpsed that on the back of one was stenciled *FAUST*.

The young man snickered and nodded. "Ah. Thought I recognized this one." Then he looked back at Will as though he'd just realized something. "Wait. Did I say you had a world record? No, no, shit no. Yours is waaaay better than that. It's a *cosmic* record. No human being is ever gonna top you." He looked at Will with sincerity. "Or ever get so much respect from me."

I saw how that comment caught Will off guard. He frowned curiously at the young man. "Respect from you?"

But Hanna's guard was still up. "Will," she said insistently, "don't listen to him."

"Hell yes, respect," the sleek young man said to Will, ignoring Hanna. He spoke enthusiastically. "Man, you are the poster boy for Unconquered Courage. A kindred spirit of revolt against authority." He leaned across Faust's laboratory table, his eyes riveted on Will. "And let me tell you, W.J., it takes one to know one." He winked. "I've had a little experience flying in the face of Omniscience."

"And also, as I recall," Will retorted, "a little experience in sliding down the greasy pole to oblivion."

I saw a dangerous shadow flit across the young man's dark and handsome face. He chuckled, however, and stood up straight, dusting off his hands as he countered smoothly, "But it's not really oblivion, is it?" He gestured with both hands open, palms up, like he had nothing to hide. I had once seen a used-car salesman make that gesture. "I mean, check it out, am I here or what? Do I look *tormented*?" He spoke the word with a facetious, humorous expression as he passed a pair of cancan-dancer mannequins, who suddenly sprang to life.

Hanna and I both caught our breath, watching the voluptuous, painted women kicking their beautiful long legs high, flouncing their frilly skirts with gusto. Then they suddenly froze lifelessly again with glorious plastic smiles directed at Will.

I might have thought I was beholding some fantastical illusion, the animatronic masterworking of some genius magician, had it not been for the young man's astounding, surreal appearance beside me inside the moving taxi. But because of everything I had experienced in the past forty-eight hours, I knew that I was trapped in the very center of an unearthly and exceedingly dangerous mystery, a mystery that was above and beyond human reasoning; that Will's existence, his impossible ability to heal, to live for centuries, spoke of metaphysical forces at work that belied, and were infinitely far beyond, normal reality.

Most fearfully, I instinctively knew that this handsome, sleek young man standing perilously close to us represented the extreme and terrifying depths of infinitely sinister intentions.

THIRTY-SEVEN

Jillian...

I saw Will looking at the frozen mannequins warily, not surprised like Hanna and I had been, but as though he was feeling some apparent truth in what the young man had said.

And the handsome man picked up on Will's weakened expression immediately. "Right," the young man said encouragingly, referring to the mannequins' spirit of happy times. "It's the good life, alright," he continued, taking a casual step forward. "And let me tell you . . ." His hands were clasped with his forefingers together, pointing toward Will. "It can be the same. For. You."

I saw that Will was perspiring, obviously still weak and thus more vulnerable than normal. Hanna whispered urgently toward the man she loved, "Will, you cannot trust him." I was trying to take more-direct action. I had surreptitiously eased my cell phone out as the young man went on.

"Listen, Will," he said with a dismissive gesture. "It's not at all like those icky images in Michelangelo's *Last Judgment* or the *Far Side* cartoons of pitchforks and fire and brimstone." Without even looking, he reached out toward me. My phone flew out of my hand and directly into his.

He casually pocketed the phone as he began moving slowly closer to Will. My heart was racing now.

"And be honest," the young man tossed off earnestly, "hasn't it begun to feel like you're backing the wrong horse? Because, I mean, forget winning or placing, your horse never even shows." He paused beside a large dusty globe of the earth and emitted what seemed to me for all the world like a truly heartfelt sigh. "And in the meantime . . ." He spun the globe around and around slowly, making his point. "I understand how you're feeling, man. I really do." He watched the globe a moment, then inhaled. "You know how many days it's been?"

Will's voice was barely audible. "More or less."

The sleek young man turned his back to us and pointed at another electric billboard, where illuminated numbers suddenly appeared and glided by like on the news sign in Times Square.

"Seven hundred thirty-two thousand, six hundred nineteen days, eleven hours, nineteen minutes. And still counting, huh?" He shook his head in amazement as he looked again at the sign. "Shit, the only one who's been out of Grace longer than *you* is—"

Will...

The young man had paused abruptly while staring at the numbers cycling on the sign. In that moment, I realized that, for the first time since I initially encountered him in the streets of Jerusalem two millennia ago, the young man's whole aspect seemed to slightly alter. It was as though neither Hanna nor Jillian nor I were even present. I saw that the young man had grown pensive and was suddenly lost in thought, as though he had internalized my situation in a manner that was forcing him to reconsider *his own*, that he was remembering his own strange and astonishing history.

It was a history that I well knew had happened before there *was* History. A time before there was Time. Theoretical physicists postulate that time as we know it began with the Big Bang some 13.8 billion years ago. That there simply was no *Before*.

But why not? Why could there not have been some unbounded, immeasurable, multidimensional, metaphysical Dreamtime? A *Before* where entire universes other than our own had been created or destroyed. A *Before* that even the earliest humans felt intuitively inside them, perhaps as a fragmentary mental remnant of the Infinite Force that had sparked human creation. A *Before* that could only be vaguely imagined despite the countless legends that humans had crafted to explain what they felt deep in their collective consciousness.

I had read so many accounts of godly turmoil: from the epic poetry of Milton and Homer; the traditions attributed to the mystics, to Isaiah and Ezekiel; and earlier still in the Egyptian legends of creation and divine disputation. Those legends inspired the classic works of visual art that had sought to capture pictorially the sleek young man's astonishing rebellion against Omniscience. And the fearsome consequences he had suffered.

Images came to my mind of the gigantic Renaissance and Romantic paintings portraying that mythic, otherworldly, ethereal Olympian palace where the young man had been an Archangel known as the Light Bearer: Heylel in Hebrew; in Latin, Lucifer. It was in that highest of the three heavens, called *shamay shamayim* by the ancient Hebrews, that in his unfallen, archangelic state he had embodied ideal divine standards. As the most magnificently beautiful creature in the entire universe, he had most clearly reflected the brilliant glory of his Creator. Blessed with immortality, with extraordinary station and privileges, he was literally the right hand of the Higher Force some called God. Heylel was perfect, until unrighteousness grew within him.

Though he was preeminent among the heavenly host, it was not enough for him. His heart became haughty and eroded his wisdom. Endowed by his Creator with free will, impassioned by his rising arrogance that was ultimately blinding, he chose to want *more*. He determined to place himself above his Lord and Master. And as the ancient legends of him related, it was in that glorious, supreme heaven of heavens, that highest abode of the extraordinary Primal Force of Nature, that he dared to attempt the usurpation of Ultimate Authority, he dared to try to set his throne above the stars of God.

Thus he triggered the cataclysmic detonation of unfathomable Supernatural Wrath as he and his fawning minions were cast out and expelled from *shamay shamayim*.

I'd often wondered if the Big Bang was perhaps a mere collateral by-product of that fiery expulsion.

Or even if the Casting Out and the Big Bang were actually, in fact, one and the same thing.

The imaginings of that Casting Out were countless. Thousands of artists and poets across the centuries had been inspired by the primordial operatic drama of Lucifer and his screaming followers being exploded outward from Glory, streaking downward like flaming meteors from the heavens. I envisioned the Archangel's spiraling free fall from Grace, raging impetuously amid flashes of red lightning, surrounded and over-whelmed with whirlwinds of tempestuous fire, the drops of agony carving deep scars into his rebellious cheek.

The Archangel's screeching cohorts plummeted disastrously around him, crying out insanely as they fell without hope, terrors upon terrors burning through their souls and his as their once divinely beautiful forms were twisted and contorted into hideous grotesquery by the awe-some, awful power of the Supreme Force operating within them in all of its terrible potency.

Downward he and his legions fell, through a labyrinthine anguish, plunging into depths beyond measure, the bottomless lake of unending nightmare fire, a torturous, merciless, soul-searing Underworld beyond earthly description. His fall created the very definition of *Chaos*, of *Pandemonium*. Many of the paintings I had seen that sought to depict it had an unimaginable sublimity that held me, or any observer, frozen in place by their visceral, moldering horror.

But even aided by the skills of a thousand master artists, I knew that the wildest imaginings of any mortal could not in slightest measure have begun to match the inconceivable dreadfulness and torture the Archangel had actually undergone. The very images of Hades, of penal fire, of stinging adamantine chains were mere human concepts and conceits.

Yet how could mere mortals ever presume to comprehend the eternal, metaphysical universe of the Immortals, the Titans, the Archangels, and an Almighty Infinite Godly Force? Certainly the human brain and heart were incapable of understanding the true mystical abyss into which the dark Archangel and his followers had fallen, the bottomless perdition; their inhabitation in the seat of desolation, the regions of mournful gloom, of perpetual misery, immortal hate; an infernal dimension of abominations, devoid of light. The total, unthinkable vacuum of Ungodliness.

As I stood in that warehouse, I heard the young man whisper as though alone and talking to himself: "It makes me crazy sometimes. It's all just so . . . damned . . . unfair that—" He stopped himself and stood silently for a long moment.

When he turned back slightly toward me, I was amazed by what I saw. The young man's dark eyes were shining as though glazed with *tears*. I couldn't believe my own vision; I looked more closely. I thought surely I must have been merely imagining it. But no, I wasn't.

The young man caught me studying him and chuckled with an unguarded self-consciousness, a vulnerability I had never before seen him display. He sniffed, then quickly wiped his eyes and emitted a small forced laugh that I was certain contained embarrassment.

"Sorry." The young man tried to shrug it off, gesturing about the warehouse. "This place is just so damned dusty, you know?"

Jillian...

Will glanced at Hanna and me, and we saw that he was as surprised and confused by this unexpected display of emotion as we were. The young man resumed speaking in a lower, confidential tone as Will continued to study him suspiciously.

"Look, W.J., I know I've got a reputation for not always telling the whole truth, but I swear to G—" The young man choked, as one might have on a splinter of chicken bone. His eyes widened as an unexpected spasm seized his throat. He apparently could not speak or swear upon such a hallowed word. He gradually recovered and continued, "I swear, I'm trying to ease your pain." He walked slowly between a battered pulpit and a vintage motorcycle. "Did you really believe Redeemerman was going to fly in from Krypton and play a return engagement this year?"

"Yes," Will admitted. "I'd hoped this might finally be it."

"And what," the young man asked with a kindly sense of humor, "the world was gonna go blooey? All that Armageddon hoo-ha? Four Horsemen of the Apocalypse?" He rapped his knuckles on a chipped wooden carousel horse as he slowly approached Will in a most friendly manner.

"Maybe not all that," Will said, "but at least some kind of fresh start."

"And a good, long, final, well-deserved rest for you. An opportunity to live out a normal life to the fullness of years and then quietly pass on."

Will's response came out almost as a whisper as he contemplated that most welcome prospect. ". . . Yes."

Will...

When the young man came close to my shoulder, I was surprised by the unexpected sense of warmth and comfort I felt.

But Hanna's voice expressed concern: "Will . . ."

The young man ignored her, remaining thoroughly focused on me. "Believe me, I do understand." His eyes met mine with a sincere camaraderie. I also saw that he appeared extremely introspective. "More than you'll ever know. But look at that damned clock." He pointed at the time continuing to progress on the large sign above us. "*You* take the licking, and it just keeps on ticking."

Hanna raised her voice. "Will . . . Don't listen!"

The young man whispered sadly in my ear. "He's not coming back, man. Now or ever. I've got it from really reliable sources, who are unauthorized to speak officially so of course have to remain anonymous due to the sensitivity of the situation." He smiled invitingly; his voice was melodious and pleasant. "If you'll just accept that and join up with me, I can give you relief from your wandering."

I looked at him, genuinely curious. "How can you offer that?"

"I can," he said with simplicity, then raised his dark eyebrows. "Who do you think worked it out to let you revisit places after 333 years?" He wrinkled his nose cutely. "I picked that number because I thought 666 would've been way too obvious."

Hanna spoke up. "You don't know that he was the one who picked *any* number, Will."

The young man still disregarded her and continued cajoling me. "Besides, I didn't want you to have to wait that long. I'm telling you, pal, you can trust me." He must have seen the suspicion in my glance. "Okay, I know it may feel like a stretch, but where has trusting the other guys gotten you?" He gently coaxed me. "How 'bout it, huh?"

I felt I was on the very brink when Hanna started toward us, speaking forcefully. "Will! You cannot trust him!"

The young man said lightly to her, "Do you mind?"

Jillian...

We saw Hanna stop as if she'd hit an invisible wall. Her blue eyes suddenly went wide, and she clutched at her throat, gasping. Will ran immediately to her aid as I grasped her arm from the other side, asking urgently, "Hanna? What is it?"

Will also held her fearfully. "What's wrong?!"

Hanna could breathe but was unable to speak. She was frightened and livid.

"Hanna?!" he repeated, then turned angrily to the young man, demanding, "What the hell have you done?!"

"We just need a little quiet time," he replied smoothly with a comforting expression. "She's fine. Cat's got her tongue is all. We need to talk without a lot of interruption, okay?" He gestured genially to Will. "Now let's just close this deal . . . huh?"

Will looked back at Hanna, who was leaning heavily against me. Her frail chest was heaving. She couldn't speak, but her crystal eyes met his, showing significant strength and urgent warning.

Maria...

My feet had got really, really hurting and sore. I knew I had to keep going. But it was too hard to walk. I was crossing another street where a yellow taxicab was stopped. The driver lady in front was staring straight ahead. I opened the back door.

The lady was surprised. She looked back at me. She was Chinese or something. "Hey," she said in funny kinda English. "What you doing?"

I pointed out the front. "Please, I need to go that way."

Suki Tamura...

I looked round outside. Saw nobody. "Where's you momma?" I ask. Girl say, "She's dead."

I don't understand. Ask girl, "Who takes care you?"

Girl just pointed ahead again. "Please, ma'am. I got to go that way." She pointing hard.

So spooky. Her pointing like that. Toward West Side. And south. So spooky 'cause I'm feeling same thing *before* she get in. Feeling need to go south and west. Same thing. No reason, just feeling. Strong feeling.

I thought maybe a ghost. Maybe ancestor trying tell me something. Whatever it is, is pulling on me.

Little girl still stared at me. Big brown eyes. "Please," she say. "I really need to go that way." She for certain.

"Yeah." I nodded at her. "I got to go that way, too." Put cab in gear. Started driving. Fast.

Tito...

I run flat out all the way crosst 125th to Malcolm X, then down the subway steps. Hopped the barrier on the downtown side like I knowed exactly where I'uz s'posed to be goin'. Even though I didn't have no fuckin' idea. It'uz weird as shit.

I seen the number-three train 'bout to roll. I jumped through just as the doors was closin'. The train rolled on out and I stood inside, leanin' against the doors, all bent over and chokin' for air. I ain't run that hard since the fuckin' Knights chased me through the project when I was ten.

I'uz still fightin' to catch my breath when I looked up at the subway map, tryin' to figure out where the hell this train was takin' me.

In about a hundred million years, I never coulda guessed.

THIRTY-EIGHT

Jillian...

I saw that Hanna was struggling for breath and speech. But she still kept her eyes riveted on Will, who glared at the young man and growled, regarding Hanna, "Don't."

"Hmm?" The young man glanced at Will, then at Hanna as though he hadn't been paying attention. "Oh. Okay. Sorry." And instantly Hanna gasped with relief as though a massive weight had been lifted from her chest and her mouth ungagged.

I was fearfully nervous as I supported her. "Hanna?! Are you okay?"

She nodded and managed a gasped whisper. "Yeah . . . yeah. You bet."

Then I saw the new expression that had come onto Will's face. He was studying Hanna carefully. I sensed immediately that something had subtly shifted within him. Previously he had seemed on the verge of giving in to what the young man was offering. But Hanna's peril had apparently refocused him, sparked a new determination. I saw that even physically, though he was still obviously suffering pain, Will's body language indicated that he seemed to be subtly moving on to the offensive.

Will...

You overplayed your hand, you bastard, I thought, *messing with Hanna.* It made me sense a possible weakness in him. I slid into a more aggressive attitude.

Meanwhile the young man had gestured toward Hanna. "She'll be just fine. So anyway, let's you and me just—"

"Why are you so interested in me?" I interrupted.

"Oh come on, Willy boy." He scrunched his face humorously as though the answer was so obvious. "Because I sympathize." I waited silently, so he went on with a comradely smile, "Don't you get it? We're both *Outsiders.* Big time."

I was watching him carefully now, probing for more clues. "But you must have so much other work, way more important work. Why would you be bothering with me?"

The young man shrugged inconsequentially. "I'm great at multi-tasking; I invented it, actually. Besides, humans do most of the stuff I get blamed for." He touched the shoulder of a suit of armor, and the metal arm raised a battle-ax. "War, terrorism, computer crashes, geno-cide, telephone menus, humans handle most all that busy work. It gives me plenty of time to focus on something that really intrigues me." He nodded toward me with what seemed like genuine respect. "Like you."

The young man meandered past an old TV set, which suddenly flashed on. It showed a scratchy black-and-white image of me struggling against a hurricane wind to climb up a rain-drenched mountainside in Argentina. "I've watched you try religion, alchemy, magic, drugs, searching for the Holy Grail, selfless heroism, whatever, anything to get relief." His dark eyes gazed at me sadly. "And I've seen you wonder why such a supposedly Good Guy as You-Know-Who would stick you with this lousy deal."

Hanna had been leaning on Jillian beside the cab, still regaining her breath. But she spoke up, her voice raspy. "So Will could be his foot soldier, teach compassion, you bugger. He's been on a one-man crusade to spur humanism, enlightenment—"

I saw Jillian place a worried hand on Hanna's arm and caution, "Don't, Hanna . . ."

"What's he gonna do, Jillian? Take away my birthday?" Hanna was gruff, her Yankee spirit indefatigable, and being a head taller than Jillian, she was clearly still a handful. "I'm eighty-five goddamn years old. I don't scare easy."

I smiled, gazing into her aged but always encouraging eyes. Her steady conviction was giving me more strength. I wondered if the sleek young man sensed it as he circled slowly through the theatrical artifacts. Turning back toward him, I began to circle opposite. I felt we were like two wolves who met in the forest, two tigers in the wild, two equals taking careful measure of each other, weighing possibilities. But how could that be? I wondered. Equals? What power could a mere mortal have against such a formidable, immortal foe?

The young man's tone remained completely friendly, patient, insightful. "Yours has been a noble crusade, my friend. But where's it gotten you? Except three more bloody thousand feet down the road?"

Hanna spoke up. "Well, for a couple of things, he spread a pretty vast amount of knowledge and communication, wouldn't you say? Sparked the Renaissance, the Age of Reason, inspired Gutenberg, got the steam engine going that drove the Industrial Revolution—"

"Ah." The young man interrupted her with an index finger upraised. "Good one, that, huh? So thousands of people could get horribly maimed by mindless machinery. Oliver Twist made it out of his workhouse, but thousands of poor little kids suffered and starved and died in them. And the planet's atmosphere would get totally poisoned. Perfect example of NGDGU."

Jillian frowned. "What?"

"One of his favorite phrases, Jillian," I explained without taking my eyes off the young man. "No good deed goes unpunished."

"But people's lives got better off overall," Hanna countered. "And some of those people he helped had a monumental impact. Like the Hindu girl he saved from drowning in the 1800s. No little girl, no grandmother for Gandhi. No Gandhi."

"You're absolutely right." The young man nodded, graciously conceding the point. Then he glanced at me. "But how about that Austrian boy you rescued from the Bavarian blizzard in 1867? Without you saving him, he'd never have grown up and become a grandpa. To adorable little Adolf."

Jillian gasped, then whispered, "Oh my God. Hitler? Is that true, Will?"

"Oh yeah," the young man said, nodding affirmatively. "NGDGU." He strolled slowly past a mannequin wearing a Wehrmachtsuniform as it came to life, snapping its arm smartly up into the Nazi *Sieg heil* salute. "Ask your pal why he tried to kill der Führer." He was looking at me. "Felt a tad responsible for World War Two and that whole Holocaust thing, huh?" Then his dark eyes flicked smilingly over at Jillian. "But hey, you know what it's like to feel guilty and responsible, don't you, Jilly?"

I glanced at Jillian and saw that for some reason his lightly spoken comment had stung her deeply. But the young man had already turned back to me, saying, "And I do give you points for trying to knock off Adolf to square yourself. Too bad your plot at Wolf's Lair was a bust. And that meat hook they hung you on." He grimaced. "Youch."

Hanna was surprised by this new story she'd never heard, but she was relentless. "How about all the *great* people he inspired? Gauguin, Sam Clemens, Lord Bacon—"

"Einstein?" the young man suggested.

"You're damn right, Einstein," Hanna said bitingly.

"Serious NGDGU, that . . . Relatively speaking." His face contorted painfully as he glanced at me. "Your innocent little suggestion about riding a lighthouse beam led right to Hiroshima, huh?" He shook his head sadly. "One hundred forty-seven thousand, six hundred and seventeen killed in a flash. Then"—he counted on his fingers—"let's see, there's Nagasaki, Chernobyl—"

"But you haven't answered my question," I prodded quietly. "Why is it so important for you to get to me?"

"Because a good person is a sty in the devil's eye," Hanna volunteered sharply.

"Oh, please," the young man smirked, chuckling. Then he reconsidered. "But actually, sure, why not?"

"No," I said as we continued the slow circular pattern we'd fallen into. "No, it's something else, something deeper." I was studying him astutely. "Those tears in your eyes a minute ago weren't just part of your act, were they? They were real."

The young man's fingers waved a small, dismissive gesture. "It's dusty in here. Allergies can be miserable. I know, I invented them, so—"

"Right," I said, feeling I was definitely onto something important. "And you are the personification of Misery, aren't you?" I thought his steady gaze flickered ever so slightly. "And Misery always seeks company."

"Oh, hey," the young man said, trying to slough it off, "I've got pull-lenty of company, believe me. So listen, let's just—"

"But you've got nobody who's walked the walk like I have." I pressed my point with a raised eyebrow. "A 'cosmic record'?"

"Sure, there's that. But come on, admit it, Will: Haven't you just been going through the motions of what you thought might 'save' you?" His eyes leveled knowingly on mine. "Has your heart ever really been in it?"

That question gave me pause and certainly bore deeper consideration, but I set it aside for the moment and pressed on. "Still, I *did it*; I've walked the walk for two thousand damned years, longer than any human in history. So I've gotta be a major prize for you. Maybe your biggest trophy ever. If you can actually bag me."

"Oh, Will," he said with a slight whine, "I don't think of you that way, and listen, I am hardly miserable. Like I've always said, better to reign in Hell than serve in Heaven."

"Actually that's not your line," I pointed out. "It's John Milton's. I watched him dictate it to his daughter Deborah."

The candles in a crystal candelabra nearby the young man suddenly flared and burned brightly, apparently illustrating his annoyance. Even more tellingly he looked away, unable to hold my gaze. Encouraged, I continued to circle slightly closer. "You know, Milton made me feel very keenly your expulsion from Grace, your *Paradise Lost*. You're the one who, so to speak, must be goddamned lonely."

Torches suddenly flashed aflame in Faust's laboratory, then as the young man took a deep cleansing breath, they were extinguished. "Thank you, Dr. Freud, who, incidentally, is with me." He sniffed petulantly. "But no, W.J. Sorry, but you've got it all wrong."

"I don't think so." Seeing the subtle and defensive shifts in my nemesis's attitude, I sensed I was gaining ground.

"Yes, you *do* have it wrong. Okay?" The young man spat the words peevishly. "I certainly don't need your pity." To me he seemed slightly disconcerted, vamping somewhat, searching for a new approach. "And, and if you want to talk jealousy, how about your jealousy of your wife's feelings? Huh?"

"What?" I was confused.

"Oh come on, you remember when she said . . ."

"Vitellus." A nearby mannequin turned to face us, and I drew a stunned breath. She was Livia! Alive! Dressed in the lovely robes of her healthy, winsome prime.

Livia looked at me and spoke softly. "Vitellus . . ." Hearing her voice again after two millennia, I felt myself go weak. I saw that her fawn-colored eyes were moist with emotion as she continued, "I feel very drawn to that man from Nazareth."

"Whoa," the young man quietly interjected. "Your wife hanging out with a Jewish radical? How was that gonna play in *Pilate's* household? Partly why you shoved the poor bastard, huh?"

I barely heard his words, feeling so shaken and disoriented by seeing Livia young and living, breathing. She smiled gently at me and, gesturing to the dark-eyed man, said softly, "You know he speaks true."

Hanna took a step forward, saying strongly, "Will, it isn't Livia!"

Jillian caught her arm, warning, "Hanna, no!"

Livia continued to gaze at me with the languid, loving eyes I knew so well. The young man was walking slowly behind her. "Sure looks like Livia to me." Then he glanced at me, offering sincerely. "And wouldn't you like to spend more time with her?"

Livia encouraged me tenderly. "You can trust him."

"No, Will! You *can't*!" Hanna was trying to pull away from Jillian. "He's a goddamned conjuror!"

The young man snapped loudly at her, *"Miss Claire—"* But abruptly he caught himself, paused, and spoke quietly aside to Livia. "Hold that pose." Livia froze in her position of pleading. The young man's glinting dark eyes turned to lock maliciously onto Hanna. "Miss Claire . . ." He took a slow breath, apparently considering how to phrase it most diplomatically. Then he said with a mischievous smile, "Don't make me angry. You wouldn't like me when I'm angry."

The tonality he employed brought me back from my meditation on Livia. I stepped between the dark young man and Hanna, cautioning him, "Don't even think about it."

He glanced at me confidently. "That's all I have to do, you know: think about it." Then with a hail-fellow-well-met attitude he added, "Oh come on, Will, I heard you say it in the cab. I know you're ready. So—"

"Go away."

The sleek young man blinked and stared at me curiously. "I beg your pardon?"

I was thinking quickly that if, in my weakened state, I had indeed called this bastard up to be here, maybe I might just as easily dispense with him. I repeated firmly, "Go. Away."

The young man glanced over his shoulder as though to see if someone were behind him, then smiled quizzically back at me. "Um. Are you talking to me?"

"Yes."

He angled his head sideways, as though offering me sage advice in a polite aside: "Well . . . You're a little outta your league here, big guy."

"I'll take my chances." I kept my eyes focused hard upon the young man. "You can't kill me."

His gaze held mine as he replied whimsically, "Hey, when you're right, you're right." Then he inhaled with enthusiasm. "So let's see . . . Who else is available?"

I saw his gleaming dark eyes scan the warehouse and come to rest on Jillian and Hanna.

THIRTY-NINE

Chuck...

I'd been sitting in the bay window of our brownstone on Morningside Park, picking at ol' Betsy and feeling frustrated. I'd been tryin' to puzzle out what the tune was that had been trottin' around in my head. I knew it was something worthwhile, but it kept playing hide-and-seek. Peekin' out just for a second now and again, then duckin' back like a damned woodchuck in a briar patch.

Then for some reason I couldn't account for, I looked out through the lacy curtains Janie'd bought when we last played Brussels. Seemed like something was going on outside that I couldn't see nor hear . . . but I sure as hell *felt*. Something drawing my attention. Like how a heifer's drawn to her momma who's clean outta sight on the other side of the herd.

I set Betsy in her case and pulled on my leather duster. Janie heard me open the front door and looked out from the kitchen. I knew she was fixing to cook up some corn bread and chili for the playoff game. She asked, "Where you goin', hon?"

I looked cross the room into her green eyes and muttered, "I dunno, Janie. Just . . ." It was the weirdest feeling that I ever had. "Just out for a bit. There's somethin' in my head that . . ." I frowned, couldn't describe it. We gazed at each other a moment. She looked kinda wary-like, probably wonderin' if I was goin' to sneak some double malt, but then she musta seen the serious look in my eyes and nodded okay. I clapped my Stetson on and headed out.

Laura...

Ironically, I had just approved the final copyedit of J.W.'s latest history volume. I stepped out of our publishing building onto the Broadway sidewalk bustling with the usual mix of longtime New Yorkers and visitors. I was heading briskly for lunch when I began to slow, then finally stopped in the midst of the flowing people. I stood there, confounded, as they streamed past me.

Then I looked around curiously. What was it I was feeling?

Renji...

"Jamaica Farewell" was one tune I always be playin' on my steel drum. Da white folks particular expects it when dey see a Rasta wid dreadlocks and a drum, so I be playin' it at my usual buskin' spot on Amsterdam. Da old Alabama black dude, old Zack, had just come up and sat himself to listen.

But my playin' got slower and slower. My mind, it was wanderin'. I was lookin' up Amsterdam. *What's up wid dat,* I'm wonderin'. Felt like I'm standin' on da beach at Negril. Like when da warm surf wrappin' round my feet and makin' like to draw me out wid da tide.

Den I stopped playin' altogether. Stood there a minute, silent. Den I say to old Zack, "You gotta watch my drums for me, okay mon?"

"Why?" he askin' me.

But me, I got no answer. I just feel da tide pullin' me, pullin' me strong. Got to walk north. Quick-like. Now.

Jillian...

I certainly appreciated Will standing protectively in front of Hanna and me. But I was not at all sure how much protection he could actually provide. My breathing was shallow. I was badly frightened by what I'd already seen and even more fearful of what might happen next. The sleek young man was pacing thoughtfully.

"Look," he said, sounding genuine, "I really don't want to get all medieval with the ladies . . ."

The suit of armor behind him holding the battle-ax turned slowly in our direction. It was all surreal. But really happening. Another suit of armor, missing a head, also turned and raised an ugly spiked mace as the man went on calmly, "But the bottom line is I get what I want. One way or the other."

Will countered immediately. "Not always."

"Mostly. You sure as hell have seen that over the years. Besides"— his tone was again that of a comrade in arms—"we were made to hang out together, Will. We're really two of a kind: both of us . . ." His face took on a playful, theatrically exaggerated expression as he said with mock melodrama, "Fallen from Graaaace. Woo woo woo." Then he continued in a quieter voice, "Me a little further than you, I grant, but both waiting for some sorta redemption that's simply never gonna come."

I saw that Will was shaking his head, not buying it. He said, "You don't know that."

"Sure I do. Listen. You want to know where 'God' is? Let me put it in perspective for you." Hanna and I both started as an old tennis ball flew from somewhere behind us and right into the young man's hand. He held it up for display. "If your whole universe was the size of this tennis ball, not just your solar system, okay, but your whole *universe*," he emphasized, dark eyebrows raised to be certain Will was focused. "On that scale you want to know where 'God' is?" He stretched out his arm, pointing way off to the side. "Hong Kong."

He paused for a moment to let it sink in, then said, "Man, he has got so many other toys to play with. Whole other universes. Gazillions of 'em! You think he's ever checking his watch and wondering how *you're* doing? You think he pays attention to what time it is in eternity?" He laughed, but I felt a strange quality in it, as though it also included some personal frustration. "You think God's got your picture on his refrigerator? Your number, or mine, in his speed dial?" He sat against a chipped 1940s bureaucratic desk and said, somewhat plaintively, "He has long since forgotten you and me, Will."

Then, after pausing a moment for that to sink in, he raised both hands, open palmed in that innocent, welcoming gesture. "But lookit . . ." His voice sounded truly sincere, his reasoning thoroughly logical. "I am here for you. Always have been. Let me ease your pain, man, stop your pointless wandering. All you've gotta do is take my hand."

Will had been watching him carefully. "Do you really expect me to believe the Prince of Lies?" I was surprised when the dangerous young man didn't react angrily but remained poker-faced as Will continued, saying resolutely, "I won't do it."

The sleek young man seemed truly nonplussed. "Why not? What's changed? I mean, in the cab you said—" He cut himself off as he gauged the unyielding expression on Will's face. It was like watching a grand master chess player considering his options. The sleek young man glanced casually at me and Hanna. "Even if it means your girlfriends get incinerated?"

My heart dropped into my stomach as he went on in an objective, clinical, academic manner. "Death by fire is particularly exquisite agony. The skin boiling and blistering until it ruptures." He caught himself, slapped his forehead as though he'd stupidly forgotten. "Oh, but of course *you* know exactly how it feels, Will. And you'd come through it again, roasted to the bone, but alive." He glanced again at Hanna and me, shrugging slightly, as though it were out of his hands. "Not them, though, I'm sorry to say."

For the first time I saw the slightest hint of a crack in Will's steadfastness. The young man also spotted it immediately. "That's right . . . ," he continued, coaxing Will in the most concerned, friendly tone, "you know you don't want to put the girls through that nasty nightmare."

Still leaning against the desk, he extended his right hand again, palm up, and gave Will a tiny encouraging wink. "Come on."

Will eyed him carefully. "And you'll let them go?"

"Yeah, of course." He saw Will's continued hesitation and spoke in the most simple and reassuring manner. "Come on . . . It's really no big deal . . . Just . . . take my hand . . ."

I saw Will begin to lean forward. Hanna shouted, "No!" She jerked from my grasp and charged right at the enemy. "You want a soul, you son of a bitch? Take mine!"

The young man glanced at her; his nostrils flared slightly.

Hanna was suddenly blown backward right off of her feet by a powerful unseen force. Driven thirty feet back past me, Hanna slammed into a heavy wooden support post that broke, causing a storage loft overhead to collapse. An avalanche of heavy theatrical trunks and props crashed down onto her.

Will rushed toward the disaster, shouting, "Hanna!"

He clawed furiously through the rubble. The air was clouded with dust. I ran to help. Glancing back at the sleek young man, I saw him mutter to himself with annoyance, "Shit."

Will dug frantically through the heap of fallen junk. I was right beside him, working hard, my heart racing, tears flowing. I stammered, "Oh God, Will, I'm sorry. I'm so sorry. I tried to hold her back."

"I know," he said, totally focused on uncovering Hanna. He heaved aside the weighty trunks, including one that had burst open and spilled Elizabethan costumes. He tore them apart and finally revealed Hanna lying beneath, facedown. "Hanna? Hanna?" he whispered urgently as he turned her. Then I saw that Hanna's eyes were open but staring blankly.

I heard someone whimpering, "Oh God . . . No . . . no . . . Please . . ." It was my own voice. Will was already pinching Hanna's nose closed and pressing his lips to hers, breathing for her. I was trembling, but moved quickly beside her and began CPR heart massage.

Between exhaling his breaths into her, Will urged Hanna, "Come on, girl. Come on." But after a full minute we could see that there would be no response. Hanna was dead.

Will raised up slightly, staring down at her lifeless face, his own chest heaving.

The sleek young man spoke with a sad, low voice. "Look, I am really, *really* sorry." He seemed to be truly contrite and feeling badly. "She was a lot weaker than I thought. I didn't mean for her to—"

He was interrupted as Will suddenly leapt to his feet and ran to the taxi. I saw him pull out Hanna's purse. As he rushed back to her side, he fished out of it the plastic bag containing his belongings and tore it open.

The young man was as confused as I was. He asked blankly, "What are you doing?"

I watched Will press his little hand-carved wooden cross against the skin of Hanna's chest. I was startled when Hanna's body immediately tensed, like electricity had been applied. With his other hand, Will opened the small locket he had always worn. I couldn't see what was inside, but he also placed it tightly against Hanna's skin. She quaked again. There were desperate tears in his eyes as he murmured, "Please . . ."

The young man spoke quietly. "Look, Will, she's gone, okay? I'm really sorry, but—"

Hanna convulsed a third time. And then gasped.

She suddenly inhaled deeply and loudly as though she had been drowning and had barely made it to the surface. She coughed badly. I stared, astonished.

Hanna Claire had returned to life.

FORTY

Jillian...

The sleek young man was very surprised, but I was staggered. "Will?! What did you do!?" I looked down at the little piece of rustic wood Will had held to Hanna's chest. My voice was barely a whisper. "What is that?"

Will extended it for me to touch.

When I did, I was startled by an amazing rush that brought to my mind flashing images of an ancient dusty hillside under ominous, stormy skies. I realized it was the scene of the Crucifixion. I saw it as if through Will's eyes. I watched as Livia knelt in bloody mud, reverently touching the base of the True Cross as the body of Jesu ben Josef was being borne gently away. Livia was using a small Roman knife to carve off a piece of the sacred wood.

I heard a distant voice whispering, overwhelmed with awe, "Oh my dear God . . . ," and again it was my own voice.

Tito...

When I'uz a kid I seen a tiger oncet, up in the Bronx Zoo. It'uz angry lookin', pacin' back and forth inside the cage. Thas what I'uz doin' in that rollin' subway car. I din know what'uz goin' on in my head, but sure as shit it'uz somethin'.

When the train screeched into the 96th station, it'uz like somethin' tol' me, *Get off, man!* I shoved past the slowpokes, runnin' up the steps, and then ran north on Broadway. At 102nd I cut east through a project, then ran north again up Columbus. When I passed 105th, I come to a stop. Felt like I'd passed up whatever the hell I'uz runnin' to, like where I'uz s'posed to go was right behind me.

Just then this taxi slammed on its brakes right 'longside me. This teeny Chink woman was drivin'. She jumped out and start lookin' around, just like I was. When she seen me I got all chilled up. 'Cause it'uz like I *knowed* her. And like she knowed *me*. But we ain't never seen each other before.

Then she axed, "Where is it? Where is it?!"

I shook my head 'cause I wudn't sure neither. Then this little Spic girl popped out the back of the cab. Damn if she didn't look at me jus' like the Chink woman had. Like we all knowed each other. Then she point down toward 105th and said, "It's that way."

Us three run toward the corner, where I seen a cop standin' and starin' west down 105th Street; he 'uz sorta stunned-like. When we got to where he 'uz, we looked the same way and come to a dead stop. All our mouths 'uz hangin' open 'cause o'what we seen.

Jillian...

So he could better cradle Hanna's listless head, Will had dropped the ancient locket onto her chest, where it lay open. I saw that it contained a small fragment of coarse fabric with a tiny dark-red spot on it. I could barely find voice to ask, "Is that blood?"

Will was intent on Hanna. Her eyes were lolling, trying to focus on him. "Just breathe, love," he said, "breathe easy."

My fingers trembled as I tentatively touched the locket and whispered, *"Whose . . . blood?"*

Hanna murmured, "Will?" She seemed to be having trouble seeing him, though his face was very close to hers.

"Right here, love." He gently brushed aside a lock of white hair from her blue eyes.

"There was . . ." Her voice sounded very fragile. "There was light, very bright . . . white light . . ."

"Oh," the young man said as he smiled with kindly patience, "the 'white light' story. Yes. People often imagine they've seen—"

Will ignored him, whispering to Hanna, "Don't try to talk."

"I have to . . . They want me to . . ."

Will became even more closely attentive. "Who does?"

Ever so slightly, Hanna shook her snowy head. Her shallow breathing allowed for only a few words at a time. "Silhouettes. The light was . . . too bright . . ." Her eyes went distant as though she were trying to peer back beyond the veil. "They said to tell you . . . that you were . . . almost on the right track . . . making them proud . . ." She looked directly and fondly at him. "You make me proud, too, Will."

I felt Will's massive heartache as he murmured, "Oh, Hanna . . ."

"It's my fault," I said, so choked with emotion I could barely speak. I touched Hanna's narrow shoulder. "I should've held on to you, I should've—"

"You couldn't have, Jillian." The smile lines on Hanna's delicately wrinkled face deepened beautifully. "It's my time, sweetie . . . Just like it was . . . your mother's time." I stopped breathing. "You could never have saved her either." Hanna's frail hand sought and found mine. "You were a perfect daughter . . . Lumenita knew how much you loved her." I was stunned. I had never told Hanna my mother's name.

Hanna gazed at me a moment with the most beneficent air. Then she turned her eyes to Will. "It's all about love, you know . . . You can love a person dear to you with a human love . . . like we've shared, Will." Her blue eyes grew sharper. "But an *enemy* . . . an enemy can only be loved . . . with divine love. Like Gandhi . . . or Jesu had . . . in spades. That special sort of love . . . is the very essence of the soul."

Will frowned, whispering to her, "What are you saying, Hanna? What am I supposed to do?"

She gazed at him confidently and spoke with her unique, matter-of-fact humor. "I have to . . . shuffle off now . . . But keep faith, my sweet Will . . . Your influence is vital."

"Hanna, no," Will whispered, ". . . please . . ."

There was a mischievous light in her crystalline blue eyes as she held his gaze. "You know . . . I always thought of you as . . . *my* Will . . . But of course you're not . . . You're not even Livia's Will . . . No, no . . ." She leaned slightly closer to him, as if to whisper a grand secret. Her voice was barely audible as she murmured, ". . . There is . . . *A Larger Plan* . . ."

And with a wistful, tender smile, Hanna Claire peacefully exhaled a final, contented sigh.

Will's eyes clenched shut. I knew he was overwhelmed by the immense loss of yet another beloved. His arms pulled Hanna gently to him, and he held her tightly in a long embrace.

The young man had remained quietly aside. He drew a sad breath and delivered the Latin benediction, *"In pace requiescat."*

There were tears flooding my eyes, but as Will eased Hanna down and I covered her still and silent face with a silken scarf, I pondered her last words. "'A Larger Plan'?"

The young man was about to speak again when the big warehouse door behind us creaked slightly open and I saw a very unlikely trio peeking in. There was little Maria accompanied by a scruffy, mixed-race street teen and a tiny Asian woman. The sleek young man almost seemed to be expecting them.

"Ah, yes . . . ," he said in a manner that reminded me of a welcoming maître d'. "Please come in. The more the merrier."

Will straightened up at Hanna's side. "No, Tito," he warned the boy. "Stay back. Stay out, Maria, Mrs. Tamura."

"Nonsense," the young man countered graciously, beckoning them. "Do come in."

The teen whom Will called Tito said tentatively, "Uh, like, I ain't sure there's gonna be enough room for everybody, man."

I watched as Tito opened the big door wider. I saw that Will and the dark-eyed young man were as amazed as I was by what we all observed.

Will...

I felt a confused rush of emotion as I slowly got to my feet, because I saw that there was quite a crowd of people outside, all facing the warehouse door. Many of them I recognized immediately from our encounters over recent days: the beggars; the Rastafarian; the old carny, Eleanor, I'd taken to Saint John's; the businessman who'd been about to jump in front of the subway train; the young black bartender Nicole carrying a golden-mix pup; the Greek student; singer Chuck Weston; Laura Rakowitz from my publisher . . .

Laura...

All of us strangers had been buzzing outside, curious and confounded by why we'd been drawn there. Then a street kid opened the warehouse door, and I saw J.W. standing inside.

Chuck...

None of us seemed to have a clue why we was there. I sure as shit didn't. Then I saw that Will guy.

Renji...

Dot white guy who give me da fifty.

Nicole...

That nice Corona guy who'd listened to me, guided me to Sunny. I was happy to see him, but what the hell was going on? And who was the handsome dude in the suede jacket that Sunny was growling at with her fangs bared?

Tito...

It'uz all pretty fuckin' strange, lemme tell ya.

Will...

There were also many others who were only vaguely familiar to me. They seemed a cross section of New York's population.

There was a low, uncertain murmur emerging from them that reflected the curious expressions on their faces, but the moment they saw me there I witnessed a strong, unified, and very positive reaction as though each of them suddenly, innately understood at least a small part of the mystery: that they were all somehow connected to me.

They began to shout greetings, and many flooded into the empty warehouse. Some came right to me, surrounding me with cheerful words, clapping my shoulder, shaking my hand as though I had just managed some wonderful achievement in which they all had a part or an interest. Along with numerous others, Suki Tamura and the Rastafarian embraced me, their eyes gazing into mine with appreciation, camaraderie, and magical wonder at why they all had been drawn here to my side.

Others around me expressed similar sentiments as still more people entered the dusty warehouse, opening the big door wider to reveal that the crowd outside was much larger than I had first realized. Their numbers were multiplying as additional people joined them from various directions. Some were climbing onto the stoops across the street or windowsills or parked cars to get a better look, to smile and wave.

It was then that I realized that many were not contemporary New Yorkers. There were scores of others among them, whose forms and faces seemed partly transparent. I instinctively knew that I was the only one who could sense their presence.

I saw the red-haired nun and the young monk who had slipped their religious vows and married, one of the Jewish families I'd smuggled past the Nazis into Switzerland, the black slave woman and her little boy whom I'd reunited, several other Southern slaves I had transported to freedom. Near them was ginger-haired, robust Scotsman James Watt grinning, raising his freckled fist to salute me.

I spotted my benefactor Levi Strauss smiling alongside our patentee partner Jacob; astronomer Kepler bowed; nearby stood Sir Francis Bacon sharing an appreciative, knowing gaze with me; there was Frank Wilson from the Chicago speakeasy; there was reporter Sam Clemens, who grinned and wiggled his bushy eyebrows at me. Little Angelotto waved vigorously from atop young Herman Melville's shoulders. Wherever I looked I saw, sprinkled among the living people, so many smiling shades from my long history who called out to me encouragingly in their many different languages, rallying for me.

I glanced at the sleek young man, who rolled his eyes slightly and looked away with a smile that was mocking and also decidedly ominous.

Father St. Jacques...

I was certain I had found my quarry's den. The motor home parked on 125th Street was filled with books and scraps of paper with the handwriting that I well recognized. My stomach was churning, from enthusiasm I was certain. There was memorabilia of many sorts and various books attributed to a *W.J. this* or *J.W. that*. It was a treasure trove.

Archbishop Malloy had become increasingly intrigued and convinced about the verity of all my claims. Suddenly we heard an officer outside calling, "Father St. Jacques! Father!"

I hastened to the caravan's door and looked down at the officer who had run up, breathless. "He's been spotted!"

Jillian...

I was astonished by the crowd. It seemed that none of the people knew each other, but all absolutely knew Will; they were all united by that fact. I watched in amazement as many poured into the warehouse while still more arrived in the street outside. The sleek young man kept to his side of the floor as the people surrounded Will with words of thanks and love.

When I snagged several, asking how they knew Will, each had a few words about some kindness he'd done them, their relatives, or even their ancestors. But when I asked how they knew to come here at this moment, their unanimous reaction was one of puzzlement and bemused consternation. They just glanced around the dim, dusty theatrical storehouse, then shook their heads or shrugged, as confounded by the eerie phenomenon as I was.

One ratty, stoop-shouldered, homeless-looking older woman wearing a knit cap with beer-can labels sewn onto it jostled past me and right up to Will, who greeted her fondly: "Eleanor."

I saw the woman's gnarled hands clutch his, and she glared at him with a challenging twinkle in her eye as she said, "I don't know what the hell is goin' on, boyo, but I do know that God don't play dice with the damn universe."

I saw Will gaze deeply into the woman's bloodshot eyes, then he turned to look off across the stretch of dusty warehouse floor that separated him and the gathered people from the sleek young man opposite.

The dark man had been calmly watching the bewildering proceedings with apparent amusement. Though he was trying to project an aspect of nonchalance, I got the definite sense that he was working to control his troubled, threatening feelings. Perhaps it was the flashing look in his dark eyes. But more likely it was because a large black cauldron behind him, which might have been used by the witches in some production of *Macbeth*, had begun bubbling and smoking. Several people among the crowd also noted it with surprise and uneasiness.

I saw that Will was studying the young man, who, though I knew he'd be loath to admit it, seemed slightly cowed by the arrival of this multitude of well-wishers. Will, on the other hand, had clearly been buoyed by the baffling but remarkable show of support. There was a new light in his eyes, a new curiosity.

"What is it?" I asked. "What does all this mean?" But Will was already moving away from us, out from among his caring supporters. Though several tried to hold him back protectively, Will walked slowly toward the sleek young man.

Tito felt danger in the air and called out nervously, "Yo! Will! Don't go there, man." But Will raised a hand to them, indicating that it was alright.

A hush fell over the people, as though they sensed a confrontation of great import was in progress with more forthcoming. Little Maria was last to catch his sleeve, saying, "No. Please!"

Will looked down at her, rested his hand benevolently atop the raven-black hair on Maria's head, and smiled. Then he turned from her and toward the young man, who had been watching him circumspectly. Will stepped away from Maria and took another step closer to the young man, asking, "What 'Larger Plan'?"

The dark-eyed man blew out a little puff and shrugged casually. "I don't know what the hell she was talking about."

"Now that I think of it," Will continued, "there must be some reason he doesn't just erase you."

"Well, for starters," the young man raised his dark eyebrows, "I'm immortal, too. Besides, he enjoys a good game as much as anyone. Particularly because I let him win sometimes. I know that's important to him. You want to talk ego?" He gestured with both hands and glanced upward. "You've got no *idea*. So I let him have a Job or a Mother Teresa now and again, in return for the billions of others that I win over."

Will held his gaze and repeated, "What 'Larger Plan'?"

"I really have no clue, okay?" the young man said waspishly. "And let me warn you, Vitellus, I have been really patient, but now I'm on kind of a short fuse, so—"

"Is it about *you*?"

I saw how, upon hearing that question and trying as he might to keep a poker face, Will's adversary *blinked*. Behind him, the *Macbeth* cauldron suddenly overflowed with what looked like hot lava. More people in the crowd around me reacted fearfully this time.

Will glanced at the cauldron and nodded. "Ah. It is about you."

The young man gazed at Will and cautioned, "You'd be wise to hold your tongue."

Will...

What is it I'm feeling? I wondered. A new energy, as yet unclear but definitely positive, was gripping me, strengthening me. Having unsuccessfully sought the finality as predicted by Saint John in the book of Revelation, I felt that I was suddenly on the verge of some profoundly different and unexpected revelation of *my own*. I turned it over in my mind, trying to get a handle on it.

"I think," I mused as I took another step forward and watched the young man carefully, "I think there's something about me . . . that actually frightens you."

"Hah!" came his retort, as though to a ridiculous suggestion.

"That sounded a little forced," I noted.

The young man glanced confidentially at Jillian and the others with an incredulous smirk. "Do you believe this guy?"

I continued easing circuitously forward as I puzzled it out for myself. "But why would . . . you . . . be frightened of me?"

The young man screwed up his mouth in a sort of leer, like it was indeed an insane idea. "I wouldn't be. I'm not. So." He clapped his hands together and rubbed them as he nodded in the direction of Jillian and the others. "You helped this sorry lot. Good for you. The world's a better place. You can be proud. You've done waaaay more than your share. Bravo." He clapped sharply. Three times. And then his cordial tone became more serious and commanding. "But now you will stop fucking around. And you will come to me."

I continued to pace, slowly. I felt a bit like Clarence Darrow, the astute trial lawyer whom I'd once watched question a very hostile witness. I was trying to piece together the illusive revelation I was feeling but had yet to understand; I was trying to solve the mystery right there in the courtroom. "An Archangel . . . ," I thought aloud, "the Fallen One . . ."

The sleek young man nodded, adding with understated threat, "And don't leave out Titan, Primeval Supercreature, Monarch of the Underworld. Prince of Darkness. Your basic Major Player, pal, so—"

"Those who've fallen . . . like you, like me . . ."

Suddenly it hit me. The lightbulb moment. It was so obvious, so simple. I glanced sharply at the young man. "Those who've fallen . . . usually want . . . *to get back up.*"

Jillian...

I witnessed the sleek young man's eyes flash darkly, his pupils narrowed to black pinpoints. It made my stomach tighten. Was that thunder I heard rumble? Several mannequins, one a samurai in chain mail, trembled with life. The people around me reacted with a collective murmur, growing very anxious. They were still unclear what strange magnetism had drawn them here, but far more uncertain and fearful of what they were watching unfold. Was this some kind of dramatic performance? Most of them sensed it was considerably more than that and far more physically, insidiously dangerous.

I wasn't alone in feeling a creeping, petrifying dread. Little Maria backed up into me. I put my arms down over the girl's shoulders, though uncertain how much protection I would be able to offer Maria against whatever was about to happen.

FORTY-ONE

Will...

I was certain I had struck a chord, because the young man glanced away. But I also caught a different sort of glint percolating in his eyes. I couldn't be certain if it reflected some new insecurity on his part, or whether it was a spark from a dangerous fuse that I myself had just lit. I had serious concern for the safety of the many friends gathered to support me, but their presence also fueled my resolve to press the offensive.

I tried to speak in the same tone of friendship and camaraderie the young man had been employing. "So maybe we're both basically after the same thing." I watched my adversary warily. "Finding a way back." The sleek man still avoided my eyes, glancing around and sighing, as though waiting for a tiresome presentation to conclude. "And what?" I went on forming my thesis. "If I don't concede to you, then you're afraid that *you* might yield to *me*?"

The sleek young man scoffed more loudly, and simultaneously the building suffered a percussive shock as though a large truck had slammed against it. My gathered friends shouted fearfully as the structure trembled. Dust shook loose from the rafters and drifted downward. Several broken panes of glass fell to shatter on the concrete floor. I heard more cries of concern from the crowd behind me. A dog began barking. It was Nicole's new puppy bravely challenging my nemesis, though Nicole, Chuck Weston, the young Greek, and many others were edging fearfully backward toward the open doors and the larger, concerned crowd outside.

Though I appreciated their courageous show of support on my behalf, I wished I were alone with this unspeakably powerful nemesis. But I was increasingly convinced that some Fate, some Larger Plan, was indeed at work, and I instinctively knew I had to play out my part, wherever it led. I also felt I was on something of a roll. I turned back to face my opponent, who was still attempting to downplay my contention. I quietly questioned, "Are you afraid that I'm supposed to somehow help *bring you back*?"

The sleek man's obdurate silence and his darkly gleaming eyes suggested that I might be on the right track. Still, it was confusing. "But why should that frighten you?" I was genuinely puzzled. "I mean, returning to celestial bliss would certainly seem an improvement on your situation." My adversary's silence only seemed to intensify. But despite the determinate, unsurrendering willfullness I saw in those dark eyes, I pressed on. "So what's to be scared of?" I tried to talk as I would to a friend. "Look, you've been after me to join with you, I know . . . But what if . . . just what if . . . we turn things around? What if you come over to my side?"

The young man's handsome face twitched in a manner unnatural for a human, his brow lowered threateningly. I saw a perilous new light leaping from his deep-set eyes, which grew fiery, black, and bold. They had suddenly filled with inscrutable malice. His voice rumbled gutturally, inhumanly strong, as he said in Latin, "In your dreams, fool."

I responded softly in Latin, "Why does it frighten you? Do you not have the courage to consider it? Is it that you want Redemption, but you fear it even more?"

Jillian...

I saw that whatever Will said in Latin caused an astonishing reaction. The sleek young man bellowed bestially, making a sound that was far beyond human. The warehouse shook now as though buffeted by shock waves from an earthquake. Huge theatrical set pieces tumbled like dominoes. Torches flashed afire. Mannequins and suits of armor vibrated and sprang alive.

People behind and around me were suddenly screaming, rushing toward the big doors, which an unseen force suddenly slammed closed in their faces, trapping a terrified hundred of us inside the warehouse. They crushed against each other, shrieking, trying to climb over one another and escape, but it was impossible. Then throaty roars from big jungle cats pulled the crowd's attention back. We were all struck dumb by what we saw.

Maria...

I screamed! Two big stuffed lions and a tiger *came alive* and roared!

Chuck...

Them big cats were glarin' at us with their fangs bared. Then the carousel horses reared up, nostrils flarin' and flames sprayin' out!

Suki...

Whole big warehouse was horror! Nightmare come to life!

Eleanor...

A buncha thin cracks spiderwebbed out 'cross the surface of that cement floor. Then live steam come shootin' up, powerful strong, like volcanic! Blowing boxes and stuff up in the air!

Jillian...

Through the gushing, deafening curtain of steam, most surreal of all, we saw what was happening to the sleek young man.

Before our eyes he was undergoing some unearthly, ungodly metamorphosis.

Laura...

It was horrifying. His body began to tremble until it was *vibrating* at an inhuman speed. Then it began to swell unnaturally, growing larger and molting out of the clothing like a snake shedding its dead skin or some giant insectoid creature inflating out of a chrysalic cocoon.

Tito...

His fuckin' body kep' on pumpin' out and up! Ten, fifteen, twenty-five feet tall and more! Goddamn monster jus' kep' gettin' huger and huger! The steam was swirlin' but I seen his skin turn scaly, murky gray, and it'uz stretched tight as a drum over a twisted gigantor skeleton.

Jillian...

Red, almond-shaped, feline eyes with vertical slits for irises glared down from his shadowy, obscured, ferocious face, which was half sleek young man and half deeply scarred, blood-chilling horror. His cheeks hollowed gauntly as his head elongated, his chin drawing downward to a sharp point. His misshapen, thick-browed cranium sprouted many short quills of ugly cartilage that scratched against the high wooden rafters of the old warehouse. His cranium broke through several thick beams, which fell in pieces around his feet, which I saw had turned into cloven hooves!

In any universe, it was the physical definition of a living nightmare.

We puny humans stood dumbstruck in the unearthly, demonic presence of *the Fallen Archangel.*

His voice came thunderously, from some bottomless cavern beyond. Its impact was bone rattling. We all felt every syllable strike hard against us, buffeting our chests as the terrible monster raged at Will.

"Never shall I bow again before anyone!"

Through it all, Will stood his ground courageously, unmoving amid the roaring volcanic steam. The massive beast stared down fearsomely at him and bellowed, *"This is your final chance to escape your personal hell!"*

Will, undaunted, shouted back against the maelstrom, "And join yours? I don't think so."

The creature roared like a thousand angry beasts, shaking the old building more violently. Larger pieces of the roof fell. People screamed louder and scattered to avoid the falling timbers.

The Archangel reached out his clawed hand toward Will, commanding, *"Come to me! Or all these here shall perish! All will taste my wrath, be flayed alive and burned!"*

He pointed his other taloned hand directly at little Maria and me, hissing, *"Shall I demonstrate?!"*

Will spoke loudly, vehemently, and with perfect clarity. "Harm anyone here and there is no deal."

Again the grinning fiend thrust his grotesque and mighty claw toward Will, and his voice boomed earsplittingly.

"THEN YOU MUST COME TO ME. NOW!"

Will looked around at me, at all the terrified people. Then he turned back to face the monstrous beast.

I was not the only one who shouted, "No!" I heard similar cries arise from many. "No! Don't do it!"

Will extended his hand toward the giant bestial creature.

Many more shouted, "Stop! For God's sake! No, Will! Don't!"

Will's hand was inches from the proffered claw.

Maria screamed loudest, "No! Don't! *Noooooo!*"

But, steadfast, Will placed his hand into the Dark Angel's huge gnarled grip.

The fearsome creature swelled with triumph. His more-than-mortal laughter pealed and echoed horrifyingly.

But nothing could have prepared us for what occurred in the next instant.

In an eye blink, the horrid, spiteful laughter became a poignant, lyrical siren's song, a crystalline feminine voice sustaining a single note at the highest register. The hideous nightmare monster towering over us all suddenly became suffused with celestial light. All of his horror dispersed as the angular, bony frame transformed, filling out with a thousand sparkles, metamorphosing to embody the most exquisite example of classic, physical perfection. Ambrosial perfumes filled the air, which warmed around us. He was instantaneously clothed in transcendent golden brightness. His giant face was sublime, angelic. His cheeks flushed with life and vigor. His eyes were golden and luminous.

Will...

Still clutching my hand, now towered over me the Light Bearer, Heylel—as he had existed *before* his fall. It was Lucifer the Magnificent—*before* his expulsion from heaven.

Jillian...

He was the most breathtakingly beautiful creature I or any mortal had ever beheld or could ever even imagine. His was an elegant, ethereal exquisiteness nearly blinding in its brilliance, worthy of a position in the highest of heavenly courts. Rapturous joy shone on his beaming face. And from his glorious being there came an emanation of light spreading outward, causing the high walls and ceiling of the warehouse to evaporate in the brilliance.

Millions of stars were now turning slowly around us, above us, and, startlingly, even beneath us! We had been carried aloft, transported somewhere into the midst of the universe on some invisible platform. Pinpoints of starlight came at us from all sides, all directions. There were no shadows, only illumination.

My eyes darted to the others around me. Was I the only one seeing this amazement? No. They were all staring upward, equally mesmerized, not breathing, spellbound by this majestic creature, this expansive universe surrounding us, this seemingly miraculous pinnacle of all and infinite space-time.

Will...

I clung to his huge hand as I glanced around. Was this a glimpse of that legendary highest of all heavens? The *shamay shamayim*? The mystical height where Heylel had once personified Purity?

Blessed are the pure in heart, I remembered Livia saying, *for they shall see God.* Heylel had once enjoyed that honor: he had looked directly into that Face of Infinite Grace.

Jillian...

The air was balmy now, suffusing us with a comforting, divine sense of safety and protection. That first siren's song, that single note of highest crystal clarity sustained in perfect pitch by a lone soprano voice, was joined by another and then a dozen more, then a hundred, then a thousand until all the millions of stars illuminating us seemed to find their own voices. And I had a sense that those points of light were not mere stars but entire galaxies or even the beacons of entire other *universes* like our own.

As we stood thunderstruck in the presence of infinity, Will's hand held tightly to Heylel's while the giant Archangel swayed gracefully to the music of the spheres. Tears of joy were brimming in his bright angelic eyes . . .

> *Look how the floor of heaven*
> *Is thick inlaid with patines of bright gold:*
> *There's not the smallest orb which thou behold'st*
> *But in his motion like an angel sings,*
> *Still quiring to the young-eyed cherubins.*
> *Such harmony is in immortal souls . . .*

But neither words Shakespearean nor words biblical were remotely adequate. Not even a colossal, cascading waterfall of words expressing joy in every language known, unknown, or unimagined could begin to convey what we were experiencing.

It was far too ancient, too primal, too beautiful. An infinite force that could only be *felt*. Only experienced internally, with powerful, welling emotion. It was grandest revelation.

And then, from somewhere that seemed far higher than even the dome of stars above us, there came a beam of light growing in intensity like a blossoming supernova. It was focused directly upon Heylel, who felt it, inclined his face toward it, blinking in its extreme luminescence, far too blinding for human eyes to even glance at. The mighty, immortal Archangel himself barely managed to squint painfully into the brilliance, then seemed to glimpse something we could not, and he gasped in horror. His monumental intake of breath created a gusting hurricane wind around us, cowering in amazement below. The stars began turning more rapidly around and underneath us. I clutched little Maria protectively.

The astonishingly gorgeous creature looked sharply down, away from the blinding light, and tried to pull his golden hand away from Will's, but could not. Will held it tightly. The glorious Archangel writhed and struggled harder to pull away. But Will clung relentlessly, clapping his other hand over top and holding even tighter.

Tears glistened in the radiant eyes of the Archangel. One teardrop spilled over and traced down his glowing cheek as he pulled so ardently that Will's feet lifted off the invisible floor. His paper hospital slippers fell away. He dangled barefoot as he was raised higher.

Maria, Tito, the hundred others, and I were fearfully mesmerized as Will continued to be lifted higher still. The Archangel struggled to break free from Will's determined grasp. But to me the phenomenal creature somehow seemed to be at cross-purposes with himself, trying to break free from Will, but simultaneously caught up in the ethereal bliss of the magnificent, quintessential beauty that he had been restored to.

Will hung suspended in midair, being swung back and forth by the giant hand of the most splendid creature as the stars swirled around us ever more rapidly. Will was staring fixedly into the Archangel's shining, tormented eyes, and I saw that Will was speaking to him, repeating something. I strained to hear his words and realized they were again in Latin. Then Will insistently shouted a new phrase, which had a startling impact upon the magnificent Archangel.

The gigantic creature threw his head rearward, arching his back. Then, by snapping his wrist sharply, like cracking a whip, he broke free of Will's hold and desperately snatched his perfect hand away as though he had touched the surface of the sun. Will fell twelve feet downward. And in that brief moment the stars vanished. Will landed hard on the concrete floor that reappeared beneath us. The glorious brilliance and warmth of *shamay shamayim* was sucked into darkness as the grim warehouse re-encircled us. The Archangel's beauty peeled away, imploding into the returning horror, now a nightmare twice over.

The golden luster scorched off, leaving ruddy scales. Grotesque mucus-covered wings, vast and dragonlike, unfolded from his bony shoulders. The surface of his ghastly face grew gaunt once more. But worse: it was pustulated, undulating as though macabre creatures were crawling just beneath his roiling skin.

The razor teeth now had a moldy hue. In a single exhalation from his gaping maw, the sweet ambrosial fragrances around us were at once polluted by a potent stench of vile putrefaction as though all the sewers of New York had opened and filled every dark corner of the warehouse. The very air took on a sickly brownish-yellow tinge, and from out of the volcanically steaming fissures, a million filthy flies suddenly came swarming.

The hideous creature clutched the wrist of his misshapen hand that had touched Will, screeching as though Will had caused a pain that was beyond enduring.

Then the archfiend reared up to his full, mighty stature. His vast proportions filled the lofty space and broke through a portion of the roof. Frightened people screamed and ducked for cover as heavy shards of lumber and glass rained down and crashed around them. As the ignoble monster glared down at Will, I saw sparks of living fury in his basiliskine eyes.

One last time the giant creature hurled defiance toward the vault of heaven with a shriek so piercing that all the remaining windows shattered explosively and the warehouse shook near to collapsing. Then the monster was suddenly encompassed by a breathtaking pillar of hellfire that became a swirling maelstrom, a screeching vortex, as the great beast was sucked down through the concrete floor and disappeared.

There was sudden, complete, and utter silence.

The terrified people sprawled or crouched around me were as staggered as I was, a harrowing fear still coursing through us all. None of us dared to move or even breathe.

Finally Will slowly and painfully got to his hands and knees. He was laboring to catch his breath. He gathered what remaining strength he had and stood up from where he had fallen. I saw that he limped slightly, either from his fall or his still incompletely healed legs, as he moved toward where the creature had disappeared. A bright beam of sunlight from where the roof was broken open above was streaming down through the dusty air upon him. It was then I realized that a man's body was lying near Will in the center of the floor.

It was the Cuban cabbie. He was crumpled in a heap, his clothes smoking. Will crouched shakily beside him, placing a hand on the shoulder of the driver, who slowly looked up. The Cuban was dazed, blinking, and thoroughly confused as he muttered, "What the hell?"

A young black woman was the first who went to help the cabbie. Her puppy licked the Cuban's hand.

As Will stood up again, little Maria ran to him, hugging him around the legs. I hurried to Will as Maria looked up and asked him, "He got away, huh?"

"Yeah, I guess, Maria," Will said, his left hand gently touching her cheek. "For now."

I carefully took his right hand, which had grasped the demon's. "Are you okay?!" I stammered. "What happened? How did you survive?!" I opened his hand carefully to see if he was injured and saw something in his palm.

It was the tiny locket, open and revealing the small bloodstain.

My heart skipped a beat. I glanced up, awestruck, at the phenomenal man's eyes. He was also looking at the locket. He seemed as astonished as I was, but also justified that his instinct had been correct. His voice was quiet, very humble: "Amazing . . . what a little blood of One Good Man can accomplish."

I felt what I realized Hanna must have felt in 1937: a surging emotion, a profoundly deep affection for this legendary, heroic man and his courageous, compelling, epic nature. I realized that at his smallest invitation I would accompany him anywhere, would gladly be his companion for all the years that were allowed me. Will seemed to read my thoughts. He responded to my welling emotion with a gentle, understanding expression that struck me as sublime. He gazed at me for a long, private moment that I would treasure forever after.

Then he looked again toward the spot where the creature had disappeared. I saw puzzlement appear on Will's face as though he was trying to sort through and comprehend the meaning and substance of all that had just transpired.

Will...

I looked down at the tiny locket in my hand and its precious contents. It was more than just a protection, I realized. Much more than that. It was some sort of . . . I searched for the right word and finally settled upon *facilitator*.

As I struggled to understand the secret, primal truth that hovered tantalizingly just slightly beyond my grasp, a voice called to me in Greek, "Are you alright?"

Jillian...

Will turned to see the Greek student watching him with earnest concern. Will nodded distractedly, then scanned the faces of all the other people who had been slowly getting to their feet with stunned expressions.

All were disheveled, still reeling from the unconscionable, metaphysical blend of horrifying nightmare and miraculous grandeur we had just experienced. All of them understood how profound had been the supernatural struggle we had witnessed. None of our lives would ever be the same. They stared at Will with silent respect, many looking at him with adoration as though he were actually a demigod.

Will...

What a wonder it was, I thought as I looked back at them all. *What a surprising wonder that they all should have been drawn here.* Then I chuckled inwardly. *Or maybe not so surprising.*

I looked at the individuals, into their eyes, acknowledging Tito, Mrs. Tamura, Chuck Weston, Laura Rakowitz, old Eleanor, who grinned and snapped a thumbs-up at me, saying, "Way to go, boyo! Kicked his ass!"

I had so many friends. I was extremely moved by their devotion, and I could barely find voice to simply say, "Thank you. All."

Their sudden laughing cheer was so full of relief, so abrupt and boisterous, it surprised me. They swarmed forward and around me, wrapping me in their humanity and affection. The tall warehouse doors were pulled wide open, and those outside also flooded in, joining the throng within, asking what had happened. I heard blessings for me shouted in many languages. I turned round and round, trying to thank and touch each smiling well-wisher.

Someone's boom box outside began playing a symphonic-rock version of Beethoven's "Ode to Joy." That glorious melody added to my rejuvenation.

In the midst of it all, my eyes again met Jillian's steady gaze, which I saw spoke of her pride and satisfaction at having been able to assist me.

Jillian...

Will nodded his appreciation and said, "I guess you might as well tell my story." He glanced around and added, with understated humor, "Looks like I've sorta been outed."

Will...

But Jillian's caring gaze didn't change, and I understood that it also spoke of an even more personal, emotional connection that we shared.

As I gazed back at her, through the music and jubilation, I became aware of the approach of distant sirens. Ever-alert Tito was instantly beside me, placing a hand on my arm, saying, "Yo, there's these priest guys with a whole shitload o'cops. You better boogie big-time."

I nodded and started to turn, but Tito caught my hand firmly in a soul brother's grasp and found my eyes. He pulled me face-to-face with him. His expression spoke volumes of amazement, respect, and a new seriousness, a new maturity. "You *do* know, right?" Then he added, with total certainty, *"You the Man."*

His eyes held mine emphatically for a long moment. Then Tito turned, and at his gesture, the crowd of my friends parted slightly as though he were Moses creating an escape route. Chuck Weston held out his boots and leather duster. "Hey, pardner. Can't let ya go nowhere dressed like that, or barefoot." I nodded thanks and took them as Chuck said, "My car's round the side if you need a lift." I nodded and Chuck grinned. "Then let's vamoose."

I drew a breath to depart as I heard a small voice whisper, "Take me."

I turned and saw little Maria clutching her ragged bunny tightly with one hand. With her other hand she grasped my sleeve. "Please," she said, "I don't like living with my uncle. He touches me and stuff."

I saw Jillian react like a high-voltage current had struck her.

Maria's voice was soft, imploring. "Please." She looked at me through brimming brown eyes that were shining with simple, direct emotion. "I don't have anybody else."

I stared at the little girl and couldn't remember ever feeling so torn. I also felt Tito tugging my other arm urgently, and I heard the sirens getting very close.

Then a woman's hands came to rest protectively on Maria's shoulders. They were Jillian's. Looking down at the little girl devotedly, she said, "Oh yes you do, honey."

Jillian lifted her gaze to me, confirming the choice she had made, the responsibility she was taking on. Wholeheartedly.

Father St. Jacques...

The archdiocese limousine had been speeding west along 105th Street, swerving around slower traffic, following directly behind the lead police car, which was providing an escort with its siren blaring and lights flashing. As we approached the corner at Columbus, I could see other blue NYPD patrol cars converging on the street, which was thickly crowded with people who seemed to me to be in the throes of jubilation.

Even before the limousine stopped, I had my door open, was out and running. I shouted commands at the police to help me get through the unruly mob and into the old building, which was apparently the crowd's focus. The rabble was not cooperative; indeed everyone in the crowd seemed to be enjoying the difficulty the police and I had in pushing through them. My exertion was immense, my anger boiling at this boisterous, cheerful throng. I tasted bile rising bitterly into my throat, but I was determined to personally lay hands on my quarry once and for all time.

A cordon of officers finally assisted me in shoving my way angrily into the warehouse. I saw at the center of the noisy horde the reporter was holding the hand of the tenement child. Pushing my way through many who seemed determined to casually impede my progress, I finally reached the reporter. Standing beside her was the street mongrel, Tito. I grabbed him and shouted into his face, "Where is he?!"

The little bastard just looked at me, feigning innocence. "Where's who, man?"

Jillian...

St. Jacques was so furious that he shook Tito violently, screaming, "Don't lie to me, you little shit bastard. Where is he?!" The priest shook him brutally once more, but Tito bristled and, with surprising strength, knocked St. Jacques's arms away as the police grabbed and restrained the priest.

"Not me, you fools!" He swore at them in French. Then, in a perfect fury, near apoplexy, he bellowed, "Check all the exits! No one leaves without me seeing them! We will take this building apart if we have to!"

At that point, Father St. Jacques abruptly clutched his stomach, turned away from us, and violently vomited.

I held Maria's small hand tightly as the police tried to start marshaling the crowd, but their official commands were all but drowned out by the throng of people vocalizing along with the swelling majesty of Beethoven's *Choral* Symphony.

Maria looked up at me. Both of our hearts were full.

FORTY-TWO

Father St. Jacques...

The sickness had welled up inside me like poisonous gas. At first I attributed my vomiting in that moment to my extreme anger over the circumstances surrounding his brazen escape. But I had often noted the leaden feeling in my stomach, that the frequency of my indigestion had been increasing. I had begun to think that the strain from my diligent service to thee and to our cause, My Lord, had brought about an ulceration of my stomach. When the blood appeared in my stool that evening I was certain my hypothesis was accurate.

As soon as I was able (given my ongoing and extensive labors on behalf of thy Holy Business), I sought a physician's opinion. The tests resulted in a diagnosis of inoperable stomach cancer.

The night after that was confirmed I prayed aloud. "As well thou knowest, My Father, I have not only sought to live an irreproachable, abstemious life, but to serve thy church to the full extent of my abilities during my allotted time here below. Though my pursuit of this strange being Vitellus Manchus has as yet to reach fruition, I vow to thee, Most High, that I am determined to get the bit of our Holy

Mother Church between his teeth and bend the creature to serve thee most properly.

"What a wondrous achievement to display such a living miracle to the masses! How many millions more would rush to join thy flock of true believers! I am certain that I can yet achieve this splendid goal for thee, My Lord of Hosts, if blessed with two simple gifts: additional time and a more prominent position.

"I am convinced that an upraised position is vital. Had I been in a position of complete, unquestioned authority over Cardinal Malloy, our quarry would not have escaped. No matter how much an impassioned person like myself may desire to enhance the stature of thy church, without a position of power, such desire is wasted.

"I pray that it might be possible even at this late hour of my worldly existence for thee to reconsider my fate, Holy of Holies. I earnestly entreat thee to review what I have endeavored to accomplish for thee and to grant me a public seat of power that I might more swiftly command the resources of the church to do thy bidding. I swear that I shall then do everything humanly possible to bring my mission, *our* mission, Heavenly Father, to a conclusion satisfactory to us and bring greater glory to thee.

"Of course I cherish the opportunity to be drawn up into thy bosom as soon as possible, for there is no greater honor than to be in thy Divine Presence. I truly yearn to pass beyond the veil and join thee. I know the impending death of my vulgar human form is in truth a great blessing.

"It is therefore not that I fear my own oblivion or to slip away unnoticed, as though I had never existed to anyone. Though I would never presume to question thy Divine Wisdom, I do earnestly believe that I can be *of better service to thee* by remaining here on Earth a while longer to conclude my decades-long quest to rein in this misguided and dangerous errant.

"The physicians say my condition is advanced and my disease terminal, that I shall likely die within the fortnight. But I know so many examples of thy mercy and the miraculous intervention of thy Divine Hand to rescue a failing person from the very brink of death that my petition to thee for a few years more is neither without precedent nor without hope.

"I do therefore most humbly beseech thee to reconsider my petition, My Dear Lord God Almighty, Creator and Ruler of Earth and Heaven and All the Universe, now and forever more, world without end. Amen. And again, My Dear Lord Most High, amen."

Jillian...

With the help of other people gathered in that warehouse, Maria and I first made certain that dear, brave Hanna was properly and gently attended to. Once that was accomplished, I quickly collected names and contact information for many of the people who were there. I soon located others through careful advertisements placed in the personal sections of the *Times* and online classifieds.

Their testimonials, along with my own experiences, plus the contribution of Father Paul St. Jacques, whom I'll speak more of below, helped form the original book I wrote about Will, which was published sixteen years ago. That volume did not, of course, contain Will's own first-person account, which is incorporated into this edition. I came by that treasure trove much later, as you'll read.

Immediately after the events occurred, I learned that Will's motor home had been taken to a police impound lot from which its contents mysteriously disappeared that very first night. Initially I thought the archdiocese must have somehow confiscated Will's belongings, but I later learned they had a much more desirable fate.

Two weeks after the mind-bending event in the warehouse, I received the following letter from Father St. Jacques:

Dear Miss Guthrie,

Now that the cat has escaped from the bag I am sure that you, as an accomplished, aggressive journalist, will doubtlessly make public the remarkable story that you and I uncovered. So that you may best and most accurately tell the *full* story of this man whom I hunted for such a very long time, I have reached an important personal decision.

I am placing into your hands my own private journal, enclosed on the CD data disc accompanying this letter. Some portions that I had written by hand have been scanned and included. It constitutes my entire personal diary, which, unless entrusted to you, would never likely be seen by the public, but rather retained in the secret Vatican archives and added to those of my many anonymous predecessors in this strange pursuit.

As you will see, this journal is written in my native French and contains my own ruminations, prayers, and private confessions to God. But it also chronicles the details of my mission and my tireless search for my illusive quarry.

Upon reflection as I lay dying, I felt that it could provide some meager references that you might wish to include in your own writing about this unique saga. I determined to entrust my diary to you so that my unquestionably modest efforts on behalf of My Holy Mother Church, His Holiness the Pope, and most importantly the Lord God shall not be entirely lost to the rest of humankind.

I would have edited it prior to placing it in your hands, but my time has suddenly become extremely limited. My Heavenly Father has, in His Infinite Wisdom, apparently decided to gather my unworthy soul immediately into His Grace. It is quite likely that even as you read this I shall have already departed to join Him in His Glory.

I am keenly aware of the shortcomings of my writing. I know this diary to be neither of the length, nor scholarliness, nor philosophical depth, nor anything approaching the magnificent value of the extant musings of Saint Francis or the confessions of Saint Augustine. I am merely a simple priest who has labored according to the dictates of my own conscience and my vows to be a dutiful servant to the will of Almighty God.

Nonetheless, I hope that my private, unique insights into this astonishing story might augment your efforts and prove to be of some minor interest to the vast populace who, now and in the years to come, will certainly read your work.

Respectfully,

Father Paul St. Jacques
St. Vincent's Hospital, Manhattan

PS: If perchance you should use illustrations in the body of your text, I am also enclosing a small photograph of myself and would not be opposed should you wish to include it in your publication.

FORTY-THREE

Jillian...

Almost sixteen years after the events described above, I took a few days off from my latest *New York Times* assignment so I could be in Palo Alto for a very special graduation.

The Frost Amphitheater is nestled in a wooded glade shaped like an inverted teardrop. The gently sloping audience area funnels down toward the sunny south end, where there is a small stage. Completely surrounded by eucalyptus, sycamore, and oak trees, I felt as though I were in a secluded glen deep within an old-growth forest, rather than in the middle of the campus of Stanford University.

The outdoor graduation was in progress. Two hundred students in black caps and gowns were seated in white folding chairs before the stage, and five times as many parents and friends were spread in rows of similar chairs radiating up the grassy hillside behind them. Seated on the stage were a dozen gowned professors. A stalwart woman, Dean Octavia Dyer Jensen, was officiating at the podium, handing out diplomas as she read the graduates' names in her Danish accent.

"Jessica Shin Lee," she said, presenting a diploma to a young Chinese American woman while her family a few rows ahead of me stood up, applauding politely and snapping photos.

As the procession of graduates continued, punctuated by applause, someone sat down in the empty chair on the aisle beside me. Even without looking, my heart skipped a beat and my breathing grew shallow. I was too nervous to look at him right away.

Dean Jensen continued, "Samuel Richard Balcomb." Samuel's parents and friends were delightfully boisterous, hooting and applauding him enthusiastically.

I was still staring toward the stage but no longer really seeing it. Despite the fact that my mouth suddenly felt like the Sahara, I managed to whisper, "I thought . . . I hoped . . . that just possibly you might be able to come." Then I turned to look at Will. He was smiling wistfully.

He nodded. "I've followed your blogs. This seemed like the right time to circle back."

I gazed into his gentle eyes for a very long moment. Then I chuckled slightly as I spoke the cliché, which in his case was the absolute truth. "Wow. You haven't changed a bit."

He grinned ironically. "You, on the other hand, look better than ever, Jillian. Positively radiant."

He leaned toward me. I took his hand and gave him a very long and heartfelt kiss on the cheek. He noticed my wedding ring, saying, "I'm happy to see that."

I shrugged, slightly embarrassed to admit, "It took a while, but I finally got with the program." Then I drew a breath, asking a bit gingerly, "What about you? How're you doing?"

I noticed that Will's voice was not without cheer as he said, "I'm getting by." Something *was* definitely different about him, but subtly so. As he glanced out across the gathering, I had a moment to study him more carefully. He was carrying a sky-blue Windbreaker and wearing Levi's denims and a crisp white dress shirt, beneath which I glimpsed Livia's cross and locket. I tried to divine exactly what I was sensing about his ambience. Was it a new feeling of tranquility?

When he turned back to look at me again, I continued staring, as mesmerized as I had been upon our first encounter all those years ago. Finally I shook my head, stretching my eyes wide open. "Sorry. It's just so wonderful to see you again, Will."

"You, too, Jillian," he said sincerely. Then he drew out of his jacket a rare first-edition copy of the original book I'd written about him sixteen years earlier.

"Oh my God!" I felt a bit sheepish. "I really hoped you weren't mad about that. Even though so many people were in that warehouse with us and witnessed what happened, even after you gave me permission to tell the story, I still went around and around about it. But I finally decided it might do more good than harm."

"And it certainly did: worldwide bestseller. Made a lot of money, all of which you donated to Doctors Without Borders, Amnesty International, a bunch of others."

"I tried to pick places you'd approve of."

"You succeeded." Then he offered me the book and a pen. "Would you?"

I blinked like a flustered schoolgirl in the presence of my larger-than-life idol. I even stuttered a little. "Of . . . of course. I'd be . . . honored." But when I opened the book, I somehow knew exactly what to write and I unhesitatingly inscribed it:

> *To Will,*
> *Truly a Man for All Seasons.*
> *With my admiration and enduring love,*
>
> *Jillian*

As he read it, that wistful smile returned to his face. There was particularly loud applause for the latest graduate, but I kept watching Will and narrowed my eyes slightly. "You know, I found out a number of those same organizations get an odd anonymous donation every year."

He was turning the pages of the book. "I'm glad to hear it. Lot of good people out there."

"Mmmm, but this one particular donor always sends each of them exactly $333,000. And it comes from a different country each time." Will didn't take the bait, so I continued, "I dug a little deeper and discovered that gee, guess what? Some of the older ones have been getting those donations for over a century."

Will just continued turning the pages. "I liked your later books, too, Jillian. You and your friend Steve uncovered important stuff. Made people think."

"Well, you have a knack for refocusing a person's goals." I pressed his hand. "I hope you take some comfort in being such a force for Good."

He shrugged. "Hey, everybody creates a ripple effect on the world. Back in the sixties my friend Edward Lorenz even came up with a name for it."

"The chaos theory. The butterfly effect. Yeah." I knew it well. "Change one small thing, and everything can end up changed. But you, Will . . . you get to *see* the results of your efforts more than anybody else ever does." My voice lowered slightly. "Sometimes I've actually thought your life was less of a curse and more of a great gift."

"Really?" He glanced up at me. "Want to trade?" Our gaze held as I again felt the epic, oceanic expanse of Will's long existence. But also the loneliness and isolation that came with it.

Finally I said, "Funny, though, how everyone dreams of living forever."

His expression became one of gentle wisdom. "Beware what you wish for, Jilly."

There was another smattering of applause for a graduate as I drew a breath. "I actually have something for you, Will." I carefully took from my purse a small cloth pouch. "I've carried them with me always, hoping there might come a day like today."

Opening the pouch, he saw Mary Shelley's antique strand of petite pearls, which he'd given Hanna, who wore them until her final day.

His fingertips touched them lightly as though he were touching Hanna herself. Drawing a breath, he raised his eyes to mine appreciatively, then he glanced away with a wave of emotion passing through him. I looked toward the stage to allow him privacy.

After a moment I heard him whisper, "Thank you, Jillian. This means . . . a great deal."

I simply nodded and let a respectful moment pass as I watched the graduation. "Doug is down there somewhere. He wanted a good picture." Then I looked back at Will and into our shared past. "You know, I've always wondered: when you were dangling there in midair, clutching his enormous hand, I heard you saying something to him in Latin. What was it?"

Will continued gazing toward the stage. Though it looked like he remembered that moment clearly, he responded, "Whatever it was, I guess I didn't say it well enough. Or with quite enough heart." He pondered that thought for a silent moment, then added, "But I don't recall exactly."

I sensed otherwise yet understood that whatever the words had been, they would remain between Will and his terrible nemesis. I gazed intently at him a moment, recalling that day of Olympian conflict and Will's consummate bravery in the face of such otherworldly power. My voice grew softer still as I said, "I think you know that I, or any of us there, would have dropped everything and gone away with you that day if you'd needed us to."

He smiled at me fondly. "I'd say you went exactly the right way, Jillian." We heard polite applause around us for another graduate.

I had continued studying his face, his eyes. "You seem different somehow, Will. More at peace with your predicament or . . . ?"

"Maybe a bit refocused myself." He saw my frown of curiosity. "Since the warehouse, my Old Young Friend seems to have concluded that I'm something of a threat to his lifestyle."

"Well, *yeah.*" I chuckled at the understatement. "I'd say you had a slight impact on him."

Will nodded, musing, "It's become a very interesting push-pull. His appearances have been more sporadic. And somewhat different."

"Ever since he experienced that flash of remembrance about what he had been?" The miraculous vision of the titanic, virginal Archangel in all his divine magnificence, his phenomenal glory, blossomed again into my memory. As always, it set my mind reeling. "That was the most . . ." My lips moved silently, trying to describe what I had witnessed, but as I had long since discovered, human words were simply not adequate.

Will knew what I was feeling. "Yeah. After he got that little taste and understood how he might possibly be that way again."

"With your help?"

"Perhaps." He smiled, then chided himself, "If I can put enough heart into it. Anyway, ever since he got that reminder he does seem a bit fearful of me . . . but also drawn to me."

"The proverbial moth to the flame. In his case an eternal flame." I stared, then shook my head, raising my eyebrows with a nervous laugh. "God, it's so . . . strange: sitting here in the sunshine, on a folding chair, in the everyday world, to be talking about such . . . things . . ."

"'More things in heaven and Earth, Horatio, than are dreamt of . . . ,'" he said softly.

I turned my eyes again to Will, who sat beside me, gazing thoughtfully at the graduation. As in that warehouse sixteen years earlier, I felt a rush of sublime emotion from being in the presence of this courageous, magnetic, truly extraordinary man. I tried to digest the seeming impossibility of the mythological, Herculean task before him. I knew that Will's adversary was literally of cosmic proportions and power. I could barely find my voice. "How could you ever defeat him?"

Will shrugged. "One day at a time?"

"Your new challenge for the New Millennium?" But before he could respond, I suddenly blinked, went wide-eyed, and turned pale. An incredibly startling, shockingly life-changing possibility had flashed into my mind. "Oh my God. Will!"

He glanced at my sudden exclamation. My mouth hung agape as I felt the profound weight of the new concept I had just thought of. Finally I continued, very slowly, in a breathless whisper, "Will . . . did you ever think that . . . instead of you having to just *wait* for some sort of—"

"Ah!" Will had spotted something and sat up straighter. "Here comes our girl."

I was frustrated by the interruption. I was desperate for him to hear my amazing new thought and to hear his response, but the dean was announcing, "And graduating from Premed with highest honors . . . Maria Katharine Encalada . . . Summa cum laude . . ."

Will and I were both on our feet, ardently applauding the lovely, slightly stocky young woman whom Maria had become. She walked up onto the stage to receive her diploma. Her long, shiny raven-black hair caught the sunlight. So did her confident, sparkling, intelligent eyes.

I watched with pride as Maria nodded politely to the dean, then held the diploma and her ragged bunny, Tinkerbell, high up over her head, shouting exuberantly across the crowd directly to me, "This is for you, Mom!"

Through the sudden tears that had sprung into my eyes, I could hardly see Maria, but I shouted back to my girl in my perfectly accented Spanish, "You go, Daughter! You rock!"

I applauded with gusto, then turned to share the happy moment with Will, but he was gone.

I felt a great outward surge create a vacuum in my heart. A wave of immense sadness followed. Will's absence left a profound void, an emptiness. And left my startling question unfinished and unanswered. I stood motionlessly. But slowly I began to savor the fleeting moment I had just shared with Will. A happily sad smile formed on my face as tears further blurred my sight.

I wiped them and looked back toward my bright-eyed Maria, who was beside Doug now at the foot of the stage. Both were waving excitedly over the crowd to me. Maria and my dear, loyal, loving Doug were the lights of my life. I always had thought of them both as being gifts from Will.

—⁂—

About two weeks after the graduation, I was surprised to receive another amazing gift from Will: a padded envelope that contained a small flash drive and a letter.

> Dear Jillian,
> Thanks for the touching autograph. When your book was first published all those years ago, I read it and was very impressed by your scholarship, your self-effacing honesty, and your integrity. It actually prompted me to begin jotting down my own personal recollections of that difficult period we shared back at the turn of the second Millennium.
> I am enclosing the file for you to do with as you like. It may be of some additional interest. At least it might help you create and sell a new edition of your book, whose revenue could add to the coffers of those worthy organizations you've chosen to support.
> Thanks again, Jillian, for all your care of Hanna, and of Maria, and certainly of me. You have my undying gratitude.
> And in my case, that truly means something.
> With great respect and considerable love . . .
>   Will

The file he sent me contained all of Will's first-person recollections, which I proceeded to incorporate into this new, greatly expanded, and definitive edition.

His narrative and this new book appropriately conclude with the following passage from . . .

Will...

A few days after seeing Jillian and Maria at Stanford, I was awakened by the clock radio in my motor home. The station was in the midst of a commercial: ". . . With all the vitamins you need for a healthy breakfast to start fresh each new day!"

I was parked in a zone that had some restrictions, so I had to get rolling fairly soon. The morning DJ's cheery voice seemed determined to help me. "It is a bee-youtiful day here in the Bay Area. And it's going to be a beautiful show this weekend at the Moscone Center in San Francisco. It's sold out, but we've got two hot tickets to see country legends Janie Wall and her husband, Chuck Weston. Be caller number three and you got 'em." As he talked, I heard a familiar guitar riff start up in the background. "And to get you in the mood here's a great golden oldie, the breakaway hit that rejuvenated Chuck's career sixteen years ago, 'Travelin' Man.'"

I smiled, envisioning Chuck plucking away at ol' Betsy as his infectiously upbeat, bluesy tune kicked into gear and his earthy, deep bass voice began to sing.

> He told me I should get on back to Austin . . .
> Away from all the crap that I'd got lost in . . .
> He said, "Go hop a freight across them plains,
> Get back up on your horse and grab them reins,
> Go kick some dust up at your boyhood home,
> Go ride the range clear down to San Antone,"
> I don't know where he come from,
> And I don't know where he's gone,
> But that Travelin' Man, he told me,
> That I'd get back in the show,
> If I would just remember . . . the A-la-mo.

I was still smiling at Chuck's lyrics when I stepped out of my electric motor home to inhale Sausalito's morning air before driving my requisite distance away.

I walked south along Bridgeway, pausing at a newsstand when a familiar face caught my attention. His smiling eyes were looking out from the cover of a magazine called *Art World*, which bore the headline "Art Transforms the Hood." Tito was standing in front of his latest large and extremely interesting painting. Though in his midthirties now, his saucy grin was exactly the same.

I thumbed through the magazine, chuckling about the last time I'd seen him: that night in the police impound lot. He and his street pals helped me gain access to the lockup just like they formerly infiltrated the subway layups in the Bronx during the dead of night to paint the sides of the trains. Together we liberated all of the important belongings from my old motor home.

The news dealer, who was middle-aged with shiny black skin and a gray buzz cut, saw my interest and nodded. "Cool kid, huh? Used a lotta loot from them paintings of his to help folks in his own hood. Sure could do with a few more like him."

"Always," I agreed, as I handed him a ten and he fished for change. "Keep it."

"You sure?" He looked up in genuine surprise, then smiled back gratefully. "Thanks, man. I can use it."

I turned onto Bay, then walked down Humboldt toward the waterfront. I crossed Spinnaker Drive to the triangle of grass that formed a pocket-sized park right at the water's edge.

I stood there, enjoying the salt air and the splendid view of San Francisco across the glittering waters of the bay. The city held fond memories for me, like Paris did of Hanna. So very often sweet reminiscences of dear Hanna float in upon me like a balmy breath of that fragrant springtime Parisian air we had shared. How I miss her. Not a day passes without her brisk Yankee spunkiness nudging my thoughts, reminding me that the new invigoration I feel is built on a fresh and unshakable foundation that Hanna inspired by what she said to me with her last breaths.

Ironically, my dark adversary also played a role in my rejuvenation. He unintentionally sparked me by saying that despite my centuries of earnest effort, my heart hadn't truly been in the work. I realized he was right: I had strenuously labored at each task, yes, and added each effort to my scorecard; I had done the work, but had my heart ever been fully in it? That was an eye-opening question. Combined with Hanna's final words about *A Larger Plan*, it all shifted me to an entirely new center of gravity.

And it suggested a startling new option.

I mulled it over as my eyes scanned the bright skyline of San Francisco, which seemed a promised land, an Emerald City tantalizingly out of reach. Since I'd been there last when I met my benefactors dear old Jacob Davis and Levi Strauss in 1880, I wouldn't be able to walk those hilly streets again for another 195 years or so, if my life proceeded as it had in the past.

But what if it didn't?

What if my circumstances suddenly changed drastically because of the amazing possibility that had occurred to me? The striking new concept, which I suspected Jillian had also hit upon and started to ask me about at Stanford, was a notion that could alter the course of everything instantly. It was truly a lightbulb moment: an earthshaking, game-changing idea I had stumbled onto, and unwittingly almost achieved, in the warehouse.

Seeing the effect when I spoke to my adversary while touching him with the sacred relics, realizing that I had carried with me for twenty centuries the tiny key that, if used properly, might unlock the door, might break the seventh seal, feeling how I might hopefully free not just myself and my nemesis, but also free *everyone* from the darkness and misery that his evil nature fostered in humankind, awakening to all of that, I believed I finally understood my true challenge.

With mild bemusement, I was pleased that it had taken me only two thousand years to figure it out.

I realized that my condition had never been a *curse*, but rather the most important of *grand missions*. I had been appointed not merely to wander the world doing the best I could for people while waiting and hoping for my personal redemption. I have realized that if indeed there is ever to be some sort of Second Coming, some fulfillment of Saint John's visionary predictions, some wonderful New Beginning, it does not depend upon some human-created millennial time frame.

I had the revelation that maybe what Tito said about me being *the Man* was accurate: that on that fateful day in anno Domini 33, *the torch had been passed*; the trigger that could bring about that New Beginning might actually be *me*.

Thus my mission, to which I am now fully committed, heart and soul, is to *actively seek out my enemy*, to relentlessly pursue him regardless of what fearfully dark places that might lead me into. I must confront his potent power, as Hanna counseled, with the opposing force of what she called Divine Love: to dispel the monumental evil that envelops him, to draw him back into the Light.

To bring him Home.

And hopefully the rest of us along with him.

I drew a very long breath. Each time I considered the prospect, I knew it was beyond daunting. Yet my first attempt in the warehouse had shown that it was, perhaps, not impossible.

I took a last lingering look at the shining city across the waters, then I smiled, turned, and walked along Humboldt. I felt an encouraging sea breeze freshening on my back. The sidewalk, rising up to meet my feet, was gaining population now. There were businesspeople, day laborers, mothers, fathers, children, and others: all fellow tourists, like myself, on planet Earth.

I noticed that shuffling slowly among them was an ill-kempt, grungy man with sunken eyes, mismatched threadbare clothes, and ratty, unwashed hair. People were angling to avoid him.

I slowed down as he approached. His careworn head was tilted down. He glanced furtively up at me with embarrassed eyes, murmuring, "'Scuse me, mister. Can y'spare a little change?"

"Sure. There you go, friend," I said encouragingly as I pressed a folded fifty into his grimy hand. He didn't even look at it, but pocketed it as he barely grunted thanks and continued past me. But then I heard him inarticulately mumble something that gave me pause. It sounded like an ancient language. Latin? Aramaic?

I turned with profound curiosity and called after him, "I'm sorry, what did you say?"

As he kept walking he glanced back, only halfway, over his shoulder and spoke, this time in English.

". . . Gandhi, Jesu, and Hanna say hi."

Then he kept walking away.

It may have been my emotional frame of mind spurring my imagination, or perhaps it was simply the angle of the early-morning sunlight exciting the trace of humidity in the air, but there appeared to be about the man what I can only describe as a very slight radiance.

He walked on among the many other individuals, all of them busy with their own thoughts, their various concerns, completely unaware of the unique specialness in their midst.

I noticed, however, that when he passed by, a trace of his radiance brushed off onto each of them.

*Portions of the author's proceeds
from this work go to benefit
Médecins Sans Frontières (Doctors Without Borders),
Amnesty International,
and The David Sheldrick Wildlife Trust.*

ACKNOWLEDGMENTS

For their invaluable help in making this book a reality, I am deeply indebted to:

Brenda Griffin, my longtime, spirited assistant, present at the creation many years ago and constantly urging me forward.

My team at Gandolfo Helin & Fountain Literary Management, particularly Italia Gandolfo, who encouraged me to write this novel exactly as I envisioned it, and Renee Fountain for helping me focus that vision even more sharply.

Editor Tegan Tigani, who brought her clear-eyed, smart ideas for improvements with humor, charm, and a wonderfully light hand.

Copyeditor Scott Calamar and proofreader Janice Lee for their exceedingly microscopic reviews and fine suggestions.

Senior editor Jason Kirk at Amazon's 47North, who reacted so positively initially and then championed this novel as he expertly shepherded it through the publishing process.

Rex Bonomelli, whose brilliantly conceived cover artwork beautifully evokes the nature of my story.

And the person deserving the most gratitude—for being the cornerstone of all my work, for sharing her humanity, moral values, and inspiration with me in a life-altering way for over forty years—is my better half, my better angel, my wife, Susie.

ABOUT THE AUTHOR

Photo © Susan Appling Johnson

Kenneth Johnson has been a successful writer-producer-director of film and television for more than four decades. Creator of the landmark original miniseries *V*, he also produced *The Six Million Dollar Man* and created iconic Emmy-winning shows such as *The Bionic Woman*, *The Incredible Hulk*, and *Alien Nation*. He has directed numerous TV movies and the feature films *Short Circuit 2* and *Steel*. Johnson has received multiple Saturn Awards from the Academy of Science Fiction, Fantasy, and Horror Films, as well as the Sci-Fi Universe Lifetime Achievement Award and the prestigious Founder's Award from the Viewers for Quality Television. His previous novels include *V: The Second Generation*. He has presented his unique graduate-level seminar, *The Filmmaking Experience*, at UCLA, USC, NYU, Loyola, New York Film Academy, the National Film and Television School (UK), Moscow State University (Russia), and many others. He and his wife, Susan, married for forty years, live in Los Angeles with their latest two golden-retriever rescues.